The Lottery

Peter Venison

Clink Street

Published by Clink Street Publishing 2021

Copyright © 2021

First edition.

ISBN: 978-1-913962-16-6 - paperback
978-1-913962-17-3 - ebook

To Diana, my life's love.

Also by Peter Venison

Managing Hotels
Heinemann Professional Publishing (London) 1983
Reprinted 1984, 1986,1988

100 Tips for Hoteliers
iUniverse, 2005

In the Shadow of the Sun
iUniverse, 2005

100 Ways to Annoy your Guests
Clink Street Publishing, 2020

Out of the Shadow of the Sun
Clink Street Publishing, 2020

Chapter 1

It all began one day in the park. Maggie and Greg were out for their early morning exercise, when Maggie, always eagle-eyed, spotted a familiar looking piece of paper nestled into the short grass at the side of the path. "What's that?" she said. "Looks like a ticket." Greg was not in the habit of picking up litter in the park but this looked clean, as if it had just been dropped. Greg bent down to pick it up. As he straightened, he saw exactly what it was. "A lottery ticket," he started, "must be an old one." Maggie took it from him and examined it carefully. "This isn't old!" she exclaimed, "I think it is for tonight's draw. Maybe this is our lucky day?" Greg took the flimsy piece of paper back from his wife and studied it again. "You're right. It is for tonight's draw. Some poor bugger must have dropped it."

Maggie and Greg lived in a leafy dormitory town, Dorking, about 30 miles from London. They had two young children, Samantha ('Sam'), who was ten and James ('Jimmy') who was six. Greg had his own small business in London; a recruitment agency for hotel and hospitality industry staff. Maggie looked after the home and the children. They led a nice middle-class life, with plenty of friends in the neighbourhood and beyond, a small boat in the driveway, annual overseas holidays and so on. They were far from rich, but managed to live a nice comfortable middle-class life. The children went to local state schools. Greg played rugby for the town team at the weekends in the winter and occasionally sailed the small boat in the summer. He was a good-looking man, blond and fit from sailing and sport. Maggie did all of the normal things that middle-class stay-at-home wives do; keep fit, bridge, socialising with her girlfriends, caring for the children, helping out at the school and so on. They were happy with the cards that life had dealt them. Together they made a handsome couple.

During the second World War, Maggie's unmarried mother, unable to make ends meet, had handed her over to foster parents, where she spent a happy childhood and her teenage years. The foster parents were both school teachers. Her foster mother, Clare, taught entry level children, and her foster dad, William, was a music teacher. They had very little money but were rich in their knowledge of the arts, which they did their best to pass on to Maggie, who like most teenagers had done her best to let it pass over her head. Luckily, some had stuck. Mostly, Maggie had been raised in the country, where she learned a lot about nature. She was really interested in the flora and fauna, and this knowledge never left her. Her foster parents recognised that Maggie was bright and they would have liked her to pursue further education at the age of 16, but there simply were not the funds available, especially since they had other foster children to feed. So, Maggie went to work, partly because that is what she wanted to do, i.e. 'get out into the world', but also so that she could contribute to the meagre resources of her foster family. After a couple of low-level office jobs, she applied for, and got, an office job in one of London's prestigious hotels, which was where, ultimately, she met Greg.

Sadly, both Clare and William had passed away, although Maggie was still in touch with her foster brother, who lived in

France. Maggie's humble roots had taught her to be kind and caring for others, but she was not without a streak of determination. Although fearful of public performances she nevertheless possessed a dash of dare devilishness that sometimes got her into trouble. She was aware of her good looks and knew how to use them. She enjoyed sex; in fact, she needed it.

Greg's upbringing was less colourful. His parents were solid lower-middle class folk, who had both risen, through their own diligence, from working class backgrounds. His mother, Ruby, had worked in a biscuit factory as an accounts clerk and his father, Roland Layburn, had won a place at the London Technical College, where he studied chemistry. He worked for the rest of his life in 'paint', in which industry he became highly respected. From a humble background he was able to provide Ruby and the two children, Jane and Greg, with a comfortable life and the opportunity to attend the local grammar schools and, thereafter, university. Both Ruby and Roland, now retired, were still alive, living an active pensioners' life in a little house at Box Hill, not far from Greg and Maggie's home in Dorking. By sheer coincidence sister Jane had married a Frenchman and lived in a little house near Paris. Greg started his working life in the hotel business. First, as a desk clerk, but he rapidly rose to be a hotel manager, one of the youngest in London. Armed with his industry knowledge, a couple of years back, he decided to open his own business as an industry recruiter. So far, things were going well and he and Maggie had been able to buy their house in 'respectable' Dorking, from where Greg commuted daily to his office in Victoria.

"I wonder who dropped it," said Maggie as she re-examined the ticket. "I bet they will be mad if it wins."

"I really don't know how we can find out," said Greg. "If we go around the park asking people, how would we know if someone said 'Yes' that it was really theirs?"

"We wouldn't," said Maggie. They both fell silent, wondering what to do.

"The post office near the park sells lottery tickets. We could ask in there if anyone has mentioned a lost ticket," suggested Maggie, after a while. "The guy at the counter will just say yes and he'll keep it."

"We could say we'll only hand it over to whomever dropped it in person."

"He could just get one of his friends to say so."

Silence fell again, as they slowly continued their walk, deep in thought. Birds tweeted their early morning chorus and the dawn dog walkers shouted silly names after their pets. Surrey was a nice place to be at seven on a sunny morning. "Listen," said Maggie, "it's really a non-problem. The chances of this ticket winning are about the same as for the tickets we normally buy; fat chance! So, it's not a big deal. Let's just keep it. If it wins, which it won't, we can worry about it then."

When they reached home, Greg slipped the ticket into the drawer where he kept their lottery tickets. The two of them had been having a small punt on the lottery for years, with nothing much to show from it. Greg bought tickets each week because he knew Maggie thought that, on the day they didn't have a ticket, their numbers would come up. Wouldn't that be a disaster? The drawer was full of failed attempts and a few pounds from the occasional small wins.

Greg headed off to the railway station to go to work and Maggie headed to the shower. She needed to freshen up, get breakfast for the children, and then whisk them off to school, before meeting up with a couple of her friends for coffee and a chat. All the normal things that ordinary housewives do.

Considering that Maggie had given birth to two babies, her body was in great shape, with firm, rounded breasts and a slim body, full lips and sparkling blue eyes. Greg thought of her in the shower as he waited for the train. Maggie was thinking of the lottery ticket. Was this a sign? Was she destined to find it? What if it won? Of course, it won't win; our tickets never have. Just forget it. Silly woman! Greg didn't give it a thought. His mind had turned from the shower to the office; there was work to be done. However, as he walked through the morning crush at Victoria station, he could not help but notice the newspaper placard, "Largest Lottery Prize in the World." He stopped to buy the paper. £450 million! "Wow, somebody is going to be happy! Maggie will be excited when she finds out."

Maggie spent the morning with her pals, Willow and Ellen. They had a good gossip about their circle of friends in Dorking and beyond. They talked about their children. They talked about the good-looking young doctor at the local surgery. They talked about their plans for summer holidays. They shared a couple of jokes. Maggie thought about telling them about the lottery ticket that she had found earlier that morning but decided to keep it to herself. Willow and Ellen were good friends and Greg and their husbands also hit it off well. Willow's husband, Ted, owned a business that distributed laundry equipment in nearby Epsom, and Ellen's husband, George, owned a small company that imported German office supplies of some sort, although Maggie didn't exactly know what. Willow was a pretty little thing, with almost a baby doll appearance. Ellen was a red head and quite voluptuous. Although they all had a fairly large circle of friends, these three were quite tight – so much so that they trusted each other with the most intimate things.

Maggie was a good friend to have. She was someone who valued her friends, particularly her 'girl' friends. Her mother had taught her that, however much she loved her husband or was involved with his circle and his activities, she should hold on to her own friends and support them when needed. "Your old friends will always be your best friends," Clare would often tell her daughter and Maggie had taken this advice to heart. She was, however, naturally warm-hearted and caring, not only for her friends but also for animals. She hated the way mankind was ruining the natural world. In her heart she was an activist, but, like many women, had not found a way to put this into practice beyond her immediate circle. Her foster parents had been ardent churchgoers. Maggie also believed in God and his power to do good but did not feel the need to prove this in a church. She wanted her children to believe as well, but also wanted them to make their own minds up about such things. Maggie was not, however, an angel. She could be quite intolerant of other's views and she could be quite cheeky. She had the advantage of being a particularly beautiful woman and she knew how to use this to get things she wanted. She could be quite a flirt and a tease, not only with her husband, Greg, but with other men, although she would never consider being unfaithful to her husband, whom she regarded as her soulmate. Maggie would be the first to admit that sex was important to her and, luckily, Greg was totally compliant. He was also a very handsome man.

Greg adored Maggie. His life revolved around making Maggie happy. To him, this meant being successful in his career. Success would bring rewards, and these would enable him to provide a nice comfortable life for his beloved and the wherewithal to educate and raise their children. Sometimes, Greg's practical resolve to be commercially successful seemed to be more important in his life than the proclaimed reason for doing so. Sometimes, Maggie even felt that Greg's job was more important than their happiness, but she understood the logic and did not make a fuss.

Greg and Maggie were synchronised in their thoughts and opinions about the state of the world, with the exception of one thing; religion. Here they simply agreed to differ and did not talk about it. Greg did not believe in God; anyone's God, but he knew that Maggie's belief was important to her, so he just stayed mute. He liked the structure that religion gave to lives and happily attended services with Maggie and the children on high days and holidays, but his body was there when his mind wasn't. Greg also liked sex. He was forever thankful that he had such a beautiful and sexy wife.

The draw for the lottery was at 10 pm that night. Apparently, media coverage of the huge amount had been so strong that many more people had bought tickets, raising the jackpot to a massive £490 million. There had been much hype about it in the evening paper and on the TV news bulletins. Maggie and Greg were not allowed to forget the ticket they had found; they were almost forced into talking about it. "I know that it is extremely unlikely, but what if the ticket is a winner? How could we find the rightful owner?" said Maggie.

"I say that the ticket holder is the owner," quipped Greg. "If we started looking for the real owner, we would have hundreds of 'applicants'. Anyway, it's not going to happen."

Although the draw for the lottery was always televised, Maggie and Greg had never bothered to watch it. After all, it wasn't exactly gripping television. That night though, because of the added intrigue of the lost ticket and the fact that the winning ticket would be worth a record amount, they decided to do so. Despite recognising that their chances of winning were millions and millions against, the two of them switched on the television with an air of ridiculous expectation. Greg had retrieved their legally bought tickets from the drawer, as well as the freshly minted 'lost in the grass' one.

When the little balls had all fallen into place on the screen, it took them a little while to realise that they had matched all five numbers – in one line. Maggie almost screamed. "We've won, we've won! Christ Almighty! We've won. Check it, Greg! It can't be true. Quick, check the numbers!" Greg could hardly see straight. His hands were actually shaking. With huge effort he disciplined himself to check and double check the numbers – five times! "It's true. We've got all the numbers on one line. I can't believe it," he stammered excitedly. "And, guess what! It's on the ticket from the park!"

"Oh my God," screamed Maggie. "What do we do? It's not our ticket!"

Excitement came to a screeching halt. "It's not our ticket, Greg. We can't keep it. Can we?" Greg was silent; his mind was whirling. "This could change their lives. It could change the lives of their children and even their extended families. They could do so much good with the money. Maybe they could figure out how to share it with the rightful owner? But how could they find the rightful owner? But aren't they now the rightful owner; they have the ticket?"

"Answer me," Maggie almost screamed, "Answer me. What do we do?"

"Nothing," Greg eventually offered. "Let's do nothing until we have thought this through. We don't have to tell anyone yet that we have won – including the kids. Let's sleep on it."

"Sleep!," you must be kidding me! How could I possibly sleep?"

"I suppose not. Nor could I, but let's not rush into any decision. Whatever we decide to do will affect the rest of our lives. Let's have a drink and talk about it."

The last thing Maggie wanted was a drink. She wanted a clear head. She had dreamed of this moment, not ever

8

believing that it would happen to her. Now, she was totally unprepared. Greg poured himself a large scotch and sat down on the couch next to Maggie. He reached out and gave her a huge hug and a long, lasting, kiss. She burst into tears, suddenly overcome with the emotion of the occasion. Greg held her tightly.

Half an hour later their debate was in full swing. They discussed all of the good they could do with the money. Even if they could find the owner of the ticket, how could they know that he or she would do any good with the money? No, the money would be better used by them. They played a game of 'what if'." What if we keep it? We could give most of it, or at least half of it, to charity. There would be plenty left to play with. Maggie could administer the charity side of things and Greg could look after investing the rest. They wouldn't have to move or change their life style. They wouldn't have to lose their friends. It needn't change the lives of their children. They needn't tell anyone that they had won. Maggie had always been concerned about endangered species, particularly elephants, which were her favourite. She could start her own 'save the elephant' fund.

The room was buzzing with ideas; exciting ideas, that could change their lives- and the lives of so many others for the better. Greg, a natural manager, could make good use and have lots of fun in managing the money they decided to keep. Their children would never have to worry about money, nor would their other close relatives. He could make sure that the money grew, whilst helping others on the way. The opportunities were enormous.

It was all very exhilarating and very exciting. But there was a real elephant in the room, not one that needed saving, but one that was hanging heavily over their excitement. The money was not theirs. It belonged to someone else. Someone that bought a ticket in good faith and filled in the numbers correctly. It was not really Maggie's and Greg's money to spend. Perhaps, if they found the ticket owner, they could do a deal with them, like, "We'll give you the ticket back, if you give us half the money. Or even 10%, as a reward?" "But how could we find the owner? Presumably the lottery people could track down where the ticket was bought, and, presumably, the 'owner' could produce the card he had marked up when he bought the ticket? But anyone could fill in a form with ticks on it, after the event. How could anyone prove that it was theirs? Maybe, if he could show that he did the same numbers every week?"

They talked deep into the night. Sleep would have been impossible. Gradually, slowly, the thought that the money was really not theirs to claim diminished and the idea that, since they possessed the ticket, the money was rightfully theirs, gained strength. Maggie became more and more excited about the 'good' she could do with it and Greg started to imagine himself as a budding Warren Buffet. If they claimed the prize, there was one thing that they absolutely agreed upon, and that was to tell nobody, not even the kids. To do this, they concurred, they would have to behave quite normally, which would not include staying up all night. The children would immediately wonder what was wrong. So, with their minds still whirling, they went to their marital bed and finally fell to sleep in each other's arms. They had often thought about what it would be like to learn that you had won the lottery; now they knew – excitement, but not without a good dose of anxiety.

Chapter Two

As dawn broke Maggie and Gregg woke up to the new feeling that they were multimillionaires. Any doubts about the ethics of claiming someone else's prize seemed to have evaporated in a couple of hours' slumber. Maggie breezily prepared Sam and Jimmy's breakfast and Dad announced that he would "Work from home today." Maggie giggled a bit, because she knew why. Greg volunteered to take the children to school; they were always happy when, on the odd occasion, he did that. So, the first day of the rest of their lives began.

Greg made his excuses with his team in the office; told them he would be working from home for a couple of days. Maggie texted her pals to call off her normal rendezvous. Coffee was made and poured and the planning began.

Greg rationalised that, before thinking about physically claiming the money they should first of all get their story straight about how they acquired the ticket. Greg was concerned that with all of the newspaper hype about the biggest ever jackpot win, the rightful owner might have started looking for the lost ticket. After all, he or she may have kept the form with the little marks on it as proof that they had bought it. Greg went on line to the lottery website and tapped in "Lottery; lost ticket." What it told him was that you could not claim the jackpot without the ticket, but that, should you mislay the ticket, you must report this to the lottery people so that they can investigate. Greg was sure that anyone realising that they had lost the winning ticket would immediately start this action, so the authorities would be alert to the fact that there might be a contest for the prize. Greg argued that this meant two things. First, that he and Maggie should claim the winnings fairly quickly, because he figured that's what most winners would do, and second, that they had better have a good story as to where and when they bought the ticket. Greg thought that it was highly possible that the lottery machine that printed the ticket would have a record of the time and date of the purchase.

Maggie agreed with this logic and quietly thanked the Lord that she had such a calm and logical partner. "The ticket looked quite new when we found it," she reasoned. "It didn't look scrunched up at all. It was almost as if it had just been bought." "You are right," agreed Greg, "and if that is the case we should check where the closest place is to the park that sells lottery tickets." "I am sure that would be the corner shop post office," said Maggie. "I just can't think of anywhere else." The two of them agreed that it must be the post office, but, nevertheless, they thought it would be prudent to jump in the car and do a little whizz around the blocks near the park, to check that there were no other lottery sellers operating in the area. Off they went in their five-year-old Range Rover, like a couple of CIA operatives, to scour the neighbourhood for lottery sellers. First passed the post office. Sure enough, there was the familiar lottery 'fingers crossed' sign. As they drove by, Greg wondered if the lottery authorities had yet notified the ticket seller that he had participated in the biggest pay-out ever. Surely the seller got some reward?

After crisscrossing the neighbourhood for ten minutes or

so, to their alarm, they found two other shops with 'fingers crossed' signs. One was the little newsagent about a mile or so to the other side of the park and one at the railway station. Both seemed unlikely culprits but it was not impossible that the ticket buyer had come from a little farther afield. "What if he came off a train?" a worried Maggie questioned. Greg did not know what to say, but he hoped that, because of the freshness of the ticket, the purchase had just occurred and that the post office corner shop was the most likely seller. It was also the shop where Greg normally purchased his tickets, which might help reinforce their claim. "Look," said Greg, "I don't think we are ever going to know for sure, but there is absolutely nothing we can do about it except take the most logical route – and that is the post office." With a certain amount of trepidation, the pair of them decided that it might be smart to delay any claim for at least another day, in case some further information came to light to guide them.

Back home in the kitchen they pondered the next steps. Despite the fact that they had yet to claim the winnings, their thoughts kept turning to what they would do with it; how they would spend it. On one thing they both agreed; they would donate half of it (well, maybe, almost half) to charity, whilst keeping the other half for the enhancement of their lives and, hopefully, their heirs. They would stay in the same modest house, so as not to arouse suspicion amongst friends and neighbours that they were suddenly wealthy, and they would try to resist the urge to splurge, for the same reason. Greg really lusted for a Bentley, but this, of course, would be like waving a flag to attract attention. He had always vowed that, if he ever won the lottery, he would join Net Jets, so that a plane would always be at their beck and call. Maybe this was possible without attracting too much attention? he mused. As for the charities, he would let

Maggie choose, but he really wanted her to fulfil her dream to help protect African elephants. Naturally, Greg would help her direct the funds.

It was not long before Maggie announced that she would need to get to the school to collect Jimmy. Greg stayed behind and googled "What to do if you win the lottery." His research was both interesting and worrying. It seemed that if you have bought the winning ticket and signed the back of it, you have the undeniable right to the prize money. There is no record kept of who actually buys a ticket, but, should a buyer lose a ticket, they can make a claim, but would have to show proof of where and when they bought the ticket, as well as some evidence that makes their claim feasible, such as a past history of betting on the same numbers. Any claim would have to be lodged within 30 days. All of this was hugely worrying to Greg, who began to feel that the risk of his and Maggie's claim to ownership might be rather easily challenged. "Is it a risk worth taking?" he asked himself over and over again. "Should we just claim the prize and hope that there is no challenge? Should we take our chances that, if the real owner came forward, he or she would reward us with the odd million?" Maggie had now returned with little Jimmy, who was, of course, completely oblivious to the torment his parents were going through, so all talk of lotteries was put on hold until the evening.

That night, after much more discussion, Greg rationalised that they should go ahead and claim because they would never come this close to being rich again. They had found the ticket; it was a lucky sign which they should grasp. They would not spend any of money until the 30 days were up, which was the time allowed for a claim to be registered, and, should they be successfully challenged, they would insist that "finding and keeping" was not an illegal act. Maggie was worried on two fronts; first, the legal one, but, more importantly, the moral issue. However, she was happy with the idea of giving the rightful owner one month to recover; that, she rationalised, was fair. The 'owner' would have had a fair chance. So, without more ado, they both signed the back of the ticket and called the number on the back to register their claim. The phone was answered promptly, even though it was now nine in the evening. After a few perfunctory questions, the voice on the other end advised that somebody would be in touch the following morning to arrange for lottery 'management' to come to the house to commence the verification process. For better or for worse, the die was cast. Greg poured Maggie a glass of French red wine and a large single malt for himself. Together, they wondered how their lives would change with £490 million. "Everything might change," said Greg, "except my love for you." Maggie wondered.

Next morning Greg did the school run. When he returned, he learned that the lottery people had already called and arranged with Maggie to visit at 11 am. Maggie had asked her friend Ellen to pick up Jimmy from school. She presumed that the lottery visit would be over by the time Sam finished school. The wait until 11 am seemed forever. Greg busied himself with some office work, but his mind he was already selecting the Bentley. Maggie had changed out of her early morning tracksuit into jeans and a pink sweater. She looked radiant. She started to google how to save elephants. On the stroke of eleven, the doorbell rang. Two men in smart suits were standing there, one with a small briefcase. The men introduced themselves; Stanley, was the officer normally designated to do the winner verification process. Stanley had a little moustache; his tie was slightly askew. The other, George, introduced himself as the Managing Director of the lottery company, and quickly explained that he was in attendance because this was a unique event – the largest ever prize of any lottery in the world. He just felt that this was a historic moment and wanted to share in the joy. Verification was quick. Greg produced the winning ticket, which was duly scrutinised and accepted. Identity proof, as in passports, were shown and accepted, and details of the bank account into which they wanted the money wired were taken. Maggie and George were then asked if they would like to remain anonymous, which, of course, they did. George looked a little disappointed, but made no effort to change their minds, other than to point out that it could be rather difficult to hide that sort of money from their friends and relatives. Offers of financial planning services were given and noted. Certain papers of acceptance of conditions were proffered and duly signed by Maggie and Greg. The couple were then advised that the money would be in their account by the end of the following day, and Stanley, George, Maggie and Greg all sat, over a cup of coffee and biscuits, supplied by Maggie, and chatted about the weather. It was all a bit surreal. Within less than three quarters of an hour, the visitors were gone. Maggie and Greg sighed with relief and embraced each other. Greg could feel Maggie's bosom pressed into his chest in her pink sweater; Maggie could tell that he really liked this. There would be just time for a quickie before Ellen showed up with little Jimmy.

"What a surprise," exclaimed Ellen, on being greeted by Greg. "Fancy seeing you at home. Now I know why Maggie couldn't make it to the school." Greg was not quite sure what the inference was. He knew that Maggie and Ellen shared their secrets. He wondered if Maggie had ever let on to Ellen that she was sometimes the subject of his arousal. He hoped not, but, on the other hand, he did not really mind. He was, however, fearful that if Maggie could share intimate thoughts with her friends, how on earth would she be able to keep the secret of the lottery win? Deep down, he suspected that she couldn't. That was something he would have to deal with later. Now, he wanted to concentrate on his little boy. It was not often that he was able to attend to him on a weekday. "Come on Jimmy. Let's go to the park with the ball!" Jimmy didn't need asking twice.

Ellen did her best to find out why Greg was at home, but Maggie deftly dealt with her questions by explaining that Greg was experimenting with working from home a couple of days each week, in the interests of global warming. Maggie thought this was rather clever, since she anticipated Greg would be spending much more time at home in the future. Greg and Jimmy returned from the park, Ellen made her farewells, Sam arrived home from school; life went on as normal; except it wasn't. Tomorrow they would have £490 million in the bank!

That evening, once the youngsters were bedded down, Maggie and Greg's conversation inevitably returned to the money. According to Greg, if they left the £490 million in the bank for one month, as they had promised each other, it would have increased through interest by another £2 million; if they left it there for a year it would increase by almost £25 million! His point was that they should really plan to spend some of it, even if it was only the interest. Greg's suggestion was that they allocate £200 million for charitable causes and keep the rest. "What happened to the fifty-fifty split?" asked Maggie. "Well it might be a challenge to get rid of £200 million to charity. After all, we do want to make sure that we only give to charities that either we control, or ones where we know the person at the sharp end. And we can always give more later. There should be plenty of the 290 left." Greg's speech seemed to satisfy Maggie. She had never seen Greg as a greedy person, but why rationalise your meanness over £45 million?

"Anyway," said Greg, "we need to think about how to set up the charity. I am sure that there are a few things we will have to do to set up a charitable vehicle. What I suggest, for starters, is that we form a charity, to be controlled by you and me. You can be the President or Chairman, or whatever. I can be a trustee. We could then use this head charity as the one that takes the decisions to donate or finance other more specific ones, such as your Save the Elephants, which you may also need to set up. We will need to do some research as to how we get this done legally but I suppose, in the end, we will need a lawyer to help us with the red tape. I expect we will also need to have trustees, which means we will have to select people we can trust and who might wonder where we got all of the money from. Sounds like having a lot of money might mean a lot of work." "Oh my God," exclaimed Maggie, "sounds too complicated to me. I am sure you can sort it all out. You are so clever at this sort of thing." Maggie gave him a hug. "I just want to make sure that, whatever we do, I can make an impact to benefit the elephants or whoever else we decide to help." Greg's arms wrapped around her body and held her tightly. "Let's go to bed and wake up in the morning with nearly half a billion pounds in the bank."

Chapter Three

Greg decided, next morning, that he had better put in an appearance at the office, partly because there were some urgent matters that needed his attention and partly because, from there, he could, perhaps, sort out the best legal advice in regard to establishing a charity. Maggie decided to return to her normal routine of keep fit and then coffee with her confidantes.

It took Greg a couple of hours to catch up with the back-log in his business. His secretary, Louise, showed a good deal of inquisitiveness about his two days of absence. Was he okay? Had he been unwell? Was everything alright at home? Greg dismissed all of the above without giving the poor girl a clue as to his rationale for what was, for him, abnormal behaviour. She concluded that, whatever it was, he did not want her to know, which, of course, made her determined to find out anyway. When Greg, later in the morning, asked her to get hold of the company lawyer, a rare occurrence, her suspicions were really aroused. She pondered over the idea of listening in to the conversation, but decided against that. Louise was an attractive brunette who was always immaculately turned out, except that she arrived at work wearing sneakers, out of which she immediately exchanged for one of two pairs of high-heeled shoes that she kept in a paper bag under her desk. Despite the fact that she had worked for Greg since he had opened the business, he knew very little about her, except that she was married to Tony, who was a poker dealer. No children. Louise, of course, knew plenty about Greg. She called the lawyer and patched him through to Greg; she decided not to eavesdrop, and, with his office door closed, she could not hear Greg making an appointment to meet later that day.

Maggie, Willow and Ellen met for coffee. They were joined by Trixie. Trixie was a colourful character. Her husband, Hal, was in partnership with Willow's husband, George and he and Trixie had been staying the night in Willow's house. Hal had first met Trixie when she was a showgirl in a London Club. As far as Maggie could make out a 'showgirl' was one step away from being a stripper, which in turn was one step away from being a prostitute. However, there was nothing sleazy about Trixie; she was glamour personified. Everybody stopped to look at Trixie; she was what men called a 'stunner'. Maggie was grateful that Trixie had joined the trio for their morning gossip session because her colourful stories kept the girls amused and there was no interest in pursuing the subject of Maggie's absence for the last couple of days. Willow described how, that morning, Trixie had appeared en flagrante in front of the master of the house on her way back from the guest bathroom. "Ted had a right eyeful," exclaimed Willow. "It must have been hard on him," quipped Ellen. Although it was Willow who was telling the story, Maggie was not sure that she was really happy about it. Maggie knew, from personal experience with Ted that he had a bit of a wandering eye and, sometimes, hands.

That evening, after the children had been despatched to bed, Greg started to relate the meeting he had had that afternoon with the lawyer. "Wait, wait!" interrupted Maggie, "the money. Did we get the money?" "Yes, my lovely, look at this!" Out of his briefcase he pulled a sheet of paper; a print-out of their bank statement. "£490 million and change. The change was there before! 'Change' had now been elevated from a few pounds to thousands." "Keep that," exclaimed Maggie with a whoop, referring to the printout, "one day we must frame it."

After the excitement had died down, Greg went into the boring details of how one sets up a charity, which involved an actual charity to dispense the money and a limited company to administer the funds. All of this would require additional directors, company secretaries and the like; people that Maggie and Greg must select. "How on earth are we going to keep this a secret?" Maggie asked, with more than a little of anxiety. "We will use professional people, who do this sort of thing for a living. Lawyers, bankers and the like. They will have to sign confidentiality agreements and so on," explained Greg. "If you say so. If that is alright, then I guess it is," she said, but sounding rather unconvinced. "Maybe we shouldn't be so paranoid about letting people know what we've won; maybe that would be alright." Maggie was really not sure, but common sense told her that if all her friends knew about the win, their relationships might change. And in addition to that, they would have no end of begging letters. Maggie didn't want to use the money to help people; they had screwed up their own lives; she wanted to help the elephants and rhinos and so on; wild animals who had had their lives screwed up by people. The evening passed strangely. They were rich; very rich, but trepidation filled the room. Although the money was in the bank, the weight of a potential challenge from the real owner of the ticket filled their living room like a dark cloud.

A couple of weeks went by; still no challenge to their win. For a few days after the world record prize had been announced, the press, across the planet, ran all sorts of speculative stories. The lottery people had announced that the winner was in England, but that was all. Articles appeared about how to spend half a billion. Advice in the press was plentiful, but, after a few days, since nobody knew who had won, the interest died down and all went quiet. Maggie and Greg dared to hope. Greg visited with the lawyer on several occasions without telling Louise why. She became quite convinced that he was planning a divorce. Several names were submitted to him as charity directors, but just to get things going, he opted for almost anonymous employees of the law firm, who, it was agreed, would agree to be replaced at a later date. Greg did allow himself one visit to Jack Barclay, the Rolls and Bentley dealer in Berkeley Square. The sales person wrote him off as a looker, not a buyer. Little did he know that Greg could have bought the showroom!

Exactly 20 days after the money had landed in their bank, they had a call from Stanley, the man from the lottery. He needed to come to see them. Apparently, someone was claiming that the lottery ticket was really theirs. "Nothing to worry about," explained Stanley, "this happens all the time. There is always some charlatan who thinks he can make a quick buck. Unfortunately, we are obliged to investigate. I am sure you understand." Stanley arrived the next day with another member of his staff, a rather stiff lady called Julia. Julia was painfully thin. Thin in the body, but also in the face. She had little round spectacles that slid down her thin nose. She carried a fat briefcase. "Now, let's run over your particulars again," started Stanley, as he sat down with the coffee and biscuit provided by Maggie. Once again Greg explained how he had bought the ticket at the corner post office, where he always buys lottery tickets. "The Indian chap there knows me," he added, as if this made any difference. "Did you buy any tickets, other than the winning one?" enquired Stanley. Greg affirmed that he had. "May I see them?," he requested, somewhat wearily. "I have no idea where they are. We never keep them. Maggie, darling, do you know where the useless tickets are?" "Probably in the garbage; long gone." She replied. "Do you recall if you bought all of the tickets at the same time?" continued Stanley. Greg smelled a trap. Of course he hadn't bought them at the same time, because he hadn't bought the winning one at all. His brain raced. "They must have a record of when each ticket is purchased," he thought, "so I'd better admit that I bought it at different times. That would sound a bit odd, so I must have a reason." Maggie came to the rescue. "Greg didn't buy the winning ticket at all," she suddenly exclaimed. "I did! I often do that. Sometimes a just get a hunch or a feeling or whatever, or think it is my lucky day, and I just go out and buy one, for luck." "If I may be so bold," interrupted Stanley, "when I came here to verify that the winning ticket was yours, you didn't say that it was you that bought the ticket." "You didn't ask me," snapped back Maggie, "you just asked it the ticket was 'ours'." "Now, look here, Stanley," Greg started, "what is this all about? Are you insinuating that the winning ticket was not ours? This is getting to be a bit annoying; what is going on here?" Stanley sighed and took a deep breath. Apparently, he explained, another customer of the shop was claiming that he had bought the ticket and had mislaid it. His details about the purchase matched up to the time of the sale as recorded on the till in the shop and he had been able to produce evidence that he always bet on the winning numbers. "Is he an Indian?" snapped Greg, instantly regretting it. "I am not at liberty to say, who he or she is," replied Stanley. "Unfortunately for him, he did not sign the back of the ticket that he claims he lost, so, his only route to claim the prize is to convince a court that the ticket is rightfully his. So, I must warn you that he may well take his case to court. Until such time as the court rules otherwise, should he take the matter there, the lottery company will continue to regard you as the rightful winners. I must also warn you, however, that should a court rule in favour of this claimant, you will be required to pay over the winnings to him. So, better not spend anything in the meantime." "Well," exclaimed Greg, with a display of increasing indignation and anger, "what a bloody shyster! There's no way he is going to steal our money! What a goddam nerve!" "Calm down, darling," said Maggie, "It's not poor Stanley's fault. Don't shoot the messenger."

Stanley thanked her for her support and intervention. Julia said nothing; in fact, she had not opened her thin mouth at all, except to sip her coffee.

Greg calmed down. "I'm sorry," he offered to Stanley, "I am just horrified about how some people can be. Anyway, what happens next?" Stanley explained that the matter was now out of the hands of the lottery company. They would supply the facts to a court, should it be necessary, but would, otherwise, not get involved. As far as they were concerned, Maggie and Greg were the owners of the ticket and the lottery company had honoured its obligations by giving them the money. Over and out. If the other individual claiming the ticket wanted to sue for the money through a court that was their prerogative, but they would have to sue Greg and Maggie to get the money, not the lottery company. Greg and Maggie would just have to wait to see if they were going to get sued. "But," said Greg, with one final thrust, "how will they know whom to sue, if you have agreed with us not to disclose who we are?" "That," replied Stanley, "is a very good question." With that, Stanley excused himself and Julia and they left. Julia had not said a word nor opened her fat briefcase. As soon as they had gone, Greg thanked Maggie for her quick thinking in claiming to have bought the ticket. "But," he quickly added, "that may cause a problem. The corner shop might have a camera recording the transactions at the counter; in which case they will not have a tape of you. We'd better check it out."

The post office shop was less than five minutes away in the car. The post office section was at the far end of the shop. The till for all of the other merchandise was near the door. There was hardly enough room in the shop to swing a cat. Although Greg had been there a thousand times before, he had never looked for cameras. "How stupid am I?" he mumbled to himself as he drove towards the shop, "I should have checked this out two weeks ago. If they have a tape of everybody at the counter, they will never find Maggie on it." Greg entered the little shop on the pretence of buying a newspaper. He had a good look around. Yes, there was a camera, but only one that he could see, and it was pointed at the post office counter, not the shop till point, which was at the other end of the space. As far as he could tell, there was no way that customers buying lottery tickets or Mars Bars, or whatever, were ever captured on tape. He pretended to be scouring the magazine rack whilst he doublechecked, until he was absolutely certain that he was right. "There was no way anybody would be able to prove on camera that they had bought a ticket or anything else in the shop, bar items bought at the post office itself. Phew!" Nevertheless, with the potential of a challenge to the rightful ownership of the winning ticket, Greg now knew that he was going to need a very good lawyer. Life, after winning the lottery, was beginning to feel much more difficult than before.

Chapter Four

About a week later, Greg and Maggie were served with court papers, alleging that they had, in effect, stolen the ticket, and demanding the payment of £490 million to the claimant as well as costs involved. This was a civil court matter, not, at this stage, a criminal affair, although, no doubt, should it be proved, the police might well get involved at a later stage. Greg had used the two weeks of heads up time to put together a strong legal team, who were willing to act on a contingency basis for a huge fee. "What's a million pounds of legal fees to save $490 million?" they had argued and he could see the point. Armed now with the identity of the claimant, their investigative team went into action. The protagonist in question appeared on the paperwork as Mr Jay Naidoo, from Bromley, in Kent. The lawyers recommended that Greg hire a detective agency to do some background checks on Naidoo. Some forensic investigation into Naidoo's history soon showed that he was an accountant, with his own small, some would say tiny, practice. His clients seemed to be mainly small shopkeepers and businesses owned by immigrants in South East London. A visit to his premises was less than impressive. Further research into his background showed that, a few years earlier, he had worked for the lottery company. Alarm bells rang in the

Greg's lawyers' chambers. Here was a man, of ethnic Indian background, with possible prior knowledge of the inner workings of the lottery, claiming to have bought a ticket in Dorking, which was a long way from Bromley, from an Indian shopkeeper. Something did not seem right. Surely, no court was going to buy this story? Yet, the court papers served, inferred that Mr Naidoo was in a position to prove that he had bought the ticket.

It was agreed that the agency should be retained for further investigative work. A number of employees at the lottery company were quietly contacted and confidentially offered an incentive to look into Naidoo's history at the company. The question was "Would Naidoo have access to the secret safeguards built in to ticket production and control?" On the other front the agency sought to find out more about the employee at the corner post office. Was there any connection between him and Naidoo, other than they both appeared to be of Indian descent? It turned out that his name was Rishi Patel. Patels in India are like Smiths in England – millions of them, so trying to get information on this one might be quite onerous and time consuming. It was agreed that the agency should keep an eye on Mr Patel for a day or so. If he were, in some way, involved with a scam over the ticket, he would, no doubt, sooner or later, make contact with Naidoo. If the agency could take a peek at Patel's phone, it might tell a few stories.

With all of this going on, Greg began to feel that he was in a movie. Life was getting more and more complicated by the minute. Here he was, paying for detective agencies to try and get dirt on a guy who, for all he knew, he had just robbed of £490 million. It all seemed so bizarre, especially compared to life pre 'win'. On top of that, Greg, was furious that the lottery company had provided Naidoo, or the Court, with his and Maggie's name, when they had agreed previously not to disclose it. Surely here was a case to sue them? His lawyers were going to look into that, but not as part of the contingency fee, of course. In the meantime, Greg was gamely trying to keep his company going, since he had come to realise that the cover of his company might be very useful in the future in shielding the fact that he had been a lottery winner.

He did his best to keep Maggie in the loop regarding Naidoo, Patel, and the lottery company, but he really did not want to unduly worry her. After all, this was the 'business' end of the lottery win, not the charitable one, although they both realised that the charity would come to nothing if the £490 went away.

Then, three weeks after receiving the court papers, and two weeks before the first hearing of the case, he got good news. The detective agency had managed to get hold of Patel's phone records (God knows how!), and, bingo! Patel had been in frequent contact with Naidoo over the last month, and before. It appeared that they had known each other well before the lottery drawing. The agency was not able to say exactly how they were going to attempt to prove that Naidoo had bought the winning ticket, but that didn't seem to matter any more. Greg's lawyers were certain that they would be able to cast serious doubt on Naidoo's claim, and, could possibly even threaten him that they would turn their findings over to the police, unless Naidoo's claim on the winnings was immediately retracted. The one and only challenge to the veracity of Maggie and Greg's right to the £490 million had, apparently, gone away. Greg and Maggie now had £489 million, the lawyers had one, and the detective agency had some of the change. Everyone, it seems, would be happy. And even poor Naidoo and Patel had no idea that Greg and Maggie were the real thieves.

Chapter Five

During the next few weeks Greg was exceptionally busy and, although he did his best to keep Maggie in the picture, she seemed content to let him get on with things, whilst she carried on with life, as normal. They had decided that it would be wise for Greg to keep going with his business. In fact, Greg had suggested that, with the new found fortune, he attempt to acquire one or more of his competitors, in order to create a business that might be large enough to mask the fact that they had won the lottery. People, he reasoned, would think that he was hugely successful in the recruitment business, and would not be suspicious of his new found wealth. As a result, to the amazement of Louise, his secretary, he entered into negotiations with two of his largest rivals to buy their businesses, and this required plenty of due diligence, and meetings with lawyers, bankers and accountants. Greg had no time to visit the Bentley showroom and decided to postpone his Net Jets application until the, hopefully, enlarged company could appear to afford it.

The money in the bank also needed some attention. It was dangerous to leave all of it in the same account and bank. What would happen if the bank went bust? Bit by bit he began to set up a series of new accounts, 20 in all, in different banks. Some of these were in offshore tax havens and they were all in his name, not the joint names of himself and Maggie, as was the original account. Not that he did this with the intention of stealing from his lovely wife, but merely, as an administrative convenience. It did not cross his mind that Maggie might, one day, see things differently. The only gamble Greg allowed himself to take was to buy a fistful of Bitcoins; 2 million of them to be precise at 50 pence per Coin. After all, taking a $1 million gamble when you have nearly £500 million was not exactly living dangerously.

All of this effort caused him to work late and at weekends. Maggie and the kids began to feel deserted. Jimmy and Sam missed their Dad's attention; Maggie also missed the sex. One weekend, in the middle of all of this extra commercial activity, Maggie and Greg were invited to a party at Willow and Ted's house. Despite it being a weekend, Greg had needed to attend a meeting in London and was running late. He called Maggie to suggest that she went on to the party and that he would join as soon as he could. She reluctantly agreed. The party was the usual small country town affair with lots of bonhomie, good hearted banter and too much booze. Willow often behaved rather provocatively at these affairs, which seemed to amuse Ted, rather than annoy him. She had been moving around the room from one man's lap to the next, encouraging the other husbands to fondle her in turn. This was not the first time that Maggie and, normally Greg, had witnessed this behaviour, although Maggie was thankful that Greg had never joined in. On this occasion, however, the whole thing seemed to arouse Maggie, who had not been serviced by her husband now for weeks. She found herself wondering if Ted was actually turned on by his wife, Willow's behaviour. Fortified by several glasses of wine she decided to find out. She sashayed over to Ted, emphasising her lovely body as she went, and sat down on Ted's lap. She immediately felt his hard member through his trousers. As they both watched his wife being fondled on the other side of the room, Maggie suddenly felt Ted's hands on her breasts. She turned to face him, but before she could speak, he was suddenly kissing her passionately. She tried to withdraw but, just at that moment, Greg walked in the room. He immediately saw what was happening and he was clearly livid. He grabbed Maggie by the arm and said, "C'mon. We're leaving," and dragged her out of the room and through the front door. By the time they reached their home, his anger had subsided; in fact, the whole episode seemed to have ignited his own sex drive. He pulled Maggie inside and they made delicious love on the thick carpet on the lounge floor. "I really needed that," breathed Maggie, when they were done, "You know, a girl does need some attention from time to time! Am I forgiven?" Greg realised that, with all the excitement of the lotter win, he had been taking Maggie for granted. He vowed not to do so again.

When Maggie met with the girls on the next Monday, she met a barrage of questions. "Was Greg cross? What happened when you got home? Are you alright?" Maggie assured them that she was more than alright. "Well, after all," said Ellen, "you were only having a bit of harmless fun." "So was Ted," piped up Willow, "You really got him going, Maggie – and I got the benefit of that later!" They all had a good laugh and the conversation turned to the kids.

Despite the fact that her friends saw the whole episode as a bit of harmless fun, deep down, Maggie was not so sure. In some ways, she thought something between her and Greg had broken and that, maybe, it would never be mended. "It was all my fault," she thought to herself, "and then, again, maybe it wasn't?"

Greg, on the other hand, determined that he would

be more attentive to his wife in future. This had been a wake-up call. He realised that, perhaps, he had gone overboard with work in the previous few weeks. What was the point of having all of this money in the bank if, by being its guardian, you neglected the ones that you love? "The time has come," he concluded, "to turn the pot of gold into some fun for Maggie and the kids." That Sunday, Greg and Maggie paid special attention to the travel section of the newspapers. They had decided to take themselves and the kids to a nice resort for a week. The school Easter break was approaching so the thought of a week of sun and sand seemed appealing. Maggie had wanted to go on safari in Africa but, after some discussion, agreed with Greg that the children were really too young to appreciate it. The thought of a five-year-old and ten-year-old getting up at dawn for a two-hour drive in a Land Cruiser was not appealing. No, they would go to a nice place with a beach. Then, when they returned they would prevail upon Greg's parents to look after the little ones for a week whilst Maggie and Greg went on safari.

Two weeks later, Maggie, Greg, Sam and Jimmy were happily ensconced at the luxurious Saint Géran Hotel on the Indian Ocean Island of Mauritius. Greg had rented the only beach villa on the property, normally occupied by the rich and famous. He explained to Maggie that it was the only accommodation available at such short notice. In truth, he had not enquired about regular rooms. He may not be famous, but he sure was rich, so why not go for the best?

Unfortunately for Greg, Air Mauritius did not offer a first-class option on the flight, so Greg had had to settle for business class. Nevertheless, this was an adventure compared to the steerage class that his family were used to on their normal holiday trips. The villa was a free-standing property, situated right on the beach, about 50 yards from the hotel proper. It had three bedrooms, including a magnificent master, a spacious lounge and a patio that incorporated a private pool, which morphed into the rocks jutting out into the finest white sandy beach and the most glorious aqua water of the warm Indian Ocean. It was truly a piece of paradise.

The hotel was also beautiful in its simplicity; unobtrusive off-white, two-storey buildings surrounded by lush landscaping and water features. Situated on a private peninsula it was almost surrounded by calm, blue, inner reef Indian Ocean water, perfect for swimming and boating. The arrival experience was into a grand high arched lobby, with a spectacular view, at the far end of the bluest part of the sea. The bars and restaurants surrounded a series of pristine pools with dining tables set on little romantic islands. Maggie and Greg were entranced. They had never before been able to afford a resort like this.

Sam and Jimmy were also in their own special paradise. The hotel had its own children's area, which comprised of a miniature house, with doors and windows that were kiddie-sized and a garden with action oriented equipment of climbing frames, roundabouts, swings and so forth. It was a supervised area with all sorts of activities for different age groups. Such a nice change from all of the screen-based things they had become used to. For much of the day, the youngsters simply disappeared into the clutches of the kids' club, which left plenty of time for Maggie and Greg to hang out together.

Although the villa came complete with private butler, an excellently groomed and handsome Mauritian called Tajen, Maggie and Greg preferred to have dinner in the hotel restaurant and the kids loved having their meals with their newfound friends from the kid's club. After the second night Sam managed to persuade Maggie to invite a couple of other little girls for a sleepover at the villa. Maggie and Greg went out to dinner, leaving the young girls in the care of Tajen. Everything seemed to go well.

It did not take Maggie and Greg long to find their own new friends. On the first night out, they were invited at the bar to join a handsome-looking couple, Sue and Ian, who in turn introduced them to Jenny and Hamish, with whom they had dined the evening before. The six of them seemed to gel and soon they had requested the maître d' to organise a dinner table for their little group, at which much wine was consumed and many stories related. The weather was delightful and the dinners, served al fresco, at the glittering pool side were wonderful. In the world of the Saint Géran, nobody knew that the little family renting the villa, were the world's largest jackpot winners; they were just a successful couple from Dorking. During the day, Maggie looked fantastic in a series of striking bathing suits, including a particularly skimpy bikini. At the villa and around their private pool, she went topless. Tajen acted as if this were normal, which perhaps it was. If he was aroused at all, he did an excellent job at concealing it. In the evenings, Maggie sported a variety of summer dresses, in which she looked not only seductive, but quite beautiful. There was no question that she turned heads and Greg was secretly pleased.

The fifth evening of their stay was to be the last night that Sue and Ian would be at the hotel. Maggie decided it would be nice to organise a dinner party at the villa for them and their two friends. Tajen was only too keen to cooperate and to organise the affair. Together, he and Maggie, planned a menu, and he agreed to be the maître d' with the enlisted help of a waiter from the restaurant. The evening was a great success. Much alcohol was consumed. Maggie worried that

Greg seemed to be flirting with Jenny, whom, she had to admit, looked really sexy with a very lowcut blouse which revealed much of her impressive breasts. Maggie knew that Greg, being a 'breast' man, would not be able to resist admiring the view, but, even so, she was mildly irritated by her husband's behaviour. When dessert had been served, Hamish suggested that the men might like to visit the hotel casino. "What about the girls?" piped up Jenny, "aren't we invited too?." "Of course, my dear," said her husband, "of course you ladies are welcome." Sue declined on the basis that she had to pack and Maggie also, on the basis that she could not leave the children. "But you go, my darling" she purred to Greg, "see if you can win us a fortune!" So off traipsed Hamish, Ian and Greg, with a slightly inebriated Jenny in tow. "I'll be back soon," offered Greg to Maggie as his little troop left the villa in search of the casino.

Given the fact that Greg had consumed at least a bottle of wine on top of some predinner cocktails, he opted for a game that required no skill – roulette. He perched himself on a stool and was joined by Jenny, whilst Ian and Hamish headed for the blackjack tables. Greg bought £500 worth of chips and started to spread them across the table. He could, it seemed, do nothing wrong. Time after time his numbers came up and soon, after a remarkable run of good fortune, he had amassed an unbelievable pile of chips in front of him. The pit boss changed the dealer, not once, but three times; but this made no difference to Greg's incredible run of good fortune. A crowd soon gathered around the table. Punters at other tables stopped playing and joined the crowd, egging Greg on to bet larger and larger until he had reached the limits set for the table. His good luck continued. The manager of the casino, believing that all good things must come to an end and that soon Greg's run of luck would change, allowing the casino to claw back the chips, decided to increase the maximum bets allowed at the table. Greg made one last huge bet. The wheel seemed to spin forever. The whole crowd was straining to see. The little metal ball seemed to hang on the rim of the wheel for an eternity until it suddenly took a dive to a number – Greg's number! He had won £100,000; far more than anyone ever had in the history of the Saint Géran Casino, and enough, several times over, to pay for their holiday, villa and all! The casino did not have enough cash on hand to pay him out, so, armed with his credit note, having bought one last round of drinks for Ian, Hamish and Jenny, he sauntered back to the villa.

It was well after midnight. The villa was quiet, so he tiptoed in, trying not to disturb Maggie and the kids. Who he did disturb, however, was Maggie and Tajen. Greg was beginning to feel that his good luck was coming at a price.

Chapter Six

That night Greg slept in the spare bedroom. This was the first time in just under 12 years of marriage that he had not slept in the same bed as his wife. 'Slept' is probably not the appropriate word, for Greg's mind was racing. He loved Maggie dearly; she was a wonderful mother to their children, a terrific and witty companion, and the most beautiful woman, who could arouse him at a stroke. He wanted her to be happy. What was he doing wrong that had found her seeking sexual comfort from others? He and she still had an active love life, so why did she want more? Strangely, as he lay awake, his mind in turmoil, the thought of her being fondled by another man, aroused him. Maybe, she was right. Maybe a 'change' every now and then, could only help to stimulate the existing relationship.

In any event, as the night wore one, Greg decided that his relationship with Maggie must be saved; it was worth saving, not just for the sake of Sam and Jimmy, but because it was something special. Everything seemed to have changed since the lottery win. But why would such good news have such a strange effect?

As dawn appeared on the sparkling Indian Ocean, Greg crept into Maggie's bed, or to be more precise, their bed. He snuggled up to her and she embraced him. "Let's not talk about it now," he offered, "I love you with all my heart."

Maggie had been crying. She was glad he was back. "I'm so sorry," she began. Greg stopped her in her tracks. "Forget it," Greg comforted her, "Let's just enjoy the rest of our holiday." There was silence, but both knew that it could not just be forgotten. There would need to be a lot of work put in to mend things.

The rest of the holiday passed uneventfully. The children continued to have a ball. Maggie was amazed to learn of Greg's success in the casino. The hotel management, stunned at their losses at the roulette table, did everything in their power to lure Greg back to the tables, but he wasn't having any of it. He was going to turn the vacation into a profit, one way or another. He cheerfully supplied Management with his bank account details, and respectfully asked them to wire his winnings forthwith. The 'change' column had just risen substantially in his accounts. Word went around the hotel about Greg's run of luck at roulette and both he and Maggie became 'celebrities' in the orbit of the Saint Géran. They were bought more celebratory drinks than they could ever have imagined. Greg was beginning to realise that money came to money.

Back at home, life returned to something like normality. Maggie was keen to organise their safari trip and set about researching destinations. Clearly it would require another long-haul journey and at least a week away from home. Since Greg's proposed acquisition of the two recruitment agencies was reaching a critical stage, Greg asked Maggie if they could postpone Africa for a few weeks. She was disappointed, but she understood. On the other hand, she asked herself, does Greg really need to take on extra work, when, given their windfall, he could stop work all together? What was really important to him? Her and the children, or work? Greg went to pains to explain again, that if he could demonstrate that his business had grown so well, nobody would question where their money was coming from. So, instead of jumping back on a plane, he should conclude the pending deals if humanly possible.

As a result, Maggie renewed her social life in Dorking with her girlfriends and busied herself with the children. At the same time, she began to put the feelers out to various organisations that were involved in the protection of wildlife. Before taking the planned safari with Greg, she wanted to find out more about the existing charitable organisations which purported to be involved with saving elephants, her special love. Over the years she had made small donations to a couple of these organisations, namely 'Trunk' and 'Shawu'. She had also heard quite a bit about the Abu Elephant Camp in the Okavango Delta, Botswana. Trunk and Shawu both had headquarters in London, which Maggie decided to visit. She called Trunk on the telephone and explained that she was a potential donor and would like to come to their offices to see what they do. The woman at the other end of the phone line tried to dissuade her from a visit, stating that there was enough information in the publicity material for Maggie to make her decision re. sponsorship. The 'voice' explained the different levels of sponsorship available but did not seem to realise that Maggie might be a bigger fish. Finally, Maggie insisted that she speak to someone in Management and was, rather reluctantly, put through to a Mr Smallbone, to whom she explained that she might be interested in a donation substantially above the advertised tiers, and would like to come to the office to discuss this. Smallbone got the message and a time was set for a meeting a few days later.

Next, Maggie phoned Shawu. This organisation, she learned, was named after one of the 'big five' elephants in the Kruger Park, all of which were now deceased. Shawu had been immortalised in a life-size bronze statue, which graces the entrance to the Lost City at Sun City in South Africa. The Shawu foundation's sole purpose was to protect wild elephants from poachers, disease, and population encroachment. Shawu had a small office in London but was operated and managed from Johannesburg. All of this was explained by the person who answered the phone in London, and who duly arranged for Maggie to meet their senior representative, conveniently, on the same day as her scheduled meeting with Trunk.

When Greg returned from the office that night Maggie excitedly told him of her plans. He was pleased for her and was full of encouragement. He too, had good news. His deal to acquire his two major competitors was complete. He had paid more than they were really worth individually, but the combined result and the elimination of any real competitors in the field, would make the whole greater than the three independent parts. The legal side of the deal was, however, just the beginning. To make the merger work would now require a lot of attention and effort, which, of course, would mean a lot of office hours for Greg. He acknowledged (to himself) that, with all of their money, he could retire, but rationalised that it was necessary to make this merger work; then he could sell it for a good sum and retire with the whole world, or at least his tiny section of it, thinking that his funds were coming from the sale. Deep down however, he relished the challenge.

Despite the weight of all of this on his mind, Greg was anxious that Maggie should also be fully engaged, and so he enthusiastically debated with her a strategy for her upcoming meetings at Shawu and Trunk. "Now that my deals seem set, we should start to plan our safari," said Greg. "Maybe your meetings will give us some clues as to where we should go." With everything going on in his life at the moment, the last thing he actually wanted to do was to take a long trip, but he knew that this is what Maggie wanted and needed. Greg's love for Maggie, after over ten years of marriage was still as strong as ever. He loved her softness, but also her determination to do the right thing. He loved her as a mother of his two little ones and he loved her as the person that she was. And he loved her as a lover. She never failed to look gorgeous for him. They were made for each other and, as Maggie's favourite psychic had once told her, they were truly soulmates. So, despite the fact that taking a long-haul trip, just as he needed to take the lead in the amalgamation of his new companies, was not the best idea, it was just too bad. Maggie came first, and, anyway, with modern technology, he would not exactly be out of touch with the office. And, there was plenty that he could do to start the ball rolling at work before they went to Africa, because the trip would take a few weeks to organise. After a pleasant and loving evening together Maggie and Greg climbed the stairs in their little house and went to bed. Maggie was ready for Greg. Greg was too tired.

Maggie's trip to London a few days later was very stimulating. Greg had agreed to work from home for the day, so that he could take care of the kids. It had been a few months since Maggie had found herself in the joyous position of being a multimillionairess and she had hardly altered her buying habits at all. "Today," she had said to herself, "will be a day for me." Since her meetings were both scheduled for the afternoon, she decided to pay a visit to the ladies' department at Harrods. Not the generic one on the 3rd floor, but to the 'designer' floor. Nothing less! She was going to buy a couple of really nice outfits for everyday use and some evening wear for parties. She was. for once in her life, about to splurge on herself. Maggie had always dressed very nicely. She was never scruffy around the house, always wore makeup when she went out, and often looked quite stunning when she really made an effort. But, despite that, it had all been achieved on a fairly strict budget. She knew which high street brands suited her and which didn't. Greg had never restricted her clothes spending; he liked her to look nice and sometimes he liked her to look sexy. Nevertheless, Maggie was not wasteful with her shopping; she had often wandered into high end luxury brand stores just to get ideas, but had never made a purchase. Today was going to be different, she told herself. "I am going to buy what I want, regardless of price. – just this once!" At the same time, she thought, perhaps to make this less about herself, she would pick up a couple of cute items for the kids.

After two and a half hours in the store, Maggie emerged with two handfuls of green Harrods bags, and was helped into a taxi by the man with the top hat and tails. A few minutes later she was struggling through the doors marked 'Trunk', in Effingham Square, near Victoria. The entrance and lobby of the offices were far from swish. Maggie felt a little out of place with her green bags, which the friendly receptionist kindly offered to keep behind her desk. "Been shopping, then? the young lady said, in a way that sprinkled guilt all over Maggie. She had often looked with envy and well-heeled ladies waltzing down Bond Street with Givenchy or Armani bags. Now she felt that she was being envied. However, it was not long before a beaming Giles Smallbone, the General Manager of Tusk, came bustling down the hallway to greet her, arm outstretched for a warm handshake. "So nice of you to visit us Mrs Layburn. Come into my office, where we can have a chat." The office was not huge, but it comfortably housed a large antique desk, totally cluttered with paperwork, and a small couch and easy chair, distanced from each other by a coffee table that had definitely seen better days. "Cup or tea – or coffee, perhaps?" enquired Giles. "A black coffee would be nice," she ventured, "Americano?"

Giles picked up the phone and ordered two coffees, presumably from the girl at the reception desk. Maggie observed. Giles was dressed in sportscoat, slacks and suede shoes. He spoke with a rather county accent. "Probably been to public school," Maggie surmised.

"Now, Mrs Layburn, I understand that you might have an interest in, shall we say, a larger than normal donation? That sounds very nice. What can I tell you about Trunk?" Maggie, somewhat guardedly explained that she had, for some time, been interested in helping save wildlife. She was particularly interested in the problems caused by poaching in Africa and wanted to do something meaningful to help. She alluded to the fact that she had been fortuitous to have received an inheritance from a relative and had decided to utilise it for good causes. She wanted to learn more about the work of Trunk and how best she could contribute.

"If I may ask, Mrs Layburn, what sort of sum are you considering in regard to supporting wildlife?" "Oh, probably, about a million pounds," said Maggie, almost not believing that these words had come out of her mouth. "How precocious that must sound," she thought to herself, but she was quietly enjoying the moment.

"I see," said Smallbone, doing his utmost to conceal his amazement at the sum mentioned, as if it were an everyday occurrence, when, in fact, nobody, in the history of Trunk had ever walked in off the street and announced that they had a million pounds to donate. "Would that be a one-off payment, Mrs. Rayburn, or are we talking about continuing support?"

"Well, Giles, may I call you Giles? That would obviously

depend on how effectively you are able to utilise it," replied Maggie, whilst thinking that what she really meant was "that would depend on how well we get on together.

"Well, I must say, Mrs Layburn, that would be a most generous contribution indeed. Should you decide to do so, I must tell you that you would be the charity's largest individual donor and, indeed, larger than many of our corporates."

"Well, Giles, why don't you spend a few minutes telling me about the work that Trunk does and its successes and failures to date. I do have another appointment at four o'clock so perhaps you could just give me a quick primer for half an hour. I would be most grateful," she smiled her brilliant smile. Her blue eyes sparkled. Giles Broadbent was captivated. Who was this pretty woman who had walked into his office holding out the possibility of a million pounds per year? Why had he never seen her name or picture on the charity rounds? Was she for real? He would need to do some fact checking as soon as she leaves. In the meantime, he would put his best foot forward and give her the run down on Trunk's history and activities, both successes and failures.

Ninety minutes after Maggie had first set foot in the Trunk offices, she found herself struggling out of the front door with her Harrods bags. She had left Giles without any commitment, but with a promise to think things over and to get back to him within a few days. Giles, in turn, had promised her that he would put forward some ideas about how the charity could put her million to good use. He had also promised himself to find out much more about this mystery woman. Was she for real? Did she really have a million pounds to offer? He certainly wanted to meet her again; he had to admit to himself that she was rather attractive.

Shawu's offices were far less grand than Trunk's. In fact, they were not 'offices' at all, but just one room, in a residential street in Pimlico. The office manager/secretary/general dog's body, and, apparently the voice at the end of the phone, was a little dynamo of a woman, Penelope Strang, who looked as if she had just stepped out of the bush. Despite the fact that Pimlico and Chelsea were bristling with hairdressers, Penelope had obviously never been to one in her life. She was a wiry woman, probably in her late forties, with a strong handshake and an arm full of bangles and beads. Maggie felt a bit awkward with her Harrods bags.

Penelope ushered Maggie into the only available chair, other than the one behind her little desk. The embarrassing and obtrusive green bags seemed to fill the room. "Now, my dear," began Penelope, "how can I help you?"

Maggie explained that ever since she had visited Africa with Greg on honeymoon she had fallen in love with elephants and really wanted to do something to help with their survival. Now, having come into a sizeable inheritance, she found herself in a position of being able to offer financial support to a charity that was doing good work in this field. Penelope listened carefully, then launched into a description of the various levels of donation that were available and the benefits attached thereto. Maggie listened politely but then explained that she thought she might be able to donate substantially more than requested. "What sort of number are we thinking of?" enquired Penelope. This time Maggie was more cautious than in the previous meeting. She had the feeling that £1 million per year might just come as a shock to Penelope, whose charity clearly existed on crumbs. "Well, I was thinking about a quarter of a million pounds," she ventured. "Good God!" exclaimed Penelope, "that's more than we raise all year! That would be marvellous." She was clearly excited about the prospect and hastily went on the explain the structure of Shawu. Apparently the headquarters were situated in a rented office from one of the game lodge companies in Johannesburg. The Managing Director of Shawu was a South African entrepreneur, Mossie Mostert, who had turned a small family farm on the border of the Kruger Park into a sanctuary for animals damaged by poachers in the Park or young animals whose parents had been shot. His aim had been to release them into the wild, but along the way, he had been shocked by the game poaching and slaughtering that was rife and had started a training facility for protective game rangers. He needed to raise about £1 million per year to finance the operation, so, for Penelope, who was his part time fund raiser in the UK, the thought of being able to inject a quarter of the annual budget from one source was like a gift from heaven.

Maggie and Penelope chatted on for quite a while. It seemed that her office was actually the converted front room of her little Pimlico house, so, when six o'clock came around, she produced a bottle of South African red wine, which the two of them downed, as if in celebration of their meeting. Pizzas were ordered from around the corner and Maggie finally wobbled out of Penelope's house to head for the station at eight o'clock. At the end of the road she hailed a black cab. "Victoria station," she instructed, and then almost instantly had second thoughts. "To hell with that, I've got all these bags. Driver, take me to Dorking, Surrey, please." She called Greg to check on the children and wish them good night. She had half-expected Greg to be a little annoyed that she had not been in contact earlier but he was charm itself. He had enjoyed his time with the children and was busy playing a computer game with Sam. So, no problem there.

Greg could tell that Maggie had been drinking, but he didn't let on. He was anxious to hear how she had got on with the charities, but he was also anxious to wrap his arms around her body. Both children were in bed asleep by the

time the taxi pulled up outside the Dorking house and dis-
gorged Maggie with her bags. She excitedly showed Greg
her purchases, including a little close-fitting number that
she thought might appeal to him. Greg was glad for her; he
was pleased that she appeared to have had such a nice day.
He really wanted her to try on the tight-fitting little dress
but realised that she needed to tell him about her whole day
and the meetings with the charities. He poured them both
a glass of red wine and listened as Maggie relived her meetings. Her descriptions of Giles Smallbone and Penelope
Pimlico were quite amusing. "Well," offered Greg, once
Maggie had finished, "It sounds as if they are completely
different organisations. Maybe we should support both to
start with, to find out which does the best work." "Do you
really think so?" said Maggie enthusiastically, "I was hoping
you would say that, because that's what I think too. Oh, I
do love you, Greg." That night their lovemaking was particularly passionate. Greg had lately been determined to pay
attention to Maggie, since the incident in Mauritius, but,
even if he hadn't, the sight of her in the cheeky looking
cocktail dress she had bought in Harrods, would have been
enough to send any man over the top. For whatever reason,
Maggie, lately, had been looking especially attractive. How
lucky Greg was, he thought, to have such a vivacious woman
as his partner.

Chapter Seven

The trip to Africa was planned to start in three weeks. They had agreed to spend a few nights at the well-established Mala Mala camp in the Sabi Sands, next to the Kruger Park. They could use this as a base to take a look at Mossie Mostert's Shawu elephant refuge. Then, they would fly up to Kazungula, in Botswana, from where they could reach one of the sanctuary operations supported by Trunk. The trip would take just under two weeks and Greg's parents had been enlisted to look after the children for the duration.

In the meantime, Greg had finally given in to his urge to buy the Bentley. He looked lovingly at the cars in the showroom at Jack Barclays in Berkeley Square, not for the first time. He had decided to buy a Continental GT Convertible. This time the salesman realised that Greg was more than just a looker and took him seriously, pulling out a long list of specifications and customisations, which he ploughed through with Greg in tow. After a little while Greg interrupted him and enquired about the delivery time, given all of the individual specs available. "About six weeks," the salesman said. Greg was now like a kid in a candy store, just itching to get at the goods. Six weeks seemed far too long to wait, now that he had actually taken the decision to buy. "What about that one?" said Greg, pointing to a gleaming silver convertible on the showroom floor. "That, sir, is a used model," replied the salesman with some disdain, as if the car had the German measles. "How used?" shot back Greg. "Three thousand miles, sir." To Greg, the car looked immaculate and after all, what's three thousand? It's just been run in. The next day, paper work completed, Greg drove his 'new' Bentley out of the showroom. One of the proudest moments of his life.

Maggie was thrilled for him. He had immediately driven the new toy to Dorking to show it to her. "It really is lovely," she exclaimed, running her hands over the soft leather seats. "But I could never drive this. I would be too frightened that I would to crash it. And I can't use it for the children; they will drop their fish fingers all over it." "But you can still use the Land Rover, like always," said Greg. "Oh, really! You get a new toy and I am left with the old bucket. That doesn't seem right." A week later, Maggie's brand new, straight out of the Dorking showroom, Mini Cooper stood gleaming in their short driveway. The house was starting to look too modest to support three cars.

Willow and Ellen were surprised to see Maggie show up at their rendezvous in her new Mini. But they were even more shocked when Willow caught sight of Greg, on Saturday morning, driving down the High Street in a silver Bentley convertible with the hood down and the kids screaming in the little back seats.

Maggie was at pains to explain that Greg had pulled off a successful merger and that things had been going well for him at work. They seemed genuinely pleased for her and they all went for a spin through the lanes in the little red car, laughing and chatting ten to the dozen. "We should have a party to celebrate," said Ellen. "Whose house?" Maggie was too embarrassed not to invite them to her house, given that it was her husband who was doing so well, so it was agreed that they would have a get together with husbands and friends on the Friday before Greg and her were due to leave for Africa. Greg was not overpleased at the thought but the image of Ellen in party clothes soon cheered him up and so he audited his booze cabinet and small rack of wine and ordered the necessary replacements in readiness for the Friday evening. It would be good to have a party. Greg had been working hard for several weeks now, sorting out the complications and opportunities following the merger. He had not had much time for recreation or socialising, so the more he thought about it, the more a good party seemed like an excellent idea.

Maggie wore the little number that she had bought from Harrods; again, she looked stunning. About 20 friends and neighbours showed up, mainly young parents or singletons from the area. Naturally, Maggie's best friends were there and Maggie was delighted that Willow had brought the lovely Trixie and her husband, Hal. The kids had been deposited with Greg's parents in preparation for the trip to Africa. Greg had suggested that Ruby and Roland move into Greg and Maggie's house, but since they only lived a few miles away at Box Hill, they had preferred to stay in their own home and drive the little ones to school each day.

Willow, after a drink or three, did her normal party trick of allowing various men to fondle her; there was no shortage of takers, although Greg was not amongst them. Trixie asked Maggie to lend her an umbrella and some underwear, without letting on to the other partygoers. She then proceeded to perform a striptease behind the umbrella to the music of the 'stripper', much to the amusement of the room. Tossed from behind the umbrella, first came the pretty blouse she had been wearing followed by other items and finally a bra and panties. As her performance progressed the men in the room yelled out all sorts of encouragement; so did some of the ladies. Greg was wondering how she would manage to leave the room completely naked; he did not recognise that it was his own wife's underwear that was being flung from behind the brolly. He found himself quite aroused. But, of course, as Trixie triumphantly folded the umbrella, much to the amusement of the women in the room and the disappointment of the men, she revealed herself with all her clothes on, bar the blouse, which she hastily retrieved and donned. Everybody laughed and clapped. Greg was disappointed; he would have liked to see Trixie's boobs.

The party was a great success. It also served a purpose, for Greg was able to explain to his men friends and neighbours about his successful business deal. He deliberately kept the whole thing vague but tried to leave the impression that, as a result of the deal, he was able to buy a new 'second hand' car and how that had forced him to buy one for Maggie. Greg deliberately only opened the subject about his new found wealth after the party was well on its way, so he was mainly talking to a well-oiled audience who probably not have cared less because they were far more interested in Trixie's and Willow's antics.

By two in the morning the party was over, leaving Maggie and Greg to clear up.

"Do you find Willow attractive?" enquired Maggie, rather teasingly, as the put away the dishes. "Not really," Greg shot back, rather non-committedly. "I mean, do you find her sexy?" "Well, sometimes," said Greg. "Like, tonight?" Maggie wouldn't let go. "Yes, her behaviour was quite sexy, didn't you think?" asked Greg. "I think she does it just to wind up Ted," said Maggie, ignoring the question.

"I know who you really think is sexy," carried on Maggie, clearly not wanting to let the subject drop. "You, I think you're sexy, very sexy," said Greg, putting his arms around her and giving her a squeeze. "Ellen," said Maggie, "You find Ellen very sexy, don't you?" "Not half as sexy as you," Greg persisted. But he knew that Maggie had hit the spot. Yes, there was something very attractive about Maggie's friend, but so be it, he was married to Maggie, not Ellen, and he had no complaints about Maggie in that department. He knew that Maggie was just trying to arouse him, and, perhaps, herself. It worked. They were soon upstairs in their empty house making passionate love. The next afternoon they flew to Johannesburg.

Naturally they flew first-class, which was really a 'first' for Maggie. "I could get used to this," Maggie thought to herself as she slotted into the wide black leather seat, surrounded by buttons and lights, which at first, meant nothing to her. Life really was taking an upward curve in the luxury department. First, shopping at Harrods; then the arrival of Greg's Bentley; now first-class on British Airways. There were more buttons surrounding her seat than in the Bentley. "Buttons must be important for rich people," thought Maggie as she experimented with her seat and entertainment console.

Eleven hours after leaving London they arrived at Oliver Tambo airport, the après apartheid, renamed, Johannesburg airport. Maggie had been pampered all of the way, even to having her bed made for her by a friendly, but overweight, flight attendant. Because of the configuration of the plane she could not sit next to Greg, but she heard him familiarly snoring through the night.

Having cleared the airport formalities, they were met by a broad smiling African dressed in khaki, with a Mala Mala baseball cap and little signboard. "Welcome to South Africa!" he exclaimed. His teeth glistened. "My name is Straightman and I shall be escorting you to Lansaria airport to take the Mala Mala private plan. It is about a half hour journey." With that they traipsed after Straightman, who chatted amiably away as he pushed their luggage and then loaded it into a minibus, in which he then drove, mainly on a highway, to the little domestic airport, thirty miles north of the city. From the highway, Maggie and Greg could see the tall buildings of Sandton, in the northern sub-urbs of Joburg, across the vast and sprawling township of Alexandra. They were later to learn that all major South African cities were not far from African townships, where people lived in 'foot out of the door' tin shacks or small brick houses.

At Lanseria they climbed into a Citation jet painted in the Mala Mala insignia. The safari had begun.

Chapter Eight

Mala Mala had been one of the first luxury lodges to be opened in South Africa. It was situated in the Sabi Sands area of Mpumalanga, which used to be the Eastern Transvaal. Some years after the formation of the massive Kruger Park, effectively owned by the South African government, a large area of land on the lower western side of the park was sold off to private enterprises, which were licensed to operate game viewing businesses without the restrictions imposed on visitors to the Kruger. In Kruger Park, visitors are allowed to drive their own cars but are obliged to stay on dedicated roads, which, in effect, only covered about 1% of the park area. In the private concessions, visitors were not allowed to use their own vehicles and were required to stay in the licensed lodges, such as Mala Mala, from whence they are taken on game viewing trips in the lodge's vehicles, driven by experienced game rangers. These vehicles are allowed to leave the roads and go cross country, giving their drivers the opportunity to locate game and, if desired, follow it for observation.

Mala Mala, being one of the first concessions was a little run down by the time Maggie and Greg were visiting, but its owners had recently built some magnificent private lodges, complete with private waterholes for game and private swimming pools for the occupants. It was possible to be basking in one's pool, with or without a costume, looking at a herd of elephants or other animals basking in theirs. Naturally, Greg had reserved one of these new villas for himself and Maggie. It came with an endless river of champagne, private Land Cruiser, and private game ranger and tracker. After the formalities of the reception, carried out in traditional African style with singing, dancing and drums, Maggie and Greg were escorted to their villa. Maggie was dumbstruck with the beauty and elegance of the place, but even happier to see a herd of seven elephants right below the porch. As soon as the driver and porter had left, she threw her arms around Greg. "Ooh, I love you. Thank you for bringing me to such a heavenly place."

Greg and Maggie were keen to freshen up. Their plan was to have a shower, change, and then take a rest before meeting up with their ranger at 4 pm, for an evening game drive. The villas had two luxurious bathrooms, both of which had indoor and outdoor showers. Although they would share a bed, they decided to each take a separate bathroom. Maggie was in heaven. Her bathroom had every amenity you could possibly want, including the thickest and softest towels she had ever held. "All this luxury," she thought, "in the middle of the African bush!" Naturally, Maggie showered outside. She found it quite exciting. "What would I do if a lion came out of the bush? I would have to run away with no clothes on." She wondered whether anyone could see her in the shower. There appeared to be no direct sight lines to any of the other villas or buildings, but what if there was a peeping tom in the bush? "Well, who cares?" she thought, "let them enjoy the view!" There was a full-length mirror adjacent to the shower. Maggie examined her body. "Not bad for a mum," she thought to herself. She was quite tanned, especially her beautifully shaped legs; but her breasts were white. From a distance it would look as if she was wearing a white bikini top. "I shall have to expose them a bit more," she thought to herself as she rubbed her hands over them. "I shall get Greg to rub some suntan lotion on them. He will enjoy that." Meanwhile Greg was using the shower in the bathroom.

When they re-joined in the master bedroom, they were both feeling tired from the heat and the journey, so they slept. When they awoke, they were hungry, but it was almost time for the game drive. Luckily the villa was loaded with snacks and drinks – all on the house, or rather, within the exorbitant price they were paying. They gobbled down some biltong and waited for the tap on the door, which came promptly at four. There, standing in the porch was the dishiest young man Maggie had ever seen. "Good afternoon, are you ready for your drive? My name is Graham, but they call me Gee, and this is Simon, your tracker for today," he announced with an air of friendly authority. "We shall go on a game drive for about two and a half hours, then will bring you back here in time for dinner. You'll find some mozzie repellent on the table just inside the door. Better spray some on before we go, especially round the wrists and ankles." Maggie was wearing fairly loose-fitting brown trousers with a flowery long-sleeved blouse. Greg was in sweat shirt and shorts. The Land Cruiser was painted in a camouflage pattern; it had, behind the driver and passenger seat, two tiered rows of seats and no roof, thus allowing great sight lines from all four passenger seats. Some blankets were piled up on the front passenger seat, as if Gee was expecting cold weather. Simon, who had only nodded a greeting checked that they were comfortably seated and then clambered into the front seat beside the blankets and then they were off. Greg and Maggie had been on safari before, eleven years ago, on their honeymoon, but they were on a self-drive trip, so had to stick to the designated roads and did not have the benefit of a guide. This evening was clearly going to be different.

The Land Cruiser crunched along the dry dirt road out of the camp and headed into the bush, following a fairly well worn track. Once it was out of sight of the lodge Gee stopped to allow Simon to climb onto the tracker seat which was attached to the front of the vehicle. Gee also pulled out his rifle from beneath his feet and placed it beside him between the front two seats, presumably within quick reach. They continued on their way, then suddenly, Gee braked, and pointed to the bushes on the right. Initially neither Greg nor Maggie could see anything except under-growth. "Springbok," said Gee, very quietly, pointing to the right at about "three o'clock." Suddenly they saw move-ment, and then, amazingly began to realise that they were staring at a small group of perhaps six or seven beautifully marked buck. It was incredible how the markings on their skin blended so cleverly into the bush – something that they were to witness time and time again, even with the largest of animals, including giraffe and elephant. They trundled on for perhaps another five minutes and saw nothing. Then, suddenly, as they emerged from a dip in the track that had been carved out by a stream, long gone, they found them-selves face to face with a huge elephant. Gee stopped the car. They were no more than the length of a cricket pitch from this massive, but somehow serene, creature. "This is the matriarch," whispered Gee, "there are probably about a dozen elephants with her. We must wait here to see." The matriarch just stood, with head half turned in our direc-tion, almost daring us to come closer. Then slowly, out of the bush on the side of the road emerged a tiny elephant, no bigger than a small pony, followed by another and then another. They were like toy elephants. "How adorable!,"

Maggie whispered, "aren't they just cute?" Slowly more elephants appeared, in all different sizes. More mothers and a whole bunch of 'teenagers', until there were 12 in all. The only sound they could hear was the sound of the elephants crunching leaves and snapping branches. For Maggie, this was the most wonderful sight. They watched the herd for several minutes, whilst Gee whispered a tale of elephant behaviour. Then, after the whole herd had safely crossed the road, the old matriarch took one more look at the intruders, tossed her head so that her huge ears flapped, turned and walked off into the bush. Within seconds she, and the rest of her gang, were invisible. You could have driven passed them, not ten feet away, and you would not have seen them.

From here on, the ride only got better. Gee weaved his way off road through the bush in search of big cats until he found a pride of lion basking under a tree and then, 15 minutes later, a lazy leopard reclining on a branch. Maggie was in heaven, and she loved Gee's quiet stories and descriptions. Clearly, he was a man who loved his job.

Just as the sun was setting, Gee suddenly pulled into a little clearing, stopped the vehicle, and clambered out. From the innards of the Land Cruiser he pulled miscellaneous tin cans, which contained, wine, beer, and a fine selection of nibbles. He set them up on a little folding table and announced that "cocktails are served." There, on a little ridge in an opening in the bush, the four of them watched the glorious sunset and listened to nature. In the distance they could hear the roar of lions and the snorting of hippos – the sounds of Africa! Gee was South African; probably about 30 years old. He had been doing this job for several years and was, therefore, extremely experienced. He was also extremely good looking. Maggie found herself imagining all of the beautiful rich young ladies that Gee must have seduced at the camp over the years. Mala Mala had entertained many of the world's most famous people. Maggie was sure that Gee could have some interesting stories to tell.

Greg and Maggie had agreed that they would not talk about the real purpose of their visit to the staff, management, or guests at Mala Mala, until they had had a chance to visit Mossie Mostert – just in case it would be a problem for him, so they just acted as tourists with Gee and Simon. When the drinks and snacks were stashed back in the Cruiser and the sun had brilliantly set, it suddenly felt cool. They climbed back into the vehicle and headed for the lodge. They were grateful for the blankets. As they arrived, other guests were also disembarking from their game drives, although most of them seemed to be in vehicles that carried four or six tourists. There was much excited chatter about who had seen what. The other guests were a truly international crowd; a melange of Europeans and Americans. The only South Africans were the rangers; clearly at $2000 per night, Mala Mala was far too expensive for those who earned rand.

Maggie wanted to change, but Greg was happy to head straight to the bar, so Gee valiantly offered to walk Maggie back to their villa. Maggie was rather pleased to have the handsome hulk accompany her. "I'll wait outside, so that I can escort you back. It is not safe to walk on your own." Gee kindly offered. "Thank you," said Maggie, "I won't be long. Come in and pour yourself a drink, while I change." Gee grabbed a beer from the fridge and plonked himself down in a huge brown leather chair. From there, he could just catch a glimpse of Maggie, who had left the bedroom door tantalisingly ajar. She emerged a couple of minutes later. The loose-fitting game spotting outfit had been replaced by some tight white slacks and a top which she knew was quite a tease for Greg. She wondered if Gee would notice. If he did, he did not let on. He was politeness itself as he escorted her back to the bar, where he found Greg in an animated conversation with a youthful young American, Jake, and his delicate little wife, Julie. J and J were on honeymoon. It was their first time in Africa. They seemed quite nervous. Maggie had been hoping for a romantic evening dinner with Greg. It turned out that Greg had already invited J and J to join their table. "How very romantic," Maggie thought.

At dinner Jake told the story of how he had met a chemist in Sherman Oaks, California, who had invented a product now called NoGrow, which, if used as a shampoo, prevented hair from growing. Jake, apparently, had been experimenting with the stuff and, just as promised, his hair had not grown a centimetre since the first shampoo. "Can you imagine," said Jake, "men will never need to go to the barber again." "That's a good idea," said Maggie cheekily, "I understand that American barbers are pretty useless anyway." "Well, be that as it may," carried on Jake, "this product will put them all out of business. If the sales of this product equal only half of what men spend at the barbers, it will be huge." "But don't men go to the barbers for a chat, as well as a haircut?" said Maggie, clearly unimpressed at the thought of the product. Jake did not have an answer. Julie never said a word. Greg, on the other hand, seemed quite taken with the idea of being able to stop the world's hair growth and said that maybe he and Jake should talk some more about it on the following day, since it clearly was not of great interest to the ladies.

Next morning, after another wonderful game drive with Gee and Simon, Maggie put in a call to Mossie Mostert. It seemed that his farm was about 60 miles due north of Sabi Sands. Apparently, it was possible to cover about half of this distance on a tarred road. A plan was made for Mossie to send his driver to Mala Mala on the following day before lunch time. Mossie explained that he had plenty of spare sleeping accommodation on the farm and would be happy to have Maggie and Greg as his guest for a couple nights. His driver would pick them up and after their visit could either drive them back to the commercial airport at Nelspruit or back to Mala Mala, whichever they preferred. Maggie was excited to be going to look at the work of Shawu. She spent the afternoon quietly sitting on the veranda of the villa, alternating between reading, nodding off, and watching various animals as they took a mid-afternoon trip to the waterhole in front of the villa. Greg had gone for a coffee with Jake in an effort to find out more about NoGrow. The concept had appealed to Greg, who during the night had been thinking about how to get in on the ground floor with whoever was planning to manufacture and market the product. Greg liked the idea of a little punt on a start-up company and NoGrow, at first glance, seemed like a novel idea. Jake explained that the newly formed NoGrow company was looking for an investment 'angel' to help them bring the product to market. It seemed that for a million dollars, an investor could own 49% of the start-up and that such an injection of capital would be enough to get things moving. Greg expressed an interest and arrangements were made for Jake's partner in the enterprise, to come to London as soon as Greg was back, in order to dig into the details.

The evening game drive was as exhilarating as Maggie could possibly have desired. Gee and Simon had been alerted to the fact that a large female elephant was about to give birth, so, as soon as Maggie and Greg had clambered on board, the four of them headed off to where the elephant had been spotted earlier. The beauty of Mala Mala was that, because it was situated on a huge concession of land abutting Kruger, there were no crowds of tourists to clutter up the privileged guests' game viewing. If an elephant were about to give birth in the Kruger Park it probably would not have been in sight of a road, but should it be so, there would be a traffic jam of tourist vehicles trying to get a glimpse. Kruger had become so crowded that even a solitary warthog attracted a bevy of onlookers. The subject elephant in Mala Mala, was giving birth in a place where only the few vehicles from the camp could get to. As it happened, three Mala Mala vehicles set off to find the elephant and when they arrived, their passengers were not disappointed. The mother had, in fact, just produced a weeny baby, about the size of a large dog. The cord was still attached and the new born was wobbling around under the belly of the mother. She, in turn, was surrounded by a herd of elephants, circling protectively. The matriarch of the group stood to one side, ever watchful. The Mala Mala vehicles took it in turns to get as near as possible to the new-born. Cameras clicked and whirred. There was a lot of delight from the onlookers, particularly the women. Gee kept his land cruiser at the site for all of half an hour during which time he captivated Maggie and Greg with stories about elephant behaviour and culture. His somewhat clipped South African accent, almost whispered, was charming to listen to. Maggie was utterly entranced.

When they eventually got back to the lodge, Gee, once again volunteered to escort Maggie back to the villa, whilst Greg opted to go straight to the bar. This time she got in first with the dinner invitations. "Are you permitted to dine with the guests?" she enquired, as they disembarked. "Of course, Maggie; we are actually encouraged to," replied Gee quickly. "Well, we would like you to be our guest tonight, to thank you for being such a wonderful guide," she said, without giving Greg a chance to object, should he have wanted to. "It would be our pleasure, wouldn't it, Greg?" she quickly added. What could Greg say?!

"Well, thank you. That would be really nice," concluded Gee. That settled, Gee escorted Maggie back to her villa. This time, he did not stay whilst she changed. "I'll be back in ten minutes. I'll just go and freshen up." Fifteen minutes later he returned to walk Maggie back to the main lodge. He was bowled over when she opened the door. Her outfit was stunning. To him, she looked like a film star. And he should know, having had many as Mala Mala guests over the last few years. Maggie was not the first woman to have taken a fancy to this rugged South African.

Because of their impending journey to the Shawu farm Greg and Maggie had decided to skip the morning game drive and have a leisurely breakfast before their mid-morning pick up. Gee and Simon were assigned some other guests, so Maggie was not sure that they would be back before she and Greg had to leave. As it happens, the morning game drive was over well before Mossie's driver appeared, so Gee stopped by for a coffee with them before they left. He told them how much he had enjoyed their company and hoped that they would be back. Over dinner the night before Maggie had told him of their plans to financially support the Shawu project, even though she and Greg had previously decided not to do this. Gee was naturally extremely interested, even enthusiastic, about this and offered whatever assistance he could give. He knew about Mossie's efforts to look after orphaned animals from Kruger and his efforts to train a force of anti-poaching "police." Needless to say, he was very supportive. "Good luck, with your visit to Shawu," said Gee as they prepared to leave. "If you want to stop by here on the way back, you will be most welcome. I can speak to the boss to get a special rate." "That's kind of you, Gee," said Greg. "We'll give you a call."

Mossie's transport was a bit more battered and far less comfortable than the Mala Mala vehicles; its suspension was shot and the paintwork somewhat rusty. Nevertheless, the driver, Chukka, was an amusing and charismatic guide. With a short round body and beaming smile, it was apparent that, if nothing else, Chukka was well fed. He was wearing khaki shorts, over which his ample belly fell and a khaki shirt where the buttons were taking a strain. His driving was erratic, although to give credit where it is due, it was mainly so from avoiding the numerous potholes in the dirt road. Both Maggie and Greg were quite relieved when they reached the tarred road, although this turned out to only have marginally less holes than the dirt one. The road led through several African villages, with houses, or rather shacks, sprawling in either side. If they had been driving through these villages just 20 years prior, there would have been no tin. The houses would all have been thatched rondavels and much prettier for that. The villages were still colourful, although very dusty. Strangely, amongst all the hubbub, poverty and general dowdiness of the villages, whenever they saw school children, they were smartly attired in school uniforms. Throughout the journey Chukka chatted away about the state of the world, or, more specifically 'his' world. From time to time he slowed to wave at or call out to a villager. He seemed to know a lot of people en route, although both Greg and Maggie noticed that they were mainly the pretty girls.

After about an hour they once again turned off on to a dirt road. A little wooden sign on a post indicated that they were on the right road. Shawu. Animal Conservancy, it proclaimed with rather scrawly black paint. "No waste on logo design," thought Greg, "that's good." The countryside, which earlier had been dotted with craggy outcrops, was now flat and brown; you could say parched. It clearly had not rained for weeks. Chukka and his passengers bounced along the potholed road for another ten minutes or so until a wire fence with a ranch type gate appeared. A uniformed security man, having seen the cloud of dust that was Chukka's jeep approaching, swung open a rusty gate to let them in. Chukka and the guard exchanged a few cheerful words in an African language that neither Greg nor Maggie understood, then with a cheery farewell, they were headed off into the Shawu estate. Rounding a bend in the track, around a little hillock, they suddenly spotted a sprawling bungalow, surrounded by outbuildings and sheds of all shapes and sizes. There, standing on the porch was a large white man, with a ruddy face, in shorts and shoes with long socks. "Welcome to Shawu," he bellowed, in a heavy Afrikaans accent. "You must be Maggie. I've heard all about you from Penelope in London. Welcome my dear, and welcome to you, sir," he boomed as he descended the steps of the stoop. "You must be Mr Layburn." "Greg," said Greg, "call me Greg. And you must be the famous Mossie Mostert."

The inside of the bungalow was surprisingly well furnished, although slightly worn. Their host escorted them to a wing on the ground floor, which he described as the 'guest wing'. There appeared to be a couple of bedrooms there. He escorted the visitors to the larger of the two, which was nicely equipped and had a bathroom en suite, albeit a bit ramshackle. "You'll find everything here that you need," said the host. "I'll leave you a moment to freshen up. When you are ready come through. We'll have a bite of lunch." Despite the fact that they had travelled with the windows closed, they were amazed to find that, not only were they both covered in sandy dust, that it had even found its way into their luggage. Despite this, they decided that now was not the time for a shower, so they dusted themselves down, Maggie ran a brush through her golden hair, repaired her make up, and then re-joined their host in the lounge. Mossie offered drinks; a cold Castle lager for Greg and a cool South African rosé for Maggie. Then they sat down in a sheltered area of the stoop for a delicious salad with cold cuts and Mrs. Ball's chutney.

Over lunch Mossie described in some detail the works of the ranch. Apparently, his family had owned this piece of land for many years. It abutted the Kruger Park, but, in fact, their ownership predated the formation of the Park. Mossie was an engineer, with a small business in Johannesburg, but his heart was in the ranch, where he had spent the bulk of his childhood. When the ugly business of game poaching in the Kruger, and elsewhere, started, Mossie had taken it upon himself to do his bit to fight it. He loved the wild animals and respected their right to live peacefully and without human encroachment. Rhino and elephant were being slaughtered wholesale by local gangs who sold the ivory to Chinese dealers for a pittance. The Kruger administrators simply did not have the manpower nor the firepower to put a stop to it. Mossie had decided to help out. He realised that many of the young offspring from the murdered animals had lost their parental and family protection and were just left to wander until they were attacked by others or starved to death. So, he built on his ranch a series of secure pens, large enough for the youngsters to exercise freely, but where they could be nurtured in safety, until they were large enough to be released and fend for themselves in the park. At the same time he built what was in effect an animal hospital, where he could treat, or operate on, other damaged species, such as the big cats. In addition to this he set up a school for local young men to train them as an auxiliary animal protection force. Once trained he effectively loaned his little army to the park's police, where they functioned as an anti-poaching unit, with enough fire power to bring down the poachers. He had named the organisation Shawu after one of the legendary big six massive elephants that had graced the Kruger. His little engineering business in Joburg was not able to completely cover the costs involved, so he had launched the Shawu charity, which sought to raise funds, mainly in the industrial heartland of South Africa. Mossie explained that his small efforts were just scratching the surface of the poaching problem, not just in the Kruger Park, but all over Africa. "Unless something more can be done," he explained, "our grandchildren will never see a live elephant."

Following lunch, Mossie took his visitors on a tour of his facilities. There were ten large pens, each about the size of half a football pitch. An elevated metal walkway had been erected in between the two banks of pens, so that workers could walk the length of the pens with a good view down into all of them. Each pen had a water hole and feeding troughs. Several of the pens were occupied with very young rhinoceros, all of them with their horns chopped off. "They will grow again," explained Mossie, "just like your fingernails. But we don't want to attract poachers here." In a couple of pens there were four baby elephants, who were obviously orphans. Then, in one of the outwardly ramshackle sheds was, effectively, an animal hospital and operating theatre, with glistening modern equipment. Mossie explained that this was used for treating wounded animals, which, after convalescence would be released back into the park, unless they had lost limbs and would not have been able to survive without protection. He explained that the rules of the park were to let nature take its course and not interfere. "Large animals live by killing smaller ones, so we must let nature take its course," he explained, "but where an animal has been maimed by homo sapiens, we have the duty to help it."

Mossie then took the couple into one of the other large sheds. Here there was a classroom, with materials for teaching about weapons and poachers' tactics and methods. At the back of this building was a practice shooting range. The targets were Chinese, even though, of course it was not actually the Chinese who did the killing; they just paid for it. There were no trainees in evidence and Mossie explained that he had temporarily shut down the 'school' due to lack of funds. Despite the fact that the whole place had a sort of Heath Robinson look about it, Greg was impressed, particularly by the dedication an apparently rough diamond like Mossie, had put in to the project. Maggie was upset to see animals in distress. She was appalled to hear the stories of the vicious and greedy poachers. She was so glad that she would be able to help and thanked God for the opportunity she had been given. "The real ticket holder probably wouldn't have done any of this," flashed across her mind.

That evening, before dinner, Mossie took the pair, with Chukka in the driving seat, into the park. Tourists are not allowed in the Kruger after sunset, but Mossie, because of his relationship with the park management, had a special dispensation to enter, which he could do through a private gate, separating his land from Kruger. To be able to go on a night drive, where you can have the whole park to yourself is a special privilege. Whilst Chukka drove slowly along, Mossie, operated a floodlight mounted on a swivel on the roof of the car. As he swung it from left to right, back and forth its beam picked up eyes, shining like reflectors on a bike. Where there were eyes, there was an animal. Somehow or other, Mossie and Chukka were often able to identify the animals and, from time to time, Maggie and Greg, having been alerted to what they were, could just about make out the dark shapes in the bush. When Mossie indicated that Chukka should stop the car, they all sat in the dark and listened. The intermittent sounds of Africa were magic, magnified by the silence. The stars were as bright as the two tourists had ever seen, shining through a clean atmosphere. The bright moon was upside down. Gradually Maggie's and Greg's ears and eyes became accustomed to these magical surroundings. After a while, Mossie switched on the swivelling spotlight and started to move it around. Suddenly he stopped it sharply. "Lion," he whispered. Maggie and Greg's eyes followed the beam, which had settled on a couple of brown eyes. Mossie moved the beam from the eyes onto the lioness's body. There, nestled up beside her were some cubs. Mossie had been hoping that the lioness would be on the prowl, looking for a kill, but it seemed that she was perfectly content to lie there with her offspring. After five minutes or so, Mossie indicated to Chukka that they should move on. On the rest of the drive our spotlight picked up all of the big game; dark shapes moving almost silently through the bush. At one point they stopped to look at a chameleon, which the swivelling spotlight had illuminated as they drove passed. Chukka got out and picked it up. He placed it onto a sheet of paper and, before their eyes, under the torchlight, it turned white. Then he moved it onto the black case of his binoculars, and it turned black. Maggie quietly marvelled at the beauty of mother nature.

That evening, after the drive, Mossie entertained his visitors to dinner, which had been prepared by his resident cook. A couple of bottles of wine were consumed and the conversation was lively. Mossie explained the financial set up of Shawu and how it was governed, as a charity, by himself and some selected trustees, all of whom were South African benefactors. He had heard from Penelope in London that Maggie might be willing to make a sizeable donation. He told her how very welcome that would be and that, if so, she should also be invited to become a Trustee. It was agreed that, due to the lateness of the hour and the quantity of wine that they had drunk, this matter should be pursued in the morning. "You're welcome to stay on the stoop for a nightcap," offered Mossie, "but I'm off to bed. Breakfast anytime from eight onwards. Sleep well."

Maggie and Greg sat on rocking chairs on the stoop; Greg nursing a single malt and Maggie with the last in the bottle of red wine. "Thank you so much for bringing me here," she said to Greg, "I do love you!" "Don't thank me, my love. Thank our lucky stars. There they are. Look at them. As clear as you will ever see them. But I am so glad that you are happy." "Happy, and sad," replied Maggie, "the thought of those bastards shooting those baby's mothers is just terrible." They drank in silence for a while. Greg could have willingly undressed Maggie right there on the porch under the African stars; he was already doing so in his head. Maggie had such beautiful breasts and the pertest of bottoms. He could feel that he was ready. "Let's turn in," he said, and she agreed. She, too, was ready, intoxicated by the beauty of Africa. Once inside their private quarters they made love – for the first time on this trip. Greg was totally immersed in Maggie's body; Maggie was fully physically engaged but, to her surprise, it was an image of Gee that she had in her head.

The next day passed pleasantly enough. Mossie produced the accounts of the charity and details of the Trustees. Greg spent a little time reviewing the numbers. They paid a visit to the animal hospital in the shed, where a lame leopard, which had been brought to the sanctuary by the Kruger rangers, was having splints applied. Greg had plenty of work that needed attention from London, so, whilst Mossie took Maggie for a trip to the local village to buy supplies, he busied himself with the issues at the office. The next morning, Maggie and Greg were due to catch an early flight from Nelspruit airstrip to Kazungula in Botswana. Since there was only one flight a week on that route, they dare not miss it, so Mossie suggested that they leave at 4 am, even before sunrise. With this in mind, all three were in bed by ten o'clock, ready for an alarm call at 3.30 am. Greg went fast asleep as soon as he hit the bed; Maggie lay enjoying the night sounds for a long time, until, she too, drifted off. She knew that she had to return to England, sooner or later, because of the children and Greg; but her heart was already lost to Africa.

Chapter Nine

Kazungula, in Botswana, turned out to be a little town, almost on the border of three other countries; Zimbabwe, Namibia, and Zambia. The Chobe River separated Namibia and Zambia from the other two. A few miles to the East the Chobe ran into the mighty Zambezi, 50 miles from where it flowed over the famous Victoria Falls. To the east of Kazungula was the Chobe National Park, home to over one hundred thousand elephants, the largest elephant population in the World. The Savuti Elephant Salvation Camp was situated about eighty miles from the Kazungula gate of the park. To get there would mean about three hours' drive on a dirt road.

For many years the airport at Kazungula had been a grass strip with a thatched hut for administration, customs, and immigration. It had been replaced a couple of years prior to the Layburn's arrival with a huge stainless steel, glass, and stone building that would have looked perfect in Nice, but was completely out of place half a mile from the Chobe River. The building looked new, but nothing seemed to work, including the officials in it. After multiple form filling and getting in line, Maggie and Greg emerged from the baggage hall, pushing trolleys with wonky wheels, to find a large, ever-smiling, black man holding a Trunk sign bearing their names. "Good morning sir and lady. My name is Sunday Times, and I will be your driver to the Savuti Camp. Please follow me." With that he took over the two wonky trolleys, and managed to manoeuvre them through a sliding door that no longer slid, in the direction of a spanking new minivan, colourfully decorated with the Trunk logo. They travelled a few miles on a tarred road, through the ramshackle little town of Kazungula, complete with its backpackers' motels, liquor stores, and mini-market, until they reached the rather grand gates marking the entrance to the Chobe National Park. With the formalities over at the gate, the three of them headed west at the maximum speed allowed, 20 miles per hour.

Because it was now approaching midday and the sun was at its hottest, they saw very few large animals as they bounced along the well-used track; the animals had the good sense to rest up in shaded spots, out of the scorching sun and out of sight of homo sapiens and their own natural enemies. There were plenty of buck, of all varieties, and the odd warthog scurrying across the road, but little else. Greg wondered how over 100,000 elephants could possibly be hiding. For a while the road hugged the Chobe River, initially passing the Chobe River Lodge, which was the only tourist lodge that had been ever built within the boundaries of the national park. At one time, it had been Africa's premier luxury lodge, situated on the banks of the river and overlooking a floodplain on the opposite bank, which attracted a multitude of thirsty animals. This was the lodge in which Elizabeth Taylor and Richard Burton had famously remarried shortly after they had divorced, much to the consternation of their lawyers and financial advisors. Apart from the fact that the travellers did not see another building for the next two hours, they saw very little at all, except for scrub and bush. Maggie, after such an early start, found herself nodding off, but kept being startled awake by bumps on the road.

After about 90 minutes Sunday Times suddenly braked sharply and stopped the van. They had just driven into an unusually wooded area. "Giraffe," he exclaimed, "plenty." Neither Maggie, not Greg, had seen them, but, lo and behold, after taking a closer look, there appeared to be dozens, no further than a stone's throw from the vehicle. At first glance, they looked like trees. If Greg had been driving, he would have gone straight passed without even noticing them. They stopped and watched for a minute or two, then proceeded. Maggie had to admit to herself, that, as gentle and elegant as they are, giraffes are actually quite boring. She imagined that, once you got to know them closely, they probably all had their own personal characteristics and stories but, apart from being amazingly beautiful, they were not very exciting to watch.

Soon after the giraffe sighting, they reached a crossroads with signage carved on a stone, announcing that Savuti was seven miles away. Maggie and Greg had had enough bouncing around for one day, so were happy to know that they were almost there. Greg had already decided that, when it came time to leave, provided that Savuti had a landing strip, he would charter something to fly them out when they were ready. As they approached the Trunk camp, he was, therefore, rather relieved to see a windsock flapping in the breeze in the distance. "Where there is a windsock, there is an aeroplane," he thought to himself.

Giles Smallbone, in London, had made sure that the potential donors were going to be looked after. The head of Trunk's operations for Africa, Gillian Gieldgud, was there to meet the van as it slowly pulled up in front of the beautiful thatched building, whose entrance was guarded, rather ironically, Greg felt, by two huge ivory tusks. Ms Gieldgud looked the part; a slender lady, dark-haired, bespectacled and business-like. She was dressed in brown slacks and cream long sleeved blouse, with a large stylish buckle on her belt. Her welcoming face cracked a broad smile as she put out her hand to greet them and introduce herself. "You must be really tired," she observed, "It is a long, hot, trip, isn't it? Let me show you to your accommodation, so that you can freshen up. When you are ready, I have arranged a light lunch because I assume you must both be starving by now?"

The Trunk Savuti camp, although having the prime purpose of rescuing elephants, was also operating as a guest lodge, in an attempt to offset some of the expenses. It turned out that there were six private suites, part tent and part rondavel, which were available to tourists. Gillian explained this as she walked the couple to the accommodation that she had had prepared for them, which appeared to be the farthest 'tent' from the lobby, down a dusty path of stepping stones. Maggie and Greg's 'room' consisted of an oblong tent in which there was a double bed, a desk/table and a couple of canvas chairs. At one end the tent was attached to a rondavel, which appeared to have mud walls and a thatched roof. This was the bathroom, or more precisely, the shower room and wc. At the other end of the tent, near the foot of the bed was an opening with a veranda which overlooked the obligatory waterhole. The whole set up was brown on brown. It looked quite basic, but seemed comfortably enough. Incongruously, a free-standing metal air conditioning unit had been plonked near the opening to the veranda. As soon as Gillian had gone and Sunday Times had delivered their bags, Greg switched it on. It immediately started to rattle.

Half an hour later, having freshened up from the dribble of water coming from the shower, Greg and Maggie presented themselves back in the lobby. Gillian was on the phone. "Giles sends his best regards," she announced, "he was just checking that you had arrived safely." "Thank you," said Greg and Maggie, in unison, both marvelling that the phone actually worked in such a desolate spot. Whilst the new arrivals had been cleaning up, Sunday Times had unloaded his Kazungula shopping from the van. This, apparently, included provisions on the cook's shopping list. Presumably Ocado nor even Amazon did not deliver to Savuti. Anyway, without really focusing on where the food came from, Maggie, Greg and Gillian tucked into a buffet of cold meat cuts and salad that was most welcome. Gillian explained the mission of the Trunk camp and why it was situated at Savuti. It appeared that it served two main functions, both related to the elephant population and nothing else. First, like Mossie Mostert's place in South Africa, it was a foster home for displaced, motherless, and often injured baby elephants, whose mothers had been the victim of poaching. Second, it was a sanctuary for elephants who had been kept elsewhere in captivity, with a goal, where possible, to return them to their rightful home in the bush. It appears that one arm of the Trunk charity reached out to zoos, circuses, and private owners of elephants to encourage their owners to give these magnificent creatures their freedom. To do this, of course, was a massive undertaking because elephants held in captivity, are logistically very difficult to release and transport. It is also very expensive and time consuming, let alone, highly specialised work. Trunk, it would appear, were inundated with requests, worldwide, from people who had identified captive elephants in need. Savuti had seemed a good place to allow release into the wild because there was very little risk of human encroachment and plenty of elephant herds for the releases to link up with, although, of course, they were not always welcomed.

Trunk had had some success with release, but, sometimes, had found that this was just not possible. Gillian also explained much of the other work that Trunk did to assist in fighting the battle against poaching, including training anti-poaching units, equipping rangers with the means to fight back, paying for fencing and patrolling and so on.

In the afternoon, Gillian gave Greg and Maggie a tour of the facility. Much like Mossie's place, there were fenced in pens for the security of the young orphans and the sick. But there was also a massive fenced area covering several square miles where previously domesticated elephants could roam and fend for themselves. Upon their return to the main lobby, Gillian produced Trunk's annual report and, more specifically, the accounts for Savuti. It would appear that Maggie's potential £1 million per year, could fund the operation of this particular camp for a year and allow the transportation of, maybe, another dozen, elephants in captivity from far flung places. It was up to Maggie to decide, but, of course, the trustees of the charity would be profoundly grateful. Maggie thanked Gillian for the information and told her that, after discussion with Greg, she would announce her decision as soon as they got back to London in a few days' time.

It seemed to Greg that not much more could be done at the camp. "Gillian, we need to get back to London as soon as possible. Is it possible to arrange a charter flight out of here back to a major airport tomorrow? I see that you have a strip here." Maggie was a little surprised that he had not consulted with her about this. She had thought they might go into the bush a couple more times before heading home. She said nothing. "Of course," replied Gillian. "As a matter of fact, I had planned to leave tomorrow, so we could organise a pick up in the morning. I need to get to Joburg, which we can do via Maun, to the south or Kazungula, where you arrived. Or there is a helicopter based at Kazungula, so that might be the smartest route, plus there are daily flights from there to Oliver Tambo. I'll get on to it now, to see what I can organise."

"Thank you," said Greg, "We will pay for the chopper, naturally." Gillian nodded her appreciation and left for the little office at the back of the lobby.

"You might have discussed that with me first," said Maggie, in a tone which reflected her annoyance. "We were due to stay here another day, then go back to Mala Mala for a couple of nights. Your parents aren't expecting us back for another five days," "Yes, I know, but I think we have accomplished what we need to know, and there are plenty of things I need to get done in the office. I just can't communicate with anyone easily from here." "I realise your frustration, and I see that I am more interested in the bush than you are," replied Maggie, "but you still should have talked to me about it before her." "I'm sorry, my love. You're right. But I really do need to get back to civilisation. Why don't you go back to Joburg for a couple of nights, and take a look around? Maybe do some shopping? I'll come there with you and then go ahead to England and you come back as planned on your original ticket. I'm fine with that, and you can enjoy yourself." "Are you sure?," said Maggie, who had already decided that was what she was going to do. "Of course, my love. You have a good time. I can see that you love it here. When we get back to England you can tell me where you want the donations to go." Maggie's heart missed a beat. She would go back to Joburg, although her head was in Mala Mala.

Gillian returned from her little office with good news. A helicopter had been arranged to pick the trio up at 9.30 next morning to take them back to Kazungula, from where they could catch the 2 pm flight to Johannesburg. This was perfect for Greg, who could then connect to the 8 pm British Airways plane to London. Greg immediately called Louise in his London office for her to make the airline reservations as well as book a hotel room in Johannesburg for his wife. Louise, ever efficient, messaged him back 15 minutes later with the necessary confirmations and a booking for three nights in the name of Maggie at the Sandton Intercontinental Hotel. All was set.

The next day, the three parted company at Oliver Tambo. Greg stayed on the non-South African side of immigration, where he bade farewell to Maggie with a big, long, hug and to Gillian with a peck on the cheek. He would have had time to go through immigration with Maggie, to make sure she was safely in a taxi, before re-embarking. However, with Maggie's assurances that she would be okay, he opted to pass a few hours in the British Airways' first-class lounge. Gillian assured him that she would help Maggie into a cab, before she took her onward flight connection from the domestic building to Cape Town, which was the home of Trunk's African headquarters. Maggie said nothing, but was just a teeny bit hurt that Greg was less than gallant about the matter. On the other hand, she thought, "It's nice to be free."

The Intercontinental Hotel turned out to be a tall skyscraper of a building with 26 floors surrounding a building-high atrium. The décor was very swish, but very masculine. Louise had booked Maggie a corner suite on the 24th floor with spectacular and panoramic views across the upmarket suburbs of Sandon and the high-rise offices, in the distance, of the more commercial centre of Johannesburg. The hotel was connected by a skywalk to Africa's most spectacular shopping mall, Sandton City. Having unpacked her things and sent off some laundry and pressing, Maggie strolled across the bridge to the Mall, in search of some things to take back to the kids. The hotel, quite naturally, abutted the luxury goods area of the Mall; all the usual suspects were there. She might as well have been in Bond Street rather than Africa. She walked quickly passed Armani, and Gucci, and Versace, thinking that she could buy all that in Europe, until she found the ordinary shops, including those full of colourful African handicrafts and toys. Her mind, however, was elsewhere. In fact, her mind was on Mala Mala, where she would far rather be than in a shopping mall. She had three days to kill, or by now, two days and a bit. Dare she take a quick trip back to the bush? What would Greg think when he found out? What could be her excuse? "Stop thinking about yourself," she suddenly admonished herself. "Concentrate on the kids, for a moment."

This trip to Africa had been wonderful, but this really was the first time that Maggie had been away for more than a weekend from her little ones. She missed them terribly. Although she had FaceTimed them every day and sent them pictures of the animals they had seen, it was not the same thing as the hugs she got at home. Some days, on the phone, they had been almost dismissive, as if to punish her for being away. They didn't seem unhappy with Grandma and Grandpa; in fact, they were obviously enjoying themselves and being, she supposed, quite spoilt. It seemed that she was missing them more than they were missing her. That sucked.

For half an hour or so she rummaged through the colourful tourist shops, until she found a few items that she thought would appeal. A car, made out of wire coat hangers for Jimmy and a wonderfully happy doll for Sam, dressed in robes, she was told by the shop assistant, from the Transkei, the birthplace of Nelson Mandela. Armed with those and a couple of African games, Maggie wandered back to the hotel. This time, however, as she passed through 'luxury alley', her eyes were taken by a striking pair of red shoes in the Versace store. They just had her name written on them. They could cheer her up.

Back in the hotel suite, sitting in splendid isolation, fiddling with the knobs on the television handset, she decided to call Mala Mala. After all, Gee had said that she would be always welcome and would arrange a special rate. Rather be alone there, with the animals, than in Sandton City. She got through immediately and asked for Gee. She had worked out that he would be back from the afternoon game ride by now. "I'm terribly sorry," replied the lady at the desk, "Gee is off duty for the next four days and is not on the property." "Can I call him?," said Maggie. "I'm not authorised to give out staff phone numbers ma'am," came the reply. "Well, could you please call him for me and give him my number in Johannesburg, please?" said Maggie, as politely as she could, knowing that she was now totally dependent on the goodwill of the lady on the other end of the phone. The receptionist agreed. Maggie thanked her and hung up. She sat and waited. She was just in the process of opening the minibar when the phone rang. "Hi Maggie, I got your call. I see you are in Joburg. Did you have a good trip? I am dying to hear all about it. How's Greg?" Gee sounded quite excited. "Guess what," Gee continued, "I'm in Joburg too; taking a few days leave. Can I get together with you and Greg, or are you too busy?" "Wow, that's great, Gee. I would love to tell you all about the trip, but it's just me here. Greg had to get back to the office in London." "Aw, well, maybe you'd rather give it a rain check, then," said Gee. "Of course not, I would just love to see you. What are you doing this evening?" "Whatever it was can wait. If you like I'll come around to the hotel and take you out to dinner. How's that?" Maggie did not let him know how happy she was with this suggestion. "What luck," she thought. "How fantastic! Maggie was strangely excited about seeing Gee again; he was so handsome. Yet, despite his ruggedness, he seemed gentle and kind. He clearly knew his animals. She wondered what he would be like in the city, away from the bush environment.

Thirty minutes later there was a call from the lobby. Gee was downstairs. "Send him up to the suite please.," she instructed. Maggie had used the 30 minutes to change into something nice for the evening and redo her make up. Before opening the suite door, she checked herself in the full-length mirror. Yes, she did look good. Bronzed from the bush, but elegant in a skirt and blouse with the bright red Versace shoes. "Come in," she beamed, and moved forward to give him a little peck on the cheek. She ushered him into the spacious lounge of the suite and offered him a drink. He chose a Castle. She opted for a glass of red wine. Like a gentleman, he got up and poured it for her. They sat and chatted. Or, rather, they sat and Maggie chatted. She related the events of the four days that had passed since she and Greg had left Mala Mala. She was thinking that she might help both charities but, in the back of her mind, an idea was forming and that was to start her own animal welfare charity, where she would not have to work through the Giles', Mossie's or Gillian's. She hadn't formulated the idea at all, but thought that talking to Gee might help her and, maybe, who knows, Gee might be a part of it. She would like that.

Gee suggested that they walk to Sandton Square, next door to the hotel, for dinner. Personally, he loved Jimmy's, the steak restaurant in the Square, but wondered if Maggie might not be keen on red meat. He did not know that she had a son called Jimmy. So, he headed for the Fishmongers Arms, where they sat on the veranda, ate, drank and chatted.

Gee told Maggie about his background and his family. He had, in fact, been born and raised in the northern suburbs of Johannesburg, not too far from where they were seated, although, at that time, Sandton Square in its present form, did not exist. Greg's dad was an accountant and his mother a homemaker, just like Maggie. Greg had attended Bryanston High School, during the time of seismic change in the South African political scene. The school catered for children from the mainly white suburbs, so, when Greg was there, by far the majority of students came from well-to-do white families. He explained that he had always loved the bush and had never wanted to do anything else as a career than to work with animals. Although he went to university in Cape Town, as soon as that was finished, he joined a safari company to be trained as a ranger. It was obvious to Maggie that Gee truly loved what he did, and Maggie could certainly sympathise with that. As he spoke, so enthusiastically about his life and, in fact, about everything Maggie was more and more enraptured by him. She could feel herself being drawn in by his easy charm. As the wine flowed, she found herself more and more attracted to him but the voice of common sense kept reminding her that she had another life, far from Africa.

The dinner finally came to an end and Gee escorted Maggie the few steps back to the hotel. Part of Maggie was really hoping that Gee would escort her upstairs to the suite. She would grab him and whisk him in for a nightcap and maybe more. Part of her was hoping that he would bid farewell in the lobby so that temptation, and possible disaster, could be averted. Gee was the epitome of a gentleman. First, although she clearly was extremely well-off, he absolutely insisted that he pay for dinner, and second, when they reached the lobby of the hotel, he politely put out his hand to say goodbye. Maggie pulled him towards her and, with another peck on his cheek, whispered that she had really enjoyed the evening and that, once she had decided what to do in regard to the charities, she would let him know and, with his permission, seek his advice. It was very hard for Maggie not to grab him right there and then and plant a big kiss on his mouth, but maybe that was the wine talking.

When she reached the suite there was a message from Greg. He had called her just as he was boarding the plane for Heathrow. He wanted to know that she was okay and promised to call in the morning. Maggie prepared herself for bed. The phone rang; it was Gee. "Maggie, I really enjoyed talking to you. Would you do lunch tomorrow? I could show you around." Maggie did not hesitate. Her heart leapt. "I'd be thrilled," she said. Maggie went to bed happily thinking about Gee's strong tanned body and his gentle manner.

She slept well, only disturbed by a strange dream. She was walking down a street when she passed a beggar dressed all in black sitting on the pavement; black cape, black hood and black face. Maggie opened her purse and gave the beggar, who appeared to be an old lady, a note. Then suddenly, there were two black caped black skinned ladies begging. She tried to walk past the newcomer, but then there were three, then four, then a whole horde, all pushing forward their begging bowls pleading for money. She started to run, but it was no good; she was surrounded by black caped beggars. There was no escape. There was an impenetrable wall of black women screaming for money. Then, Maggie woke up; shaken and a bit confused. Soon, however, she was rationalising the experience as a meaningless dream and went back to sleep, thinking once more about her happy evening with Gee.

Chapter Ten

Whilst he waited at the airport Greg took stock of things. It had been three months now since £490 million had been deposited in their account. In that time he had acquired two rival companies for £12 million, but the synergy of these two additions to his company had probably added about £3 million of net worth to his portfolio. He had spent £1 million on lawyer's fees to fend of the false ticket claim, and around £300,000 on an almost new Bentley and a new Mini Cooper. Meanwhile his investment of one million on Bitcoins was, temporarily, at least, in a short three months, now worth £4 million and the interest on the £490 million, for three months was £6 million. According to his calculations the original $490 million had now grown, in a short three months by roughly £11 million. Furthermore, as yet, he had not spent anything on Maggie's charities. "Well," he thought, "even if the rightful ticket holder shows up now, we are still £11 million to the good." Greg was in a good mood as he boarded the plane. He had started to think about how to shield his gains from the taxman. He also decided, that since Bitcoins seemed to be on an upward trajectory, he would buy some more. He would round off the million pounds investment to £10 million. "After all," he rationalised, it only represents 1% of our net worth, so it is not really a big gamble." Before boarding the plane he had called Maggie to check that she was okay, but she had not picked up. "Probably out to dinner somewhere," he thought. "What a shame she is on her own."

Next morning, he went straight from Heathrow to the office, where he quickly took hold of the reins of the consolidation process. His arrival, however, so early in the morning had not been expected by Louise, who thought that he was going to go home to Dorking to pick up the kids. Whilst innocently looking for some files that he needed, he searched Louise's desk and file cabinet. He was surprised and somewhat shocked to stumble across some notes that she had made. Clearly, she had been attempting to get a look at his personal finances. Nobody in the office was aware of the 20 different accounts that he had set up and certainly, nobody knew how much was in them. But here, tucked away on some papers was a partial list of the names of the banks involved and, in some cases, some account numbers. Louise had been prying. Louise was gone before the coffee break. "Better to start with a new girl," said Greg to himself. "Maybe there is someone appropriate from the merging firms?"

Whilst waiting at the airport in Johannesburg, Greg had also been doing some strategising about how to make the merged companies work to take advantage of the synergy. It was true that now there was little competition in his field, but that did not necessarily grow the market. The need for recruitment in the hotel and hospitality field was fairly static, so the only real advantage of having all three of the agencies, would be to cut costs. Maybe there was some room for increasing the fee structure, since he was now close to a monopoly, but he would have to be careful not to create a gap for a new start up into the field. After all, the barriers to entry in his business were not high. No, the most sensible thing to do would be to rationalise cost. This could be done by amalgamating the offices, or at least, some of the functions of the offices. Greg's thinking was that it made sense for each of the brands to be maintained because they each had dedicated customers. In fact, it would probably be a negative thing to even advertise the fact that the three agencies were now one. On the other hand, the three companies as merged, would only need one General Manager, one Chief Accountant and accounting office, and maybe, even one switchboard and so on. So, one way to add value, was to cut costs whilst retaining the pre-merger appearance. Another way forward, not necessarily exclusive of cutting costs, would be to branch out from hospitality into other industries. This, thought Greg, should be examined carefully. Maybe each of the three agencies could expand in a different direction. In short, there was plenty of work ahead to make the whole merger work and to increase its value, which was, of course, Greg's goal.

Now Greg was back in London, he was itching to get on with the job. Maybe the three days before Maggie returned could be very productive. Much as he wanted to see Sam and Jimmy, he knew that his folks had planned on having them for another four days, so it would be easier for him if they stayed for the intended period, so that he did not have to play 'housewife, mother, kids taxi' and so on, with all of this workload on his plate. He called his mother in Box Hill and explained. She was perfectly understanding. In fact, she seemed quite pleased, and assured Greg that the children were not tiring her, nor their grandfather. That done, he called Maggie in South Africa, as he had promised. He explained his plan and she approved. The call was fairly short; neither Greg nor Maggie minded. Greg's parting shot on the phone was "Have you been behaving yourself?" said in a rather teasing manner. This was their personal code for "Did you masturbate last night?" "Of course I have," said Maggie. She lied. "What about you?" asked Maggie. "I was on a plane!"

That done, he returned to the task at hand.

Halfway through the afternoon Greg located the slip of paper he had been carrying with Jake's numbers. After checking the phone to see what time it was in California, he shut his office door and dialled the number. Jake was thrilled to hear from him and, after a brief conversation, it was agreed that Greg should fly to LA as soon as possible to meet with the NoGrow inventor, Curtis Burchfield, rather than have him fly to London. Burchfield lived in the Palisades, not far from Santa Monica. Greg had never been to California; he was excited at the thought. In the meantime, Jake promised to email Greg a nondisclosure form for signature, before mailing him more details about the product. By seven o'clock that evening, Greg was feeling really tired. After a night on the plane, even though he slept well, and a tiring day in the office he had had enough. He decided to stay in town. Why traipse all the way to Dorking to an empty house with no supplies when he was already equipped with a suitcase full of everything he needed? He called the Goring Hotel, which was round the corner from his office. Yes, they did have a room available. Greg booked it for three nights.

Maggie's day in Johannesburg was wonderful. She woke early. From her panoramic windows she watched the sun rise over the suburbs of Johannesburg. She was amazed how green everything was. There had been no rain for months but, as far as she could see was green, intertwined with red and grey tile roofs. Joburg was not naturally green, but many of the suburban houses still had a minimum of half an acre of land and quite a few, much larger plots with pools and tennis courts. These back yards had been planted with trees which were clearly being watered by the garden 'boys'.

There were probably more swimming pools and tennis courts per square mile in Sandton than in any other city in the world, including Beverly Hills. Maggie was looking forward to exploring the city with Gee. She showered and dressed. Luckily her clothes had been returned by the hotel, clean and pressed. She picked out some suitable sightseeing clothes, making sure that the top two buttons of her blouse were left undone. She applied her makeup with special care, cursing about the impracticality of the mirror in the bathroom. She breakfasted on the Club Floor, where she was served by a very amiable black waiter with a name badge 'Alfred'. She flicked through the morning newspaper. She was interested to see how many lovely homes there were for sale at 'giveaway' prices.

On the dot of 10 am, as promised, the phone in the suite rang. Gee was downstairs waiting. As she descended in the glass elevator to the lobby, she could see Gee standing below, first a little dot, which grew larger and larger as she went down. There was a uniformed air crew milling in the lobby, presumably waiting for their transport. The girls looked very smart in their bright red uniforms. Maggie saw several of them admiring Gee. Yes, he certainly was handsome! With a peck on the cheek, and the warmest and widest smile imaginable, Gee greeted her, and whisked her through the revolving doors to a white Mercedes in the driveway. He thanked the doorman with a twenty rand note for holding his car at the door, then escorted Maggie to the passenger side and held the door whilst she climbed into the soft leather interior. "Borrowed my dad's car," said Gee. "Thought you would prefer it to my dirty boneshaker of a Suzuki." With that, he drove off. "There are not too many tourist sites in Joburg," he started, "there was nothing here before the mines. But after gold was discovered, the little mining town quickly became the industrial and financial capital of South Africa, even the continent of Africa. Up until the 1970s all of the businesses were in downtown Joburg, with a few affluent suburbs just to the north, like Houghton. In the late seventies, business started to move north and the suburbs and shopping malls of Sandton were developed. These were exclusively occupied by whites; in fact, blacks needed a permit to be allowed to work in the area, and, if they were domestic workers, they lived in servants' quarters in the whites' houses. Sometimes these quarters had no heating nor hot water for ablutions. With most of the population moving away from downtown it took a hit and became very black. I thought today I could show you some of the grand palaces that the whites live in, and now, many wealthy blacks, but also where the majority of the blacks live. Maybe, if we have time, we could visit the Apartheid Museum; you might be interested in that." Maggie, listened to every word intently. She was, of course, interested, but she would still have listened even if he had been narrating nursery rhymes. At lunchtime they stopped at a café near the Wanderers cricket ground. Gee was a member of Wanderers, but it was out of season, so there would be nobody there. But Blinis, the café, was buzzing with well-heeled whites, all attempting to look ultra-casual. The tour included the northern suburbs, the downtown financial district, the ruined inner suburbs, and, very briefly, a glimpse at the edge of Alexandra township, the closest black township to the city. "Maybe, too close," thought Maggie.

Gee was bubbling with information, not only about Joburg, as he called it, but also about South Africa, of which he was clearly proud. Maggie just loved his exuberance. When they finally arrived back at the Intercontinental, she invited him in to tea. Gee made Maggie try the rooibos. They laughed a lot.

In the middle of 'tea', Gee suddenly became serious. "Maggie, I do so enjoy your company. Will you have dinner with me again? I do so want to talk to you about the protection of the wildlife. That really is my passion and I sense it will be yours too." Maggie did not need to be asked. She only had one day left with this beautiful man. Why would she miss a minute? Also, she had, as expected, noticed Gee's glances at her undone top buttons on more than one occasion during the day. He had been the ultimate gentleman throughout the day but he was, after all, a man. She just knew that he fancied her and she was pleased. Here was a man who could have had any pretty young thing, here was a man, who had probably seduced many an actress at Mala Mala. Why would he take a shine to a 31-year-old married mother of two? Well, for whatever reason, she just knew that he had. She was frightened. Maybe she should turn back now? She had had a lovely time with Gee; maybe now was the time to step away? But strong forces pulled her towards him. His love of wildlife, his pride in his country, his strong but gentlemanly ways, not to say his astounding good looks, made her hesitate to say goodbye. "I'd love to," she said, "What time should I be ready?"

A rendezvous was arranged for 7.30 pm. Maggie repaired to her suite. It had been a busy day so far. A couple of hours to rest and reflect would be welcome. She took off her clothes and shoes and wrapped herself in the luxurious towelling robe that was hanging on the bathroom door. "Are you completely mad?" she asked herself as she contemplated the escalating liaison with Gee. Until the incident in Mauritius with Tajen, Maggie had never been unfaithful to Greg. Maybe a bit of a fumble or two on a dance floor at a party, but never to the point of an intimate relationship. She knew that her best friends had – or at least they claimed so. Willow was always putting herself about, although Maggie actually thought that she only did it to arouse her husband, and that she never actually carried through with anything. Ellen was different. She had had several affairs. Indeed, after one such fling with the plumber that came to fix their sink, she actually left George for a month or two, but soon realised where she was best off and came home. Maggie didn't want to be like that but she was, after all, only a woman, and one that needed sex as part of her loving relationship. Lately, Greg had not been too active in that department. She even wondered if Greg had another woman. She never really trusted that Louise in the office. "Well, I guess I must just go slowly," she said out loud. "Let's just take it easy with Gee. Anyway, he's not the one that's doing the chasing. He is behaving like a real gentleman. On the other hand, I just know that he wants me; I just know it."

During all of this time in Africa, Maggie had not given one thought to the fact that she was a rich woman. The fact that she could have and buy whatever she wanted had not crossed her mind. The fact that this had come about on the back of someone else's loss had not been an issue for her on the trip. At home, she thought about this at least once a day. A little voice of conscience popped up from time to time and she had to shove it back into its box. Here, in Africa, she felt free. She did need to focus, however, on the charities she had been investigating because, when she got home, she would need to make some decisions. She decided to use the evening with Gee to get his opinion; who else could be more knowledgeable than him? It also gave her an excuse to keep seeing him, especially when she had to explain to Greg one day that she was still in touch with him.

That evening Gee came again with his dad's Mercedes. He took Maggie to a small casual Portuguese restaurant in Bryanston, about four miles from the hotel. It was quiet, but convivial. Maggie had dressed in blue jeans and a sweater that really emphasised her figure. With her blonde hair and blue eyes, she looked like a film star, which is what she intended. Gee, too, wore blue jeans and a plain cream shirt that emphasised his tan. They talked about poaching and what needed to be done to stop it. Not only, according to Gee, did the frontline park's police need equipment and training, but the people from the villages needed education as to why animals' lives mattered, and secondly, good alternative ways to earn enough to support their families or their habits. Work also needed to be done from an international political and legal point of view. Nations must come together to make the sale and consumption of tusks illegal. In other words, much money would be needed to cover all of the basis, not least of which would be lobbying at the world's highest levels to create a common anti-poaching policy. In Gee's words, "It will need a ton of money."

"I have a ton of money," Maggie thought to herself. "I have some money I am willing to spend," she said out loud. "I was thinking of donating £1 million to Trunk and a quarter of a million to Shawu," she said, quite softly. "That's incredibly generous and very sweet of you," said Gee, who was astounded, "but this is going to take hundreds of millions." Maggie was on the absolute verge of saying that she had hundreds of millions, but bit her tongue. It turned out that Gee had all sorts of ideas as to how to go about convincing the world how to stop poaching and Maggie lapped them up like an eager schoolgirl.

They ordered and ate, without even really noticing it. They were so wrapped up in the subject; and it would appear, to those around them in the restaurant, wrapped up in each other. When it came time to pay the bill, Maggie insisted that it was her turn. Gee, absolutely refused to allow her. Maggie liked that masculinity. When all was done and dusted, Maggie reached out her hand and grasped

Gee's. "Thank you. You are such a wonderful man. I so want you to be part of my life. I just need time to figure out how." Inexplicably, she burst into tears. Gee offered a clean napkin, put his arm around her and escorted her out of the restaurant. When they reached the Mercedes and he had flipped a coin to the African boy 'guarding' it, he pulled Maggie to him and kissed her, a full blooded emotionally charged kiss on the lips. She hugged him tight. He took her back to the hotel and up to the suite. They made love. Greg had called; Maggie ignored it.

Chapter Eleven

Maggie walked off the plane at Heathrow at 6 am with a spring in her step. She had slept so well on the flight in the comfort of 'first' that the journey had passed very quickly. The day before, her last in Johannesburg had passed without incident. Gee had had to return to Mala Mala to work. Their parting had been gentle and loving. Maggie was sad to see him leave. When he was out of sight she could not hold back the tears. She thought she should feel guilty but, strangely, she felt exhilarated. She decided to renew her shopping trip to look for some more interesting things to take the kids, plus she needed a thankyou gift for Greg' parents for childminding. Now, back in England, she was still glowing from her encounter, but was also harbouring wonderful memories of the bush. She was excited to be seeing Sam and Jimmy. On leaving the terminal she went straight to the taxi rank and negotiated a fare to Dorking. Greg had called her the evening before to explain that he was still at the Goring and had an important breakfast meeting, so could not pick her up. For once in her life, she was actually pleased not to see him; life would now need to make a little adjustment, but that realism had not yet sunk in. Something told her that you can't have your cake and eat it, whatever that means, but it had yet to sink in. Anyway, she was now free to head straight to Box Hill, see the little ones and maybe even drop them off at school. She would compose herself before Greg came home that evening. She was pleased that he was so busy and inattentive.

Sam and Jimmy leapt all over her when she arrived. "I dare not lose these darlings," she thought to herself as she hugged and kissed them. "Did you have a great time with Grandma and Granddad? I expect they absolutely spoiled you, didn't they?" The kids were not listening. "Did you bring us a present?" they both squealed. "Of course, my darlings," said Maggie as she rummaged in her bags. "You can have one thing each before I take you to school, and something else when I take you home later." The youngsters squealed with joy and it was quite difficult for Maggie to get them out of the door to head for school. Maggie thanked Ruby and Roland for their kindness and insisted that Sam and Jimmy give them big hugs and kisses, which they willingly did. Clearly, they had had a wonderful time with Grandma and Granddad; no doubt they had been utterly spoilt.

When Maggie finally reached their little home, she found that the familiarity was comforting, but there was something missing. She was still glowing from her encounter in Johannesburg, but, as she showered in familiar surroundings, she started to ponder upon how much she had to lose. She had a comfortable life here in Dorking; a clever, handsome and loving husband, two wonderful offspring, a nice home, and many lovely friends. Was she mad to want more? As she stepped out of the shower the phone rang. Her heart leapt. "Is it Gee? Of course not, you silly woman! Is it Greg to welcome her home? No, he is probably too busy." She grabbed the phone with a wet hand. It was Ellen. "You must tell me all about your trip," she gushed, "did you have a great time in the jungle? I bet you met some dishy game rangers." "My God," thought Maggie, "Ellen has hit a hole in one." They chatted excitedly for at least half an hour and arranged to meet for coffee on the following day. No sooner had Maggie put down the phone, then it rang again. This time it was Willow and, again, the chat went on for at least half an hour, like two excited schoolgirls. "Thank God for friends," said Maggie to herself, when she was finally off the phone. "Whatever happens, I must not lose my friends. If everything changes in my life, I must always treasure my friends."

Greg came home that evening in a jolly mood, obviously pleased that he had achieved a lot at work over the last three days. The hood was down on the Bentley and the radio was blaring out. Maggie and the kids heard him as he pulled up outside. "Daddy, daddy; have you bought us anything from Africa?" they both yelled as the ran to meet him. Of course, he hadn't. "Mummy had brought it back for you, my little darlings," he said, hopefully. "Of course," interjected Maggie, "Your presents were from both of us." Greg gave Maggie a big hug, opened a can of beer, and proceeded to tell her how well he had got on with the business. "Let's talk about it later," said Maggie, "the children need us now." Suddenly, it struck her that Greg was self-engrossed; it was all about him. "Not like Gee, she thought. But maybe he's just excited. Yes, it's nice to see him so enthusiastic. I must support him." Later, when the kids went to bed, they insisted on Greg reading the stories. Maggie listened outside the bedroom door. Greg read so well, with all sorts of different voices for the characters on the books. The children loved it when he did that. They loved their father so much.

For the rest of the evening Maggie and Greg played 'catch up'. Maggie told Greg that she had, by chance, bumped into Gee on his day off in Johannesburg and that they had discussed the problems of poaching. She made out that this lucky encounter had helped her understand the potential there was to help. She told Greg that she intended to move forward with both Shawu and Trunk, if only to use them as a learning laboratory before working out how to tackle the issue from a more global perspective. Greg was impressed and agreed to organise the one and a quarter million that she would need. Greg, whilst nursing his single malt, then related the progress he had made with the amalgamation, including the firing of Louise. Maggie was pleased that Louise had gone. Somehow, ridiculous as it was, she had seen her as some sort of rival for Greg's attention. "If he is having an affair, or whatever, it obviously was not with Louise," she thought. Then, almost as an afterthought, Greg mentioned that he planned to go to Los Angeles on the following week to meet with the NoGrow people. No mention that he was sorry to be going away so soon after she had just returned. At around eleven o'clock they went to bed. With a peck on the cheek, Greg was asleep. "Something is making him tired," thought Maggie, but for once, she was actually quite pleased.

It took Maggie a long time to nod off. She had so much to think about. Gee's muscular body and brilliant smile kept flashing in her mind. She tried to think of other things. She decided that she would, the next day, call up Penelope at Shawu and Giles at Trunk to give them the good news. She rehearsed what she would want in return. Gee still kept appearing. Maggie had obtained some sleeping pills from her GP to take on the overnight flight. Finally, she slid out of bed, without waking Greg, broke one to the pills in half, and popped a piece into her mouth. At last, she slept.

Greg left early in the morning. The long flight and the pill had caught up with Maggie, who sleep-walked through breakfast with the little ones and drove them to school like a zombie. A cup of strong coffee with Ellen soon fixed the problem. Ellen was all ears. She wanted to know every detail about the trip. There was not one ounce of envy in her voice. She was just excited that Maggie had had such a good time. "What about the game rangers?" she asked, "were they all they are cracked up to be?" "Absolutely," replied Maggie, "and they were so knowledgeable." Ellen sensed that her question had been batted away. She also sensed a slight blush. Maggie changed the subject. "Greg has got to go to Los Angeles next week on business," she said. "I think he's quite excited about it. He's never been there before." "Does he need a secretary to go with him? I could be available," said Ellen with a wicked smile. "Funny you should say that. He has just fired his secretary, Louise. I never did like her."

On returning home, Maggie called Giles to make arrangements to see him and to thank him for Trunk's hospitality at Savuti. Naturally, Giles was extremely interested to find out about Maggie's decision. Maggie was going to wait until their meeting to inform him of her decision to support Trunk with a million pounds. She wanted to secure some sort of policy making role in the organisation in exchange and considered that it was better to handle that face to face. However, she had never ever been in a position of giving away a million and her excitement got the better of her. She blurted it out. "I've decided to donate £1 million to Trunk this year but I would like you to think of what role I might play in the organisation, since I will have such a big interest in it." Giles was ecstatic with appreciation. "This is a great day for Trunk. We are so grateful," he effused. "Of course, you must be involved in how it is spent. I will think about the best way to handle this and we can discuss it when we meet." They arranged to meet up on the following Tuesday, whilst Greg would be away in Los Angeles.

Then Maggie called Penelope at Shawu in Pimlico. She was answered by a recorded message. Presumably Penelope had popped out to the shops or the wine merchant. Maggie asked her to call back, which she eventually did, just as Maggie was collecting the children from school. Eventually, that afternoon, Penelope and Maggie had a chat and similarly arranged for a follow up meeting for late Tuesday afternoon. That done, Maggie turned to her duties as a housewife. The laundry had been piling up and the fridge was bare. It crossed her mind that, with all of her money, she could actually get someone else to do some of these things.

By the time Greg returned from London, the children were in bed and the house was restocked and tidy. Maggie was on the phone to her brother, James, in France, who, of course, had no idea about Maggie's good fortune.

James was a school teacher, married to Marie Claire, a vivacious French woman, who taught at the same school. They had no children of their own, but were both very active people with hiking and cycling and gardening and everything else that one could do in the open air. They lived near Etienne, a place with very hot summers and very cold winters. Maggie rarely visited them and, likewise, they almost never came to Dorking. As far as Maggie's children were concerned, they could have lived on another planet. Maggie excitedly related her recent experiences in Africa. She was not sure that James was really listening. Perhaps he was a little envious? Maggie had been contemplating helping them out with some of her new found wealth. Now, she was not sure that she wanted to; elephants seemed more important than her brother. Maggie held her hand over the phone and whispered to Greg that his dinner was ready. All he had to do was pop it into the microwave. Greg poured himself a whisky and sat down, alone, to eat, whilst Maggie finished up on the phone. The evening was passed uneventfully, in fact, by watching a movie on the television. There was not much discussion between the two, each, it would seem, with their own thoughts. The weekend was much the same. Greg played rugby and stayed at the club after for a few beers. Sometimes Maggie would watch the game and join the lads for a drink in the club house. She was very popular with the boys in the team. This time she excused herself; Sam was going to a friend's party so she would stay with Jimmy. In the evening they all went to Pizza Express. On Sunday, Greg spent most of the day working on his boat, getting it ready for the summer season. Jimmy helped out until he got bored.

On Monday, Greg left early for the airport. He could have flown from Gatwick on the one class Norwegian Air to LAX. Instead he opted to leave from Heathrow, which was slightly further away, so that he could travel First Class, something he was rapidly becoming accustomed to. Somehow, the weekend had been awkward at home. Maggie had seemed a bit distant. Greg thought it may have been an anti-climax after the excitement of the bush and Africa; he knew how much she had loved it. He decided to buy her something nice in LA. He realised that he had been very occupied for the past few months but Maggie must under-stand that it was for the good of their family.

The flight to LAX from Heathrow is a long one, but worse, it crosses eight time zones. There is plenty of time to think about things whilst sitting in splendid isolation at the front of the plane. Nevertheless, for once, the flight crew were pretty, and he enjoyed flirting with them. The food service was also excellent. Greg had still not fulfilled his dream of joining NetJets, but, with service like this, one had to wonder, why bother? He was soon to find out why. NetJets uses the General Aviation terminal in LAX, and elsewhere, where there are no immigration or customs lines-just a welcoming cup of coffee and a quick wave through. In the international arrivals terminal at LAX there are no special favours, be you American, foreign, black, white, brown or yellow. You just get in line, and that line can take between one and two hours before you emerge from the other end into the baggage claim area, where, if you are lucky, your bag will still be going round and round on the claim rotunda, by now buried under the luggage from the next flight. Then, you line up again to hand a slip of paper to a uniformed and bored customs official, who knows, that by the time you have reached him, that you are utterly pissed off. "From now on I charter," swore Greg to himself under his breath, as he pushed his luggage up the ramp from customs to the awaiting throng of 'greeters' blocking the exit to the street. Greg had booked into the Peninsula Hotel on South Santa Monica Boulevard, Beverly Hills, but had omitted to avail himself of their pickup limousine service. He instantly regretted it when he saw the length of the line for the taxis, and, once he reached the front of it, the condition of the vehicles themselves. The terminals at LAX are spread around a squashed U-shaped one way only road, which is normally full of shuttle buses and limos; it is always chaotically busy and noisy. The international arrivals terminal is right at the curve of the U which means it is quite a long way from the exit to the highway. Most people that arrive there are naturally tired and bad tempered after the shambles of immigration. Greg was not alone.

He finally climbed into a cab and instructed the driver to take him to the Peninsula. Luckily, the driver, who spoke little English, knew where it was, so, 40 minutes later, Greg found himself being driven through the white gates of the hotel, which is a little oasis of calm amongst the bustle of the surrounding streets.

It was now early evening. Greg was shown to a very elegantly furnished suite overlooking a palm fringed pool, which was graced by several very attractive bikini-clad young ladies and a few bronzed men. This was Beverly Hills as he had imagined it, the Beverly Hills he had seen on the silver screen since he was a little boy. Greg had 'arrived'! After a quick shower and an exploration of the public areas of the hotel, Greg went for a stroll. The 'golden triangle' that stretches from Santa Monica to Wilshire is home to the world's most exclusive shops. It is America's answer to Bond Street, but unlike Bond Street, it was teeming with cars. Not just any cars, but a succession of prowling Rollers, Bentleys, Ferraris, Lamborghinis, McLarens and so on. Without question, this was show-off city. Even its only supermarket, Whole Foods, into which Greg wandered, seemed to be full of ageing Hollywood actresses and young botoxed starlets. Mixed incongruously with the Rollers, from time to time, were open topped tourist minivans touting 'tours of the stars', which presumably took people to gawk at film stars homes, or at least, the walls of their homes, as Greg would later find out. "No sweat here, then, to find a nice present for Maggie," thought Greg as he walked up Rodeo and then back down Canon. Having found a cute looking restaurant/ wine bar, called Wally's, Greg stopped for an evening snack and a glass of California Cabernet Sauvignon. He found himself seated at a communal table. The other people at it did not talk to him. That did not matter; there was plenty to look at. After two glasses of an excellent red, he wandered back to the Peninsula. The air was warm and pleasant. In one direction he could see the Hollywood Hills, and beyond them high mountains; in the other direction loomed the tower blocks of Century City. On the other side of the road he recognised the old Beverly Hilton, where the annual Golden Globes awards take place. It was a weird feeling, being in a place that you had seen so many times before on countless TV shows and movies. One more glass, this time scotch, at the pretty poolside bar, then back to his suite, where he to checked his messages and turned in. It was too late in the day to call England, where it would be the middle of the night.

Next morning, as he waited under the porte cochere, watching with interest the coming and going of the hotel's wealthy clientele, a less than pristine Cadillac pulled into the driveway. Driving it was Charles (call me 'Chuck') Chambers, the man, who claimed to have invented NoGrow. Greg's first thought was that Charles could benefit from his own product, looking at the thick curly hair that cascaded almost to his shoulders. Chuck clambered out of the low sedan, and thrust his hand out to Greg. The concierge and car valets of the Peninsula eyed him suspiciously. "You must be Greg. Pleased to meet you. I'm Charles; my friends call me Chuck." "Nice to meet you too," said Greg. Charles, indicated for Greg to climb in, manoeuvred himself back into the driving seat, and off they went, heading west down Santa Monica in the direction of the Pacific Ocean. As he weaved his way down the straight road, flanked with low rise stores, Chuck explained that he owned a small laboratory, located near Venice Beach, a few blocks from the ocean. He also was a visiting professor at UCLA, the sprawling college situated between Beverly Hills and Brentwood. Actually, he was a chemist who had, whilst engaged on some other research, stumbled across a formula which, he claimed, prevented hair growth. After much careful research and experimentation, he claimed, he was certain that this was a safe and practical discovery and had set about the long and arduous task of seeking government approval to market and sell it to the public. This, he explained, had been a two-year exercise, which was now nearing its end. Within a few months, Chuck, explained he would be ready to bring it to market. He had identified a manufacturing partner and his plan was to launch the product in California, before going through all of the regulatory steps elsewhere. What he was lacking, were the funds to get going. In his estimation, it would take a million dollars. If it took off in California, then he saw no difficulty in finding the funds to conquer the world.

By the time Chuck had explained all of this they were pulling in to the backyard of his lab. Venice Beach seemed quite run down, compared to neighbouring Santa Monica, and the lab was located in an area of low-rise buildings, some in dirty grey concrete, some in black-stained wood. The lab consisted of a tiled room, no bigger than the average house kitchen, a couple of store rooms and a corner office, partitioned from the main room by a glass wall. There was just enough space in the lab office for Chuck and Greg to sit and talk. "One thing is for sure," thought Greg to himself, "this man does not waste money." Chuck fired up his computer screen and proceeded to baffle Greg for half an hour about the science involved in the formula and the multiple tests that he had carried out. He was clearly convinced that the formula worked. Then he proceeded to explain the costs involved in production, the possible need for an industrial partner and a marketing plan and so on. As explained in Mala Mala by Jake, they had budgeted that these start-up costs would be close to a million dollars, and that was just to get going in California. Despite the rather ramshackle premises where the magic potion had been conceived, Greg remained impressed with the concept. He figured that if only 1% of the male population of the USA spent only $1 in a year on the product, the revenue would be $4 million. If that formula were to be extended to South and Central America, that would add another $3 million and if extended to Europe, another $4 million. "Surely 1% of the male population of the Western World would be quite happy to never go to the barber again," he tried to persuade himself, "and surely they would spend more than one dollar per year on it?"

That evening Greg had dinner with Jake and Jill, last seen at Mala Mala. J and J lived in one of the canyons which run from Beverly Hills to Sherman Oaks in the 'valley'. The property on the Beverly Hills/Hollywood side of the hills is very expensive, both on the flat portion close to Beverly Hills and in the upper reaches of the canyons, close to the famous Mulholland Drive. Mulholland Drive has two price categories; extremely expensive to the west, overlooking, in the distance, and often through the smog, the Pacific Ocean, and just plain expensive to the east, overlooking the Valley. Jake and Jill's house was near the top of their canyon and was cantilevered out from the hill, giving it wonderful views from almost all of the rooms. Being invited to dinner in the USA, as Greg was to find out, does not usually mean that one is going to eat in the hosts' house. That is what restaurants are for. So, after a couple of cocktails on the splendid deck, when the threesome reminisced about their trip to Africa, Greg was suddenly whisked off to a restaurant, somewhere on Wilshire Boulevard. There, in front of a rather bored looking Jill, Greg and Jake discussed the next steps in moving forward Greg's potential investment in NoGrow. It turned out that Jake had been funding Professor Chuck up til now, but did not have the appetite to carry on doing so. Greg announced that, based upon everything he had learned from Chuck earlier in the day, he was ready to invest. Jake called for the champagne and arrangements were made to meet at his attorney's office in Century City the next day. After dinner, J and J dropped Greg off at the Peninsula and he went for his nightcap at the poolside bar. "Damn it," he suddenly thought, "I'm too late now to call Maggie."

Greg stayed two more days in Los Angeles. Apart from

sorting out the paperwork to invest in NoGrow, he decided
to wear his hospitality recruitment hat and visit some of
the hotels in the area, in an attempt to leave his calling
card with management. What he discovered interested
him greatly. There seemed to be no dominant recruitment
agency operating in the field. Instead, there appeared to be a
bevy of small firms, all charging much higher commissions
that his three companies back in the UK. Greg paid careful
attention and gathered a wealth of information. "Perhaps,"
he thought to himself, "there is room to clean up in this
market?" He decided that, once he was through with the
NoGrow paperwork, he would stop off in New York on the
way back to England, to see how his industry worked there.
He had an old friend who was the Manager of the Pierre
Hotel. He called him to make a reservation and changed his
flight plans, thereby delaying his return home. Greg called
Maggie to let her know that he would be delayed. She said
the right things about missing him, as were the kids. She
peppered him with questions about Los Angeles. She asked
him about the 'deal'. She couldn't stay on the phone because
she had to get the children's supper. She let him speak to
them. And that was that. All about facts and little about
feelings. Thankfully, he did not ask her if she had been
behaving herself.

Greg left Beverly Hills having signed a Letter of Intent
with Chuck and Jake to proceed with his investment. For
$1 million, Greg would own 49% of NoGrow, and a part-
nership between Chuck and Jake would own the balance.
Greg would return to LA in three weeks' time to sign the
final paperwork and to agree to a game plan of how to move
things forward. Before leaving, Greg remembered that he
had promised himself that he would buy Maggie a gift
from Rodeo Drive. He wandered in and out of the famous
fashion boutiques, trying to imagine Maggie in a variety

of outfits. The thought of his beautiful wife in some of the skimpy offerings aroused him. "It has been too long," he thought, as he imagined her taking off some of the clothes on show. This led him to a famous lingerie shop. He knew her bra was size 36, but he had no clue in regard to the Ds or DDs. He would just have to take a chance. He left with the most expensive and smallest package of 'clothing' that he had ever bought, but he knew Maggie would look spectacular. It did not occur to him that this was actually a gift for himself, not Maggie.

That done, Greg packed and checked out of the Peninsula. This time he had ordered the hotel car to take him to the airport. The big back Cadillac was waiting for him at the entrance. Not one, but three, fawning uniformed bellhops helped him into the vehicle. Gregory, the smartly suited black driver, introduced himself, and off they went, accompanied by a running commentary on the state of Los Angeles, the state of California, the state of the USA, and the world at large. Greg stayed silent. Gregory, the chauffeur, checked the bags in at the kerbside and drove off with a smile and a $50 note. Greg proceeded to the first-class lounge which was completely overcrowded with far more passengers than can ever have bought tickets for the front of the plane. After some time, he found an empty seat, took out his tablet, and googled NetJets. The 'starting' membership was $200,000. He filled out the online forms – and joined.

Chapter Twelve

Maggie could not get Gee out of her mind. It was as if he had invaded her senses, her very being. No matter how hard she tried to concentrate on other things, the touch of him, the smell of him, the sound of him, kept intruding. She just could not seem to shut him out of her consciousness. He was totally distracting and she was totally distracted. Thankfully the children did not seem to notice as they busied themselves with children's things, but both Willow and Ellen sensed it. When they asked her what was wrong she explained how she had been affected by the plight of the animals and that she was struggling with thoughts of how she could get involved to help. She did not mention the huge donations she was about to make, because, in any event she was going to insist that the recipients should not disclose them. Nor, of course, did she mention her infatuation with the handsome game ranger, though, deep in her heart, she knew she had to talk to someone about it.

She made arrangements for Ellen to look after the kids on Tuesday whilst she went to her meetings in London. She warned Ellen that she might not be back until around their bed time so Ellen had kindly volunteered to have them on a sleepover. Maggie felt bad about this because she had only just sprung them from the in laws, but the wild life projects were important to her, so she rationalised that this was okay. So, off the London she went, catching an after rush hour train from Dorking to Victoria, on which she rehearsed the conditions for the upcoming donations. Number one, she wanted them to be anonymous, at least beyond the knowledge of persons outside the charity trusteeship and management. Number two, she wanted to become a Trustee of both organisations, so that she could have a seat at the decision-making table and also in a position to learn. Number three, in the case of Shawu, she also wanted Gee to be appointed as a Trustee.

The first meeting with Giles at Trunk could not have gone better. Before she was able to enumerate her conditions of the donation, he surprised her by announcing that there had been a hastily convened meeting of the Trustees, at which they unanimously agreed that she should join their ranks. There were 11 Trustees, including one junior member of the Royal Family, two peers, two members of parliament, one television personality who specialised in wildlife programmes, one Cambridge professor, one professional fundraiser, and four, what could best be described as 'leaders of industry'. Of these, there were five women and four men. Giles, although not a Trustee, apparently sat on the Board, representing the management. "Having another woman on the Board will be great, especially one as charming and generous as you," beamed Giles. "I do hope you will accept to join us." In regard to the privacy clause, Giles was not so enthusiastic. He had hoped to gain some valuable publicity from the huge gift, but he understood and respected Maggie's reasoning. That all settled, the balance of the meeting involved the signing of various documents required under the Charities Act regarding the role of a Trustee and other clerical matters. Then Giles took Maggie on a tour of the building and introduced her to the staff. That done, he invited her to the Goring for lunch. Maggie had selected a navy-blue suit and blue high heels for the day; elegant, but with a skirt short enough to show off her shapely legs. They walked from the office to the restaurant. Giles noticed a few heads turn as they walked past. He could thoroughly understand why. He knew that he was going to enjoy working with Maggie; she would be a breath of fresh air from some of the aristocratic ladies or empty-headed debutantes, that he had to deal with as a norm. Whilst they sipped a pre-lunch cocktail Giles asked Maggie if she and her husband would agree to attend the Trunk ball, which was due to take place in three weeks' time at the Grosvenor House Hotel. This was an annual fundraising dinner, which was normally attended by the high society. Maggie recalled seeing pictures of it in *Hello* magazine. From what she had observed it was something of a fashion show put on by the rich and famous. Maggie accepted the invitation graciously, but with trepidation. "I suppose I shall have to get used to this sort of thing," she thought, even as she accepted.

After a very pleasant lunch with the charming Giles in the appropriately formal dining room of the Goring, Maggie found herself in the Victoria area with an hour or so to spare before heading to Pimlico for her meeting with Penelope. Since there were no shops in the area that appealed to her, she decided to make use of the time by using the conference room at Greg's office to digest some of the literature that she had picked up at Trunk. She rarely visited Greg's office but, naturally, had been there on the odd occasion to rendezvous with Greg before a theatre visit or restaurant date in London. A receptionist sat at a desk inside the glass office doors. Maggie had forgotten her name and she knew that Louise, his secretary, had gone, so actually she did not know any of the administrative staff and, of course, nobody knew her. She introduced herself to the receptionist, and asked to use the meeting room. The young lady welcomed her and told her that she would call Greg's assistant to escort her to the room. "Assistant!" thought Maggie, "that's a new name for a secretary. He didn't tell me that he had already replaced Louise." Suddenly, down the hallway a stunning black-haired beauty appeared, sashaying towards a surprised Maggie as if she were parading at the Miss World pageant. In the few short steps from Greg' office to the reception area Maggie took her in. She was tall and slender, with long and shapely legs. If Maggie had to guess she would say Spanish, or maybe South American. Maggie thought she was beautiful, dangerously so. "Good afternoon, Mrs Layburn. Such a pleasure to meet you. I am Maria, Mr Layburn's personal assistant." "I bet you are," thought Maggie as she shook Maria's outstretched hand. "Nice to meet you," she offered, "I was in the neighbourhood and between meetings. I thought I might borrow your meeting room for an hour." "But of course you may. It is free at the moment. Can I get you a coffee or tea?." Maria was quite charming. "A little too charming." thought Maggie. "I wonder why Greg did not tell me that he had found a replacement for Louise?"

Two hours later, Maggie found herself, once again, knocking on the door of Penelope's little terraced house in Pimlico to talk about Shawu and how her quarter of a million could be deployed. Penelope had, of course, heard all about the visit to the farm from Mossie Mostert. She was so excited that they could now make some real plans. Maggie explained that she would like to appoint the young game ranger from Mala Mala to be her representative on the ground, so to speak, in Africa, and that he would be a great benefit to the cause with his detailed knowledge of the area and his passion for saving wildlife. What could Penelope say? She would have let her propose bringing Micky Mouse onto the board for a quarter of a million. Once again various forms needed to be completed for Maggie to become a Trustee of the charity and bank details and so forth needed to be sorted. With that done, it was time to open the red wine, something, Maggie noted, Penelope seemed to do with alacrity and great experience.

After three glasses Maggie thought she should be heading home and called for a cab. She realised that she had not even discussed with Gee the idea of him becoming a Trustee of Shawu. She had been doing everything to resist the temptation of calling him, but no matter how hard she had tried, he was constantly on her mind. Part of her had been hoping that his effect on her would wear off. She had too much to lose by encouraging him. But now she had opened the dangerous route of planning to work with him; a good cover, she thought, for her relationship with him. Now she would have to talk to him because, she needed his agreement to be a Trustee and, thereafter, would need the information required by law to make him so. She wondered how much the weakening her resolve to call Gee, was related to the fact that Greg now had a Maria in his office. "Don't be stupid," she told herself, "Maria is probably not what I think."

In the cab, on the way home, Maggie's phone buzzed. It was Greg, calling to see how her meetings had gone. Maggie filled him in and told him that he needed to arrange the payments to the two charities as agreed. She told him that she would email the bank details and he promised to arrange the transfers on the following day. "You didn't tell me that you had already replaced Louise," said Maggie, almost accusingly. "No, I was really lucky to find someone so quickly," replied Greg, without reference to his 'negligence' in not informing his wife. Maggie had guessed correctly that by the time Greg was making this call, his 'assistant' would already have tipped him off that Maggie had been to the office. He did not, however, let on. "Well, I hope she works out," offered Maggie, "she seems like a very nice young lady." "I hope so too," came the reply down the phone. Maggie changed the subject and told Greg about the Trunk gala dinner, asking him to put the date into his calendar, which he agreed to do, even though it appeared to clash with his planned trip to the West Coast. A few minutes later, Maggie was home, having said goodbye to Greg with her normal love and kisses.

Once inside, with no children to worry about due to the sleepover, she called Gee. If Greg were to look at the phone bill, he would see that the call lasted for two hours. Neither Gee nor Maggie could say goodbye. They basked in each other's voice. Maggie accomplished what she needed in terms of Gee's agreement to act as a Trustee and advisor, but in her heart, she knew that this was just an excuse to keep Gee close. She kept telling herself that his was a dangerous game but she just could not seem to help herself. She finally went to bed, both happy and troubled. Sleep eluded her. When she closed her eyes she could still see Gee's handsome body. Finally she drifted off, only to be awakened, once again, by the strange dream of the black beggars. It was odd, she thought, to have a recurring dream. She wondered what this meant.

By the time Greg returned at the weekend, Maggie was determined to blank Gee out of her mind and to concentrate on Greg, in the interest of their marriage and the children. Sam would soon be 11 and that meant a change of school with all the accompanying tension. Maggie told herself not to be selfish. Greg was full of his trip to the USA. Not only was he excited about the prospect of NoGrow, he had also seen a gap for the international expansion of the recruitment agency. He poured his thoughts out to Maggie, who made a real effort to listen. Maggie also related her thoughts about the charities she was supporting. She explained that she wanted to be active in both, which could mean substantial travel. She realised that Greg too would need to travel to satisfy his ambitions. "I think we will need a housekeeper or a nanny," she announced, "and she will need to live in. Obviously we cannot cope in this house, so it looks as if we should start looking around for a more suitable place." Greg was so glad that Maggie had come to that conclusion because he too felt that they needed to upgrade. "Well, why don't you start looking, my love?" he said. "That's okay with me."

Maggie felt that it was important for the stability of the children that they stay in the same area. She also wanted to be close to her friends. Although they could afford a mansion with acres and acres of ground, she wanted their planned 'upgrade' to be as unobtrusive as possible. She would limit her search to properties less than £3 million and only an acre or two of land. "Nothing too fancy," she told the real estate agent. She enlisted Willow and Ellen to accompany her on the search and together they giggled their way through quite a few local properties, sometimes just to be inquisitive and sometimes to see how the other half live. After a couple of weeks, Maggie found the perfect place. A Georgian country house, set in three acres with stables/garage attached. Above the stables was a self-contained apartment, just ideal for a nanny. Asking price; £4 million. "My God," exclaimed Ellen, "can Greg spring for that? Isn't it a bit over your budget?" "Probably," said Maggie, "he'll just have to work harder, won't he?"

Greg loved the house. They both took the children to see it. It was only three miles from their present home, so the kids could still keep the same friends. There was a bedroom for both of them and a spare, each with their own tiny bathrooms. The youngsters approved; they were even quite excited. The die was cast. Now, all Maggie had to do was to sell their current home and find a nanny. Then, she felt, she would be free to travel.

The Trunk Ball came and went. It was a glittering affair. Maggie and Greg dazzled as brightly as the stars; Maggie in a Givenchy dress that she had bought in Bond Street and Greg in an Armani tuxedo. The photographers who had come to shoot the celebrities wondered who they were, but Maggie looked so alluring and Greg, so debonair, that they took plenty of pictures. Ellen and Willow were thrilled when *Hello* magazine showed, not one, but three pictures of Maggie; maybe they were also a little bit jealous. The Trustees of Trunk were delighted to have such a glamourous donor and fellow Trustee; always good for publicity and for drawing attention to the charity. The welfare of African animals needed to be in front of everybody; Maggie's charm and good looks would make her a fantastic ambassador.

It did not take long for Maggie to locate and hire a nanny. She had contacted Norland Nannies, who immediately despatched the perfect candidate for her to interview. Fanny, a delightful 24-year-old South African girl arrived. Maggie and Fanny clicked immediately. Maggie watched as Fanny met and played with the children; it seemed like a natural fit. Fanny suggested that, for the times that Maggie planned to be away, they make use of a housekeeping agency, which Norland recommended. That way Fanny could give her sole attention to the children. Maggie concurred and everything was arranged to kick into place as soon as they were able to move into the new home. In the meantime, Fanny started helping out on a non-live-in basis at the old home just so that the children could get used to her. Greg was too busy to get involved.

Maggie now set about planning her trip back to Africa. She needed to spend time with Mossie Mostert and, of course, Gee, to start to widen the scope of Shawu's activity. She also planned to visit the five other sites in Africa where Trunk was operating. The most efficient way to do this, she explained to Greg, would be by utilising NetJets. She didn't mind using a commercial plane to Joburg, but thereafter, for all of the shorter hops, she would charter a plane. Greg asked if the charity would pay for that. "No," said Maggie firmly, "we will."

Although Maggie had promised herself not to think about Gee, she just could not stop herself. The days could not go fast enough before she could see him again. To some extent this whole planned trip was not about animal welfare or charities, it was about being held again in his strong arms.

Maggie did not want to wait until after the house move and Greg needed to be in America for about ten days, so Fanny agreed to move in whilst they were both away. She stayed in the tiny spare room for a couple of days whilst Maggie was still home, just so that the kids would get used to her, and then moved into Greg and Maggie's room for the rest of her stay. Maggie introduced her to Willow, who promised to be on hand if required. All seemed set, so finally Maggie jetted off to Johannesburg, tingling with anticipation. It had now been two months since she had waved goodbye to Gee in Sandton. She was as excited as a schoolgirl on her first date. This time she had used the secretarial services at Trunk to book her accommodation. Maria, the Assistant, had liaised with NetJets to book the charter flights, but, needless to say, she had not been asked to add Gee's name to the manifest; Maggie had decided to fix that herself. Maggie also did not want Maria to know that she had reserved 'their' suite at the Intercontinental. Maggie was not planning to travel to Mala Mala for two nights, but Gee was not going to be there anyway. As Maggie flew through the night, Gee was on his way to Johannesburg.

Chapter Thirteen

Word reached Giles, in London, that their beautiful donor, was travelling to their sites in Africa with her personal game ranger in tow. He had to smile. So, there is more to the lady than he had thought. "Be careful, my dear," he said out loud, "the world is a village." Meanwhile, in Los Angeles, Greg was so overwhelmed with the workload that he suddenly found the need to have his assistant in attendance at the Peninsula. Sam and Jimmy's parents were both having affairs at the same time on opposite sides of the world. This sort of thing does not end well. Despite this, certain pretences were kept up. Greg called Maggie almost every day for a chat. He did not know that Gee had joined the flight manifest and Maria was too occupied to find out. Likewise, Maggie did not know that the assistant was giving more than a helping hand. Maggie called Greg and felt guilty that she was cheating. Likewise, Greg felt guilty when he called Maggie. At least they still had feelings for each other's feelings, even if they were unnecessary.

Maria was just 'hot'. Greg was not in love with her; he just loved having her around. She was the perfect plaything, a very sexy lady. He did not realise that she was playing him. Maggie, on the other hand, was in love. And so was Gee. This was no seven-year itch fling. This was real heart-stopping love. This was serious. But so were Maggie's intentions regarding the animals. They were both impressed with the programmes being run by Shawu and could see instantly where more resources were required.

Back in South Africa, Mossie had been delighted to meet Gee. He was pleased that here was a young man who shared his passion and could help him immensely to beef up his programme and allow himself more time back in Joburg to run his company. Mossie and Maggie listened with interest to Gee's suggestions for improving the work at Shawu and getting the anti-poaching training school up and running again, now that funds were available. Mossie offered rooms to Maggie and Gee, but Maggie opted to stay one last time at Mala Mala before jetting back to London. She did not think that it would be smart to make love to Gee in Mossie's house, preferring the privacy, and luxury of the Presidential Lodge. She was also anxious to experience at least one more game drive after her whistle stop tour of Trunk's African activities, which had been quite a structured affair. The thought of being alone with Gee incognito and in the bush really appealed. So, once certain plans had been drawn up with Mossie, in which Gee agreed to assist, both Maggie and Gee headed back to Mala Mala, where, in any event, Gee was overdue at returning to his job as a ranger.

It was around lunchtime that Maggie checked into the now familiar suite at Mala Mala. Having helped her with the formalities, Gee reported for duty, leaving Maggie a free afternoon for relaxation after the busy trip. They had agreed that Gee would take her that evening for a game drive; he would pick her up at 4.30. The receptionist accompanied Maggie to the suite. She did not need the normal welcome explanations, so dismissed the clerk at the door with a 20 rand tip. A few minutes later her luggage arrived. The porter placed the bags where she requested and left, also beaming with satisfaction for his generous tip. Finally, Maggie was alone. She threw off her clothes and lowered herself, naked, except for her panties, into the cool leather arm chair. The air conditioning and the soft leather on her skin sent a shiver through her body, but the coolness was delicious after the midday heat outside. She decided to take a shower, although, this time, inside. It was just too hot outside to consider the shower by the pool. Having washed off the dust from the travel, Maggie stretched out on the massive bed in the master bedroom. She had no company, so she needed no clothes. She could see herself in the mirror. She imagined Gee looking at her. Soon, she had nodded off.

At 4.30 there was a tap at the door. The naked Maggie was still sleeping. Clearly the hectic schedule had tired her; her body was telling her that she needed this rest. Grabbing a bathrobe, she went to the door. It was Gee; ready for the drive. This time, he was alone with the Land Cruiser. This would be a private trip. "Thank goodness," thought Maggie, "Just me and Gee in the bush, for my last evening in Africa. What a treat." Gee waited in the lounge, whilst Maggie brushed her teeth and threw on some safari gear. Since it would be just Gee and her, and because it was so hot, she decided to do without a bra. Gee looked at her approvingly when she appeared from the bedroom and announced that she was ready. Maggie wondered how many women Gee had waited for in this room.

Maggie opted to sit next to Gee in the Land Cruiser. This somewhat interfered with his vision, whilst scanning for animals, and also his flexibility in handling the rifle, but they were not insurmountable problems for him to contend with. Maggie also knew that the view of her unrestrained breasts under her blouse might be nicer for him to look at than the bush. Maggie's long snooze had been good for her; she was ready for action. There was something terribly sexy about being alone in the bush with a handsome man with a rifle. The game viewing that evening was as good as ever. They tracked a lioness for several miles seeking a kill, without success. They had wonderful sightings of a hungry leopard, who was also unsuccessful in the hunt. They saw the smallest rhinoceros ever, about the size of a dog. Clearly, it had just been born and was wobbling around under its mother's belly. In short, Gee's ability to ferret out interesting sights, without attracting a crowd of other game viewers was astounding. Maggie knew that Gee was really supposed to radio any good sightings to his colleagues so that the other guests at the lodge could share in the experience, but, for once, he did not do this, preferring, obviously to give his lover a special and private experience.

As is the custom, just as the sun was about to set, Gee pulled into a little glade and cut the engine. Time for the sundowners. He climbed out of the vehicle, then held his hand up to help Maggie. Her breasts fell forward towards him as she leaned over the side of the vehicle. Gee enjoyed that. All alone, as the sun slowly sank towards the horizon, the two lovers, sipped their drinks, wrapped in each other's arms. It was very romantic. After a while, just as the sun touched the horizon, Gee announced that they should move on. As he started to pack up the glasses and tins of nibbles Maggie moved to the other side of the vehicle, and, in a flash, removed her blouse and skirt. She lay there, on a patch of soft grass, naked, apart from her little white panties, smiling at Gee with a come-hither look. "C'mon Maggie. Jeez, it's getting dark. It's dangerous to stay out here." "Don't you like it when there is a bit of danger? Doesn't it turn you on?" Maggie had her fingers inside her panties. The danger of the bush clearly excited her. "Maggie, we can't stay here now," pleaded Gee, though his body told him otherwise. Maggie, the beautiful Maggie, was just irresistible. As the sun disappeared over the horizon, he grabbed his rifle, pulled down his shorts, and engaged with Maggie on her grassy patch.

It is amazing in Africa, how darkness follows light so quickly. There is no such thing as twilight. It is either light or it is dark. By the time Maggie had removed her little white panties, the two lovers were enveloped in blackness and the night sounds of Africa accompanied their lovemaking. The fact that this was potentially dangerous made it all the more exciting, particularly for Maggie. Gee still had his ranger's eyes and ears. When they were done, the two lovers lay there, entwined, in the dark for perhaps half an hour, listening to the night sounds, interrupted only by the odd crackle of Gee's walkie talkie. Maggie could have stayed there all night but Gee explained that, if they did not return to base soon, they would be the subject of a search party. Maggie reflected on how exciting it felt to make love in the open, or in places where she shouldn't. This, she hoped, would be something they could repeat. Until then, she could enjoy herself from time to time with the happy memory.

Chapter Fourteen

Fast forward two years. Jimmy was now seven and Sam, at 13, was at Dorking Grammar School. Both had retained most of their friends, but the house that they lived in, spacious and substantial as it was, was no longer a home. Fanny had become a fixture and, although they were really both beyond the 'nanny' stage, she represented real stability. From Maggie and Greg's point of view she was a Godsend. There was also a permanent housekeeper, Betsy King, who lived in Dorking but worked at the house from 8 am to 5 pm every weekday. The reason for all of this was that both Greg and Maggie travelled excessively with their separate pursuits.

Greg's recruitment agencies now had branches in London, Manchester, New York, Chicago and Los Angeles. Its reach had spread beyond the hospitality business into top executive search, specialising in board level appointments. NoGrow had taken off like a rocket. Greg had hoped that in their trial state introduction that at least 1% of the male population would spend one dollar each per year on the product. As it turned out 5% of males in California spent $4 each, which translated into $60 million revenues against his projection of $3 million – and that was just for California. The product was now being rolled out in the rest of the USA, with plans for export into South America and Europe. Within another year Greg reckoned that NoGrow sales could be over $200 million per year. If Greg wanted to cash in he could have sold his share in the business for almost $500 million, or roughly £400 million. On top of this the Bitcoin price had shot up to £8000; Greg's blended average purchase price of the 6,500,000 was just under £2 per coin, so his potential capital gain was humungous at over £50 billion, a staggering amount. If Greg were to cash in on the agencies, NoGrow, and his Bitcoins, he would easily be listed in the top 20 wealthiest men in the United Kingdom. All of this in three short, busy, years.

Greg's personal life though had not been quite so successful. His affair with Maria had blossomed and then withered. Maria was sexy and cunning. Maggie's first instinct about her was absolutely accurate. For the first year of their relationship, after their fling in Los Angeles, Greg's sexual appetite for Maria knew no bounds, so much so that he had little left to give Maggie. Maria would do anything to give Greg an exciting sexual time. She was an artist in how to please him. He had been used to Maggie, who, although beautiful, had engaged in sex with him as an act of love, and sometimes fun, if she really wanted to arouse him. Maria's sexual performance was sensual, almost dark, as she found more and more ways to excite and entertain him. To accommodate Maria and her performances Greg had acquired an apartment in Mayfair. He had hidden the ownership of it in an offshore company to keep it from Maggie. "Working late," for Greg, was spending erotic evenings in the apartment with Maria, particularly when Maggie was travelling. However, Greg was not in love with Maria, nor she with him. Maria was aware that she could not hold him and Greg found that his eyes were often wandering. Gradually, their ways parted. Maria hooked herself another rich 'client' and Greg stopped using the flat. In the interests of Maria's continued 'cooperation', Greg ceded the offshore company that owned the flat to Maria and returned to the Goring for his evenings in town. What he really wanted, he decided, was something that he could not have.

Greg and Maggie's home life was shot. There were extended periods when either one or other of them was away, or even both of them. For the sake of the children they remained together and, when they were both in residence, they maintained a cordial relationship. Greg could no longer pretend that he did not have love interests elsewhere and Maggie made no secret of the fact that she had found the love that he did not provide, in Africa. Although they shared a bedroom to keep up appearances, they were no longer intimate. The warmth had left their relationship. They were jointly now worth billions of pounds but their love for each other was worth nothing.

Maggie had become quite the poster girl for Trunk and the international fight against poaching of ivory and rhino horns. She was beautiful and passionate about it and, after a while, as she conquered her nerves, became extremely articulate on the subject. If the anti-poaching lobby wanted a spokesperson for the press or television, they found themselves turning to Maggie. She spoke from the heart and she looked good. In addition to this, she was the only Trustee of Trunk that was actually physically engaged in anti-poaching activities, with frequent visits to Africa to support the frontline efforts. Bit by bit, Maggie had become the most prominent spokesperson in the international anti-poaching movement, with a schedule of impassioned but logical speeches at the United Nations and the European Union. Her goal, in alliance with Trunk, was to dent the demand for tusks and horns by making it illegal everywhere. Sam and Jimmy, although sad that their Mummy was away so often, were old enough to be proud of her when they saw her on the front of magazines or speaking on the television. Not everyone in their schools has a mummy that everybody admired.

The anti-poaching training facility at the Shawu farm, under the overall direction of Gee, was giving employment to many men and women from the villages. Poachers in the Kruger were finding life harder. Maggie also had a business interest in the area. An opportunity had arisen for Maggie to buy her own game viewing lodge. Gee had alerted her to the fact that the game viewing concession, just north of Mala Mala was going to be sold. The land involved butted onto Mala Mala's land and was almost the same size. The lodge itself consisted of 30 thatched cottages and a lobby/restaurant/bar/ admin building. It was not as luxurious as Mala Mala, but it had great potential to be improved and the game viewing was identical. Maggie told Greg that she wanted to buy it. At the time he was hot and heavy with Maria, so whether through guilt or disinterest or the fact that the cost was a mere drop in his bucket, he immediately wrote the cheque. Maggie installed Gee as the Manager and rechristened the place 'Sam's' after her daughter. Sam's would be Maggie's and Gee's love nest in the bush. It needed plenty of renovation work but that might even be fun too. The game viewing was first class and so would be the future.

Maggie and Gee's love life was as delicately poised as it was lovely. There was a tenderness and a passion about their feelings for each other that transcended all of the difficulties that their relationship had and would encounter. In the depths of the bush, away from the normal constraints that would apply to their relationship in London or Johannesburg, their friendship flourished both emotionally and sexually. They had created their own little world, far apart from the real one. In reality, they were hiding from the real world of Maggie's husband and children; they would not simply go away and God forbid that the children should. Somehow Maggie was hoping that she could share her good fortune with them, but she did not know how.

Sam was thrilled that her mum had named a game lodge after her. The relationship she had with her mother was typical of any young teenage girl. A mixture of outright rebellion tinged with moments of love. Sam was not too interested in school work; she was more interested in the boys at school. The fact that she had a beautiful and, now, well known, mother was difficult for her. When your mum is appearing with regularity in *Vogue* and *Tatler*, not to mention *Hello*, there is a sort of threat implied. How could this chrysalis of a girl be worthy of such a glamourous mum? For much of the time she hated her mother, or at least thought she did. One thing, however, did bring the two of them together, and that was their love of wildlife. Maggie had now taken Sam and Jimmy on a couple of trips to Africa. Jimmy still preferred cars, but Sam just adored everything to do with animals. So, for her to have a wildlife concession in Africa named after her was just lovely. In fact, she was slightly embarrassed at the thought of it and definitely did not want her friends at school to know of the connection. Deep down, though, she was pleased as punch and thanked her mum effusively.

Sam also got to like Gee. She was no fool. She had witnessed the deterioration in the relationship between her dad and mum. They no longer seemed to have fun together; they no longer seemed to be connected. Yes, when it came to disciplinary affairs in the house in Surrey, they worked as a team, but the tenderness between them had disappeared. When Sam got to meet Gee, she knew why. At first, she wanted to hate Gee. After all, he appeared to be the reason that her mum no longer connected to her dad. By all rights she should hate Gee's guts – but she didn't. Mum was clearly very happy in Gee's presence, and she liked her mum when she was happy. And Gee seemed such a nice gentle person. Not someone driven by success and money, like her dad, but someone who genuinely loved her mum and clearly was passionate about the wildlife that he had spent his life trying to help. To Sam, this was far more worthwhile and meaningful that buying Bitcoins or selling shampoo. No, much as logic told her that she should hate the man who had broken up her parents' marriage, she could not bring herself to do so. In fact, she longed for these trips to Africa. Gee was a wonderful guide and teacher as well as a warm and kind person. Yes, it was true that he was screwing her mum, but, since her dad did not seem to mind, why should she? Her little brother, on the other hand, seemed quite confused about the situation. Much as he could be a little brat and pest, Sam worried about him. He said very little.

When Maggie and the kids returned to England, Greg, both husband and dad, was there to greet them. The arrangement with Maria seemed to be over and it appeared that he had decided to make the most of family life, and married life, again. It was not, however, just his decision to make. Maggie remained cool. Her heart was elsewhere. She thought about suggesting a divorce and a split of the wealth, but was worried about the effect it would have on the children, particularly young Jimmy. She decided to continue, as is, at least for a while longer. She had discussed this with Gee, who, ever the understander, understood, or at least said he did.

Maggie's 35th birthday was approaching and Greg announced that he was going to throw a party for her. He told her that she did not have to worry about the catering or any of the arrangements. This would be the party to end all parties and all she need do was to show up looking pretty.

She tried to resist; the last thing she wanted was a party without Gee, but what could she do? She just shut up and let him get on with it. Also, the children seemed to be all for it; maybe they thought it would bring their mum and dad back together.

Tents were erected, portaloos where installed, a firework display was prepared, bands were contracted, DJs hired, and caterers came and went. Maggie, who at first was completely disinterested, now saw this as an opportunity to thank all of her friends around Dorking for their loyalty, so she had enthusiastically invited them all. She had been in the bush for quite a while, so had not changed much out of safari gear in the day and slacks and blouses in the evenings. It would be nice to dress up for the occasion, so she, with Sam in tow, went to Bond Street to 'do' the shops. Sam, of course, opted for teenager stuff, which was not too easy in Bond Street, but Maggie finished up in her favourite Givenchy store, where she selected a stunning gold number, which showed off her tan, her boobs, and her legs to perfection. When she modelled it for Sam, she gasped. "Mum, you look like a film star!" Maggie was satisfied. Greg could eat his heart out. She was not going to let him back in the door after the Assistant.

The party was fantastic. Everyone seemed to be having fun. As well as many of the friends and neighbours, Maggie had also invited the Trustees of Trunk and, of course, Pimlico Penelope. Greg had invited a host of bankers and offshore lawyers, as well as the senior staff form the recruitment agencies. Everybody wanted to dance with Maggie, she looked so delectable, and sexy. Greg too, thought so but Maggie politely turned him down whenever he asked, and moved on to another fawning guest. At ten o'clock, after the fireworks display, Fanny the nanny took Jimmy off to the flat above the stables, where she put him to bed. Sam was allowed to stay up until midnight, by which time many of the guests, particularly Greg's invitees from London were leaving. But the party rocked on, as did many of the locals. Finally, Greg gave up on Maggie and asked her friends to dance. Willow was only too happy to press her body into Greg's as he held her close on the dance floor. So were one or two other friends and neighbours. Finally, Greg found Ellen, who was literally dressed to seduce. Her sliver of a dress clung to her shapely body like clingfilm. Her heels were so high that her bottom wiggled whenever she walked. Greg just had to have her. Maggie was well aware how Greg had always lusted for her sexy friend. "Well, tonight," Maggie thought, "she can have him." The thought of this turned Maggie on. For the first time in the evening, she felt aroused, but she was not thinking of her husband and best friend on the dance floor. Both Greg and Ellen had imbibed plenty. Maggie watched as his hands literally explored her body. If there had been any hope for their marriage, or if Greg had been thinking that, by throwing a party, there might be hope, there was none now. She now knew that she didn't care if her husband was about to screw one of her best friends. She had her own lover who was far away. She would go to him as soon as possible because there was nothing left for her here.

Chapter Fifteen

Sandy had been born in Anguilla, the most northerly of the Leeward Islands in the Caribbean. She was named after Sandy Point, a beautiful bay in that tiny country. Anguilla, at the time, had been offloaded by the British into a political association with neighbouring St Kitts and Nevis. This arrangement had not suited the Anguillans, who attempted to leave the so-called West Indian Federation. The 8000 citizens were united in their insistence that their little island should be reinstated as a British Protectorate. Demonstrations and some rioting took place and since Anguilla had no military, indeed, no police force, a few troops from the UK were deployed to keep order, followed by a small force of 50 British policemen. Eventually the peaceful life of the Anguillans was resumed and Britain welcomed Anguilla back into the fold.

One of the British police was a man called John Coltrane. PC Coltrane, being far away from home, had been rather taken with the 17-year-old, Sandy. When time came for the British to pull out of Anguilla, John Coltrane, was summoned to Sandy's parents' little home to be informed that their daughter was pregnant and to enquire what he intended to do about it. Being churchgoing folk they insisted that he do the right thing and marry their daughter. Arrangements were made and PC Coltrane found himself returning to England with more than he left. John Junior was born at the London Hospital a few months later. However, by then PC Coltrane had abandoned his new wife in favour of another woman. Sandy was now alone, far from home and family, with a new born to care for; she was just 18. Because she was still, technically, married to a policeman, she qualified for a council flat and moved into a two-bedroom flat on the 12th floor of a tower block in Battersea, about as far removed from Sandy Point as one could imagine. PC Coltrane never came to visit his son and, in many ways, Sandy was pleased that he didn't. Sandy was a young girl in a foreign country and had no understanding of her rights. Even before John Junior was one year old, PC Coltrane has asked for a divorce, or rather, he had told Sandy that he was going to get divorced. A neighbour told Sandy that she must seek legal advice from someone at the Wandsworth Town Hall, and offered to go with her. There, they were advised that, even if the father divorced her, he still had a financial responsibility to his son, and that Sandy should make sure that she secured some sort of agreement from him before allowing him to divorce her. Sandy was fearful that, if she were no longer married to a police constable, that she would lose the right to live in the council flat. Her mind was put at ease by the lady at the Town Hall. She had the right to stay in her little flat.

For the first few months following John's birth, Sandy felt all alone. PC Coltrane sent a pittance, the minimum required by law, as maintenance payment for his son but, with baby John to look after, it was very difficult for her to work. She longed to go back to Anguilla, but she had no money to get there and, in any event, did not want to endure the shame of being, first an unmarried, then divorced, mother. Her neighbours were helpful, but they all had their own set of worries to contend with. She noticed that the local corner shop had a board on which one could advertise services, such as babysitting or cleaning and the like. So, one day, she neatly printed her name and address on a card, offering her services as a cleaner, and pinned it, with the permission of the shopkeeper, on the board. She had no telephone, so had to call into the shop every day to find out whether anyone had enquired. After almost a month of fruitless visits to the shop, when she kept having to re pin her card to stop it from being covered over, the shopkeeper handed her a slip of paper with a name and address on it – 'Mr David Jackson, Forbes House, Battersea Church Road.'

The house was an imposing Georgian building with an unobstructed view over the Thames. An elderly lady wearing a pinafore, opened the door. Sandy was a pretty little thing, standing there with tiny John wrapped in a blanket on her back, African style. She was holding her little advertising card. "Mrs Jackson?" she enquired, "the shopkeeper on the corner said that you might have some work?" "Well, my dear," said the lady, "I'm not Mrs Jackson. There is no Mrs Jackson, as far as I know. I'm Mrs. Braintree, the Housekeeper. And who might this little cutie be?" she said, obviously referring to John Junior, not Sandy. "He's my little boy, John," replied Sandy, clearly encouraged that Mrs Jackson was so friendly. Mrs Braintree was quick to notice that John Junior was not as black as his mother, but said nothing. It turned out that Forbes House was pretty big; six bedrooms, numerous bathrooms, huge dining room, sitting room, library and rambling kitchen. Mrs Braintree, now of advancing years, had prevailed upon the owner, Mr Jackson, to allow her to hire a part-time assistant, to do the heavy cleaning work and laundry, maybe three times a week. For Sandy, this could be a perfect arrangement, especially since Mrs Braintree seemed to like babies. "Maybe, she would let me bring John Junior with me," she thought. Mrs Braintree listened to Sandy's story about Anguilla, the policeman and so on. She felt sorry for this young girl, all alone in a huge city, after her sheltered life on an island. She also thought that, since Sandy was not from the neighbourhood, she would not have been corrupted by the local youth, for whom she had zero tolerance. On top of this, Mrs Braintree thought John Junior was adorable.

"You'll have to meet with Mr Jackson. I can recommend you, but he must approve. There are a lot of valuable things in this house. He must know who will be working here." The 'interview' with Mrs Braintree had been in the kitchen. She now asked Sandy to wait whilst she went to disturb the boss in his office upstairs. John Junior had woken up and was starting to niggle. Sandy knew that he would want her breast, but she couldn't possibly start to feed him with the impending arrival of the boss. John's niggles became louder. She had no option but to put him onto her right nipple. He stopped niggling and drank. Almost immediately Mrs Braintree appeared, followed by a huge man, presumably Mr Jackson, himself. "Well, this is a first!" he boomed as he entered the kitchen, "I've interviewed many people in my life, but this is the first who has been breastfeeding." Sandy was terribly embarrassed. She thought that any chance she had of getting the work was gone. "I'm so sorry, sir," she stammered, "I didn't want him to disturb you." "Quite alright, young lady," boomed Jackson, "Won't be the first bit of breast that I've seen, -and hopefully won't be the last," he guffawed.

There was no interview. Jackson simply stated that if Mrs Braintree was happy to employ Sandy, then so was he. "What do we call you, young lady?" he enquired, "and what do we call the little lad?" Sandy answered politely and thanked him for giving her the chance – and that was that.

Mrs Braintree let Sandy finish feeding the baby, and made the arrangements for Sandy to start the very next day. Mrs Braintree turned out to be the first real friend that Sandy had in England and for John Junior she was as good as the Grandma that he never saw in the Caribbean.

David Jackson was a descendant of an illustrious British family, who had made their fortune from candles, which were obviously big business, before the invention of gas light and then electric. Jackson, himself, did not know one end of a candle from another. He was a Professor of English Literature at Cambridge, where he lived during term time. Forbes House in Battersea was the Jackson family home, which had been entrusted to him. He had been married, but the union had not lasted and had produced no offspring. When Sandy first met him, he was a large, loud man, with a very hairy face. His ruddy complexion indicated that he liked a tipple or two. His loud laugh, which was never far away, was infectious. His reliance on Mrs Braintree to keep house for him, which included the cooking and shopping was complete. From time to time he would throw dinner parties in the grand old house and, on these occasions, Sandy was called to help out by serving at the table. Jackson's guests were always delighted with the delicate little Sandy with the shy smile. From time to time Jackson would bring a lady friend home to dinner; they normally stayed for the night. Mrs Braintree and Sandy would always have a little giggle together as they evaluated the guest sleepers. Sandy didn't earn a great deal, but it was steady employment, and both Jackson and Mrs Braintree were good to her. They were also good to John Junior, who grew up thinking they were family.

John Junior turned out to be a bright little thing. At two, he was running around and speaking nonstop. He was a handsome little boy, who had taken on the best physical attributes of his mixed parentage. There was no doubt that he had a white father, but he grew up thinking of himself as black, probably because he lived with his black mother and never saw his white dad.

Sandy was a good mother. She was devoted to John Junior and showered him with love. Her work as a cleaner and housekeeper did not bring in much money, and the payments from PC Coltrane were not as regular as she would have liked, but not so irregular that it would be worthwhile taking him to court or even registering an official complaint. One way or other Sandy scraped by, with just enough money to feed and clothe her growing boy, but never enough to spend on anything nice for herself. Her clothes came from the charity shops and from time to time she took advantage of the church food bank. The was no time for dalliance with another man. Love, outside of her son and the church would have been a luxury.

Sandy's social life, such as it was, revolved around the Church. Her parents, back in Anguilla, had been devout Methodists; so Sandy had been made as a child to attend services held every Sunday in the little Methodist hall in the Valley, the only town in Anguilla. She was obliged to walk to and from the hall at least once, and sometimes, twice, each Sunday, which was a round trip of five miles. Religion and the fear of God had played a large part in her early life and that is why, when she became pregnant at the age of 17, her fall from grace was so devastating for her parents. Relations with them had been frosty since she fled, pregnant, to England. By the time John was five years old, he had never met his grandparents, nor had they communicated with him. He and his mother were alone in a foreign land. For this reason Sandy's 'home' in England became the Methodist Church in Wandsworth and the kind folk at Forbes House.

Professor Jackson was impressed with the quietly spoken

Anguillan girl. She never failed to show up for work on time and was always available to help at his occasional soirees. Mrs Braintree had taught her to cook and sew and, perhaps, more importantly, to read. Not that she did not know how to actually read when she first started at the Forbes House, because her basic education in Anguilla had been very good; but David Jackson, being a Professor of Literature, had a huge library in the house, to which Mrs Braintree had carte blanche to use. "What use are books," Jackson would say, "unless someone reads them?" So, Mrs Braintree gradually coaxed Sandy into reading. She and her employer, actively encouraged Sandy to take books home and guided her on their selection. Sandy's television in her council flat became books. Her mundane existence was enhanced and illuminated by the wonders from her employer's wonderful library. Gradually Sandy became knowledgeable. She absorbed knowledge. What she lacked in a social life, outside of the Church, she made up for in the fantasy, and sometimes factual, world of books.

As the years went by, Mrs Braintree became more and more impressed with the range and complexity of the books that Sandy borrowed. Professor Jackson, too, had watched Sandy's prowess and from time to time, would ask her to come to his office to discuss what she had read, as if he were giving a tutorial at Cambridge. Little did Sandy realise, but she started to receive an education fit for a Cambridge undergraduate. It was, therefore, in this strangely academic world that John Junior grew up. He was a cute little youngster, but, unlike most of the lads on the council estate, he was more interested in books than in football. He attended the local government school, where the teachers recognised his prowess with the written and spoken word. Many of his fellow students found great difficulty in learning to read and write. Many were not interested to try, and clearly had no encouragement to do so, at home. John Junior, although not popular from his exploits on the sports field, had demonstrated a kindness to others that many of his schoolmates admired. He would help anyone who asked with their assignments, and do so willingly. This is what his mother would have liked and this is what he was taught at church.

At the age of 11, John secured a place at Putney High School, a prestigious government school for which there was much competition to attend. Sandy was thrilled. It would be a stretch for her in providing the school uniform and the daily fares and so on, but, somehow, she would make it work. John Junior was her life and she was determined that he would be successful, in whatever he chose to do. David Jackson and Mrs Braintree were also delighted for John and Jackson told him that, if he ever wanted a quiet place to study, the library at the house would always be available. As a reward for his achievement the kindly professor bought a brand-new bicycle for John, with a seat that would adjust as he grew. John was the envy of the estate. It was also a little difficult for him there, because he was the only boy there who had passed the entry exam to a good school. Achievement of this sort could make you a pariah on a council estate, but John's easy going, friendly and unthreatening manner, seemed to carry him through and the roughnecks left him alone. He was seen as a professor rather than as a threat or challenge to the ruffians and drug dealers.

When John was 15, his mum, Sandy, received a rare letter from Anguilla. When she opened it she cried. Her mother had passed on. She was only 65. The funeral had already taken place. Her father, now 70 years old, was still living in the small cottage, which had been Sandy's childhood home. Sandy's tears soon gave way to anger. "Why hadn't her father contacted her earlier? Maybe Sandy and John could have gone to the funeral. Why had it taken the death of her mother to receive news from the family?" Suddenly, she was homesick. And cross with herself. John had never been to the country in which he had been conceived; he had never known his grandparents nor any of his cousins. She had deprived him of this. She was ashamed. When John came home from school that evening Sandy had made up her mind; she was going to take him to Anguilla. He deserved to see his true home. It might take a while for her to save up enough for the tickets, but that was her goal. She would take on an evening cleaning job until she had enough money for the fares. This would be her new goal.

A year later, in the school summer holidays, the plane carrying Sandy and her son touched down at St. Maarten's airport. From there they had to take a taxi to the little town of Marigot on the French side of the island, where they could get a ferry to Anguilla. This was the first time that John had been out of England and now, in a couple of short hours he had been from Dutch Sint Maarten, through French Saint-Martin, to British Anguilla. Saint-Martin is a small mountainous island, divided by the colonialist between France and Britain. Its wealth had come from sugar and its hills were dotted with plantations. Anguilla is situated about ten miles across the water from the French side of Saint-Martin. It is a small, flat, elongated strip of unfertile land whose name is derived from the French word for an eel. Although scenically it is undistinguished, it does have the advantage, on one side, of glorious views across the water to the mountains of Saint-Martin. It also possesses some of the most beautiful sand beaches in the Caribbean, if not the world, and the most glorious blue water in its bays. When Sandy left for England there were only 8000 inhabitants. Now, 15 years later, there were a mere 10,000.

As Sandy and John stepped off the ferry, Sandy scanned the handful of people waiting on the dock. She had thought that her father might be there to greet them; she wondered if she would even recognise him. But alas, nobody came forward to greet the mum and her boy, so they climbed into a waiting taxi and instructed him to drive to the family home. John was tired, but excited. The road was narrow but in reasonable condition. It wound its way along a little ridge which seemed to run down the centre of the island like a spine. On either side were dotted little houses, some with tin roofs and some with colourful tiles. Most of them seemed to have a water storage tank attached to catch the scarce rain from the roofs, Sandy explained to her son. After a few minutes the road went around a sharp bend and revealed, down below, the most magnificent bay that John had ever seen. Brilliant blue water, in several shades, was met with a beach of the whitest sand he had ever seen, wedged between two rocky promontories. A handful of little homes were dotted along the beach and a few fishing vessels were anchored offshore. To John, from Battersea, this place looked like heaven.

As the taxi pulled up outside one of the smallest tin roofed houses, an old black man shuffled out. As he hugged his daughter Sandy, they were both crying. Sandy, who had been holding back her emotions since learning of the death of her mother, was overcome with the memories of her home and her childhood, which had been so abruptly ended. Her father, who had basically thrown her out for crossing the line of his Methodist principles, had long since regretted it. For a full minute he held her tightly, almost oblivious of his strapping young grandson. Then, he broke free. "So man. You must be John Junior. Welcome to Sandy Point. It is wonderful that you are here!" John held out his hand to greet his grandfather for the first time in his life. Granddad, brushed it aside, threw his arms around the lad, who was now taller than him, and hugged him. "Welcome home, my boy. I am so happy to meet you at last."

Chapter Sixteen

John had a fantastic holiday. His grandfather, Moses, spoiled him royally. In these magical three weeks, John learned to sail, to fish, to lay out lobster pots, to windsurf and to garner the salt from the local salt 'farm'. Sandy and John were also warmly welcomed by relatives from across the little country. It seemed to John that everyone was related to everyone else. In fact, so many of the surnames were the same, or similar, that it became quite confusing, even to an intelligent young man like John. He also learned how the little island was governed, since it had returned to the British Commonwealth of nations. There were eight political constituencies, he learned, and each one voted for a Member of Parliament. There were two main political parties, basically one to the left and one to the right. Elections were held every five years and the ruling party handed out the political jobs, such as Prime Minister and other ministries. The truth was, however, that the only viable industry was tourism, and that had yet to really take off. The bottom line, John discovered, was that the little independent island was totally dependent upon subsidies from the UK. Notwithstanding this, John absolutely loved the place. He loved the sunshine, he loved the blue water and the sandy beaches, and he loved the warm welcoming people. He was so grateful to his mum,

Sandy, for having used her savings to bring him here. One day, he vowed to himself, he would pay her back and make her proud.

Sandy's relationship with her dad had healed. She understood that it was his religion that had forced her to leave, not the person. She forgave him. For two pins Sandy would have swapped her life in London for one on the island, but she had John's future to consider. He was doing so well at the high school, always top or near the top of his class. He was a serious boy who had great potential. The teachers at the school had him marked down, in their minds, for Oxford or Cambridge. That would be amazing for a mixed-race boy from a council estate. All of this was ahead for John, but only if they stayed in London. A return to the sleepy island of Anguilla would be wonderful, but only at the expense of the future of her son; it could not even be contemplated. She had come so far with John Junior. He had been the reason for her life. She could not let him down now.

So, at the end of the three weeks, Sandy and John bade their farewell to Moses. The afternoon before, all of the cousins and aunts and uncles that were still alive, had descended upon their little cottage with food and bottles of beer. Somebody had a guitar and made music. There had been much laughter and promises were made that they would all see Sandy and John again. Nobody said so, but mostly they wondered whether this could ever happen. When they reached the airport at Sint Maarten, waiting for the plane to take them back to Gatwick in England, John suddenly reached for his mum and gave her the warmest of hugs. "Thank you, Mum," he said, "thank you for bringing me here. I will never forget it."

Back in Battersea, life returned to normal. There were still a couple of weeks left of summer holiday for John. He had answered an advert asking for temporary labour to harvest grapes in Surrey, a county not too far from London. There, just outside Dorking, a vineyard had been set up, and, as global warming had gradually improved the weather in south of England, these tentative projects had been expanding rapidly, as British wines started to make their mark on restaurant wine lists across the country. The Dorking vineyard was one of the first and largest in the UK. Every year a small temporary army of pickers were required for a short period. John was lucky enough to be selected as one of them.

When John turned seventeen, he began the process of college applications. His teachers at Putney were insistent that he aim for the top. Professor Jackson, who had had so much to do with encouraging John, was adamant that he should apply to Cambridge. He maintained that he was not allowed to pull any strings, but, unknown to John Junior, he had had a quiet word with the principal at Putney, with an indication that an application from John just might be well received, subject of course to his A level results. When the results came in John had absolutely 'smashed' it. Jackson told his cleaning lady that she had nothing to worry about. Her son would make it to one of the most prestigious universities in the world, with a scholarship and financial assistance that would make it all possible. "One day, my dear," he told Sandy, "this boy will make you very proud." "Oh, but he already has!" thought Sandy. "Thank you, sir, thank you so much for all you have done for him. It is your encouragement that has got him there. We will never forget it, and may God bless you."

After one year at Cambridge, John had figured out that he wanted to do something for his mother's homeland, Anguilla. He had decided, in a very mature way, for a young man of nineteen, that he could help Anguilla become an international banking haven. To do this, someone there would need to understand international banking and tax law. Anguilla had little to offer, outside of beaches and sunshine. It needed a financial and banking infrastructure to be able to attract wealthy clients, who in turn could bring riches to the little island, by investing in second homes and upmarket tourist facilities. John Junior had decided to become that man. He would study law, particularly international tax law, and take his expertise 'home'. This would be a long haul in terms of education but to him, the goal was clear, and he never wavered from it.

By his mid-twenties, John had proudly opened "Anguillan Tax Advisors," a company with a small office near St. Paul's Cathedral in London, and another in The Valley, Anguilla. He was no longer picking grapes in Dorking. He, together with the eight elected men in Anguilla, was drawing up a roadmap that would make Anguilla one of the most wanted and desirable tax havens in the World.

By the age of 28, John Coltrane was Anguilla's de facto Chancellor of the Exchequer. By the time he was 31, he was the Prime Minister and Anguilla boasted two of the finest resort hotels in the World and an exclusive housing estate to rival Lyford Cay in the Bahamas. Sandy's little boy had come home. Sandy, herself, finally stopped cleaning Professor Jackson's house and moved back to her homeland in the sunshine.

Chapter Seventeen

The morning after Maggie's birthday party, Greg had not come home. The last Maggie had seen or heard of him and Ellen had been the grey Bentley scrunching off down the drive; she knew not where. Maggie had not slept well, but she had made a decision. This farce of a marriage could not go on. She had thought that she was protecting the children but that was clearly no longer the case. She lay in bed cursing the day that they had won the lottery. Before that, she mused, life had been normal. Now everything had gone wrong. But something kept telling her that 'everything' had not. Without this dramatic change in their fortune, she would never have met Gee. Her life would never have been complete. Now, however, happiness for herself and her children, was up to her. There seemed no way back to the days of normality before they had found the lottery ticket, so she must just make the most of the hand she had been dealt.

Sam appeared for breakfast. "Hey mum, it was a great party, wasn't it? Where's Dad?" "He had to go to work early," lied Maggie. "What? And leave you with all this mess to clear up? How could he?" said Sam, indignantly. "Well, you know how important the business is to Dad," said Maggie, half meaning it. Maggie wanted to tell Sam that she was planning to get a divorce, but thought better of it. "Better discuss it with him first," she counselled herself. This week was to be a big one for Maggie. She was due to address the National Assembly of the United Nations in New York on Thursday. Giles was scheduled to fly with her, where they were representing Trunk in its campaign to make the sale of tusks illegal. Maggie did not want this week to be spoiled by domestic upheaval. She explained to Sam and Jimmy that she needed to go to New York later in the week, but that Fanny would be on hand to look after them. After breakfast, she ran them to school and then returned to supervise the clean-up. Ellen did not show up for the morning friend's coffee reunion; only Willow and Trixie. They raved about the party. Nothing like it had happened in Dorking for a long while. They gossiped about who did what to whom. They were silent about Ellen's disappearance, as good friends might be.

When Maggie returned to the house just before one o'clock, the Bentley was back. Greg was taking a shower. She watched his toned body as he scrubbed off the lust from the night before. She had no regrets about her decision. A light lunch passed without much conversation. Maggie waited to see if Greg would say anything; anything at all; maybe where he had been or even an apology. But, nothing. It was as if it were perfectly normal to spend the night with your wife's best friend. Finally, Maggie broke the silence. "Was her body as nice as you've always dreamed of?" she started rather contemptuously. Greg cut her off. "Don't start," he barked. "It was just a fling. After all, I don't get any at home!" "No, you're right, and you are not going to any more. I have decided that it is time to end this sham. My Greg ceased to exist after we won the lottery. I think we should split permanently. I have only stayed because of Sam and Jimmy. Now, I think that we are actually doing them harm. I don't want to row with you. We have a job to

do with our kids. We must work out how to do it apart."
Maggie's voice was surprisingly strong and steely. She was
determined not to cry. She wanted him to understand that
she meant what she said. Greg let her finish. He was not
surprised. He had not behaved well, but then, nor had she.
"Perhaps," he thought, "she is right. Perhaps it would be
for the best." Maggie reached out her hand and placed it
on his arm. "I'm sorry, my love," she said softly, "I am so
sorry that it has to end like this." With that she stood and
left him at the table. He sat there, wondering what would
happen next. After a while, he got up and buried himself in
his den, immersed in paperwork. He emerged a few hours
later. Maggie had continued with the after party clear up.
Instructions had to be given to a host of helpers; the catering staff, the Porto John people and so on. When Greg
finally emerged from his little home office, his eyes were
red – either, Maggie thought, from the heavy night before
of maybe from the news. "I think we must tell the children,"
he said, "before they hear it from somewhere else."

"Yes," agreed Maggie. "Let's do it this evening."

Before flying to New York, Maggie made a visit to the
lawyers to instigate the divorce proceedings. After some
research on Google she had selected the prestigious firm of
Bishkon de Playa, divorce attorneys to the stars. She had
often seen their name in high profile divorce cases. She reasoned that if they were good enough for Elizabeth Taylor,
they would be good enough for her. Maggie May, the firm's
divorce specialist, often pictured herself in *Tatler*, had agreed
to meet. Maggie had not really focussed on the fact that Mrs
(or Ms) May, shared her name; maybe this was a good sign.
Maggie May ran through the procedure's that would need
to be followed to set the ball in motion, then proceeded to
ask Maggie loads of questions, mainly about her knowledge
of the couple's financial affairs, bank accounts, companies

and company accounts, offshore arrangements and so on. Maggie realised that she knew very little about their joint financial affairs. She explained that she trusted Greg and always had. "Trust has no place in divorce proceedings," Maggie May pronounced rather solemnly. "How do you have access to money, when you need it?" she continued. "We have a joint bank account. There is always money in it," replied Maggie. "And what is the current bank balance in this account, may I ask?" Maggie did not have the first idea. She just wrote cheques or transferred money on line as required, sometimes for quite large sums. No cheque had ever bounced and why should it? After all, she and Greg were multimillionaires. Maggie May was incredulous at her client's naivety. There was something quite charming about it. Maggie May decided that she would do all she could to help her but knew that this could be a bumpy and difficult ride. "We will have to start by requesting bank account details of all of your accounts, be they in joint names, your name singularly or your husbands. We will also need to get details of all offshore accounts, share ownership, and other arrangements. How much do you think you are jointly worth, Maggie?"

"Well, I do know that a few years ago we had £500 million in the bank," replied Maggie, without explaining how it had got there. The other Maggie's jaw dropped. "Well, we need to fill in a few forms and I will need you to put up a security deposit regarding our fees of, say £30,000. Then we can get started." Maggie May was ready for a fight. "No man," she thought to herself, "ever leaves £500 million in a joint account with his wife."

Having started the ball rolling, Maggie jetted off to the Big Apple with Giles in tow. The charity did not usually spring for first-class tickets on planes, quite rightly, Maggie had thought, so she paid for Giles's upgrade herself. There was no way she was going to fly to New York at the back. Maggie did not want to stay at the Pierre, where Greg's friend was the Manager, so had asked Trunk to book her and Giles into the Grammercy Park, at the end of Lexington Avenue. She had been told that, because the Avenue is not a through road going south, there is little traffic and, therefore, less noise at this address. Also, being on the East Side it was reasonably close to the iconic UN building. Maggie was by now used to giving speeches about the devastation caused by poaching in Africa, so this was not new territory for her. The General Assembly of the United Nations, however, was breaking new ground for her. She was a complete bundle of nerves as she approached the dais, in a business-like and demure pale blue suit with plain blue half height shoes. She need not have worried. Her reputation as an animal rights activist had proceeded her and she was given a standing ovation that seemed to go on for minutes. This was both comforting and a little overwhelming. She composed herself as she felt the pride that comes from recognition. She made a slight gesture with her hand and started to speak. Her presentation was at first full of facts; awful facts about the devastation caused by those who insisted on trading in wild animal tusks and horns. It was also full of passion. Her description of the poor orphan animals that she personally had cared for, and her description of the suffering animals left to die by the poachers in the bush, brought tears to her eyes and to many of the packed house of delegates. "This must stop," she almost shouted from the rostrum. "It is your duty as citizens of the world to stop this terrible trade. Do your duty!" The applause was thunderous. Maggie had made her mark.

The next day, the papers, not just in America, but all over the world, showed front page pictures of this beautiful English lady berating the international law makers. Every

British newspaper had photographs of Maggie, not only on the front, but also in countless articles within. Maggie had been well known in fashionable circles before. Now she was a national treasure; the English 'rose' who had taken the UN to task. The Trustees of Trunk were over the moon with praise, and several called her in New York to congratulate her. Donations started to pour into Trunk's coffers and bumper stickers began to appear on cars. Back in England Sam and Jimmy were so proud of their mum. Their teachers had shared the newspaper headlines with the school; they were happy that some of her glory had rubbed off on them. They did not want to lose her.

Greg too could not help but notice Maggie's sympathetic press coverage. People in his recruitment business did nothing but congratulate him. He could not bring himself to admit to them that it was all over between him and Maggie. He just accepted their praise graciously. He had worked from home since the divorce discussion with Maggie, partly so that he could keep an eye on the children, to whom Maggie and he had levelled with at the beginning of the week, and partly because he did not want to face the world. He had plenty to think about concerning potential divorce arrangements, in addition to how it would affect the children. He was, of course, also thinking about how it could affect his bank accounts. He took stock of the situation. Maybe he needed to do a little pre-planning to defend his portfolio. At no point did it cross his mind that it was 'their' portfolio.

Sitting in his home den, he drew up a chart of his net worth. For starters, the value of his recruitment business, based upon a reasonable multiple of earnings was around £80 million. His NoGrow investment was doing really well. The product was available now for 50% of the world's population, either directly or on line. Since it obviously only really appealed to men, this meant that a quarter of the world's population could get hold of NoGrow, should they desire. If only 1% of a quarter of the world's male population were to spend just $1 per year on the product, the profit would be $15 million per year. Last year, NoGrow had obviously soared past these projections, reporting a profit of $25 million and still on a sharp upward curve. Greg reckoned that he could sell his stake now for $100 million, not bad for a $1 million investment six years ago. "Maybe I should get out now whilst the projections are still on the up?" he thought. These shares were safely hidden in a company, ultimately owned by Greg, in a Caribbean tax haven. If he sold them now, in theory there would be no tax to pay. The more that Greg thought about his situation, the more vulnerable he thought he might be during any divorce 'discovery' process. He did not want Maggie to open a can of worms. He would have to be very careful.

Then, of course, there were the Bitcoins. Here, Greg had really hit the jackpot. When he first got into the market a Bitcoin was worth 50 pence. His second and larger purchase had been at £2 per 'coin', giving him a melded purchase rate of around £1.80 for 6.5 million coins. One Bitcoin was now worth an astounding £8000, so his total holding of Bitcoins was currently worth a colossal and staggering amount of £52 billion. This made Greg the richest man in England, although he would never want anyone to know that. Luckily, the *Sunday Times* Rich List was never accurate. Everyday Greg awoke with the fear that the Bitcoin price would crash, but every day the price went higher. Tulips had nothing on this. But when would be the time to get out?

Finally, and this really seemed like chickenshit to Greg, there was the interest on the £500 million lottery win. At a cumulative 5% of interest per year, this pile had now grown by £170 million and stood at plus minus £670 million. Out of the small change, Greg had paid out around £7 million to Maggie's pet charities, around £4 million on their house, £10 million on Sam's Lodge and maybe another £10 million on miscellaneous living expenses and other small investments. Greg considered that his net worth at this moment was somewhere in the region of £54 billion, give or take a few million, here and there. Now was the time to protect this from Maggie. He would not be ungenerous, but, after all, it was him that had made the money, not her. All she wanted to do was to give it away.

Greg picked up the phone and instructed his lawyers and tax advisors to reinforce the protection of his wealth. "Find me the most bullet proof tax haven. Tell me where you think I should register domicile. Ring fence my assets from my wife. And, finally, start unloading the Bitcoins, slowly, so as not to disturb the market." One month later, half of the Bitcoins had been sold for £26 billion, which was now sitting in accounts in Anguilla. The remaining £26 billion worth's value had increased by another few billion as the price of the 'coin' increased to around £10,000, up 20% in a few weeks.

When the papers arrived from Bishkon de Playa, Greg's people were ready for them.

Chapter Eighteen

As soon as Maggie was back from New York, she asked Greg to move out. He had agreed that it was important that the children's lives should be uprooted as little as possible and that it would be best for them to stay at the same schools and live in the same house – at least for the time being. Greg accepted that it would be better for Maggie to live there with them; he did not relish the idea of being in charge of the household. Since Maria was now in the London flat and out of bounds, he moved temporarily to a suite at the Goring, close to his office. He was not in too much of a hurry to find a permanent place of residence, having been advised by the lawyers that it might be better for him to 'go offshore'. When he signed over the Dorking house to Maggie, she was astounded, thinking that this was an act of kindness and consideration, rarely shown, of late, by Greg. She did not realise that he was ring fencing his position as it concerned their real wealth.

Maggie continued to meet with her friends. She even forgave Ellen for her brazenness. In fact, in some strange way, she felt grateful to Ellen for forcing her to come to her senses. However, she knew that she could never really trust Ellen again; their relationship going forward would be different, which was a shame, because they had had a lot of fun together. Even her relationship with Willow and Trixie had been impaired. She did not want them to take sides between her and Ellen, but she wondered how frank and intimate she could be with them in the future, whilst they were still good friends with Ellen. Time might tell.

Maggie was desperate to get back to Africa and now that Greg was no longer a consideration, she decided to do so as soon as possible. Not only was she aching to see Gee, with whom she talked for hours each night on the phone, but there was work to do at Sam's Lodge, as well as on the Shawu farm. The Easter holidays were approaching. She asked the children if they would like to spend them in Sabi Sands, having given no thought to the fact that perhaps, by law, she would need to get Greg's permission. That sort of thing was new territory for her; something she might need to navigate in the future, but, surely, not now? Sam was thrilled at the idea of going back to 'her' camp. Jimmy, less so, rather preferring to hang out with his friends in Dorking. He did not, however, under the new circumstances, want to upset his mum, so agreed to come along. Maggie made it clear that she was not forcing him to do so; he could have stayed in the house with Fanny and she was sure that Dad would visit, but she also was pleased that he had chosen to come and told him so, with a huge hug of love. She knew, at times like these, that there would be plenty of need for hugs. Greg did not seem to mind. It had not crossed his mind that Maggie might not return with his children. However, when he casually mentioned this to the lawyers handling the divorce, they were quite concerned. He told them not to worry, but decided that, in future, there would have to be some protocols in regard to the movement of the kids.

Maggie had decided that she could not hide her love for Gee from the children; in any event, it would have been impossible. Her love for Gee could not be hidden. When the three of them emerged from the baggage claim hall at Oliver Tambo, Maggie could not stop herself from running towards him, a child clinging on to each hand, to embrace him. The warmth and strength of his body flowed through her. It had been weeks since she had felt his flesh; very difficult weeks, full of stress and tension. As she hugged and kissed him, almost oblivious of the two offspring, the tension flowed from her body. She was in the safe hands of the man that she loved. Gee eventually prised himself away, and pulled the two youngsters towards him. He did not want to usurp their Dad, but he wanted to be a great alternative. He did not need a route to Maggie's heart, but neither did he need her to have to choose. He would do his best to be their friend. One day, maybe, they would think of him as a second Dad. He was also anxious that they should have a brother and/or a sister. Neither he nor Maggie were too old. Now that she was getting divorced, there was nothing to stop them.

The Easter holidays at Sam's Camp, passed quickly. Gee had made huge progress with drawing up plans for its renovation and upgrade for Maggie to review with him. Shawu Farm was also going gangbusters. Mossie Mostert had been delighted with the progress as a result of Maggie's donation and Gee's thoughtful management. The anti-poaching school currently had 24 cadets. The pens were full of orphaned animals. There was plenty to keep Sam and Jimmy occupied. On top of that the sun shone every day. The evenings were spent around a campfire, often with guests from the Lodge, always under the clear African sky, with its upside-down moon. What was there not to like? Gee went out of his way to make sure the kids were taken care of. He organised soccer matches for Jimmy with the local African boys and, when they visited the Shawu Farm, arranged for Sam to feed the cubs. Maggie watched his involvement with her children with joy. But, at night, when the children, tired from the African sun, were finally in bed, the two lovers were, truly, wholly, as one. They made love with abandon. The fact that Maggie had made her decision had liberated them. True, she was not yet divorced, but this was just a formality. From now on they would be together. It didn't seem to matter at that moment, where or how. They just knew that they really were soul mates and nothing could get in the way of their love.

All good things must come to an end. The three weeks sped by. The children were due back at school and Maggie was scheduled to continue with her campaigning, this time at the heart of the trouble, China. Much as she loved Sabi Sands, she knew that she could not abandon her, and Trunk's, campaign to make the sale of tusks and horns illegal. Gee, completely understood. He was proud of her and wanted her to continue with the work. Meanwhile, he told her, there was so much to do at Sam's, especially since, during Maggie's stay, they had put in some long hours on the renovation plans. Maggie also was determined to get the divorce process moving as fast as possible, and Gee, naturally, understood and supported that. So, it was with some sadness, that two suntanned youngsters and their radiant mother, walked down the jetway to board the plane to Heathrow, back to their life of tension.

On the morning of their return, Maggie received a call from Maggie May, who wanted to see her as soon as possible. Apparently, Bishkons had received some responses from "the other side," and wanted to review things with Maggie in person. Maggie, as keen as mustard to get the divorce over, agreed to go to London on the next day to meet them. As it happened she also needed to go to Trunk to review with Giles the plans for the trip to China.

Maggie May looked quite serious. "Initially, we were

stonewalled in our request for financial information. However, we exercised a little pressure on the co-respondent's lawyers and finally got some information, which, I have to say, is quite disturbing." Maggie, who had arrived, it seemed, without a care on the world, suddenly looked a little worried. "Tell me," she said, "what is wrong?" "Well, my dear, it appears that, apart from the house in Dorking, which was recently signed over to you, you own nothing. That is to say that all of the bank accounts, bar one, that we have discovered are in the sole name of your husband. The only account that you are able to draw from has a balance of about £40,000. In addition to that the only other sterling accounts that we could locate, which are in his sole name, have total balances of approximately £5 million. If you were right that there should be in excess of £500 million then I am afraid that this is now 'off shore' and, maybe, technically, beyond your reach." "But that can't be right," insisted Maggie, "we had an agreement that we would be donating £200 million to charities of my choice. So far as I am aware, we have only donated £1 million per year to Trunk, and maybe half a million to Shawu farm in Africa. That can't come to as much as the interest on the £200 million. You must be wrong." Maggie May took a deep breath. "Maggie, I am sorry to tell you that we are not wrong. We have tracked back on the activities of your joint account. It would appear that, about seven years ago, you had a balance of just under £500 million, just as you told us. About a month after that money was deposited your husband moved it into some 20 other bank accounts on which he is the sole signatory. We were able to force the other side to let us have sight of these accounts. It would seem that a couple of them have been utilised to acquire legitimate recruitment agencies, and one to buy Bitcoins, and some smaller transactions to buy shares in NoGrow, a company in the USA. None of the shareholdings in these companies nor the owners of the Bitcoins are actually in the name of your husband, although, of course, we assume that he controls the actual shareholders. Finally, we must tell you that your husband recently became a citizen of Anguilla in the Leeward Islands, one of the most aggressive tax havens in the world, which is probably why he did not want to be seen as the owner of your home in Dorking." Maggie was aghast. "How could he do this? This means he has been planning to keep my money all along. What can we do?"

"Well, it may not all be bad news. The moves he has made may not have been to steal your share of the marital funds, but to protect them from UK taxation. For example, if he wanted to sell Bitcoins, which have increased in value dramatically, as a resident of the UK he would have been subjected to huge capital gains tax, so it was just prudent of him to avoid that. The real question here will be his willingness to accept that half of the initial balance and any gains thereafter, are your property, wherever they are now located." "He should have told me that he was doing this," said Maggie, a little wistfully, "It doesn't seem as if he wanted to share, does it?" "Maybe not," responded Maggie May, "we will soon find out."

"Under English law," Maggie May explained, "you are entitled to 50% of the net worth of any wealth acquired during the course of your marriage. That may not be so for any assets brought separately by either of you to the marriage, that is to say, that were yours or his before you tied the knot. We know for a fact that you, seven years ago, jointly had £500 million in the bank. I need to ask you if this money was acquired during your marriage or did either one of you bring it to the union?." "My God, no," said Maggie, "neither of us had a penny when we got married. It is true that Greg was the wage earner and provider for the family, but the £500 million was a gift to both of us." Maggie had promised Greg that she would never reveal the source of their wealth, not even to the children. But now, she realised that it might help Maggie May to understand the true source of the money. She knew that whatever she discussed with her lawyers would remain secret, so, as she thought about it, it made sense to come clean with Maggie May. "Well, it wasn't exactly a gift," she finally said, "We actually won the lottery and we had both signed the ticket." Maggie May took a deep breath. Now she understood. At the back of her mind she remembered news stories about the biggest ever jackpot winners, whose identity was never disclosed. Now she knew. "Well, if this is the case there can be no doubt that you are entitled to half of those winnings, plus any interest they may have attracted." She took out a calculator and quickly worked out the compound interest at 5% on £500 million. "Unless your husband has frittered away some very large sums without telling you, the £500 million that he removed from your joint account should be now worth about £670 million. At the very least, we should be suing him for a settlement of £335 million. Then we need to find out how well he has invested this money and claim your half of that."

Maggie explained to the lawyer that she really did not need £335 million and certainly not her share of further gains. She repeated that Greg and her had agreed to give £200 million to charities, but that they had been slow to do this. As she saw it her share of the donation 'agreement' would be £100 million, so she definitely needed that amount from any settlement. Beyond that, she was happy with her house in Dorking and Sam's Lodge in Sabi Sands. "Maggie," interjected the lawyer, "with the greatest respect, I have a lot of experience in these matters, although I must admit that these sums are larger than normal. I have seen many women, anxious to get the whole settlement done and dusted, often hoping to minimise damage to the children, settle for less than they were entitled to and live to regret it. I know that I am here to follow your instructions, but I am also here to give you advice. Do you really believe that if you leave large sums with your husband that are really yours, that he will honour his pledge to give them away to charity? My experience tells me that he won't. My suggestion is that we advise the other side that, in agreeing to a divorce, you might consider settling for the £335 million that you are clearly owed. If they will agree to that we will indicate that we will not request further disclosure of his other offshore assets. Why don't we see where that takes us?" Speech over, Maggie May smiled at her client. Her experience told her that, by taking this perfectly reasonable approach, Maggie would hold the moral upper ground. It also told her that Greg would almost certainly haggle about this, which would give Maggie good grounds to pursue the real offshore wealth. "This," thought the lawyer, "is where the real wealth lies." Although uncomfortable, Maggie agreed to demand 50% of the lottery win, as advised. After all, that did seem fair.

It took less than a week for Greg's attorneys to respond. Greg would be prepared to allow Maggie to keep 100% ownership of Dorking and Sam's Lodge, to pay for all future education of the children, and to pay Maggie £12.5 million per year as alimony (which Maggie May pointed out, happened to be equal to the potential interest at 5% per year on the original £500 million win), but only until she remarried, if ever. "Basically, Maggie," the lawyer pointed out, when they met to discuss things, "he keeps all the money and puts a set of handcuffs on you regarding your future." She did not need to point this out. Maggie was astounded at Greg's greed. "You know what?" she exclaimed to Maggie May, "I would like to know just how much he is hiding from me, wherever it is." Suddenly, Maggie had been transformed from the woman who would settle for a quick and painless exit from the marriage into one who actually wanted some sort of revenge; a woman scorned! Beware! "I'm going to call him and tell him to go to hell," she fumed at the lawyer. Maggie May attempted to calm her down. After all this was not the first badly treated wife that she had dealt with; in fact, it was more the norm. "The richer they are, the less they want to share," she thought. "I think it would be more prudent if you let the lawyers deal with him," cautioned Maggie May. "Keeping emotions out of it is normally helpful." Maggie stewed for a moment and then nodded her agreement. "Okay, but you can tell him this; if he doesn't play fair then I will tell the world about our lottery win. I know that is the last thing he wants people to know; he wants them all to think that he is a self-made genius." Maggie, of course stopped short in regard to the full information about the lottery win. She knew that Greg would not want her to spill the beans, so just the mention of the lottery from the lawyers might make him see sense.

Unbeknown to Maggie, whilst she was fuming in Bishkon's offices in London, Greg was relaxing on his new yacht, which he had acquired whilst Maggie had been in Africa with the children. As yachts go, it was not super fancy – you don't get too much for £10 million – because he did not want to attract too much attention, but, nevertheless, it had three sleeping cabins, one of which was very plush, a beautifully appointed lounge and dining area, a superb and spacious aft deck, and accommodation for three crew. He had acquired it with the help of Ellen, who, when Bishkon's message reached him, was sunbathing topless in full view of the crew, as was her habit. This, after all, was the South of France; it was de rigeur to go topless on your yacht. Ellen had plenty to show off. Although her breasts were not quite as firm as Maggie's they were beautifully shaped and Greg loved to watch her; so did the crew. Greg was clearly irritated by the call. Ellen sat up and pulled a towel over her upper body, or almost over it. Greg put the phone down with a scowl. He did not want to discuss this with Ellen. She was a wonderful and witty companion. She had left, George, her husband back in Dorking, not for the first time. She had been more than a sexy plaything for Greg, even though she could arouse him as much as any other woman ever had, but, he did not want to let her into his business life and, in this case, his personal affairs. "It was just a work call. Something I need to sort out and think about.," which meant, "Keep your nose out of my affairs." Ellen got the message. She would be a good girl now, but sooner or later she was determined to be his confidante. She was aware that Maggie was suing for divorce. She was hoping that this could all end amicably. She really liked Maggie, and missed her friend.

That night, despite Ellen dressing for dinner most provocatively, she could not get any reaction from Greg. His mind was elsewhere. If there wasn't so much to lose, Ellen would have sought her kicks elsewhere. She really fancied the skipper of the yacht, but any action there would be just plain foolish. No, Greg was brooding over something; she would just have to be patient. After a fitful night, Greg announced that he needed to make some business calls and suggested that Ellen pay a visit to the antiques market in Nice, which he thought she might find interesting. "I've asked the skipper if he wouldn't mind escorting you," announced Greg, "I am sure you will find it interesting." "That's fine, my love," said Ellen. "obviously I would have preferred to go with you, but never mind, some other time." With the skipper and Ellen gone, Greg got straight on to the phone. He had clearly got the message about the lottery. He wanted to talk to Maggie directly, "Screw the lawyers!"

After his third attempt Maggie picked up the phone. She was cool. Greg almost immediately went off at her about the lottery. "Surely you haven't been crazy enough to tell them about the lottery?" he shouted down the phone. "You know that could get you into as much trouble as me." Maggie calmly explained that she had told them about the lottery win, but not about the lost and found ticket. However, she made it quite clear that this was the next step, if he did not treat him fairly, which meant 'equally'. Without letting him speak she told him how angry she was that he had not shared with her the movement of 'their' money into 'his' money. She told him that she had trusted him but that now this trust had been betrayed. Greg started to say that he had done what he did to protect her. Maggie was having none of it. "If that is the case you will have no difficulty in giving me my half of what you have been protecting, including all of the interest on it, and any profits we have made from using it." Greg had never heard Maggie so angry, but he recognised that she was also calm and determined. He thought that if he tried apologising, instead of arguing, it might be helpful. "I see where you're coming from, Maggie, and I want to say that I am sorry. When I first moved the money it really was to protect us. I realise that I should have told you but, to be fair, you were never really interested in handling the money. If this has upset you, I apologise." "That's fine," said Maggie, "I accept your apology, but what has really pissed me off, is the fact that you thought you could just fob me off with a paltry payment, plus control my future life. But worse, you obviously had no intention of following through with our agreement to give to charity. No, Greg, I am afraid that I will not be fobbed off. I don't trust you anymore and I want half of everything you and

I have. Nothing less!" With that Maggie cut the phone off. When it rang again, she ignored it.

Two days went by. Greg had been silenced. Then, at ten in the morning of the third day Maggie May called Maggie. "We have a new offer. You can keep the house in Dorking and the Lodge in Africa, plus he will make a cash settlement with you of £250 million, on the understanding that there will be no public disclosures. His lawyer says, that this was "further to his discussion with you. Did you talk to him?" Maggie explained to Maggie May what had happened. "You did well, Maggie; I am proud of you," said the lawyer. "What do you think of this offer?" "How much interest would my half of the winnings over seven years come to?" said Maggie, ignoring the lawyer's question. "Because, whatever it is should be added to the £250 million. Then I might be prepared to settle." "Okay, Maggie, I understand. But there is just one thing you should know. We were able to trace the usage of the 20 accounts that he opened with the original deposit. It would appear that, with some of the money, he bought Bitcoins, apparently, at least £10 million of them. Are you familiar with Bitcoins?" "No," replied Maggie, "educate me." Maggie May knew that no explanation of how Bitcoins work would be easy for her client to grasp; she had difficulty in understanding them herself. All she knew was that the price of a Bitcoin had gone from around 50 pence per coin when Greg was in the market to £8000 now. She had no idea when or if Greg had sold the coins he had acquired, but, if he had not, they could now be worth billions. It could well be that Maggie's potential share of Bitcoin profits could make her acceptance of £250 million plus interest look like a huge underpayment. This she explained to her client. "Are you telling me that if Greg bought £10 million worth of Bitcoins shortly after we won the lottery, they could now be worth billions and billions of pounds?" she asked incredulously. "Well, we may not be able to find out when he sold them, unless we threaten him with court proceedings, but yes, he could be worth billions." Maggie was dumbstruck. She was also furious all over again. It looked as if Greg had once again tried to short-change her.

"Here's what I think we should do," said Maggie May. "We should tell him that we accept his offer of £250 million plus interest, which by the way totals £320, plus 50% of the Bitcoins he still owns or 50% of any proceeds from the sale of Bitcoins plus 5% interest." "Go for it, Maggie," said her client, "go for it! I have to go to Beijing for a few days. See if you can get this sorted whilst I am away."

Chapter Nineteen

Three weeks later, it was all over. The papers were signed, money was transferred, and the official divorce was a mere formality. Greg's lawyers had argued that Bishkon would need an army of forensic accountants to figure out the history of Greg's Bitcoin dealings (even though, in reality, there were only a couple!) and that the whole process could take years. Also, Maggie may have to force Greg in to court in order to get access to his bank accounts. This would be a spectacular case for the press. Maggie, the well-known and beautiful wildlife protagonist, arguing over billions would attract a lot of press attention. This would be the last thing that Greg would want. Greg had offered Maggie 50% of the original lottery winnings plus cumulative 5% interest, plus a whopping £6 billion in lieu of any Bitcoins or Bitcoin profits that he might have. Maggie May who had, rightly, assumed that there could be more to come, kept negotiating. She eventually settled on £15 billion. She did not know that his left Greg with a mere £37 billion, but the numbers were so dizzying that it a billion or two here or there no longer seemed to matter. Maggie, to her amazement, was now the richest woman in England, even though the riches were, on the advice of Bishkon's tax department, safely stashed away elsewhere. It was just too much for Maggie to absorb. It has been hard enough for her to think about distributing £250 million to charities. She just could not get her mind around a sum 60 times larger.

Although the children were still at school, and, therefore, living with Maggie in the house in Dorking, once the paperwork had been signed, Maggie was desperate to head south to be with Gee. Sam, now 17, had been very understanding and comforting to Maggie during the whole divorce procedure. Mother and daughter had become close. She was now old enough to understand her Mum's desire to see Gee. She assured Maggie that she and Jimmy would be perfectly okay for a couple of weeks with Fanny, who was still on the family payroll, even if she had morphed into being part of the family itself. Besides, Sam now had a boyfriend. It might be easier for her if her Mum was away for a while. Maggie was a little nervous to leave the kids. Sam was quickly becoming a beauty in her own right; slightly shorter than her mum, but just as well proportioned; clearly a magnet for the young men in the sixth form at Dorking. Maggie had been open with her daughter about sex; she wanted her to be safe and careful. Sam seemed mature enough to understand. Maggie had also discussed her dilemma regarding her future. She desperately wanted to live with Gee and to work with the animals, but she knew that she had a responsibility as a parent. Sam came to her rescue. "Mum," she ventured one day during the divorce wrangling, "why don't we all go to live in South Africa? I can apply to Uni at Cape Town; I would like to study ecology. You know how much I too love the 'wild'. Getting a degree in Cape Town would be just as good for me as one here in England. We could all live there." "But what about Jimmy?" said Maggie. "We have to think of his future. I am not sure that it would be right for him to go to school in South Africa. It may not be fair, and in any case, I would have to get agreement to this from his Dad." Sam's view had been that her Dad didn't care where Jimmy went to school, but Maggie was not so sure. Up until then, Maggie had not discussed any of this with Jimmy. She decided to wait until she could really talk to Gee.

When Maggie emerged from the now familiar baggage claim, faithful Gee was there to greet her. This time, with no children in tow, she was really able to demonstrate her affection for him, with a hug that lasted so long that passers-by stared. Greg could feel Maggie's bosom through his thin cotton shirt. She could feel his erection. They clearly needed each other; they had been several weeks apart. Although this had not been the plan, at Maggie's suggestion, they walked across the road to the Airport Sun Hotel, registered as Mr and Mrs Fishburn and took the elevator to the sixth-floor room. Their embrace was disturbed by the luggage porter, but, after that, the 'do not disturb' sign went straight on the doorknob, and within seconds they were naked and rediscovering each other's bodies on the king-sized bed. After several orgasms a jet-lagged Maggie fell asleep, even though it was only ten in the morning. The tension of the past few weeks had evaporated. She woke up once, at noon; made love to Gee again and then slept again. Finally, at about three in the afternoon, after a shower and a change of clothes, the new Maggie was ready to take on Africa. They decided not to drive up to the Sabi Sands because it would be dark by the time they arrived and the roads around Kruger were littered with dangerous potholes. The idea of spending the night at the airport had no appeal either, so they proceeded to Sandton, where they checked into the familiar surroundings of the Intercontinental. The hotel's guest history worked wonders and they were delighted to find themselves in the very suite where they had first made love. Dinner in Sandton Square, this time in

Jimmy's, and then back to the love nest. Life could not have been better. But then came the dream; the same unpleasant nightmare with the black clad beggars. But this time the noise and screaming were so frightening that Maggie woke up with a start. Although shocked, Maggie did not share her dream with Gee.

The next morning the two lovers headed for Sabi Sands. Maggie was keen to see what Gee had achieved at Sam's Camp; she was also keen to see the game in the concession. It seemed to be such a long time since she had been on a game drive. They arrived at the Sam's around lunchtime. Maggie could immediately see that Gee had made all sorts of improvements, including the lunch menu and service equipment. The place was beginning to be competition to Mala Mala, not that there wasn't a place for both of them. Gee was also excited to review with Maggie the bids he had received for the new work they were going to undergo in the guest lodges and the public areas. Maggie could see that he was totally involved in the place and she was glad. That evening Gee took Maggie on a personal game drive. They had wonderful sightings and shared a cocktail or two in the dying light of an amazing African sunset. All around Maggie were the sounds of Africa – the magical sounds of Africa, which she loved so much. She could not wait until the time she could move there.

Maggie had planned to stay for two weeks. She needed the time to think through her future. She needed to work out how to have Gee, how to advance her work with Trunk, how to do the best for her children, and how to give away £200 million. "Nothing complicated," she said quietly to herself. Gee was also keen to show her the work that he had done at Mossie's place. The Shawu anti-poaching training school had been a great success under his guidance and the Kruger Park police were very pleased with their local boy, Gee. "You really do love your country, don't you?" she both stated and asked Gee, one day. "I guess I do, Maggie," replied Gee, "I could never live anywhere else." Maggie knew that Gee would be like a fish out of water anywhere but the bush. She knew that she would have to rule out any idea of getting him to England; it just would not work. On another occasion, whilst Maggie was relating her trip to the United Nations and then the meeting with the Government officials in China, Gee had said, "I don't know how you can do that; I would never be able to do what you do. Don't get me wrong, I am 100% for it and you are a heroine to me for what you do, but I could never do that. Jus, man, two days away from the bush and I am twitchy. The thought of New York and Beijing; just couldn't do it." Maggie loved Gee for his honesty. She loved him for his love of wildlife and the bush. She loved him for being a considerate and passionate lover. But the thought of giving up her ambitions to rid the world of trading animal parts for the idyllic life in the bush troubled her. After all, she pondered, if someone doesn't do anything to stop this poaching, there will be no animals left in the bush to view. In fact, there may be no bush at all. What troubled her was the fact that she had been blessed with the means to do something about it. She was truly worried, and sometimes ashamed, about how she had acquired these means; she now felt it her responsibility to use them wisely.

In between their work and their lovemaking Maggie and Gee talked and talked about their situation. Gee was pleased that Maggie's divorce was about to happen. He truly wanted to marry her. He wanted to have children with her. He loved her deeply, but he wondered if he would be able to make her truly happy. They talked about it for days. They thought about it for days. Maggie was torn in two. But she began to see that Gee was not. Gee wanted

Maggie and he wanted his life in South Africa; he did not want a life with Maggie somewhere else. Gradually Maggie came to see that, if she gave Gee what he wanted, indeed, what she wanted too, that she would be the one doing all of the giving. She was the one who might lose her family, notwithstanding Sam's thoughtful offer to come to Cape Town; she was the one who would give up her global ambitions to improve the world. She had learned that, for a marriage to work, both parties may have to give something up. She had made a mistake the first time. She did not want to repeat it. Perhaps Gee was frightened of the world beyond his animals and South Africa? Perhaps he was nervous of her wealth, even though he had no idea of its huge extent? If that was the case, it was better that he stayed where he was. She could still love him, she could still let him have the means to operate Sam's Camp, and, indeed would be grateful if he did, but she should not make the mistake of trying to change him.

Before the two weeks had passed, Gee and Maggie had talked the thing through that there was nothing much left to say. Maggie would return to her 'career' and motherhood and Gee would do what he did best – in Africa. They pledged to be constant to each other, even though they would be on different continents. Maggie would visit as frequently as she could. Any thoughts of marriage would be put on ice, as would any thoughts of children. Their last night together was passionate. Despite all that had been said Maggie left the next day with a heavy heart. In fact, her heart had been left, once again, in Africa. As the wheels of the jet left the runway Maggie could not hold back the tears. Luckily, as the big plane lifted into the evening thunderstorm, the seat belts stayed on for a long time. By the time they reached clean air and the familiar 'ping' freed the captured passengers, Maggie had regained control and wiped her wet face.

She did not care about the blurred makeup because she was going to clean her face and go to sleep. Several nights of lovemaking with Gee meant that she had a lot of sleep to catch up on. The hostess was used to the fact that most people in first-class do not want to eat on night flights, so, when Maggie set off to brush her teeth, she returned to find her bed already made up. She sunk into the soft pillows and duvet, popped a sleeping pill, and slept soundly for seven hours. The first flight in from Johannesburg arrives at Heathrow at 5.30 am, so Maggie was back in Dorking by 8.15, just in time to greet the kids before school.

Fanny made Maggie breakfast and filled her in on the events of the last two weeks. Sam, had showed up a few times with the boyfriend, who Fanny described, worryingly for Maggie, as 'dishy'. Fanny kept her promise to Sam and did not mention that 'dishy' had stayed over one night. Jimmy had behaved himself. He had captained two school team rugby matches, both of which his team had won and spent a lot of time at the training ground. Over all, Fanny said that the kids had been well behaved and cooperative. Maggie was pleased. Maggie asked Fanny about their father. "As far as I am aware, he has not called once, Maggie," replied Fanny, "According to Jimmy, he is overseas on business. Sam thinks that he is now living overseas. In any event he seems to be too busy to talk to his children." Maggie was sad, but also glad. She was happy to have her children to herself for a while. She made a mental note that she would attend Jimmy's next rugby match. She was proud of him for having been made Captain.

Now that the alimony payment had been made and her coffers were full, Maggie was determined to set about spending it, or, at least, giving a load of it to charity. Bishkon had put her in touch with a financial management firm, Stokes and Stokes, in the city. They were highly recommended as financial advisors, something which Maggie obviously needed. Maggie's account was so large that the Managing Director of Stokes and Stokes, James Cambridge, had suggested to Maggie that he and one of his senior associates, should come to the house in Dorking for their first meeting, so that Maggie did not have to travel to the City. Maggie was thankful for this considerate thought, especially because she had been travelling. So, two days after Maggie's return from Johannesburg, James Cambridge and his colleague, Shea Briscoe, arrived at Maggie's home. They were somewhat surprised how modest the home was, considering that Maggie was now their largest personal client, but, needless to say, they did not show it. Maggie, too, was somewhat surprised at the bankers, or whatever they were. First, they were much younger than she had imagined, and second, much better looking. At a guess she would put them at the same as her age, 37. Shea was possibly a little younger. She offered them coffee, which they accepted. She did not ask Fanny to serve. She wanted this meeting to be private.

Maggie explained that she had very little experience in handling money; that her ex-husband had always attended to matters financial. She therefor needed advice on where to keep the £15 billion, not necessarily so that it would grow, but so that it could be preserved. She also explained that her passion was animal protection and anti-poaching and that she had plans to spend up to £200 million for this cause. She made it clear that, for her, this was a priority. Mr Cambridge ("Call me James") explained that Mr Briscoe ("Call me Shea") would be her account executive, who would be available to her at any time, day or night. "Night might be good," thought Maggie, naughtily, as she looked at the handsome man in her lounge. Maggie nodded her understanding, but Shea thought that he caught a twinkle in her eye. Together, the two bankers laid out an investment strategy, which included extra safe investments, bonds, and a few gold shares, just for fun. They did, however, suggest that they take £1 billion of the 15 for a 'flutter' on some start-up companies and identified Amazon and Tesla for a punt. Maggie had no real idea what either Amazon or Tesla did but she listened to their explanation and rationale, then agreed. They also suggested that the £200 million earmarked for charity should actually be put into a charity owned by Maggie for the purpose of making charitable donations. They said they would arrange this with Bishkon de Playa. It was agreed that, once the paperwork was in place, Maggie would visit their offices, maybe for lunch in their board-room. Maggie accepted. They also agreed that it might be judicious for them to review the portfolio once per month in person. Maggie also agreed. Finally, they discussed the concept of tax avoidance, wherein they could shield much of Maggie's money by moving it offshore. Maggie, who had been horrified to find out that her Greg had been doing just that, and was now, apparently, forced to live overseas, emphatically stated that she was not interested. "This coun-try has been good to me. I am perfectly willing to pay my share in taxes," she pronounced quite firmly. The two bank-ers, whilst maybe not agreeing with that principle, roundly congratulated her on her stance. "That is so good to hear." lied James, "we don't have many clients like you."

Business done, Maggie offered to drive the two bankers to the station. They politely declined on the basis that they had a driver waiting outside. Maggie had not noticed the black Roller when they arrived. Even though she had plenty of money, she now wondered about their fees. The percentage quoted seemed very low, but Rolls Royce don't come cheap.

Maggie now turned her attention to her real interest. She called Giles at Trunk, her long-time admirer, to arrange a meeting. She wanted to get serious about giving money away.

Chapter Twenty

John 'Junior' Coltrane, firstly as advisor to the Anguillan Government, and thereafter as Prime Minister, had transformed his little island homeland into one of the most efficient tax havens in the world. It had quickly become apparent to the eight members of parliament on the island that this young man who had come to settle in their homeland was a genius. Although he had not been born in Anguilla, his mother had. Futhermore, John had been conceived there. Never mind that his father was a British policeman, as far as they were concerned, John was an Anguillan, and fit, therefore, to stand for the Anguillan parliament. One of the eight was due for retirement, so he had gladly stepped aside to allow John to be elected as MP for Sandy Point. Within months, his small, but ruling party, asked him to be their leader, which he gladly accepted. Sandy Coltrane was the proudest mother in the land. After 20 years of scrimping and saving to educate her gifted son, she was now reaping the rewards; not necessarily with money, but with something far more important to her, respect from her country men and women. When Sandy had been forced to leave, she had left in shame; a pregnant, unmarried, girl, fresh out of school. She had now returned with her head held high. She was the mother of the Prime Minister, the Mother of the Nation.

Part of John's political plans had been to offer Anguillan citizenship to foreigners in exchange for investment in the Anguillan economy. To obtain Anguillan residence, and therefore an Anguillan passport, foreigners would need to keep large deposits in Anguillan banks but also to lease parcels of land, on which they would be required to build homes withing two years of signing the leases. Since there had been no real construction companies on the island, this had meant the establishment of a whole new industry, offering good employment to the local population. Three large, empty, tracts of land, had been acquired by the Government to be designated as residential areas for 'new Anguillans'. These had been offered to wealthy foreign investors for large sums. The purchase of one leased plot would secure the buyer an Anguillan passport for himself and a partner. This would be forfeited if building work on the plot had not commenced within two years. The scheme had been very successful and some magnificent new homes were popping up on the three walled estates. Greg Layburn had bought a double lot and was busy with architects and Ellen in designing a spectacular island home.

John Coltrane had also recognised the upside in a state-of-the-art marina. He knew that all good billionaires had floating palaces, so he set about transforming Sandy Point into one of the world's most desirable marinas. He did not want to destroy the charm of the little village, where he still lived in Moses' little house with Sandy, his mum, but he had earmarked the unsightly area of the salt pans to create the Caribbean's 'San Tropez'. In John's opinion, the revenue that could be generated for his people, from a marina and marina village would far exceed the revenue from salt. At the moment, the development of Sandy Point was still a figment of his imagination. What John needed, was an expert in that particular sphere of tourism development. That was when Greg came into his life.

Greg had been busy trying to reorganise his life. He had felt defeated by Maggie over the divorce wrangling, even though he still had a fortune. It wasn't so much the money, it was the fact that during the haggling he had begun to see what he had lost. Maggie had turned out to be a formidable opponent. He should not have underestimated her. He should have involved her more in his decisions. Perhaps he should have involved her more in his life? Perhaps he had been greedy and thoughtless? In any event, he now saw that he had lost a partner, and one that he would rather have had on his side to share his life with. Instead, he had, at least for the moment, one of her best friends, which was not the same. Certainly, his current partner, Ellen, was a glamorous and witty woman. She could be incredibly sexy and he liked that. She was also clever; he liked that too. However, Maggie was clever and could also be sexy, but Maggie had a softness about her, a thoughtfulness, a concern for others, that was not part of Ellen's make up. He was not in love with Ellen in the same way that he had been (or, maybe, still was) with Maggie. Ellen was great company and her exceptional looks and sensuousness were a great asset. He knew that she sometimes played 'away'. He even encouraged it. She liked putting threesomes together and he had to admit that, at the time, it was a lot of fun. He drew the line with the skipper of the yacht, which she had once proposed, but that had not stopped her having the odd fling with the chap. The fact that Greg could have Ellen anytime he wanted in the close proximity of the skipper just maintained the fable of who was actually in charge; at least, that's the way Greg saw it. All of this, however, felt shallow to Greg. Since they had won the lottery life had truly changed but was it, he sometimes thought to himself, really better than the family life he had before?

In any event, Greg reasoned, you must play the hand that

has been dealt and right now he was trying to establish a new domicile in the sunshine of the Caribbean. His financial advisors and lawyers had all recommended this tiny island, Anguilla, especially because it fell under the British umbrella. "Less chance of a coup or a security risk," they had advised. Greg and Ellen were staying at Cap Juluca, an elegant white low-level resort, which spread out on, perhaps, Anguilla's loveliest beach, on an island of lovely beaches. One of the designated areas that John Coltrane's government had acquired for foreign investors, was situated on a peninsula that looked across the Cap Juluca beach. Greg, had leased two adjacent plots there. They were absolutely the best two pieces of real estate available on the island. Greg had brought a team of architects and interior designers with him from America. They were all staying at Cap Juluca, where they had taken over the only meeting room to design Greg's new residence. The General Manager of the resort, Clive Ricketts, had got to know Greg. As far as he knew, Greg was the owner of one of the biggest international recruitment agencies in the hospitality industry. In fact, he had often used Greg's companies to find staff, which was not always an easy task for a seasonal property on a small island. Clive, of course, knew Prime Minister Coltrane, who had discussed with him his plan to build a marina village at Sandy Point. Clive had called Coltrane. "The man that bought the two plots at Point Juluca is staying here with a team of American architects. I was wondering if you would like to meet him. He has a lot of experience in the hospitality business and lots of contacts. It may be presumptuous of me, but I thought he might be a useful resource for your marina village project." "Not at all, Clive," said the PM. "Sounds good to me. Please set it up. Maybe a dinner at the hotel?"

And so, this is how John Coltrane, Prime Minsiter of

Anguilla and Greg Layburn, the world's secret largest lottery winner, came to meet. Greg consulted with Clive, the hotel manager, about the format of the dinner and, as a result, decided to include the chief architect, a well-known resort hotel designer, and Ellen to attend. A table of four, he believed, would be appropriate, with a little melange of business and pleasure. John Coltrane described his vision for Sandy Point. Greg, was familiar with the bay, which he agreed, was spectacular and ideal for the purpose mentioned. Coltrane was impressed with the knowledge and experience of the two men. He was not so impressed with Ellen; far too forward for him. Nevertheless, they had a good conversation and John could see that their combined experience in the hospitality industry could be very useful. Also, when he discovered that Greg was also a yacht owner, he was even more pleased. He wondered if Greg would, or could afford to, invest in the project. At the conclusion of dinner, Greg agreed to meet the Prime Minister the following afternoon for a site visit. He would bring with him his design team, minus the decoration or distraction of Ellen, even though Greg knew that Ellen would, as always, have plenty of good ideas. All of the visitors to the island were very impressed with the site and lots of ideas were kicked around. At the end of the afternoon, Greg invited John back to the hotel for a one-on-one discussion. Greg had immediately seen the potential commercial opportunity of this project; he wanted to be involved and where better place to start than the beginning?

Although John did not drink alcohol, he had no problem taking a virgin sundowner with Greg; he was interested to get Greg's opinion. He was, therefore, delighted when Greg offered to put together a professional team, at his expense, to explore design and content possibilities for a marina, marina resort hotel, spa, and other commercial facilities.

These facilities, in Greg's mind, included a casino. Greg had already sensed that the suggestion of a casino in such a small and God fearing community might be a big ask, so he chose to keep silent about this idea for the moment. The cherry on the cake for John was that Greg alluded to the fact that, if they could make the numbers work, he could well be interested in investing personally in the project or raising the money from others. John went home to his mother, Sandy, feeling good.

Greg had dinner with his team of professionals and Ellen. They bounced around ideas for the project and it was agreed that the designers would go back to their office in Fort Lauderdale to work on concepts and that Ellen and Greg would join them in a week for a preliminary review. In the meantime Greg promised to give thought to the scope of the project and its finances.

Greg was energised by the project. Ellen was amazed. She had felt that Greg was getting a little introspective over the last few months, particularly during the divorce wrangling with Maggie. The thought of being able to design, build, and maybe even own, a new marina resort in such a beautiful spot had obviously sparked a chord in Greg. She was pleased too, that he seemed to want her to be involved and valued her input. The only thing that troubled her was that Greg seemed to want to keep her away from Coltrane; she had yet to cotton on to his inert nervousness in the face of women, but Greg had picked up this vibe good and strong.

By the time Greg and his team reappeared in Anguilla, ready for a presentation to the Prime Minister, they had already produced two sets of drawings and two sets of financial projections. The first showed a one hundred berth marina, a 120-room hotel, and marina village of shops and restaurants. It looked very picturesque and completely in sync with the nature of the island. In fact, it made a very pretty picture and the architects had produced some colourful renderings that were quite stunning. The second set of drawings and renderings showed a 300-room hotel, all of the other things and a casino with 200 slot machines and 20 gaming tables. Although quite large, the proposed casino was not huge; there was no major airport on Anguilla, at the moment, so there was little point in building a thousand slot casino. Greg's proposal was not to turn Anguilla into the Bahamas, or Las Vegas, but more into the Monte Carlo of the Caribbean.

The meeting began with just the Prime Minister in attendance. The venue was Cap Juluca, which rather surprised Greg, who had thought it would be at Government House in The Valley. Apparently, at this stage, the PM, he had not shared his thinking with the rest of his colleagues. Greg wondered why.

Presentation number one went down extremely well. John Coltrane absolutely loved it. Greg ran through the financial projections, both the capital costs and the potential returns. The rewards were not spectacular, but they would be good enough, Greg explained, to attract banking finance and maybe investors. Then came presentation number two. The addition of the casino and the doubling of size of the hotel made a huge difference to the costs, but an even bigger difference to the profits. John Coltrane looked on in silence; he could see the point. "You are presenting me with a difficult dilemma," he said, after thanking the team profusely and sincerely for their work. "I do not think that I can allow a casino on Anguilla. We have a very strong religious background here. The people follow the guidance of the Church. Without the backing of the Church I would not be Prime Minister, do you understand? I can see the benefit for my people, but at what cost will that benefit come? Getting something for nothing is not a good principle. Like

winning the lottery does not always bring happiness." Greg
was taken aback. "Why did he refer to the lottery? Was that
just a turn of phrase, or does he know something?"

"Well, Mr Prime Minister, here you have it. We can help
you with plan A, but it will be much harder to put the finance
together. Or we can go to plan B, in which case I will personally put up 50% of the funds required in exchange for
a 49% stake in the business and a long term management
contract. Something for you to think about." It truly was
something for John Coltrane to think about. Up until now
he had not really shared his vision for Sandy Point with his
more conservative party members. There would certainly be
some negative reaction to the commercialisation of one of
the islands beauty spots, Sandy Point, but to throw the 'evil'
of a casino into that particular pot, would be really tricky.
John, personally, was not too bothered about the morality or
otherwise of a casino. "After all," he thought to himself, the
island was already prostituting itself by selling residences to
a group of people who were basically cheating on their own
country's tax laws, so what was so diabolical about taking
more money from them in a casino? Perfectly respectable
places, like Monaco, operated casinos and nobody thought
twice about it, including the Catholic Church, so why get
twisted out of shape about Anguilla? Nevertheless, he was
smart enough to know that casinos could attract the wrong
sort of customer. He was happy for Anguilla to be a well-reg-
ulated tax haven but not an unregulated money laundering
centre, as if there really were a difference. In addition to this
the development, although originally his own idea (without
the casino) was now being hijacked by a man of whom John
realised he knew very little about. For all John knew, at this
stage, Greg could have been money laundering for the mafia
or the Pope. Prime Minister Coltrane needed more time;
time to do some due diligence on this unlikely benefactor.

"This is fantastic work," he started, after a long thoughtful moment. "I really like your designs. In fact, the whole project is amazing. More than I could have hoped for. But, you will understand, that I need to move cautiously. As I told you, the religious element on the island is very strong. At this point there will be a lot of questions asked, such as "who are our partners? Where do they get their money from?" "We have no casino legislation on the island, which means there is no process for vetting investors. If I am to move forward, I will need the answers to many questions and there will be much preparatory work."

"I fully understand that," said Greg, "it is perfectly reasonable and absolutely correct that you must be careful. But I think you will find that the sort of information that you will require about me, if I take on the role of the sole investor here, is very similar to the information your country required before it granted me residence. I have nothing to hide about the source of my wealth and, in any event, have already shared it with your Immigration Minister. As for the formulation of casino regulations, and laws, I can help you by recommending experts in this field, who can be your government's employees, completely distanced from me, the investor. I am at your disposal in all of these regards, but I do think that you have a magnificent opportunity to position Anguilla as the Monte Carlo of the Caribbean. You are a small nation, but so too is Monaco." John Coltrane left the meeting with plenty to contemplate. He went home to his modest cottage, which he shared with his mum, Sandy. He was tempted to share the content of the meeting with her. Despite her humble life she was still one of the smartest persons that he knew. This time he decided it was too early. Greg left the meeting with the feeling that he had a foot in the door. Yes, he could see a good return on his potential investment, even if he did not lay most it off on others, which was his intent. But he was more excited to be involved in the project; something to get his teeth into. Something to make his children proud. Something to prove that he was not where he was in the world through pure luck. He also had a long-term vision. Anguilla, was actually larger than Monaco. Its buildings were mainly one or two storey. Just think how many towers you could build here. And who says the casino should stay so small?"

Chapter Twenty-One

Maggie and Giles were now meeting frequently. Maggie had shared with Giles her ambition to fund the anti-poaching programme with £200 million. Nothing that Maggie did or said now surprised Giles. His organisation, Trunk, had already received £8 million from the lady, by far and away the largest donation in the history of the charity. It had enabled them to do so much, and the goal of wiping out the poaching industry was, inch by inch, getting closer. Without Maggie's help they would be nowhere. She had been a wonderful spokesperson for the charity and a pleasure to work with. Giles had been in love with her from the day she had walked into his office, carrying her Harrods bags, but he would never let her know. Giles was not one to mix business with pleasure. Maggie knew he was a bachelor. She actually thought that he might be gay. However, he had always been a complete gentleman in her presence, be it on international lobbying trips or at the frequent fundraising events with the rich and famous. Unbeknown to her, he had collected all of the photos that had appeared in the press of lovely Maggie, often with him on her arm. However, when he heard the number she was talking about, £200 million, he thought he had misheard. Twenty million would be incredible, but £200 million was just off the charts.

"I don't want to put all of this into Trunk," explained Maggie, "but I do want you, Giles, to help me oversee it, even if it is for another charitable organisation. Do you think we can work that out with Trunk?" "Maggie, my dear lady, you can work anything out you like with Trunk. The trustees all love you."

What Maggie had in mind was to attack the problem of poaching on two fronts. First, she wanted to stop the demand for tusks and horns. If she could secure a worldwide ban on the purchase, sale, or movement of tusks and horns, then this should have a dampening effect on demand. She understood that an illicit market might still exist, but, overall, she felt that a ban would drastically cut down on demand. To do this, she had learned, she would need to bring endless pressure on several governments, many of whose members were profiting from the trade. What might help could be sustained public relations efforts in many countries, where demand was the highest, as well as an organised lobbying effort to get politicians to change direction. All of this was going to take a lot of money, which she had, but also well organised professional management. It would be useless to throw money at the problem unless it were done in an organised and professional manner. This, she had concluded, was beyond hers, or even Giles' expertise. She would need to recruit and pay for a top professional manager.

The second front in the war against poaching would be at the supply end of the chain. If Maggie could find a way to make it more difficult to poach, then she might be able to limit the supply. In her view this meant a massive education programme in rural Africa, as well as reinforcement of the physical protection of animals. This meant more money for schooling and anti-poaching indoctrination, as well as more money for men and equipment in the game parks of Africa.

Maggie had decided that schools were the place to start. It might be a drop in the bucket of the problem, but she was thinking about setting up a chain of new schools in villages near game parks. Her initial goal was to establish a school adjacent to major parks in Tanzania, Namibia, Botswana, Mozambique, Zimbabwe, Malawi and South Africa. She was willing to budget £10 million per school to get them up and running, and, thereafter, their annual running costs. However, just as in the case of the lobbying project, she needed a professional educator to oversee the project. It would clearly require someone with the professional ability to locate and negotiate site ownership, design and build multiple premises, and plan curricula for several ages of pupils. In short, a massive and complicated operation, but not one that was impossible under the right leadership.

What Maggie now needed from Trunk was assistance in recruiting the right individuals to oversee these ambitious programmes. Giles listened to Maggie's vision with increasing enthusiasm. As far as he could see, this initiative, was exactly the sort of thing that Trunk had been fighting for. It mattered not to him that the schools might be called Layburn Academies or that the international lobbying programme be called the Layburn Initiative because they supported fully the goals of Trunk. Indeed, Trunk could take credit for being the surrogate parent of the idea and, in any event, Maggie was looking to Trunk to effectively monitor the two initiatives. Maggie was delighted with Giles' reaction to her game plan. She wanted Giles and his team to be helpful critics of her ideas, to add practicality to her idealism. Instead, at least initially, all she got was unbridled and enthusiastic support. Giles immediately proposed that he and his staff would produce a document, outlining in detail Maggie's plans so that they could formulate job descriptions for two heavyweight candidates to manage Maggie's initiatives. Maggie left London that day, happy that her cherished initiatives were at last gaining some traction.

Life in Dorking had changed. Sam had dropped her ideas of applying to Cape Town University and opted for a programme in ecology at Leeds University. Jimmy was still at Dorking High, but teenage boys' interests do not always gel with their mother's, unless you count the occasional cuddle. Maggie, without Greg, and without the proximity of Gee was a bit of a lost soul. Gee called her frequently and was extremely enthusiastic about her big picture plans. He also wanted to keep her in the picture regarding the refurb programme at Sam's Camp. But, she noticed, his calls were no longer daily. He was the same Gee that she knew when they did speak, but the conversations were not quite so intimate – or was this just Maggie's imagination? The truth is that Maggie was lonely. She missed the company of a man in the house. She missed the little intimate touches that pass between two lovers. She missed the sex. Since one of her best friends had run off with her ex, the little trio of good friends had been reduced to two. Ellen's husband, George, was still in town, now living in the house on his own. Willow, ever willing to share in the sexual department, had suggested to Maggie that George might be able to give her a good time. Maggie liked George, she always had, but her relationship with Ellen has been damaged by Ellen's pursuit of Greg, so she did not want to make matters even worse by dating Ellen's ex. Yet George was an attractive man. "Ellen would only go for an attractive man," thought Maggie, but dating him would be just making a complicated matter even more fraught. "Besides," thought Maggie, "my heart is still with Gee. Nobody can replace him."

Willow and Ted did their best to entertain Maggie. They had no children so their house was very much an adult place. Willow quite often threw dinner parties and always invited Maggie. Each time she did so, Willow did her utmost to pair of Maggie with one of the other guests, including George. Maggie could not make out if George had actually divorced Ellen. In any event, she continued to resist any attempt to get her in to bed with George. Ted, Willow's husband was a different matter. Maggie had always felt that he was rather attractive. She recalled the time that she had deliberately sat on his lap, whilst Willow was busy enjoying herself. Ted had fondled her breasts and kissed her, but was rudely interrupted by a jealous Greg, who had yanked her off home. She had no intention of doing anything about this matter; as far as she was concerned Ted was untouchable, the husband of her remaining best friend. Now, if her best friend wanted that, it would be a different matter, but her best friend would have to give her the signal.

Maggie did, however, enjoy the company of Penelope in Pimlico. Penelope still busied herself in raising funds for the Shawu Farm, even though Maggie remained the biggest donor. Nevertheless, Penelope was loyal and hard working. She was also fun to be with. She knew her way around the bars and restaurants of Pimlico and Chelsea. She had a group of interesting, if not a bit Bohemian, friends. It was always fun to hang out with Penelope and, from time to time, Maggie had her to stay in Dorking. Both Sam and Jimmy loved her. She was like something from a different world; like a character from a television series. She treated them both as adults; they reacted well. She had a friend who, in his prime, had captained the English rugby team. She brought him with her one day to watch Jimmy captain his school team. The boys were awed and Jimmy glowed with pride.

Despite all of this Maggie was missing Gee. She longed to feel his arms around her. She wondered if she had made the right choice. She wondered if they would ever be close again. Her loneliness intensified. She was the richest woman in England and yet, she was alone.

Chapter Twenty-Two

Prime Minister Coltrane's due diligence research into the source of Greg's wealth had not revealed very much. It was true what Clive Ricketts at Cap Juluca had told him; Greg was the owner of a chain of recruitment companies world-wide, but that did not explain the source of his wealth, which John had discovered was extensive. To start with, although Greg's accounts in banks trading in Anguilla were supposed to be absolutely secret, as Prime Minister, John had obtained access to the balances held in his country. He may not have located all of Greg's wealth but he had discovered that Greg had over £20 billion stashed away in Anguillan accounts. John had also commissioned an agency to check whether Greg had any criminal charges against him or even a sniff of scandal regarding drugs or crime in any form. The reports all came back negative. Greg was as clean as a whistle, a very, very, rich one.

Satisfied that Anguilla might have caught a big fish, who could help his country establish itself at the top end of the world tourist market, John decided the time was ripe to talk to his colleagues. He knew that in Anguilla, any discussion he had with his parliamentary colleagues would, within hours, be discussion at every dinner table and bar in the country. Nothing stayed a secret for very long in Anguilla.

Nevertheless, he had no option but to share his thinking with the other members of parliament. Sometimes the fact that everybody got to know what was being considered could be a positive factor. If Greg had been serious that the Project Sandy Point could not be financed without a casino, then John needed to convince his colleagues that this was the case. Although John, as Prime Minister, was still the de facto Finance Minister and Treasurer, due to the fact that he was the only Member trained in this area, he did have a colleague, James Brown, who held the title, Minister of Finance. James was grateful to John Coltrane for the leg up to ministerial office, so it was to him that John first explained the proposed project. John wanted to make sure that James understood the numbers fully so that he could throw his weight behind them. Having convinced James, John summoned a full cabinet meeting, which in the case of Anguilla, meant all of the eight elected Members. There was a lot of opposition and considerable concern about how such a development could eventually ruin the quiet lifestyle of the islanders. On the other hand, there was much interest in the jobs that would be created, particularly for the young folk. It did not take long for the persuasive Prime Minister to convince his Members that the development at Sandy Point would be a massive boost to the community and would certainly help them be re-elected, should it all go well. The biggest concern from the entire group was the reaction of the Church. It would not be good for any politician on the island, to make an enemy of the Church. What the priest said from the pulpit on Sunday would be listened to intently by the God-fearing population, or, at least, the older ones. The problem was that they would not be dealing with the Catholic Church, which had always found a way to accommodate money making, but with Methodists who were in search of a simple and pure existence, where worldly wealth was less important. There were eight churches in Anguilla. They were small, simple, buildings with tin roofs and rather squat bell towers. They were not well maintained; in fact, they were in pretty poor shape with leaking roofs and rotting wood. The climate under the Anguillan sun could be harsh on buildings, unless they were well maintained and that any damage was rectified before it became catastrophic. John hatched a plan. He had learned in his research about the casino industry that a key to development was the level of taxation implied on gaming profits, not from the individual winners, but from the establishments operating the casinos. It was within the power of governments to set casino tax levels. If set too high, they would discourage development projects, but even at a commercially attractive rate, they could produce substantial revenue for the taxing authority. John had James draw up some numbers based upon Greg Layburn's projections. Should all go well there would be plenty of money available to carry out all of the much-needed repairs to the churches, as well as fund the choir activities, and support the church run care home for needy citizens. There might even be enough, once the repair work was done, to fund the church school. "Surely this will be a way of serving God, of doing God's work?" he argued, a few days later, with the group of ministers that he had convened. The ministers did not race to agree, as the Members of Parliament had done. Ministers of the Church do not need to be re-elected every four years; they do not look over their shoulders at the electorate; they look up to God. John left the meeting with the ministers and then offered his personal prayer to God.

It was hard for Prime Minister Coltrane to explain to Greg, on his next visit, that things were good with the government but they would not enter in to serious negotiations with Greg, until God had given the green light. Greg was not in a position to talk to God. He felt very frustrated and somewhat helpless. John assured him that, in his view, the clerics would come around. "We must just be a little patient. This is an island. Nothing moves fast." Greg decided to take a positive view. Perhaps, if he moved the planning process along, the momentum would keep things bubbling. People would start to see that jobs were being created and that the future, economically for their children, could be great. Soon, the designated site started buzzing with men with hardhats and rolls of plans. A site office was erected. Posters appeared depicting a beautiful marina with adjacent village shops and a hotel. The marina in the poster pictures was full of super yachts and the people depicted strolling around were well heeled. The 'support the project' movement gained momentum. It looked as if money might be more important than God, although almost everyone picked up on the logic that development on the island would bring benefits of which God would wholeheartedly want. After a month of internal debate, and presumably, many prayers, the Ministers of the Church gave way. They appreciated that any taxes raised from the casino should be for the benefit of the nation, but recommended that one third of these be steered directly to the Church. John and James agreed on 25% and all of the green lights went on.

Greg was thrilled. He and Ellen had taken an apartment in Monaco, where he was temporally keeping the yacht. He informed Ellen that they were going to move to Anguilla. They would take the yacht and moor it at Sandy Point, from where they could oversee the construction of their villa, and Greg could supervise the planning and development of the marina/casino project. Whereas Ellen understood the necessity for Greg to take up residence on the tinpot island, and she understood his enthusiasm for the development project ("A bit like a boy with a Lego set," she had told her friend, the skipper) she did not fancy, in the slightest, being castaway on a tiny God-fearing island, miles from civilisation. "But we are going to create the civilisation," explained Greg. "One day, Anguilla will be the Monte Carlo of the Americas." To Ellen, Anguilla was a tiny dusty dry flat spot of land at the end of the earth. Monte Carlo was not. "Why don't you move your tax residence here?" asked Ellen. "Monte Carlo has already been built. You don't have to do it. The whole world is here. You will never budge them." Greg decided not to argue. He had made up his mind. He was excited to be able to create something; to put his stamp onto something. Maybe she would understand later. In the meantime, he could let her stay in the apartment in Monaco and just visit Anguilla from time to time. He didn't want to lose her from his life. He had come to realise that he did not love her like he had Maggie, but she was good for him. She was very gregarious. She made friends easily, sometimes too easily, in his view. She was great to be seen out with socially. She was cheeky and she was sexy. He needed that in his life. He reached out an pulled her to him. She wanted to get her way, so she let him get his. No more arguments that night; just a mutual understanding that somehow they would both need to get what they wanted.

It was agreed that Greg would head off in the yacht across the ocean to the Leeward Isles, where he would use the it as a temporary home and office and that Ellen would remain in Monaco. Ellen would visit him there several times a year and he, of course, would need to be in Europe quite frequently to oversee his other interests. That seemed to suit both of them. Neither really realised that such separations are the death knell of close romantic relationships. The first problem, of course, was that Greg would need the skipper. He knew that Ellen was attracted to the chap; he didn't know that Ellen had been the first one on the yacht every time Greg's back was turned. However, much as the skipper enjoyed screwing the boss's wife, he also enjoyed his job and intended to keep it. He was sure he would find a pretty young thing in the tropics; sailors always did.

It would have been sensible to Greg to fly back to Anguilla to finalise the negotiations with the Government and get on with the projects, but he had never done an ocean crossing and, as a sailor at heart, it has always been on his bucket list. "A few days at sea for contemplation will be good for me," he convinced himself. Part of him thought that it might have been better for him to have used the time to visit his kids. He had not seen Jimmy or Sam now for several months. They had chatted from time to time on the phone but he knew that he should do better than just call. He excused himself by believing that he was just too busy, but he knew, that nobody can ever be too busy to attend to their children. He decided he had to find a way to make amends. At the next school or college holidays he would fly them over to Anguilla to spend time on the yacht. He would have quality time with them.

The yacht journey was, in fact, quite boring. Greg used some of the time to receive instruction from the skipper on how to drive the boat, but other than that he was on his own. He spent a lot of time working on the resort plans, developing a long list of questions for the architects and engineers. He also spent a long time reviewing the progress and plans for the continued roll out of NoGrow. He had heard on social media a couple of negative comments about its safety. Somebody in Taiwan had claimed that all his hair fell out after NoGrow application. This sort of talk needed to be nipped in the bud and counteracted. But for much of the time, Greg spent staring out to sea, thinking about the state of his life, since his luck with the lottery. Yes, he had a bucket full of money and all of the trappings, but he had, along the way, lost his beautiful wife, and perhaps his children. He missed Maggie. He could not really understand what had gone wrong. He had heard of her fame in the war on poaching. He could see that she was actually doing something positive with her share of the winnings. What was he doing, except chasing the dollar?

However, life had to go on. The momentum that he had caused was now self-sustaining, but it needed feeding. First with his money, but more importantly with his ability to push and pull to get something done. Once you have started a project you can't just leave it alone. You have to follow up on every detail. You have to look at every line on the plans to make sure that, once built, it will work. There are thousands of details to attend to. Then, you have to put together the right crew to turn the plans into a real project and after all that you have to find someone to run it all properly. All of this is twice as hard on an island than it is in the middle of a well-developed city. Greg threw himself into the task with fervour. He had been in the bay at Sandy Point for almost a month before Ellen paid a visit. By then, he had assembled a team. He was pleased to have Ellen in his bed on the yacht, but there was not too much privacy from the crew, especially since he knew that Ellen fancied one of them. Also, although he tried to engage Ellen in the planning and design process, because he respected her sense of style and flair, she clearly irritated the rest of the planning professionals, who did not like their work challenged by this glamourous party girl – especially when her ideas were really worth listening to. The upshot was that Ellen did not stay long. Greg had his fill of sex, Ellen did her duty because, after all, he was financing her luxurious life, and then hotfooted it back to the real glamour of Monte Carlo, where it had not been long before she had developed a whole coterie of new friends.

Greg had made a greater effort to communicate with his children, just as he had vowed on the yacht crossing the ocean. He invited them for the summer holidays to stay with him on the yacht. As teenagers are, they had plenty to do at home. They wanted to please their dad, but, on the other hand wanted to be with their friends. They absolutely did not want to be on the yacht together. When all of these teenage complications and considerations were sorted out, it was agreed that Sam would come to stay with her Dad for two weeks in July and Jimmy for two in August. "Could Jimmy please bring a friend?" Greg was not pleased at this request but conceded that it might be for the best.

When Sam showed up in July at the ferry dock, Greg was blown away. It was as if her mother, Maggie, was clambering off the boat. Despite the long journey from England, Sam looked absolutely gorgeous. Now 18 years old, her body was fully mature and through the rumpled travel clothes Greg could see her mother when they first met. "My God," he thought to himself, "my little girl has become a woman." Sam flashed her Dad a big wide smile, dropped her bags on the jetty, and gave him a warm hug. "So good to see you Dad. I've missed you." "I've missed you to, my love. It's been too long. Anyway, welcome to Anguilla. You are going to love it!"

Chapter Twenty-Three

The renovation of Sam's Camp in South Africa had come on well. All of the guest lodges and public areas had been beautifully reworked according to the plans that Maggie and Gee had agreed. Gee had done a first-class job of supervising the work, whilst continuing to keep the business operating. He was now ready to receive guests of the same calibre as those that visited his neighbour, Mala Mala. Gee, after several years of experience there, knew exactly which buttons to press in the international safari trade to bring Sam's Camp to the notice of the right people, who could provide him with business. The word was out that Sam's Camp was now *the* place to see game and that Gee was one of the dishiest Camp managers around. Gee had kept Maggie abreast of progress at the Camp, speaking to her frequently, but Maggie had not visited for over a year. Maggie could not let her contact with Gee die, but at the same time she could not trust herself to resist him if she returned. She often picked Gee's brain in regard to the curriculum to be for the Layburn Academies, and he was extremely helpful. Often, though, she just called to hear his voice; despite everything that she had, she was still lonely. So too was Gee. Not that he had remained celibate during that year. That would have been almost impossible for him. He was a young man with plenty of opportunity to fool around; physically he needed to. Maggie had made her choice and he respected it, but he could not be expected to become a monk. In most cases there was very little chance of him ever meeting the women that he slept with again. Since the Camp had elevated its prices to those of Mala Mala, only the rich could afford to stay. The charges for the Camp were all set in US dollars; this made it out of the reach of most South Africans, particularly unmarried young ladies. Most of his conquests were married women, either from Europe or the USA. These were wives of rich businessmen, who often visited in pairs, whilst their husbands got on with the task of earning the money to pay for them. To them, Gee was the hunting trophy. It was easy for them to fall for Gee. He was young, tanned, handsome, charming, and free.

On one occasion an actress from Hollywood, unmarried at the time, had taken a shine to Greg. She was a stunning beauty. Her long legs mesmerised Gee on the personal game drives. The only 'game' she was really interested in was Gee. She stayed for three nights in the most deluxe of the lodges; Gee stayed with her on the last night. She went on three game drives, each one in the late afternoon. Whilst Gee got up at 4.30 to organise the morning viewing, she stayed in bed and slept. Her name was Gloria. Gee enjoyed her company; her background and experience were so different from his. He found her witty and interesting and exceptionally good between the sheets. Gloria too, must have found Gee different from her usual suitors, because, no sooner than she returned to Los Angeles, she called to rebook another three days at Sam's in a month's time. Gee had not told Maggie about Gloria or, for that matter, any of the other conquests in his 'wives' club. Gloria returned and the schedule of the previous visit was repeated, except, this time Gee found himself sharing her bed on all three nights. The other difference was, that, on this occasion, Gloria had not taken proper precautions. A couple of months later, she called from Los Angeles to announce that she was pregnant. Gee was dumbstruck.

Gloria was not messing around. She insisted that the baby had been fathered by Gee. He had no way of knowing for sure, but he knew, of course, that it was a possibility. She also insisted that she would not abort the baby; she intended to have it and she expected him to move to Los Angeles to be with her. There was no way that she was going to spend her life in the bush in Africa. Gee did not know what to do. He desperately wanted to seek Maggie's advice, but he knew that this was not possible. Gloria was nonstop on the phone. When was he coming to Los Angeles? He should be with her at this time. She wanted to introduce him to her family and friends. He shouldn't worry about money; she had plenty. After a week of indecision Gee called Maggie and explained the situation. It was like an arrow piercing Maggie's heart, but she knew that it was a catastrophe of her own making, so she could not be critical; she must try to be helpful. There were also practical issues to confront. If Gee went to Los Angeles and stayed there, who would run Sam's Camp? Maggie's advice to Gee was unselfish. "I think you should go to Los Angeles to try to come to some arrangement with the woman. See if you can persuade her to abort. If not, get her to understand that you cannot live in LA. You know, Gee, even if you loved her, you could never live in Los Angeles. It is about as far removed from the things that you love than any place I could think of. You must make her understand that. You cannot do that on the phone. You must go there. Your assistant can run Sam's for a couple of weeks. I understand the situation."

When Maggie came off the phone, all her practicality and firmness dissipated and she burst into tears. It was just too much to bear that the man that she loved had sired a child with a brazen hussy of a film star. But she blamed herself. All her troubles seemed to start with the lottery. Why did they win the lottery? If that hadn't happened none of this would.

Gee had no option but to fly to California. A limo was waiting for him at LAX to whisk him up the Interstate to Beverly Hills. Gloria lived in a mansion overlooking the Los Angeles Country Club. Her neighbour was a famous black singer, although a neighbour in this community might as well have been on the moon, since the lots embraced several acres and were separated by high walls and even higher perfectly trimmed hedges. As the limo swept up the driveway Gee noticed the heavily manicured gardens, so different from the wild natural forms of the bush. Every little bush and tree here had been immaculately shaped and pruned. The flowerbeds were arranged in a well-planned pattern. It all looked beautiful, but in a manmade fashion; nothing to do with nature. Suddenly a colonnade of white pillars appeared, springing from a raised deck, in the middle of which were two huge white doors. As the car pulled up at the turning circle near the doors, they swung open and, standing there was Gloria. Gee had to admit that she was aptly named; she did look absolutely glorious; no sign of pregnancy at all. He climbed out of the vehicle, his clothes crumpled from the journey, but his tan intact. Gloria did not move. She stood there with her arms outstretched, her long legs peeking through the slit in her dress. Gee hastened up the steps and she embraced him with a warm and pleasing hug, followed by a passionate kiss. Gloria obviously was not shy in front of the staff. "Welcome home, my lovely man," drawled Gloria, "I am so excited that you are here."

For the first two days Gloria did not really talk about her pregnancy or their future. She had just sort of assumed that they would have a future – together. She showed Gee around Beverly Hills, and its neighbouring Brentwood and Bel Air. She took him visiting to some of her friends in the neighbourhood and in Malibu, by the Pacific Ocean, which Gee was seeing for the first time. Gee was tired from the trip. The time difference from LA to Joburg is huge; the time difference from LA to civilisation anywhere is huge. As Gee was about to find out, Los Angeles is on another planet. Whether jet lag or nervousness was causing it, Gee was finding it difficult to confront Gloria with the truth. He did not want to spend his life away from the bush; he was not in love with her. He had not yet had the courage to tell her that he was only staying for two weeks; that he could not just drop everything at Sam's Camp; that he had responsibilities that he could not just abandon.

Gee had not jumped into bed with Gloria as soon as he saw her. Indeed for the first two nights that he was in her house, he did not make love to her at all. She put it down to jetlag, or his consideration that it might affect her pregnancy. On the third day Gloria addressed the issue. "You know, the doctor has told me that it is okay to make love when you are pregnant," she said over coffee. Gloria was looking especially alluring in a see-through wrap, having just emerged from an inactive bed. "I know," said Gee, "it is not just that; before we pick up where we were, we need to talk. There is so much to talk about."

"I know, honey," said Gloria, "but there's no rush, honey. We have all the time in the world to talk, now that you are here." It seemed to come as a shock to Gloria when Gee announced that he was only 'here' for two weeks, and that he could not see his way to living in America. "If the baby is mine," he explained, "I do not have a problem with you coming back with me to Africa and we can raise it there. If you don't want to do that then I am happy to shoulder my responsibilities, not that it seems you are short of money. I would be happy to raise the baby myself in the bush, or I could come on regular visits here, but I cannot live here. Nor, Gloria, do I think we should marry, at least, not at the moment. In truth, we hardly know each other. It could be a disaster for both of us, and the child. Under these difficult circumstances, I really think you should consider and abortion." It all came tumbling out. Gloria, ever the actress, made a good show of being totally upset and stunned by his speech, but she knew that he was right. The truth was that she didn't really want to marry him either. She was at an age where she really wanted a baby and she was glad to have one sired by a great looking man, who would not become a drag on her career or her life. So Gee had been a great choice. A handsome specimen of a man who could impregnate her, then go away. You could say that she had used him as a stud.

Gee held her tight while she sobbed her Hollywood tears. He was so relieved that he had been honest with her. When she had calmed, still wrapped in his strong arms, they talked. Gloria said that she understood. She was not sorry that they had had a relationship and she was not sorry that it was going to produce a baby. She was determined to have the child. She wanted a child, and she was pleased that it was his. She did not need anything from Gee. He could go back to the bush. She did not expect him, nor need him, to marry her. She did not expect him to pay for the baby and, if he wished, he need play no active role in the child's life; this would be up to him. This was a completely different woman speaking from the one who had called him in Africa and more or less demanded that he appear. Gee could not work out whether this Gloria was really a compassionate woman, who understood and had sympathy with his predicament, or whether she was just a selfish bitch who had used him to get what she wanted. "After all," he thought to himself, "if a local actor had sired her baby, he may not have been so willing as to push off and not complicate her life." Whatever her reasoning, Gee was relieved. He would have to think through what role he could, or should, play in their baby's life, but this could wait for now. He was relieved that he did not have to marry Gloria and that he did not have to leave Africa. She was letting him off the hook.

Gee did not stay the full two weeks. Gloria had tried to get him into her bed again but he has resisted, not wishing to complicate the matter further. Ten days later he was back at Sam's Camp. He had considered flying back via England to see Maggie but had decided against it. Instead he phoned her and thanked her for her advice. She was more relieved to hear the outcome than he knew.

Chapter Twenty-Four

Sam's vacation with her father in Anguilla went well. It was a good opportunity for them to bond, especially since Ellen was not there to complicate things. Greg allowed her to sit in on the construction planning meetings both for the villa and for the Sandy Point marina project. Both she and her dad stayed on the yacht, although they worked from a site office that had been erected near the beach. All the men on the site fell for Sam. She was only 18, but she was such a stunner that she had no end of male admirers. The holiday was not all work. Greg had introduced Sam to the manager of the Cap Juluca, Clive, who, like all men, was captivated with her fresh beauty. He told her that she would be welcome to use the facilities of the hotel at any time. He could provide her with a day room in a cottage on the beach, so she could swim and sunbathe to her heart's content. Since the long beach with a sweeping curve was, without question, the most beautiful beach on the island, with brilliant blue water and white fine sand, Sam was quick to take him up on the offer. But, apart from the wonderful beaches, there was really not much for a young woman to see or do in Anguilla, so Greg suggested that the skipper take the yacht on a short trip for three nights to visit the neighbouring islands of Saint-Martin, and St-Barth, where there was much more action. Greg would stay in Anguilla to push forward with the work.

Well aware of the randy reputation of his skipper and the attractiveness of his daughter, Greg, before proposing this trip, had taken him aside and warned him, in the bluntest possible manner, to keep his hands off his daughter. "You are the chaperone. You are there to protect her. Do you understand? No monkey business!" The skipper completely understood. His job was on the line. Sam loved St-Barth. Unlike Anguilla it was quite mountainous, and very pretty. The harbour was bustling with yachts, some of them even larger than her dad's. Needless to say, she attracted plenty of attention, especially in her skimpy bikini. The skipper had his work cut out swatting the flies. But, strangely, he thought, Sam was not too interested in any of the good-looking men that tried to impress her. She even seemed quite keen to get back to Anguilla. What he did not realise was that, during the planning meetings at Sandy Point, she had been introduced to John Coltrane, who, after that, had suddenly taken a great deal of interest in the process of the development of the project. John had been told about the arrival of Greg's beautiful blonde daughter and wanted to see for himself. The reports were not an exaggeration. John was bowled over by her beauty and impressed by her contribution to the design process. He decided to attend more meetings. Sam had felt the spark of John's curiosity, and wanted to get back to Anguilla to explore it. She had been quite smitten by this handsome black man. It was clear that he was highly intelligent and insightful, but he also seemed gentle. She wondered why he had not been snapped up; he must be one of the most eligible bachelors in the Caribbean. He certainly was the youngest Prime Minister. St-Barths was a buzzy place. It seemed like the King's Road in Chelsea had been transported there, but Sam wanted to get back to

Anguilla. Every time she closed her eyes, she could see John Coltrane. What was happening to her?

John had heard that Sam was back. He decided to invite her to Sandy's little cottage for a simple island style supper. He wanted her to meet his mother. Being a politician John had concluded that he could not invite Sam without her father and, in any event, Sandy had never met Greg, apart from passing him on the dusty road that ran along the back of Sandy Point. Obviously, she had heard a great deal about him; everybody in Anguilla had. Sandy was not nervous about having a multimillionaire to supper. After all, she had spent many evenings helping Mrs Braintree prepare and serve meals to Professor Jackson's guests in the Forbes House in Battersea. And, in any event, she was only going to serve local dishes, which meant basically a barbecue, proceeded by conch chowder. Greg was pleased to receive the invitation and pleased, too, that it included his Sam. Since he had last seen his daughter in England, she had changed from being a stroppy teenager into a delightful woman. He was proud of how she handled herself in the planning meetings. Her contribution had been outstanding and, clearly, she had gained the respect of his planning team. He could already see how his beautiful daughter, so reminiscent of Maggie, may be a very useful addition to his team.

Sam couldn't find any flowers to buy in Anguilla. She really wanted to take some for Sandy, so she jumped on the speedboat taxi and whizzed over to Saint Martin to see what she could find. There, in the little French town of Marigot, she found a flower shop, or rather a multipurpose shop that also sold flowers. She also found a fashion boutique, which carried limited lines of all the best French fashion houses, presumably to tempt the wealthy clientele from the yachts. "What a good idea," she thought, "I will treat myself to a dress to wear this evening." Sam had not come to Anguilla with a wardrobe equipped for dining with a Prime Minister. On the other hand, since they were not dining at the Cap Juluca, but in, what appeared to be a very humble home, she did not want to overdo it. Luckily, after flicking through the rather limited selection in her size, she came across a little summer polka dot dress that fitted her perfectly. It had a short skirt and a top that covered her nicely. The only thing was that the shoulder straps were so thing, she wondered how they would cover her bra straps. "That's alright, missy," said the helpful assistant, "you don't need a bra. With your lovely breasts." Sam wondered whether it was right to go to dinner with the Prime Minister's mother without a bra. She bought the dress anyway.

Sandy was delighted to be given flowers. There were not many times in her life when this had happened. On the other hand, there were not many times when she had invited a millionaire to her little cottage. Sandy thought young Sam was just beautiful, and charming too. Her father, Greg, was also gracious. After all, she discovered, he had once been the manager of a famous London hotel, so why would he not have good manners? Sandy asked Greg about the Sandy Point development. She had not been keen herself, because of the changes it would bring to her little hamlet. This was the place that she had been born and spent her childhood. It had remained unchanged for centuries, so naturally, she had been fearful of change. Nevertheless, her son, John, had convinced her that the economic benefits to the people of Anguilla, in the form of improvements to the hospital, the schools, and, not least, her beloved Church, would be worth the sacrifice. She took the opportunity to impress upon Greg and Sam that the actual historic beach village, should be preserved. Greg promised that it would.

Sam was interested in learning more about John's mother. Sandy resisted the questions, but John intervened and told her that she had nothing to be ashamed of. She still was shy to speak up, so John did. He proudly told Sam and Greg how his mother had been forced to leave her native land; how she had battled to raise him by working for years as a char lady; how she had scrimped and saved to send him to university, and how he owed everything to his dear mum. There were tears in Sandy's eyes as he spoke. Sam reached out and squeezed her hand. John noticed and was pleased.

John was interested to learn more about Anguilla's benefactor; more that is, than he had been able to glean from his financial espionage. He was interested in John's background, and education. Greg was happy to oblige. He related his early start as a young hotel manager, and how he had branched out into the recruitment business. He related the story of how he had met Sam's mother and how she was as beautiful as her daughter. Sam blushed. "And where is your mother?" Sandy asked. "Sadly, we are divorced," interjected Greg, before Sam could answer. "She now lives in the old family home in Dorking in Surrey. She is very active as a wildlife lobbyist." "Good for her," said Sandy. "We know Dorking," she continued, "John used to pick grapes there."

"Oh," said a surprised Sam, "so did I." They all laughed at the coincidence. After dinner John suggested they turned out the lights to look at the night sky in the darkness of Sandy's tiny backyard. He pointed out various planets and, in so doing, found himself very close to Sam in the dark. He wanted to hold her. He was completely in her thrall. Never mind she was over ten years his junior; she had the mind of a mature woman, and she hadn't yet started college. "So what," he thought to himself, "Sandy was only 17 when she had me."

When the evening was over, Greg and Sam walked in the moonlight back to the dock, where their tender was moored. John accompanied them. When he gave Sam a peck on the cheek to say goodbye his hand squeezed hers; he was definitely sending her a signal. Her heart leaped. Back on the yacht, she thanked her father for a nice evening and went to her cabin. John Coltrane was still in her mind. Greg too, was pleased with how the evening had gone. He was happy to be close to the most senior politician in the country that he intended to make his personal fiefdom.

The next day, which was to be the last one of Sam's vacation, she did not attend the planning meeting, having told her father that she would like to spend her last day on the beach at Cap Juluca. When she got to the hotel desk to pick up the key to her beach cottage room she noticed John Coltrane, deep in conversation with two other black men in the breakfast room. She wondered whether to interrupt to thank him for the evening before, but decided that he may not want his guests to know that she had visited his house. So, she slipped passed the dining room and headed down the beach, making absolutely sure that he had seen her. She changed into her bikini, went for a dip in the blue sea, and then spread herself out topless on the cottage deck to catch one last day of sun. An hour later, there was a tapping on the little gate from the beach to the terrace. It was, of course, John. Sam's heart raced. She sat up, attempting to cover her top with a towel. "I just came to say goodbye," he started, "and how much I have enjoyed your company. I do hope that you will come back." "Of course, I will," replied Sam, "Come here. I want to say goodbye properly." He went through the little gate. She rose to greet him, holding the towel as tightly as she could. He put out his hand to shake hers. "I shall have to kiss you," said Sam, "if I let go of this towel there could be trouble," she said with a cheeky smile. She pulled him towards her with her free hand and kissed him on his lips. The kiss, that started as a peck, became something else. She embraced him with both arms, pulling his body into hers. The towel fell to the deck. No words were spoken until after they had made love. They were both in a state of shock. They were both as happy as they had ever been. They had thrown all caution to the wind. In neither case was this wise. John, the respected black Prime Minister, scholar, and diplomat and a young white girl, yet to go to university, making love in the midmorning sun. This was indeed stuff for the tabloids. Neither cared; they were both so happy.

Chapter Twenty-Five

When Sam got back to Dorking she had gone, in two short weeks, from a girl to a woman. Maggie, of course, noticed. She did not bombard her daughter with questions about her vacation, but she just knew that something important had occurred. Maggie assumed that it had been a boy; she would not have dreamt that it had been a man, never mind a black man. Instead Maggie helped her daughter get her things ready for university and, at the appropriate time, packed her in the Mini, and drove her to Leeds. It is always a difficult moment for a parent to send a child off to university. It is one of the moments in the life of a parent, that one remembers as the day you lost your baby. Maggie did not, of course, realise that her 'baby' had already gone, so for her it was a day of sadness mixed with pride. Maggie was so happy that her daughter had matured into a beautiful and sensible woman, far older, it seemed, and wiser, than her years. Maggie found herself wishing that Greg could have shared in the moment.

Fortunately, Maggie had plenty to keep her mind off losing a daughter. She had made good progress in hiring two top rate executives to head up her main initiatives, The Layburn Academies and the international lobbying effort, which she had named 'Hope'. The Academy man, whose name was Peter Oxford, had a first class academic background, but he has also been involved in an initiative in Pakistan to build schools. He was about Maggie's age, married with two sons and living in Wimbledon. The other new hire, James Burchfield, had worked as the Managing Director of an international public relations firm, but had wanted to turn his career to doing something more useful than merely promoting commercial enterprises. James was extremely experienced, being an older man in his mid-50s. He had worked in London, New York and Hong Kong during an illustrious career. He knew his way around the politics and politicians of the West and the East. He was also passionate about wildlife and had taken many safaris with his wife, in Africa and South America. Maggie was so pleased that he had agreed to join her and knew that she could learn a lot from him. James's plan was to appoint public relations agencies in the world's most influential capitals, to lobby their governments into banning the sale of wild animal parts and also to put pressure on the United Nations to take firmer action. He had already undertaken a trip to select agencies in the USA, France, Berlin, New Delhi, Beijing, Johannesburg, Canberra, Abu Dhabi, Rio and, of course, the UK. Maggie had agreed to fund each agency, on average, with $2 million a year for a three year period, i.e. $60 million in total The goal was to get banning laws in place in all of these regions before the end of the three years.

Now, James wanted Maggie to fly with him to meet the teams at all of the agencies. He considered her to be the best salesperson he had to motivate and kick start their activities. He had witnessed her addressing the United Nations General Assembly. He knew that she could melt an iceberg with her charm. This would mean a trip that circumnavigated the world. Luckily, Greg had kept his NetJets membership, which, due to a laxness unlike him, still included Maggie as a family member. It seemed to Maggie that the only way she could tackle this global sales pitch would be in a chartered aircraft. James was rather thankful. Net Jets came up with the smallest wide body plane with an intercontinental range, a Bombardier, which would ensure that Maggie and James had comfort, privacy and a place each to sleep.

James and Maggie decided to cut out the European offices for the round the world trip; they would tackle them separately later. So their itinerary took them first to New York, then Rio, and then Joburg, where Maggie had told James that they needed to break it for a couple of days. She wanted James to see the work that had been done at Shawu Farm and she also wanted to take the opportunity to inspect the completed renovations at Sam's Camp, which, of course, she still owned. What she really wanted of course was to see Gee, but she didn't trust herself not to be derailed by him. By taking James with her she could, hopefully, keep things on an even keel. But, also, it would be a good education for James to see what havoc and cruelty are created by poaching. Gee was delighted that Maggie was coming to see him, even if it was with a chaperone. He picked them up at Lanseria private airport near Johannesburg and drove them to Sabi Sands. The three-hour drive gave him plenty of time to explain to James what they were doing at Shawu to help eliminate poaching. Maggie had chosen to sit in the back, which allowed Gee to chat more easily to James. It also helped her from disclosing her real feelings of love for Gee as he chatted on in his lovely relaxed manner. When they reached Sam's camp, Gee proudly showed them round. The newly reconstructed lodges were wonderful, far better, Maggie thought, than the tired ones at Mala Mala. Although Gee had driven all the way to Lanseria and back, he still was keen to take the pair on a game drive. As usual, it was an exquisite experience. It was so wonderful to be out in the bush again, having been cooped up in a jet. The magic of the night sounds of the bush came rushing back to Maggie. She had needed this to remind her why her work was so important. She was also so happy in the presence of Gee. When they stopped for a sundowner and were sharing a bottle of good South African wine, Gee suddenly put his arms around her. She wanted him so badly, but James was there. With the utmost self-discipline, she released herself from Gee and started to pack up the snacks. Back at the Camp, the three of them had dinner in the moonlight. As soon as the meal was done, James excused himself; he could feel the chemistry between the two. He did not know that they had been lovers, but he sure thought that they should be.

Gee did not sleep with Maggie. He escorted her through the dark to her accommodation and kissed her goodnight at the door. She so desperately wanted him to come in with her but she knew that Gee was right. They both had work to do. Gee understood that, much as he would like to, he should not upset the programme. He so badly wanted Maggie to stay, but he knew that she couldn't. If he had entered that room, who knows what would have happened? Maggie went to bed and cried.

When Maggie and James climbed back onto the Bombardier, headed for Australia, with a refuelling stop in Mauritius, James took Maggie's hand. "You love that man, don't you, Maggie?" Maggie nodded. She could not speak. If she did, she knew she would cry. "You must find a way to be with him," said James, "and I am going to help you. We will win this battle with the lawmakers. You will be successful. And then you must stop. Stop doing things for everyone else. Stop trying to save the world. You must follow your heart and be with Gee. Maggie, I promise you that you will be happy." Maggie did not know what to say. This man was working for her, but he had so much more experience of life than her. She would learn from him. He seemed so wise and kind." "Thank you," was all she could muster, and gave him a big hug of gratitude.

The rest of the trip went well. In each of the chosen offices, the staff were delighted to meet Maggie. She lit up their rooms with enthusiasm. She listened intently to their different plans and approaches. She gave sensible advice, to which they listened. Best of all, she was able to paint a personal picture of the horror, created by the ruthless poachers. For them to be with someone who had witnessed such cruelty focussed their minds. They all thought that she was beautiful; a beautiful person with a beautiful mind. They promised her over and over again that they would get the job done.

Maggie arrived back in Dorking to an empty house. Well, not quite, because loyal Fanny was still in the stable flat, even though there were no kiddies to look after. Jimmy was taking his turn to be with his dad on the yacht. She wondered how that was going. Feeling rather down, after a good night's sleep, she called Willow to let her know that she was back. Willow was delighted and asked her to come to lunch the next day; she said she would call up a few friends so that they could all have a laugh and a chat. She did not mention that Ellen was staying with her, taking a break from Monte Carlo. Willow wanted to see her friend Maggie so much, but she was not sure what to do. Should she include Ellen in the lunch party? What should she do with Ellen if she didn't invite her? She decided to discuss it with Ellen directly; to confront the elephant in the room. Ellen had been seeing much less of Maggie's ex. She spent most of her time in Monaco. The regular visits to Anguilla had not taken place. She hated it there; there was absolutely nothing to do and all Greg did was to work. She had found a very active social life in Monaco. The only trouble was that Greg was paying for it. In regard to Maggie, she had been her closest friend. She rationalised that Greg and Maggie's marriage was effectively over before she allegedly wrecked it. She could now see why, and had some sympathy for Maggie. Greg was all work and only play when it suited him. "Maybe," thought Ellen, "if I meet Maggie again with Willow and her friends, we can pick up where we were." After all, she was sure that Maggie had had lovers in the meantime and she was divorced. Maggie, in Ellen's view, was the prettiest of all her girlfriends. She would have had no trouble nailing a lover. "Okay," said Ellen, "I am very happy to have lunch with Maggie. I would really like to be her friend again."

When Maggie walked into Willow's house, she found a group of four other girls, all old friends. She was startled to see Ellen amongst them, looking as glamorous as ever. She could have turned and left, but she didn't. Either she was too tired from the long trip or she just didn't care anymore about Greg. She decided to brazen it out. She didn't know whether she hated Ellen or loved her. Yes, Ellen hadn't waited a second before she moved in with Greg as soon as he had moved out from Maggie, but did Maggie really care? She would have preferred it if it had been someone else but by that time there already had been someone else in Greg's life and bed, and, to be fair, there had already been some-one in Maggie's. Ellen moved towards Maggie and reached out her arms to hug her. "Is all forgiven?" she whispered in Maggie's ear, as they hugged. "I'm honestly not sure," Maggie whispered back, "that depends."

Of course, Maggie did not know if Ellen was still living with Greg or what she was doing. She didn't even know if she was actually divorced from George. Before she was to allow Ellen back into her life, there was plenty she needed to know.

Both women re-joined the others and they all had a jolly time talking about everything but Ellen and Greg. They were all anxious to hear about Maggie's 'fabulous' trip. "What was Rio like? What about Canberra?" and so on. They were amazed that Maggie couldn't tell them anything about anywhere, because all she had done was fly in, conduct her meetings, and fly out. "I can tell you about plenty of airport hotels, if you like, but they all look the same." The rest of the girls were disappointed, even puzzled. Why would anyone fly around the world and not stop to see anything? After two bottles of wine and lots of laughter, nobody cared. At around four, the party broke up. Before Maggie left, she asked Ellen to call her. Maggie departed for the supermarket, before returning to the empty house in Dorking. She was tired; she shut off the phones and slept.

Peter Oxford, the new Director of the Layburn Academies had rented offices in an inconspicuous block in Battersea, London. Unbeknown to him, of course, the offices were only 50 yards from the house that Sandy Coltrane had cleaned for many years. Peter was a very serious young man but also an adventurer at heart. For him, this was a dream job; the opportunity to build from scratch a group of much needed schools in Africa was incredible, both from the point of view of developing an educational programme, but also from the viewpoint of physically designing and building the schools. The job would entail much travel to Africa, a continent that he knew well and loved. Peter was tall, almost lanky. He was bronzed from his time in Pakistan and he was clearly an outdoor person. He was not handsome and muscular like Gee, but he had a softness in his personality. He was keen for Maggie to see his new offices, but Maggie, still tired from her trip, had asked him to come to Dorking to report on his progress. This was unlike Maggie, who normally was most accommodating and curious, but the intensity of the trip around the world had somehow sapped her energy. Her enthusiasm was, however, as strong as ever, as Peter found out in their meeting. He had located various potential sites in several of the targeted countries. He wondered if Maggie would want to come with him to investigate further. Maggie suggested that, maybe, initially he should make the first inspection and enquiries alone, but he was quick to point out that his expertise was in education, not deal making. To evaluate each deal, in regard to the acquisition of the land and the potential to develop a site, were beyond his expertise. Maggie suggested that maybe Giles at Trunk, would be willing to go with him. She agreed to call Giles to see if she could persuade him to help. Quietly, she thought that Giles would do anything to help her, so she was pretty sure that this would be a good plan. Peter left Dorking feeling well pleased. He would soon be on his way to accomplishing the first step on a long journey. Maggie promised that their next meeting would be in Battersea.

Ellen had called. Maggie debated with herself as to whether to return the call or not. Did she really want to start up a relationship with Ellen after all that had happened? While she was still thinking about it there was a ring on the door bell. It was Ted, Willow's husband. He had been sent round, he claimed, by Willow because Maggie had left her sunglasses on the table after yesterday's girly get together. Ted looked very handsome standing on the porch. "Thank you so much," said Maggie, taking the glasses from him. "Do you have time for a coffee?" Ted accepted with alacrity. He really got turned on by Maggie; she had such a beautiful body. And, in any event, he would be quite glad to get away from Willow and Ellen, who did nothing but chat and giggle, whilst he was trying to get some work done. Willow, of course, knew that Ted fancied Maggie: she knew that he was one of Ted's dream girls in his fantasies. Willow, of course, had shared this piece of vital information with Ellen and, together, they had hatched a plan to send Ted round to Maggie's with the sunglasses. "Half an hour alone with his dream girl will do him good," quipped Willow, "might even spice him up for tonight."

Maggie took Ted into the kitchen and busied herself with the coffee pot, whilst Ted sat on a stool and watched her. He particularly liked it when she had to reach up for the cups in a cupboard; her dress rose as she stretched to display her lovely legs and the top of the dress stretched tight across her breasts. "Wow," thought Ted, "she is so pretty." Maggie, aware that she was being ogled, turned the conversation to Ellen. "How are you getting on with your house guest?," she enquired. "Well, she is a lively person to have around, but, between her and Willow, there is plenty of chatter all day long. It is quite nice to escape for a while." "She wants to be friends with me," said Maggie, "what do you think I should do?." Ted was as noncommittal as he possibly could be. "It's not for me to say," was the best he could do, or, at least, the best that he was willing to do. "From what I understand, it is pretty well all over between her and your ex. She has told Willow that she wants to come home to George. Poor bloke. I wouldn't have her back again. I know that she's sexy and all that, but she is always going off with someone. No offence meant. No, Maggie, you will have to decide this one for yourself."

The pair sat in the kitchen and chatted over their cups of coffee. Maggie really liked Ted, but she had always been intrigued by the relationship he had with Willow, that is to say, the sexual relationship. Willow had always confided in Maggie that Ted liked to watch. "He just loves the idea of me with another man," Willow had once confided with her. "The thought of it really gets him going." Maggie used to think that that was a bit weird. She had discussed it with

Greg during their marriage. "Would you like to see me with another man?" she had teasingly asked Greg, who had replied that he would have preferred to see her with another woman. She had thought he was joking, of course. Now Ted was with her, all alone in her kitchen. She knew that if she wanted, she could have him. "Maybe the thought of that would turn on Willow. Maybe that's why Willow had sent him round? Who knows?" As far as Maggie was concerned, this was not going to happen. Ted was a striking man. Maggie had always thought so, but the idea of doing something behind Willow's back, her friend's back, was just not a starter as far as Maggie was concerned.

Coffee over, Ted got up to leave. "Ellen is leaving tomorrow to go back to Monaco. Why don't you come around for supper tomorrow night with me and Willow? We could have some fun." Maggie did not know exactly what sort of fun he was talking about, but she needed a bit of fun in her life at the moment, so she graciously accepted. Ellen did call again that afternoon. "I want to be friends again," Maggie told her over the phone, "but it is just too soon for me. There is too much for me to process at the moment. Next time you come back to England, why don't you stay here? I have got plenty of room. Maybe we can work it out then."

Maggie went to bed that evening in the house on her own. She had called Penelope for a chat, but, as usual Penelope was out, presumably drinking. She called her daughter Sam in Leeds. "Please leave a message after the beep."

"Damn it," she said out loud to no-one but herself. "I will go to Willow's tomorrow. It's time I had some fun."

Chapter Twenty-Six

Little Jimmy's turn with his Dad in Anguilla did not go so well as his sister's. He had asked if he could bring a friend, which seemed like a good idea to Greg, who had agreed, and even picked up the extra air fare. Jimmy brought a friend from the rugby team, Darryl. Both Jimmy and Darryl were at the grunting age. Greg found it almost impossible to get more than two words at a time out of them, particularly out of his son. Darryl was polite when spoken to and clearly loved the idea of being on a luxurious yacht, but Jimmy remained very tight-lipped. Not so, of course, when the two boys were alone together. Greg could hear them chattering away ten to the dozen in the privacy of the cabin they had opted to share. Clive Ricketts kindly offered the boys the same facility at Cap Juluca that he had for Sam, which they gratefully accepted but, as Sam had found initially, there was very little action for two teenage boys on the island; in fact, there was none. So, the days went well with the sun and the sea, but the evenings were an invitation to provide self amusement. It had not been hard for them to acquire a little dope from one of the boat hands at Sandy Point.

During the days Greg continued to be busy with the planning processes. At the outset he took the trouble of walking the boys through the plans and renderings, but they were clearly not interested, so he did not press it. He also had a few other pressing matters on hand that kept him pretty busy. NoGrow was running into some stormy waters and needed attention. It would appear that the number of budding lawsuits against the company was growing. Although Greg personally was shielded from any potential damages the value of his 49% in the company needed to be protected. NoGrow was still not listed so any rumours about lawsuits could not affect a share price, but if substantial payouts had to be made, it would be the death of the company and Greg's 49% would be worth zilch. Firstly, Greg needed to find out whether there was any substance in the claims; did NoGrow actually cause hair to fall out, rather than just inhibit growth, or was there some peculiarity with the few people, whose hair had come out? At first Jake and Chuck, the inventor, in Los Angeles had not been worried about these claims. The product had now been in use for several years with no reported problems. The mailbox was full of letters praising it. It seemed strange to the guys in Los Angeles that the first reported cases of hair falling out were all in the same place, Thailand. What was going on in Thailand that was not going on elsewhere? Maybe there was something in the water or the atmosphere that negatively impacted the product? However, when lawsuits started to pop up in Japan as well the owning trio started to worry. Finally, when a law firm in Texas declared that it was preparing a class action in the USA, and started to contact all known purchasers of the product to join in, Greg knew that they really did have a problem, even if all of the allegations were untrue. He decided that as soon as Jimmy and his mate had finished their holiday, he would fly to Los Angeles to try to manage the process of defence. He realised that his partner and the professor, were not the right people to be mounting a defence. He also suspected that they may not have told him the full story. He might have to distance himself from them, but whatever was going to transpire, he needed to brief his own legal team. So, whilst Jimmy and his pal smoked their pot, Greg concentrated on putting together the people and information he would need in LA. He also instructed a senior partner of Brentwood, Mattheson, and Kaplan, to go to Japan and Thailand, where they had legal partnership arrangements, on a fact-finding mission.

Luckily for Greg, John Coltrane, was off island. Greg was happy about this because he was pretty preoccupied with NoGrow and also did not think that Jimmy and his mate would make such a good impression as Sam had done. Greg was not party to John Coltrane's travel plans since they were on Government business. He had no way of knowing that John's itinerary took him to Leeds, and nobody on the island told him.

Since Sam had left, John almost had nothing else on his mind. He had to see her again. Their cell phones glowed with each other's numbers. John had organised a personal phone for himself with a different number from his official one. He had never found the need to do that before, but the Anguilla phone company found nothing unusual in the request. It was easier for John to fly in to Manchester, rather than Leeds. Anyway, Sam, wise beyond her years, thought it would be smarter to keep him away from the campus in Leeds. Although his face was not well known in the UK, he was the Prime Minister of a British Overseas Territory and someone, somewhere would know that he had entered England. The last thing Sam wanted at this stage was her parents to know that she intended to have an affair with John. Likewise, at this stage, it was not something that John thought wise to publicise. John had booked a suite at the Central hotel in Manchester. The "official" schedule that he had hastily put together meant that he had to attend meetings with banks and the foreign office in London, but he had blocked off two days and nights for free time. He did not include where, or just how free, on the itinerary. So, one could say that this was a secret tryst in Manchester. John arrived at the hotel before Sam. He checked in for himself and 'Mrs' Coltrane and asked for two keys. Once ensconced in the suite he texted Sam and gave her the room number. An hour later, after John had freshened up from the journey, Sam was knocking on the door. "Room service," she called out cheekily. He opened the door and swept her into his arms. Her little suitcase fell to the floor. He pulled her into the room, hung 'do not disturb' on the doorknob, and shut the door. That was the last Manchester saw of John and Sam for two days and nights. They had so much to talk about and so much to explore about each other. Sam had brought with her a nice couple of outfits; she did not need them. They laughed about it.

On the second day, knowing that this tryst would soon end, their mood of elation began to be more serious. There was no doubt in their minds that this was love, not lust, but love. Why should they keep their love for each other a secret? They wanted to shout about it from the rooftop. They were so carried away with the moment that they thought everyone would be pleased for them. Then, there were moments of reality. Of course, nobody would agree with them. Sam was too young for John. Sam had three years of college ahead of her; she must not toss that away for a man. John was the Prime Minister in a deeply religious community. What would his voters think about him with a young girl, barely out of high school? Question after question came tumbling from their lips and through their thoughts but the answer was always "Who cares what anyone else thinks? It is our lives, our bodies, our right. Who cares what anyone else thinks? We are in love, and it is beautiful." Strangely, the one thought that never crossed either's minds was that John was black, albeit half black, and Sam was white. They discussed their age difference, their experience difference, their cultural difference, but never, not once, their colour difference. To them colour was invisible.

Late in the second night, after they had made love for the umpteenth time, John made a proposal. Not a proposal of marriage, but a proposal that they hold off on announcing their liaison until they could plan it properly. For a split-second Sam thought that John may be backtracking, but he quickly assured her that it would be for the best. They must prepare the ground so that they did things in the right order. He needed to tell Sandy that he had found the girl he wanted to marry. He also thought it would be correct for him to first meet Sam's mother, whom he had, of course, never met. He just did not think it was right to spring this whole thing on either of them. Of course, John's mother Sandy had met Sam in Anguilla, but Maggie did not have the first clue that her daughter had fallen in love with an older man. John insisted that he meet Maggie first; then he would feel free to propose marriage to her, which is what he intended to do. Strangely, John did not seem so bothered about discussing the matter with Greg. Sam was so happy. This had not been a proposal with ring on bended knee; things had been far too rapid for that, but it had been notification that a proposal would be forthcoming. She also realised that she must cool off a bit and think a little more of the practicalities that his liaison would throw up. One thing she was sure about. Whatever the difficulties ahead, she would work them out. She was in love.

Parting the next morning was hard, but they both knew that it would be brief. Theirs was a love that would not, could not, wait. Sam was to call Maggie, to let her know that she was coming home to see her next weekend. John would still be in the country, but only for a few days more. When Maggie got the call from her daughter on Monday morning, she was a little under the weather as a result of a weekend party at Willow and Ted's house. She was so pleased to hear from Sam, who had not been answering her calls, but was a little alarmed to learn that Sam was coming home for the weekend, so shortly after she had enrolled in Leeds. "Is everything alright, my love?." "Of course," replied her daughter, "things could not be better. I just want your advice on something and I don't want to do it on the phone." Maggie arranged to pick Sam up at Gatwick airport on Friday evening and that was that. Maggie knew it was about a boy. Sam did not have to tell her. She knew that something had happened to her daughter when she was away with her dad. She just hoped it was not something too serious. The week seemed to pass very slowly for Maggie. Whilst Maggie waited for her daughter at the baggage claim she was curious, even anxious, to see what Sam looked like. She feared that Sam would be looking anxious or distraught. After all, something serious must have happened that Sam felt unable to discuss it on the phone. She was, therefore, amazed to see the happiest looking young lady sauntering towards her as if she were on top of the world. "Whatever it is," thought Maggie, "it can't be bad." Sam saw her mum and rushed towards her, flinging her bag down and her arms around her. They were not even out of the car park before the whole story had come tumbling out. Maggie was taken aback, but did her utmost to stay calm and not overreact. Inside, she was churning. Her lovely daughter, with her whole life ahead of her, was sitting in the car explaining that she was so much in love that she wanted to get married. It was a lot to take in. Too much. Maggie listened as Sam bubbled on. "I must be so careful how I respond," thought Maggie, as she desperately considered what to say and how to react. "I do not want to lose my daughter over this." But Maggie needed time. Time to absorb it. Time to figure out how to be a real mother.

They reached home and Maggie organised some coffee. Sam had now talked herself out. She was desperate for a reaction from her mum; desperate for her approval; desperate for her to say she wanted to meet John. Finally, Maggie spoke – in very measured terms. "Sam, my love, you know that I love you. You know that I only want for your happiness. So I am glad that you have found happiness. It is wonderful to see you so excited and happy. But, I must admit that this all comes as a bit of a shock. I am sure you realise that. As a mother, I obviously only want happiness for my child, but I believe, as a mother, I must also try to give you advice. First loves are often the most passionate of all loves. They do, however, have a history of falling apart. I am not saying that yours will, because who am I to say; I haven't even met John, and if he loves you, he must be a wonderful man. But first loves, more often than not, are things of passing beauty. To think of marriage based upon such a short period of intense love would be risky. However, I am not in a position to judge, because, as I say, I have not met John. You are of an age where you are free to do whatever you please, but if you are looking for my approval, I cannot give it until I have met him. Where is he now?" "He's in London, Mum, waiting to hear from me. He wants to meet you." "Then, my love, what are we waiting for?" said Maggie with the warmest smile she could muster, "Let's get him down here for lunch."

"Oh, thank you, Mum. I knew you would understand. I know you are going to love him." Maggie was far from sure. Maggie did not want to alienate her daughter; that would be the worst possible thing. The best thing she thought she could do is buy time. She must fight herself, she thought, from being, or appearing to be, unreasonable. "Time sorts out a lot of problems," thought Maggie, "I must try to use it wisely."

John caught the first train available from Victoria to Dorking. He was there by one o'clock. An excited Sam met him at the station and drove him back to the house. Whilst he had been travelling, Sam had filled Maggie in on John's background. In her first flush of excitement she had not mentioned that John was black. Nor had she mentioned that he was the Prime Minister. This news was a lot for Maggie to absorb whilst John was taking the short train ride. Now, it seemed, she had the whole picture. This news was so astounding that poor Maggie did not feel there could possibly be anything else to shock her. She was reeling with bad news, but she knew that she must play and pray for time.

When John walked in, despite all to the deep suspicions that had been building in her mind over the past few hours, Maggie immediately fell under his spell. She knew that he was going to be black, so no surprises there, but she did not know that he had film star good looks. He was also so gracious, so polite, so utterly respectful. His easy manner did not hide his confidence and sureness. It did not take long for Maggie to find that she really liked him and she could see why her daughter had fallen for him. Naturally, there were many unanswered questions, which could not, in all fairness, be settled at their first meeting. "Has he had previous relationships?" she wondered, "he must have; a handsome man like that. What happened to those?" Questions for another day. Maggie did, however, learn about John's humble background, Sandy's travails, his life at Cambridge, and his career. It was all terribly impressive and related with complete humility. In short, Maggie liked him a lot. But it was all too fast. Maggie knew, only too well, how loving relationships can fade. The chances of such a swift affair lasting seemed to Maggie to be very slim. And then there was the matter of Sam's university career, which had hardly started. She wondered what he thought of that. It just seemed that these two lovers had not thought about anything except their obvious passion for each other. Maggie did not know what to do.

After a long lunch, which had been hastily prepared by the housekeeper, Sam decided that she needed to have a nap; she had been up very early to catch the plane. John offered to stay with Maggie, to help her with the dishes. "I realise that this must all have come as a shock to you, Maggie (she had insisted that he call her by her first name), but I have had the chance to think about this very clearly. I do intend to marry your daughter. I do not expect to have your approval right away because I am sure that this is too much to absorb in one day. You have been extremely gracious in receiving me and listening to me. I know that Sam is young, but she is mature far beyond her years – you know that. You have done a remarkable job as her mother. I am as concerned as you must be about her education. I am as concerned as you must be about taking away her right to have fun. But I love her. And because I love her we will find a way that will allow her to do whatever she must or wants to do with her career. One way we will work it out. I promise you."

"All I ask," said Maggie, quite softly, "is that you don't rush it. Promise me that you will allow some time to pass to see if you still feel the same about each other a year from now." The reply was instant and firm, "I promise you."

Chapter Twenty-Seven

The following year passed quickly for Maggie. She had a very busy schedule with her two executives in Hope and the Layburn Academy, which involved many meetings in London to review progress and a fair amount of international travel. It was good that she had so much to concentrate on because her personal life was at a crossroads. There was every sign that her daughter would get married and be whisked off to the Caribbean. She was worried about Jimmy, who seemed far more introverted than seemed right and her sex life was confused, to say the least. At a time when she had been feeling particularly lonely, she had been lured into a threesome with Willow and Ted, which, after initial embarrassment, she had enjoyed; at least she had enjoyed the sexual release. Willow had been keen to repeat the act, but, Maggie, realising that it had been an alcohol-fuelled happening, was far from sure that it was wise and resisted. Her heart still ached for Gee and although she had agreed with him that they were free to follow their respective lives, she thought of him every day. Whenever she was able to fabricate an opportunity in her schedule to visit South Africa, she took it. Needless to say, her mentor, James, at Hope, understood her reasons and encouraged her to follow her heart. As a result, during the year following her meeting with John Coltrane, Maggie had found reasons to go to Joburg on four occasions.

On the first visit, she did not have the time to get up to Sabi Sands. Gee picked her up outside baggage claim and together they proceeded to their favourite suite at the Intercontinental. The hotel staff now recognised Maggie and welcomed her back effusively. She had featured frequently in newspaper reports, so her face was quite familiar. The staff had figured out that she came there to meet her lover, but, since she was always so nice to them, they only wished the loving couple well and nobody, so far, had informed the press. Maggie only had time on her itinerary for one night there. She and Gee made the most of it. Their love for each other seemed indestructible. From the minute they met again to the second of their departure they were as one. Maggie just longed for the day when all of the commitments she had made would be over so that she could just be by Gee's side.

On three other occasions during the year Maggie found a way to see her lover. If anything, rather than allowing their relationship to cool off, it was heating up. Maggie did not seem to know how to take it off the boil; she was not sure that she wanted to. Her daughter came to the rescue. Sam had asked her mother for help in organising her wedding; there would be little time for weekends in South Africa, at least, not for a while. Maggie knew that she only had one daughter. Now was the time to think about her.

Sam and John's wedding took place almost exactly one year after Maggie had met John. He had kept his word, but only just. The ceremony was in the Dorking Methodist Hall, where the minister was enthralled that the groom was actually a Prime Minister, albeit of the smallest country in the Commonwealth. The reception was held at Wotton House, a rambling hotel near Dorking with a large and pretty garden. Maggie had invited all of her friends from Trunk and the associated charities as well as her loyal local Dorking mates, including Ellen, who claimed to have left Greg. Maggie was interested to see their body language when they met. Maggie had wanted to invite Gee, but he wisely suggested that the two of them might be a centre of attention and that this day ought to be about her daughter. Greg had invited far fewer people; they tended to be law-yers and accountants rather than true friends, at least, that's what Maggie felt. Sam, of course, had invited lots of her mates from school and college, which she had attended for the first year, and John had invited half of Anguilla, or so it seemed. Sandy had come ahead of the pack and Maggie had invited her to stay at the house in Dorking. Maggie and Sandy really clicked. Maggie liked, and admired Sandy, and Sandy, in turn, was amazed at all that Maggie had achieved. She also admired how Maggie had maintained her fitness and beauty. Maggie, now pushing 40, looked ten years younger. Her daughter Sam, at nineteen, could have passed for 25. Indeed, the two of them could have been sisters.

John had kept his promise to Maggie. He had proposed to Sam before returning to Anguilla after the conversation in the kitchen with her mother. His proposal came with a proviso; that Sam finish at least her first year at university and that their marriage must wait until that condition had been fulfilled. He would fly her out to Anguilla for the hol-idays and he would visit her as often as his position allowed, but she must agree to wait. She had agreed. Their passion for each other did not abate. It seemed that Sam would not be attending her second year at university. Unbeknown to any of the guests, including her mother, by the time the wedding took place, Sam was two months pregnant.

Greg had mixed feelings about his daughter's marriage. She was definitely too young; she had not had time to enjoy her young adulthood. She would be missing out on a whole chapter of life. On the other hand, he liked John Coltrane a lot, and, a marriage to the Prime Minister of the island he wanted to use as his catapult to fame and further riches ought to be good for business. Nevertheless, he was uneasy. He was also tired. He had been battling increasing lawsuits involving NoGrow. Although there appeared to be little scientific evidence to support the growing claims that the product was dangerous, the cost of defending the company and the damage to its reputation had been hugely draining. Luckily Greg's net worth was determined in the main by the price of Bitcoins, which continued to rise, rather than in NoGrow. The way things were going NoGrow might soon be bankrupt and Greg's future battle would be to protect his other assets from litigious users of the shampoo. Greg had not been pleased to see Ellen, flaunting herself at the wedding. She had not stood by him as he fought his battles, but she had enjoyed a good life, at his expense, in Monte Carlo. Luckily, her sexual drive had got the better of her, and she had finally left the security of Greg's apartment, and gone to live with a Russian. The Russian did not appear to be at the wedding.

Since neither Sandy nor Maggie had a partner at the wedding, they went together. Sandy, of course, was considerably older than Maggie, but since Maggie's parents had passed away many years ago, she was delighted to have Sandy's support. Maggie was losing a daughter, but Sandy was gaining one; this somehow brought them together. Because Anguilla was really Greg's stomping ground, Maggie had never actually been there. She had no intention of making use of Greg's yacht, nor the villa that he had now moved in to. As far as she was concerned these two acquisitions had been prompted by Ellen, and even though the two of them had patched up, to some extent, their friendship, to use these two properties did not sit well with Maggie. Besides that, she had been far too busy travelling for the Academies, Hope and Sam's Camp, to allow her time to add a destination where there was no wildlife to save. Now, however, she felt that, in Sandy, she had a friend. Also, since John and Sam were planning to set up home there, Maggie would have no choice but to visit, yacht or no yacht. Little did Maggie know that, by the time the wedding took place, the patter of tiny Anguillan feet, would not be far away.

Maggie had helped Sam with the preparations for the big day. Sam had been pretty bogged down with her college work and, being in Leeds, did not make it easy to organise an event in Dorking. There were also a few weekends when John had found a reason or excuse to fly into England for a covert weekend. Maggie had, however, consulted her daughter every step of the way, so there had been absolutely no friction in the process. In fact Sam was extremely thankful to have her mother around. In her first break from college, Sam, quite naturally had flown to Anguilla to be with her beau, but in the break before the wedding, she had come home to Dorking to help her mother with the plans and to choose a wedding dress. Mother and daughter spend a wonderful day together in Bond Street. There were plenty of laughs as they tried on dresses, although they finally found the perfect wedding dress in a boutique in Chelsea on the Fulham Road. Maggie was determined not to outshine her daughter at the wedding, although she wanted to look elegant. After much searching, and much fun together, they finally selected a beautiful dress for Maggie in Armani in Sloane Street. Sam was so thrilled; her mother looked stunning.

Greg had offered the yacht to the couple for a honeymoon, and they had gratefully accepted, since John could only spare a week; he had been in England for the week before, so did not want to be out of office for too much longer. They had agreed that Sam would not return to college, and Leeds had kindly agreed, under pressure from a Prime Minister, that Sam could restart her course at some time in the future. Greg had offered Sam and John the use of his villa, until they had selected or built a home of their own; he had offered to stay on the yacht when he came there to work. In the meantime, he knew that he would probably have to base himself in Los Angeles for a while until the NoGrow problem had been sorted.

The wedding was a joyous occasion. Clearly the couple were madly in love and the high spirits of the Anguillans made the whole affair great fun. Rarely had Dorking, buried deep in the white stockbroker belt of Surrey, seen such undiluted and infectious celebration. The reception room rocked with music and laughter. Black mixed freely with white, young with old, Surrey with Anguilla. The bride and groom looked so happy together that the room was filled with hope. Sam and John were to spend one night at a mystery destination before jetting off from Gatwick on the following morning.

When the evening was over and the guests were gone, Maggie sat down and cried. Months of pent up emotion were released. She sobbed and sobbed. Sandy held her and consoled her. She had not known Sandy for long but she was turning out to be a lovely friend. Maggie could not explain why she was crying. She had so much to be happy about. Her beautiful daughter was so happy; her new son-in-law was a wonderful man, his mother was an angel; what more could she want? She kept thinking how she had missed Gee. She needed him at a time like this. He should have been there.

Chapter Twenty-Eight

Three weeks after their return from honeymoon on the yacht, Sam and John called Maggie in England to tell them that they were expecting a baby. They explained that she was the first to know, but they were planning to visit with Sandy that evening to give her the good news. They asked her not to share the news until they had had a chance to see Sandy. Maggie was so happy for them. She had, of course, hoped that they might enjoy a few years of married life unencumbered by children, but, once she heard the news, she was actually thrilled. Maggie, who was still under 40 did not look, or feel, like a grandmother and her daughter was so young. But she realised that, at John's age, it would be better for the child. She was pleased that John could still be a 'young' father. Maggie agreed to resist spreading the news, until the following day. After an hour or so, she just had to tell someone. She wanted to call Willow, but she knew that the news would then spread like wildfire, so she stopped short at that. Should she tell Gee? Maybe he wouldn't like the idea of having a grandmother as a lover? She had to talk to someone. She called Pimlico Penelope. "I just have to tell someone. But you must keep the secret. Promise?" "Of course," said an intrigued Penelope, "what has happened?" "Sam is pregnant!" burst out Maggie. "Wow, wonderful news!" said Penelope, as she quickly counted on her fingers. "That's great. I am so pleased for you. I promise I won't let on to anyone until you say so. Why don't you come up to town? We could celebrate together." Maggie agreed. It would be nice for her to be with a friend. She would see her at 6 pm.

Penelope and Maggie downed two bottles of Penelope's best red wine. Since Sam's Camp had been named after Maggie's daughter, Penelope had been dying to call Gee, to give him the good news, but she had resisted. She told Maggie so and, as a result, they started to talk about Gee. Obviously, at some time, Gee had shared his feelings about Maggie with Penelope. She knew that they were lovers. Maggie, her tongue loosened with the alcohol and the emotion of the news from Sam, poured her heart out to her friend. "You must go to him," said Penelope, "You have plenty of competent people now running your schools and lobbying. You must follow your heart. You are still young. You deserve happiness." "But I worry about Jimmy. I can't just leave him here and he needs to finish school. No, Penelope, I can't be that selfish." Penelope could see the problem. She did not have an answer, at least, not for the moment. "Maybe, when he goes to college," she said, "maybe I can move to Africa then." "But that is four years away," said Penelope. "I know," replied Maggie, "I can't do anything about it." It was sad how what should have been a happy day had turned to this. In the taxi, on her way home, Maggie wondered once again, if life would have been simpler without the winning lottery ticket. "It certainly would have been happier," she said, almost out loud. "Are you okay, lady?" asked the driver. "Not really," she replied, "but just take me home, please." Her phone buzzed. It was Sandy from Anguilla. "Hello, my dear. I just had to call you to congratulate you. What wonderful news. We are going to be Grannies!" Sandy's cheerful, bubbly, enthusiastic voice literally shamed Maggie out of her moroseness. "Of course, it is a wonderful day. And congratulations to you, Grandma; you are so lucky to be close to the happy couple. I know you will take care of my daughter. I so wish I could be closer" "You can come here whenever you want, my dear. You will always be welcome." "Thank you, Sandy. You are a kind person. I am so lucky to have you in my life."

A few weeks after learning of her daughter's pregnancy, Maggie had bad news. The Headmaster of Jimmy's school, Dorking High, called her and asked her to pop into the school as soon as possible. He wanted to discuss Jimmy with her. "Is there anything wrong?" said an alarmed Maggie. "Of course, there must be something wrong, you stupid woman," she thought to herself, "Why would the headmaster call personally unless there was something wrong?" "I can come now, if it suits you?" said Maggie. They arranged that they would meet at noon. Maggie, worried out of her mind, tidied herself up, and drove to the school. "I am afraid I have bad news, Mrs Layburn, and I thought I had better tell you personally," "Oh my God," thought Maggie, "Jimmy must have done something awful." "It has come to our notice that Jimmy has been using drugs. Not only using them but also trafficking them. He has been running a small business here, selling drugs to other students, including much younger ones. The police have been involved, but in deference to your standing in the community and internationally, they have opted not to pursue the matter, provided that you get him the help that he needs. Unfortunately, it is a policy of our school that such offences cannot be tolerated. I have no option but to expel him from the school forthwith." Maggie was stunned. She had been concerned about Jimmy. He had been quite introverted of late. Now she knew why. Maggie did her best to get the headmaster to change his mind about the expulsion, but to no avail. He did, however, have some recommendations for Jimmy's further education and, most importantly, agreed that the offences would not be a matter of record. If Maggie would agree to remove Jimmy from the school, in order for him to pursue his education elsewhere, then there would be no need for an expulsion and not need for a record of it. It seemed that Maggie had no choice. She thanked the Head for his compassion and advice and asked if she may have the grace of a day, so that she could contact Jimmy' father. It was agreed that the removal of Jimmy would officially wait until the following day. "You do realise Mrs Layburn, that I am giving young Jimmy a chance by not pressing this matter further and by not recording it fully. Our records will show that you have knowingly removed him from the school to place him into paid education. It is not unusual for boys to be placed in prep schools at his age to prepare them for their O levels exams. God knows why they think the public-school sector will be better for them, but that is what people do. If I were you, I would see if you can get him into Epsom College or the Abbey School. He could do well there. At the same time, you should see that he gets help for the drug problem. In his case, I tend to think that he has been more interested in dealing the stuff to make money, rather than being dependent on it personally. Must be his father's entrepreneurial example. Anyway, better that way than being dependent. I am sorry that we have such a strict policy in these matters. My board of Governors would never allow me to deviate from our policy, no matter who has broken the rules. There can be no exceptions." "I understand, Mr Barnes – and I appreciate your kindness. I will get back with you tomorrow." With that, a stunned Maggie, stood up, shook hands with the headmaster, and left.

By the time she had reached the car park, Maggie had

decided to call her ex. "This is your problem as well as mine," she pronounced to herself in the car. "You can jolly well help me solve it." It was a frustrating exercise getting hold of Greg. His secretary in the London office was quite evasive. Maggie explained that this was an emergency but she could not get any information out of the girl as to Greg's whereabouts. She gave no clues as to whether he was in the UK, the USA, Anguilla, or elsewhere. However, within a few minutes of her ringing off from the secretary her phone buzzed. She was still in the parking lot, so she took the call. Staying as calm as possible, Maggie explained the situation to Greg. He was clearly shocked, but, having pulled himself together, discussed their options quite calmly. He offered to stop whatever he was doing at the moment to make some calls re the public schools the Head had recommended. It was just possible, he explained, that amongst his myriad of financial and legal advisors, there was someone who could pull strings to get Jimmy into one or other of the schools or, at least, somewhere equally acceptable. He also offered to come to Dorking that evening so that they could talk together to Jimmy to explain what was going to happen. Maggie had no wish to see Greg, but, for the sake of Jimmy, she agreed.

When Jimmy came home from school that afternoon, she tackled him. She told him about her visit with the headmaster. At first, Jimmy, attempted to deny it, but he already knew that he had been rumbled, since the police had caught him. He was frightened that he would be prosecuted. In fact he was petrified. To Maggie, this was not a hardened drug dealer in her living room, it was a scared little boy. "Your father is coming here this evening so that we can work out what is best. You must know that they will not let you back into Dorking High, so we are all going to have to make a plan. You are very lucky that the police and the school have agreed not to record the evidence. They are giving you a chance to make amends. It is up to you if you take it. If you do, I am sure your dad will agree to help in whatever way he can. Me too. Now, let's not talk about it again until Dad gets here. What would you like for your tea?"

"I'm sorry Mum," said Jimmy, close to tears, "I am sorry that I have let you down." "No, Jimmy," replied Maggie, "I am sorry that your dad and I have let you down. Having a broken home cannot be easy. We will do our best to pull together to help you through this, but you must promise me that this is the last time you will have anything to do with drugs." "I promise." Said Jimmy and reached out to his Mum for a hug.

Greg did arrive that evening. The second-hand Bentley had long gone; he was now in a tank of a Roller. Maggie explained to him on the doorstep the previous discussion that she had had with their son and asked Greg not to be too hard on him. "We're here to solve the problem, not make it worse." she said, hoping that he had heard her. Before his arrival Greg had located a couple of excellent contacts who were alumni of Epsom College. Indeed, one of them was on the Board of Governors. He expected that, given some time, he could locate many more Governors of other good prep schools. Jimmy was a bit scared of what his father would say, but Greg had heeded the request of Maggie, and approached the matter as a problem to be solved. "Lessons must be learned, my boy," he said, "but there is no use in crying over spilt milk. We must turn this event into a positive." Jimmy was not in the mood to argue. He did request that whatever school they sent him to should have good sports teams and, surprisingly, and a bit hurtfully for Maggie, said that he did not mind being a boarder, if that would help. Jimmy never went back to Dorking to collect his things and never said goodbye to his mates. That both surprised and worried

Maggie. "Is he really repentant, or is he playing a game? Why is he keen to board?" Maggie was suspicious, but she kept her thoughts to herself.

Greg did the business. After all, that's what Greg did. Having 'sold' the story that he was unhappy with the education his son was receiving from the State school, he was able to secure Jimmy a boarder's place at Epsom. For a fairly large donation to the school funds, he was able to arrange for Jimmy to start right away and not wait until the next term. Jimmy was a bit surprised at that, having anticipated a bit of a holiday, but he had no option other than to go along with it. "Maybe," he thought, "it will be easier to do business as a boarder?"

Maggie, at first, was upset that she was going to have an empty house. For her it was a double whammy. First Sam, and now Jimmy. She just prayed that Jimmy would pull his weight. She put on a brave face. She had collected Jimmy's things from Dorking High. She had been able to speak to the Head to thank him again and to explain what arrangements they had made. She had prepared Jimmy's belongings ready for Epsom and that was that. Greg had offered to pick Jimmy up to take him to the school; he thought it would be good for business to personally thank the hierarchy there. So, Maggie was now on her own. Suddenly she had an idea. "I think it's time to see Anguilla!"

Chapter Twenty-Nine

Sam was thrilled that her mother was coming to see her. Now, three months along with the pregnancy, she had been really suffering. Shortly after the wedding she had begun to feel very sick. She had not been able to enjoy the honeymoon having thrown up for much of the time. The motion of a yacht was not the ideal antidote to prenatal sickness. To have her own mother at hand for a while would be a blessing. Much as she loved Sandy, she was not her Mum. There was plenty of room at Greg's villa for Maggie to stay. In fact, there were five empty bedrooms. The place was like a palace. There could be no doubt that Ellen had had a hand in the design. However, Maggie decided to give the newlyweds their space and opted instead to stay with Sandy. Sandy had explained that she lived in the same humble abode that she had inherited from her mother and Moses, but Maggie told her not to be so silly, and that she would be delighted to accept her invitation. Sandy was thrilled to have the company, especially since Maggie had been so good to her in Dorking.

Maggie had taken a private jet from Farnborough, England to Saint-Martin. The runway at Anguilla was still not long enough to handle a jet, so she had to land at Saint-Martin's international airport, from whence she was whisked onto a private speedboat which was anchored in the harbour adjacent to the airstrip. No customs nor immigration formalities were required at the request of the neighbouring Prime Minister. Mother-in-law was coming to visit and mothers-in-law are formidable presences in the Caribbean. Instead of using the public landing point that the regular water taxis used near the Valley, this craft whisked Maggie straight to Sandy Point, where she was able to use the same little dock that Greg did when he was staying on the yacht, and which was only 100 yards from Sandy's little home. As the little craft bounced along passed Cap Juluca, Maggie was astounded to see the colour of the water, lapping onto the beautiful beach, but she was even more amazed as the rounded the promontory into Sandy Point. There, in the bay, was anchored a sole yacht, gleaming in the sunshine. "This must be Greg's," thought Maggie. The sea colour was just breath taking. Suddenly she saw two figures waving on the little jetty. Sam and Sandy were there to meet her, both excited as little children; Sam to see the mother that she adored, and Sandy to see her newest friend. Sandy was so pleased that Maggie had opted to stay in her humble home, rather that the splendour of Greg's sumptuous villa. Little did she know that Maggie had no interest in even seeing the 'house that Ellen had built'.

Once on shore they walked the short distance to Moses's old house, talking excitedly about the new baby to be. Sandy had prepared supper; John would join them as soon as he could. Maggie told them that she had not brought lots of baby things. She explained that it was bad luck to do that until the baby or babies were born. Sam was just pleased to see her Mum. She was also anxious and concerned to hear about Jimmy and promised to keep in touch with him on a more regular basis. When John arrived the three ladies were happily chatting ten to the dozen; he felt like an intruder.

Maggie realised that she was now the mother in law and must take a bit of a back seat. That would be hard. She realised that she actually did not really know her new son-in-law, having spent so little time with him prior to the wedding. She made a promise to herself that on this trip, she would really try hard to bond with him. After a delicious dinner, Maggie, now quite tired, excused herself and retired to her modest bedroom, feeling the glow of a welcoming family. She did not sleep well. Whether it was jetlag or the unwelcome return of her nightmare, she could not tell.

Over the next few days Sandy showed Maggie over the tiny island and introduced her to many of her friends. It seemed that everyone in the island loved Sandy. It also seemed to Maggie that almost everyone was a cousin or aunty or uncle. She wondered just how many surnames there were on the island because everybody seemed to be a Stephens or a Dandridge. Sam's day trips with Maggie were a little more adventurous. They explored together the island of St Martin, both the French and the Dutch side. And, despite Maggie's reluctance to do so, they shopped; that is, they shopped for baby. Maggie was concerned as to where Sam would give birth, especially after she had seen the cottage hospital that served Anguilla. "Don't worry, Mum," said Sam, "look at how many healthy babies there are on the island. And, I am the wife of the Prime Minister. I am sure I will be well looked after. And, if there are any complications, we have a backup plan in Miami. So, stop worrying." Maggie could not believe how mature her nineteen-year-old daughter was.

Everything went well for about a week. Then Greg arrived. Unbeknown to Maggie, Greg had scheduled a whole bunch of meetings with the architects, builders and quantity surveyors in regard to the Sandy Point development. He had texted Sam to say that he would be arriving the next day and that he would stay on the yacht, which was still anchored in the bay. He did not seem to know that Maggie was on the island. Sam alerted Maggie and asked her if she should warn Greg that she was there. Maggie was a little put out that her personal time with her daughter was about to be invaded, but what could she do? Greg, was, after all, Sam's father and he did obviously have legitimate business on the island. "No, we'll give him a surprise. Might be a nasty one," said Maggie.

Greg had had been having a difficult time in America, trying to organise a defence against the class action lawyers. It was not going to be easy and it would not be cheap. On the other hand, since the lawyers were involved, it clearly was going to take a long, long time to sort out, so there was no point in hanging around in Los Angeles looking at paper. Besides, Greg's main interest in life at the moment was his pet project in Anguilla. Above all, he wanted to prove that he could design, build, and operate a first-class marina and resort, so he needed to be there. Also, at the moment, he did not have a young lady in tow, so there was nothing to stop him from concentrating on the job. He was not anticipating the presence of Maggie.

It was impossible for Greg and Maggie not to meet. He was staying on the yacht, which was moored less than 300 yards from Sandy's house and his site office was even closer. Also, Sam, maybe in the hope that she could mend their relationship, decided to invite both of them to dinner at the villa. Neither thought they could let their daughter down. Maggie, who had been happy to stroll around the island in the most casual of clothes, decided that she would pretty herself up for the dinner. "Show him what his is missing," she wickedly thought to herself as she got ready to go. Sandy had also been invited, but, diplomatically, had declined. "I get to see them all of the time," she told Maggie, "You just go and have a family affair." When Maggie emerged from her room Sandy clapped her hands for joy. "You look just beautiful, my darling. Your ex will see just what he is missing," she laughed. "I hope you have a lovely evening."

John served drinks on the patio. Conversation between Maggie and Greg was a little stiff, but John, being an accomplished politician handled the situation well by getting everybody engaged in a discussion about world affairs. Maggie thought that Greg looked really tired. Greg thought that Maggie was looking magnificent. Her dress was cut low enough for him to catch glimpses of her, still beautiful, breasts. To him, she had always been the most beautiful girl in the world. "I must have been mad to let her go," he thought as they sipped the cocktails. "it is so nice to see her again. I do miss her." Sam had hired a cook/housekeeper. With the pregnancy she needed the help and John had insisted that she did. The cook served a delicious meal and John was on hand to pour the wine. Needless to say, the pregnant Sam did not drink alcohol, nor did John, but that did not stop Maggie and Greg, who between them downed two bottles of red wine. The meal over, with no obvious disasters having occurred, John drove them back to Sandy Point. He was a little surprised when Maggie accepted Greg's offer to look at the yacht, especially since she had previously shown a complete disinterest in the thing. He was also concerned about Greg driving the tender dinghy, after the cocktails and the wine. "I'll get the skipper to bring Maggie back to your mum's," said Greg, waving John away. John watched the tender weave its way across the water. He waited until he saw the skipper help Greg and Maggie aboard and then left.

Greg poured himself a large whisky. Maggie rarely drank spirits but decided to take a limoncello. Greg told Maggie that she looked beautiful. She brushed away his comment, but had to admit to herself that Greg was still a handsome man. Maggie had not had sex now for quite a while and she really missed it. But, in her inebriated state, she fought against an urge to pull Greg towards her and kiss him. She just knew that that was exactly what he wanted. "I'd better get out of here," she suddenly found herself thinking, "before I do something I will regret." "Greg, it has been a lovely evening, but I need to go now. Sandy will be worrying." Greg did not resist. Through his somewhat blurred mind, he reckoned that they were going to be on this island for at least a few days more, so that he would have other chances to see his beautiful ex-wife. "Okay, my love. I understand. I will ask the skipper to escort you home. But be careful of him – he's a randy chap." He then had another thought." I would like to show you the plans for the resort. Maybe you could come to the office tomorrow, then I will buy you lunch." Maggie nodded, with some relief. That said, Greg went to find the skipper, and Maggie duly left, giving Greg a little peck on the cheek as she clambered, unladylike, into the tender.

It took three days for Greg to get Maggie into bed. It happened in the middle of the afternoon, when the skipper and the deck hands were off duty and Sandy had gone to the Valley for supplies. Maggie had done it because she needed sex; Greg, because he realised that he was still in love with Maggie. When it was over, Maggie instantly regretted what she had done announced that she would not see him again until she left in two day's time. She was not sure that she could stick to her word. Sandy had been an observer. Not, of course, to their actual lovemaking, but to their body language when they were together. Sandy thought that it was as shame that they had split up, especially for the little baby that was soon to arrive. Sandy knew though, that she could not interfere, not even to offer advice. She did not know enough about Greg to have the right to an opinion or even give advice. On Maggie's last evening on the island, she decided to spend the evening with Sandy to thank her for her hospitality, kindness, and friendship. She was so glad for Sam that this wonderful lady, Sandy, would be on hand during the pregnancy. It had really put Maggie's mind at rest.

During their last dinner together the two of them talked openly about their respective lives. Maggie explained to Sandy all about her charity work with the animals and her worries for Jimmy. Sandy was a good listener. Maggie poured her heart out about her thwarted love affair with Gee. She did not mention that she had just been intimate with Greg; she was too confused to take this on board for the moment. But Maggie also wanted to hear about Sandy. She wanted to understand how someone who's life had been so difficult for so many years had coped. She wanted Sandy to talk, not just listen. Maggie felt that she owed at least that to Sandy. What emerged was astounding and deeply troubling for Maggie. Although Sandy never grumbled, never complained, nor regretted the years she had scrimped, saved, and worked to give John his education, she did admit that things could have been different if, on one occasion, she had been more fairly treated. She told a story to Maggie, that she claimed she had never told anyone before. When Sandy was trying to put together the money to buy air tickets to take her son to his homeland, she had the opportunity to pick grapes at the vineyard in Dorking. One day, on her way to the railway station she had stopped to buy a lottery ticket because she had read that it was the largest jackpot that had ever been offered. She had never bought a ticket before in her whole life, and none since. It was definitely against the teachings of her Church. She did not have a television at home, so when the draw was announced, she did not know that her numbers had come up. It was only two days later that she saw what they were when she went to the post office in Battersea. Naturally she couldn't, at first, believe what she was seeing. She was sure that she had the right numbers because they were the birthdate of John, never to be forgotten. She had looked excitedly for her ticket but could not find it anywhere. It had slowly dawned on her that she must have lost it. She asked at the post office what she should do and they told her that she must call the lottery office to let them know her predicament. However, without any proof of her purchase, it had turned out to be impossible to convince the lottery company that she had bought the ticket. She could not prove anything. The lottery people had said that the best she could hope for would be that someone who had found her ticket would come forward and say that it was not theirs. Even then, they explained, they would not be able to give her the winnings because anyone could walk up and say what the numbers were after the event. They had agreed that it would be strange that the numbers matched exactly the numbers of her son's birth, but that could be a coincidence. Anyway, any further discussion was useless, because, whoever claimed the winning ticket did not disclose that they had found it. So there was nothing that Sandy could do. She knew that she had been robbed, but also knew that she was silly to have lost the ticket. She put it down to God's will. She had been a sinner to even buy the ticket. She had not deserved to win. And look how well God had looked after her now.

Maggie listened to this story in horror. All her selfish blabbing about her own love life seemed petty in the face of this story. Her head was spinning with self-hate. How cruel had she and Greg been? How could she ever make amends? What on earth could she say? Stunned as she was, Maggie managed to say nothing. She needed time to think. She knew that she could never give Sandy back the hours of hard work she had endured as a result of not collecting her winnings, but she felt just awful about the whole thing.

Suddenly she saw what her nightmare meant. Sandy was the lady in the nightmare. How incredible!

"Are you alright, my dear?" asked Sandy, suddenly alarmed that Maggie looked deathly pale. "You look so pale. Are you sure that you are alright?" Maggie pulled herself together. "No, Sandy, I suppose I am just tired – and maybe a bit sad at having to leave tomorrow." "Then, off you go to bed, my dear. Enough talking for one day. I so rarely have anyone to talk to in the evenings. I am sorry if I have tired you." "Not at all," Maggie managed, "I love hearing your stories. You have been so brave." "No, my dear, I have been lucky. God has been good to me."

Maggie just could not sleep. Over and over again she heard Sandy relating her story. It was just so incredible that such a coincidence could have occurred. Maybe there was a God after all. After all of these years to discover that the person you had stolen £500 million from was now your daughter's mother-in-law. What would happen to their relationship if Sam and John found out the truth? Maggie knew that Sam was aware that her parents had won the lottery, but she did not know the details. It was only a matter of time, thought Maggie, before John and Sam put two and two together and realised that the biggest winners of the lottery ever lived in Dorking, the same town that Sandy had bought and lost the winning ticket in. Sandy had said that she had never told this story to anyone, including John, so, for the moment it was still a secret. But Maggie knew that it was a secret that could blow the family apart if it did come to light. Maggie had to find a way to prevent that. The more she lay in bed thinking about it the more concerned she became. Finally, she decided on an action plan. She would visit with her financial advisors as soon as she got back to London to ascertain the state of her finances. She intended to pay Sandy back with interest. She knew that she could never make up for the years of back breaking work endured by Sandy because she did not have the money, but if she could somehow make things right and ask Sandy to keep quiet about the whole thing, she might be able to keep things on an even keel. It would just be a secret between her and Sandy. "But how will Sandy explain that she had suddenly come into half a billion pounds?" thought Maggie. "That will be impossible to hide on such a tiny island. Sooner or later John will ask questions and sooner or later Sam, her precious daughter, will get to know that her mother was a thief. Oh, what a nightmare! Is this God's way of punishing me?"

Greg had offered to take Sandy to the airport in his yacht, rather than in the speedboat. She was grateful because it meant that Sam could come too. She would not be allowed in the speedboat due to her pregnancy. Also, having Sam there would prevent her from having to say goodbye to Greg on his own. Clearly, through lack of sleep, Maggie did not look too well. Sam was concerned, but Maggie brushed it off. She had decided not to let Greg know about the problem even though he was as guilty as her. "Nobody else must know until I have worked it out with Sandy. If three people know, then the whole world will," Maggie rationalised. So, she just kept quiet and promised to Sam that she would return soon, which, of course, she now intended to do.

As soon as she reached Dorking, Maggie called the accountants, Stokes and Stokes, to arrange a meeting as soon as possible. Shea, the good looking one, agreed to come to Dorking the next day with copies of all her recent balances. As it turned out, Maggie's finances were in excellent shape. As a result of playing safe with 14 billion of the 15 she had been awarded from the divorce, this had grown with interest to an amazing 17 billion. With the other 1 billion, Shea had invested most wisely in two stocks, both of which had literally zoomed upwards in value; Amazon and Tesla. They could not have invested more brilliantly. This billion had grown to 5 billion, making her net worth now over £22 billion. In short, there were plenty of funds to be able to give Sandy what was rightfully hers. Maggie was minded to offer Sandy £1 billion, double what the lottery ticket was worth. Her initial thought, to clear her conscience, had been to give all of her net worth to Sandy, but she had begun to recognise, now with a clear head, that it was not actually Greg and Maggie's fault that Sandy had lost the ticket, nor that she had not signed it. It was now apparent that even if they had handed in the ticket, the lottery company would never have paid the prize out to Sandy, for lack of proof that she had bought it. In effect, Maggie could now be Sandy's saviour. Furthermore, it was Greg's business acumen and hard work that had grown the original half a billion into so much more, so why should Sandy be rewarded by something that she would not have been able to achieve? Just as Maggie's shame at not disclosing that the ticket was not theirs on day one had dissipated by the next morning, her shock at listening to Sandy's story was now being rationalised. "The name of the game now," thought Maggie, "is to find a way to neutralise Sandy; to prevent Sandy from spilling the beans and ripping, albeit innocently, the family apart." Maggie had concluded that an offer to pay back Sandy at double the original loss was fair. The question would be, how could Sandy accept this money and explain where it had come from? One thing Maggie knew for sure; if Sandy ever mentioned her bad luck to Sam, she would put two and two together and that could have disastrous consequences for her relationship with her mother and father and would put John Coltrane in a very difficult position. Maggie just hoped that, if she could make amends with Sandy, that Sandy would see the potential breakdown of family relationships in the same way.

Chapter Thirty

Maggie had not been back in Dorking long when she received some terrific news, which, at least for a while, stopped her brooding about the problems of the lost lottery ticket. James called from Hope. There had been a breakthrough at the United Nations. Leaked information to the New York lobbyists on Hope's payroll had informed him that enough votes had been secured to implement a worldwide ban on the sale, import and export of elephant and rhino tusks. The vote would be taken imminently. Even China, apparently, was going to ratify the new law, which all signatories of the UN Charter would agree to implement. This was an historic moment and one, in James' words was entirely due to the thoughtfulness, doggedness and generosity of Maggie. Maggie was over the moon with joy. She immediately called Sam and Jimmy to give them the good news. She just had to share it. Then, something told her that she should let Greg know. After all, he had condoned and encouraged her anti-poaching activity right at the start. Greg was still in Anguilla, managing his marina/casino development. Things had not been going well for Greg with the escalating NoGrow law suits, so he was delighted to hear some good news. He knew how much this would mean to Maggie and he was genuinely pleased for her. Maggie immediately found herself wondering why she had called Greg before Gee. After all, Gee was the person who had encouraged her more than anyone to fight the poachers and it was Gee who would be most personally affected by a total ban. She was right. When Gee received her call with the good news, he was overjoyed. "That's fantastic, Maggie. That's the best news ever. Jeez. Well done. It's all due to you. I absolutely love you. You are incredible. I don't know what to say!" Maggie was so happy that she had made Gee happy too. "It's not just me," she interjected, "James and the PR teams did a great job."

Next, Maggie called Willow, who absolutely whooped for joy. "We must have a party!," she shrieked, "This is terrific news. We must celebrate." "Yes," said Maggie, "but we must wait until the vote. I think it will be in a few days. Just in case something goes wrong." "Nothing will go wrong, my dear," said Willow, "you've come so far. Nothing will go wrong now. Next Saturday; big party, my house! No arguments." Maggie smiled to herself. "Willow will do anything for a party," she thought. In fact, Maggie was so happy about the news that she couldn't stop smiling all day. She called back James at Hope, to get more details. He told her that the crucial vote would take place in the UN in three days' time. "Fingers crossed," he added, "but I do not think there is anything to worry about."

And, for once in Maggie's life, there wasn't anything to worry about. The vote sailed through. It was unanimous. Maggie's face was plastered all over the press in practically every country in the world. For one brief moment she was probably the most famous woman in the world. The phone just would not stop ringing with the written and broadcast media all wanting to do articles or obtain interviews with Maggie. The housekeeper in Dorking became a switchboard operator. So much so that Maggie decided to change telephone numbers and directed all calls to Hope in London. James suggested that the London public relations firm that they had been using handle all press enquiries. They took control of the situation and organised a series of interviews and appearances for Maggie. She used the opportunity to thank all those activists that had supported her but also to draw attention to the practices that had not been banned, including the breeding and sale of lions and tigers for 'medicinal' reasons. Maggie's world became a whirlwind for at least three weeks; she had no time to think about Sandy nor returning to Anguilla. The task of the Hope's international public relations agencies and lobbyists had been fulfilled. Now it was time to wind down the organisation that had been so successful. Maggie had long debates with James about the future of Hope. She wanted it, and him, to continue to fight wild life injustices. James agreed that he would and that he would stay on for another couple of years with a much-reduced budget from Maggie. "I will continue on one condition," he stated, "and that is that you now withdraw and get on with your personal life. Go to South Africa to be with your love. I and my team will carry on your work. It is time for you to look after you." Maggie really loved this man. He had been like a second father to her and she was sincerely grateful. "Okay, James, I'll go quietly."

About three weeks after the historic UN vote, a letter landed on Maggie's doormat. The postmark immediately caught Maggie's attention. It was from Buckingham Palace. She had never had a letter from Buckingham Palace before, so she opened it eagerly. The contents of the letter overwhelmed her, so much so that she started to cry. "What on earth is the matter, my dear?" said the housekeeper. "My letter is from the Queen. I am going to be Dame Maggie. I can't believe it," Maggie tried to say between her sobs of joy. She passed the letter to the astounded housekeeper, who read it in amazement. It was from the Lord Chancellor, stating that Her Majesty the Queen intended to name Maggie in the next Honours List. She was not to tell anybody until the official list was published, except her immediate family. She would shortly be receiving more information about the arrangements. A covering letter advised her that she would be allowed to take three guests with her to the ceremony, to be held in Buckingham Palace. Maggie was in a state of shock. She had always read that 'recognition' was one of the most important motivators. Now she knew what that meant. To Maggie, this impending honour was the most important event of her life. It was hard for her to deal with because this simple act of recognition seemed to mean more to her than even the birth of her children. It was a remarkable feeling and one which she would never forget.

The next day's post brought more letters from Buckingham Palace; letters of congratulation from HRH The Duke of Edinburgh, HRH The Duke of Cambridge and from the Princess Royal and HRH The Earl of Wessex. Clearly the Honours List meant a lot to the Royal Family as well. Maggie immediately started to worry about who her three guests should be at the Palace. Definitely her children, she thought, but who should she have on her arm. It would mean a great deal to Gee, she thought, after all, he is the one most involved in wildlife. The thought of Gee having to dress in a morning suit to visit the Palace brought a smile to her face. Also, he was so handsome. He would look great. Yes, she would ask Gee. Then, another thought hit here. Why not invite Sandy? Surely this would be a huge thrill for her? That was it. No need to think further. This would be a great opportunity for her to cement her bonds with the lady she had robbed.

As it turned out the investiture took place six months

after the notification letter had dropped on the doorstep. This had wiped out any possibility of Sam attending; she would be exactly nine months pregnant! So, much as Maggie was disappointed, she understood completely. In the meantime, Maggie had been back to Anguilla to help out her pregnant daughter. Whilst there she had, once again, stayed with Sandy, who was absolutely thrilled to be asked to attend the investiture. Maggie had thought that this was enough for Sandy to absorb for the moment, so she resisted mentioning the billion pounds that she was planning to give Sandy. "Best to do this when Sandy comes to England," she thought. The dropping out of Sam cleared the way for Maggie to invite Gee to the ceremony. Maggie did not think that this was Gee's sort of thing, but, to her surprise and delight, he jumped at the invitation. He wanted to share Maggie's happiness.

Maggie wanted so much to have Gee stay at the house in Dorking, but she just couldn't. First, because Jimmy would be there, and second, because of Sandy. Although Maggie was perfectly entitled to have whoever she wanted to stay, she could not trust herself to have Gee in the house without jumping on him, which she did not think would be right in front of her son and her daughter's mother-in-law. So, she booked Gee in to the Goring, just around the corner from the Palace. She also booked the function room there for an after investiture celebration lunch.

The day of the investiture was one blur of happiness for Maggie. There had been plenty to do in the weeks before. Both Jimmy and Gee had to be fitted for morning suits. Maggie was not sure which of the two objected most to dressing up. Both claimed that it was not necessary, but Maggie insisted and dragged them both off to the suit hire company in Lower Sloane Street. They both looked so handsome in their grey suits, that, even they, had to admit that it made them feel good. Maggie picked herself out a beautiful satin suit from the designer floor in Harrods. Her problem was the hat, which was obligatory. Maggie never, ever, wore hats. She hated them. She searched in the most exclusive stores but nothing suited her. Then Willow told her about a hat rental shop in Fulham. "Why buy something that you will never use again?" argued Willow, "let's go to Fulham to see what we can find. It's 50 quid for a week's hire. Everybody who goes to Ascot uses the place." Sure enough, Maggie found just what she was looking for; something so flimsy that it almost wasn't a hat at all, but, according to the lady in the store, passed the test for Buckingham Palace. When Sandy arrived, Maggie had enormous pleasure kitting her out. Sandy had never before been in such luxurious stores, but she was determined to look her best for Maggie's big day and, of course, for her Queen. Sandy had no problems with the hat; she loved hats.

Maggie had been sent four passes to get into the Palace. She decided to splurge and rent a Roller with a chauffeur for the day. They passed easily through the gates of the Palace, having been waved through by a bevy of policemen, who recognised their windscreen sticker, under the little archway and into the inner courtyard of the Palace. As they alighted from the gleaming Rolls Royce, the photographers instantly recognised Maggie and clamoured for pictures. Maggie's little entourage was certainly eclectic. There was Maggie herself, looking absolutely beautiful; happy and radiant. The perfect front page picture for tomorrow's press and *Hello* magazine. Then there was a diminutive and somewhat older black lady with a flamboyant hat, a skinny and somewhat self-conscious schoolboy and probably the most handsome and tanned man in the Palace that day.

As Maggie's little group mounted the few steps from the courtyard to the Palace lobby, the three observers were separated from her. Maggie was sent to a 'rehearsal' room and the guests were directed to the ballroom where the investitures were to take place, having been asked to deposit their cell phones and cameras at a cloakroom on the ground floor. There appeared to be hundreds of people entering the Palace that morning; actually, there were 80 recipients of gongs but each, presumably, with three guests meant that there was quite a crowd. At the top of the grand staircase, Maggie was asked to deviate from the route that most people were travelling, and to step into an ornate room, where three other potential awardees were waiting. "The reason we are gathered here," stated a magnificently attired officer, "is for a rehearsal. This little group will be receiving honours that require Her Majesty, the Queen, to touch you with a sword or hang a medal around your neck. All other medals being awarded today will be pinned on. Your group will be honoured first, because the Her Majesty will be standing on a small raised platform, which will later be removed. To make sure that all goes smoothly we are going to have a short rehearsal." With that he proceeded, like a sergeant major, to make them practice the short walk to the dais, bow, bend their heads, get on one knee etc., not once, but twice, before allowing any questions.

Once sure that there would be no slip-ups, the small group of four were escorted to a side room adjacent to the real investiture room, which was now filled with the guest of all the potential recipients.

Maggie was the second out of 80 to be called forward. Her Majesty the Queen, even whilst standing on the little raised platform, was shorter than Maggie had realised. Having touched a bending Maggie slightly with the sword Her Majesty allowed herself a short conversation with Maggie, about whose exploits she seemed quite aware. Her Majesty thanked Maggie for her work which she said was "Dear to my heart, and that of my family." Maggie was so overawed by the occasion, that she was actually at a loss for words. She managed a rather weak, "Thank you, your Majesty," then took the three steps back that she had rehearsed, and moved off to allow the next recipient to step forward. This whole ceremony, with its sense of history, its colours, its wonderful ambience, was a highlight of Maggie's life and one which she would never forget. For the first time Maggie allowed herself to be proud of her own achievements. She proceeded to the adjacent room, where she was guided by a man in a bright red tunic to some special seats, where she was reunited with Sandy, Gee and Jimmy. Sandy gave her a big hug. Maggie could see that Sandy had been crying. Jimmy too gave his Mum a little self-conscious hug too. Gee kissed her gently on her lips, took hold of her hand, and did not let go. Maggie had never been so happy.

When the ceremony was over Maggie and her little entourage emerged into the sunlit courtyard, this time with Maggie displaying her magnificent medal of honour. Now the press could have the photo they really wanted; Dame Maggie Layburn. Maggie obliged them graciously. She felt so good about herself that she would have obliged anyone at that moment. She looked absolutely radiant, and so happy. The pictures whizzed their way across the world and by the next day every newsstand across the world was graced with Maggie's beaming face, proudly displaying her medal of honour. When the photographers were through the Rolls Royce whisked the little party round the corner to the Goring, where Maggie's invitees were gathered and already celebrating with Klug. Sandy suggested to Jimmy that they let Mum go first, escorted by Gee. As they reached the function room, Gee stepped back to allow Maggie a solo entrance. The room, which was packed with her friends from Dorking and all of the Trustees and staff of Trunk,

Shawu, Hope, and the Layburn Academy, erupted into a cacophony of clapping, cheering and whooping in honour of their benefactor and heroine. The sheer warmth of the welcome was overcoming. The Maggie that had held herself together so well for the photographers at the Palace, was now so overwhelmed with the astounding welcome that she could no longer hold back the tears. Gee put his arms around her to steady her and Sandy produced some tissues to repair the mascara. After a minute or two, Maggie had recovered and began moving her way around the throng, greeting everyone as she went. After 30 minutes or so the headwaiter announced that luncheon was being served and ushered the guests to a room packed with round tables of eight, beautifully decorated with memorabilia from the Buckingham Palace shop around the corner. No speeches had been planned, but, as the meal proceeded, one by one, each table pushed one of their number forward to make a little tribute to Maggie. It was a wonderful occasion, not just for Maggie but for all of her friends who were so genuinely happy for her and for all of the workers for the charities, who had, for once, seen their efforts rewarded. Pimlico Penelope made a hilarious speech, James from Hope was exceptionally eloquent, and even little Jimmy stood up to thank his mum for being his mum. Sandy spoke with exceptional warmth and read out a short message from Sam and John, and when all were done, Gee, made a wonderful speech, littered with South African jokes but ending with the sincerest expression of his love for Maggie, which moved the room to tears.

When all was done and the last guest had left with a hug or handshake from Maggie and Gee, the award party of Sandy, Jimmy, Gee and Maggie collapsed into the big leather chairs in the Goring lounge bar. Sandy, ever thoughtful, had considered that Maggie might like to have some time alone with Gee, so had had a quiet word with the chauffeur to take her and Jimmy back to Dorking ahead of Maggie. Sandy thought that a stop at McDonald's, or the like, might appeal to Jimmy. She had not really considered that a Rolls Royce with a young lad in morning suit and a little black lady with flowers in her hat might look incongruous in a fast food restaurant, but she didn't care. This had been the most wonderful day in Sandy's life. She had never ever dreamt of being inside Buckingham Palace, let alone at an award ceremony. She could not have cared less if the whole of the restaurant stared at them. She actually wanted to share her happiness. After all, Buckingham Palace was a long way from a Battersea housing estate.

Inevitably, with young Jimmy and Sandy gone, Maggie and Gee found themselves in Gee's suite. Maggie was exhausted and absolutely dying to take of her shoes. In fact, she was quite happy to take everything off, and since the hotel supplied magnificent bath robes, Maggie was soon naked under the robe. Gee watched her as she disrobed. Since he had known her, she had maintained her body in wonderful shape. He had never met a woman as beautiful as his Maggie, and, as Maggie suspected, he had met quite a few. He wanted to make love to her; in fact, he was desperate to do so, but he could see that she was emotionally spent. Maggie lay on the huge bed, wrapped in the towelling robe, and almost instantly went to sleep. Gee lay beside her and pulled her body to his. She snuggled up next to him and slept. Two hours later, at eight o'clock Maggie came to. Now she was ready to make love. The perfect end to a perfect day.

Chapter Thirty-One

Exactly one week after the investiture Sam, now only 19 years old, gave birth to a healthy baby girl in the cottage hospital in The Valley, Anguilla. Six pounds, four ounces; no problems with the baby or mother. John was so happy, and so proud of his darling young wife. Luckily, his mother Sandy had made it back to the island two days earlier. She, of course, was thrilled. The first person that John called to announce the birth was Maggie, even before he notified Greg, who was in the beach office a few miles away. Gee, who had stayed on in London for a few days, at Maggie's request, had just left for South Africa, so Maggie had been feeling a little deflated. The news from John was just what she needed. She was so sorry that she had not been there for her daughter, but she was sensitive to the fact that she wanted to give the young couple the space to enjoy their firstborn alone – at least for a few days. John, of course, told Maggie that she could come over as soon as she liked and Maggie felt like jumping on a plane immediately, but she resisted the urge to do so. A few hours after John's call, Sam phoned. "Oh, she's such a little darling, Mum. You must come immediately to see her." "Do you have a name yet, my darling?" asked Maggie. "Penelope," said Sam, "and we shall be asking Penelope Pimlico to be a godmother."

"That's nice," said Maggie, thinking that Penelope had probably never been in a church in her life except through necessity. "That's a lovely choice, my darling." "When are you coming, Mum? You must see the little darling before she gets too big!" "I'm going to give you some space with John. Then I will come. Probably in ten days or so. How would that be?" "You're welcome anytime, Mum. You know that, don't you?" "Of course, my darling. Now, you get some rest. I will call you tomorrow."

Greg was delighted to hear the news. He stopped his meeting with the development team and headed to the Valley to see his first grandchild. The Sandy Point project had now broken ground. The sound of the pile drivers had been sending the villagers mad for several weeks now. Greg was excited about the development. He had put an enormous amount of thought into the design. As bad news piled on bad news in America and the Far East in connection with the law suits, concentrating on Sandy Point had become a sort of therapy; something to keep his mind off NoGrow. Since the quickie with Maggie a few months back, Greg's love life had been slow; in fact, it had stopped. He thought of Maggie frequently. He was disappointed that she had not invited him to her investiture, but had said nothing. He was pleased that Sam had given birth, not least because he knew that it would attract Maggie back to the island. He believed that there was still a spark between her and him. Otherwise, why would she have made love to him on the yacht? He looked forward to her showing up again soon.

Before Greg reached the hospital, his phone buzzed with some very bad news. The lawyers in Los Angeles had been notified of a case in Thailand of a NoGrow user claiming to have contracted cancer as a result of using the shampoo. There appeared to be no hard evidence that NoGrow had contributed in any way to the man's condition, but the lawyers were worried. They did not want this to be a band-wagon that every male cancer victim would climb on. If NoGrow use caused cancer, Greg would need very deep pockets indeed to satisfy the claims. It would certainly bankrupt his partners and maybe, even himself, if the ringfencing of his wealth did not hold up. Concern for the cancer victim did not appear on Greg's agenda.

Sam and baby Penelope came out of the hospital three days later; John drove his precious cargo home in triumph and Penelope was installed in her newly decorated bedroom in the villa. The place was awash with cards from well-wishers on the island; John and Sam were a popular couple. Sandy was on hand to help. It had been so many years since she had nursed her son, back in England, but mothers do not forget. Penelope was a beautiful baby; the prettiest little thing that Sandy had ever seen, with a bronze skin and bright blue eyes. "She is going to be a stunner," said Sandy, "the boys will be lining up to take her out. You wait and see," she chuckled.

Maggie arrived ten days later, by which time Sam had managed to get baby Penelope into some sort of routine. Feed, sleep, feed again! Maggie, too, was delighted with Sam and John's work. This time, Sam insisted that Maggie stay in the villa and Maggie agreed enthusiastically. She wanted to be as much help as possible; after all, this was her first grand-child. Greg was keen to reconnect with Maggie. The arrival of the baby, of course, meant that they were thrust together. Both grandparents were enraptured with little Penelope and, in this sense, they were re-joined. Sandy, sensed that there might be a slight whiff of potential reunion. She thought that this would be nice for Sam and little Penelope, so decided to invite the pair of them to dinner at her little cottage. Maggie was not keen on the idea but Sandy seemed so determined that Maggie did not want to reject her. So it was that, a few days after, her arrival in Anguilla, Grandma and Grandfather found themselves seated round Sandy's kitchen table, consuming far too many glasses of wine. This time Maggie did resist Greg's invitation to share a nightcap on the yacht – she knew where that would lead – and insisted that he escort her back to the villa. She did, however, agree to meet him again to look at the progress of the construction. Maggie remembered well the last time she had seen Greg. He had wanted his way with her, but it suited her at the time since she had been months without sex. Effectively, she had seduced him and then, sexually fulfilled, had dropped him, just as many men do to women. Greg had been particularly frustrated. To be given sexual access to one of the world's most beautiful women, only to be cast aside immediately, had continued to frustrate him. This time, he thought, I will make her want to stay. "She will be begging to have more of me" he repeated to himself. This time, however, Maggie had not been enduring a sexual drought. Indeed, she had just finished almost a week of passionate lovemaking with Gee, in London. After Gee, Maggie wondered what she had ever seen in Greg. Nevertheless, she did visit the site office and Greg took her, hard hat and all, on a tour of the embryonic construction site. What she saw was very impressive. "You've not seen anything yet," said Greg as Maggie marvelled at what had been achieved do far. "Come with me to the yacht. I will show you phase two and phase three of my plan."

"You can't be serious," gasped Maggie, when Greg unveiled a series of drawings, plans and models for the area. The planned second and third phases dwarfed phase one. What she found herself looking at were pictures of a completely changed Anguilla. The whole western end of Anguilla, abutting a hugely enlarged marina, looked like Monte Carlo. High rise building after high rise building surrounded the lower areas as they tapered towards to ocean. There were several impressive looking squares, complete with gardens, shops, hotels, restaurants and bars. The original casino, from the current phase, had been turned into a convention centre and a new, larger and grander building dominated the sky line. This would be the biggest casino in the Caribbean, far larger than any would be competitors in the Bahamas. Maggie was looking at millions and millions worth of real estate. This would be a complete transformation of the island and, of course, of the way of life of the islanders.

"Has Sandy seen these plans?" asked Maggie. "Absolutely not. Nobody else has seen them. Except John." "What does he think?," asked Maggie. "He is nervous, but also excited. On balance he approves." "I bet his mum doesn't," said Maggie, "and, frankly, I am not sure that I do either." Notwithstanding her initial shock, Maggie could see the reason and the possible economic benefits for Anguilla. "After all," she reasoned to herself, "apart from the beaches, it is a pretty barren slip of land, so there is not much to spoil. Except," and this was in Maggie's mind, a very large exception, "their way of life." Greg had asked the skipper to lay on some snacks and drinks for Maggie. He has hoped first to impress her, then to wine her, and then, if all went well, to bed her. All had not gone well. As soon as the show and tell session was over, Maggie requested to be taken back to the villa, where she was happy to spend the rest of the evening baby watching.

Maggie was also determined to square things away with Sandy, whilst she had the chance. Now, their futures where even more inseparable, bound together by the little bundle in the villa. Sandy might relate her lost ticket story at any time, just as she had one evening to Maggie. Sam was too smart not to put two and two together, so Maggie must find a way to kill the story forever. But, the more Maggie thought about it, the more her thinking switched. As she saw it Sandy, having lost her ticket, would never have been able to prove that it was hers, apart from a possible coincidence that the numbers matched John's birthday. Maggie and Greg had not spent any of the money for 30 days, awaiting the rightful owner to make a claim, which they never did. So, if Maggie were to give Sandy £500 million now, she could be seen as an angel from heaven, turning up, later rather than sooner she had to admit, to make sure that Sandy received her rightful prize. It was not Maggie's fault, she rationalised, that Sandy had lost her ticket, nor had any proof of ownership. It was just her absolute good fortune that she had, later in life, run into Maggie, who was prepared to let her have the prize at last. And for all of the years of hardship, Maggie was willing to pay extra. "No," thought Maggie, "I am the saint here, not the sinner."

So, with that convenient truth firmly in her mind, Maggie invited herself to Sandy's one evening, with the intention of raising the matter of the lottery.

"There's something you should know Sandy. I have a confession to make." Sandy, realising that Maggie had something serious to say, by the tone of her voice, sat down and waited. "You remember your lottery story?" Sandy nodded. "Well, I have a lottery story as well. By an amazing coincidence Greg and I were the ones who found your lost ticket in Dorking. We admitted that we had not bought it," she lied, "but we had signed the back, so, according to the lottery authorities, unless anyone else came forward who could prove that it was theirs, the rules were clear; the person in possession of a signed winning lottery ticket was entitled to the money. We waited for the requisite 30 days during which time there were several challenges, one of them so serious, that we had to hire a private eye to prove that they were fraudsters. When no one came forward, other than pranksters, we, and the lottery company, accepted that we were the winners, and life went on." Sandy sat there dumb-founded, trying to absorb what Maggie was saying. "Why didn't you say something when I told you the story?" she asked. "Because, first I was stunned to hear what you had to say and second, I wanted to check the dates to see if our ticket had really been yours. When I checked, and it was, I felt so awful, I did not know what to say or do. Then, when I thought about it, it seemed that we were destined to meet, and I am so glad we did. You were denied access to your prize and it would seem, they were never going to give it to you. Now, in a roundabout way, you have found me – and I am going to give you the prize with a big slug of interest to make up for the time that you did not have it" Sandy tried to interrupt. "No, Sandy, let me finish, please. I am going to give you £1 billion on one condition; that you do not tell anyone that I have done so. You can have the money imme-diately, but you must promise to me that this will always remain just between us; not even the children must know." Sandy was dumbstruck. Finally, she managed to speak. "My dear Maggie, I don't know what to do or say. As I told you it was God's will that I lost my ticket, he told me that to gamble is a sin; I paid for my sin and I have always accepted that. I cannot take your money now; money that has been acquired through sin. You could have said noth-ing, but you are right, as a friend to admit what you had done. It was all a long time ago. Having the money now will not bring me happiness; I am already blessed with John and Sam and, now, Penelope. I am also blessed with you, but it will not make matters any better by me accepting the money." Maggie went to Sandy and put her arms around her. "Then," she said, "I have an idea. Will you allow me to make a contribution to your church, the Methodists, of £1 billion. If you like, it could be an anonymous donation.

I am sure it will do a lot of good and I am sure that God will know that it was from you, Sandy." Sandy was silent. Maggie thought that she was crying, but she was praying. Sandy was asking for guidance from her God. After all, this was still money that had been acquired in a sinful way. Could the church accept it? Finally, after what seemed an eternity to Maggie, Sandy spoke. "I think that would be a very nice thing to do. We can make an anonymous gift to the Church, but we can make some recommendations or stipulations on how it should be spent. We wouldn't want the priests to spend it on their boyfriends, would we?"

Maggie was so relieved, first at Sandy's acceptance and secondly that she could make a small joke about it. Surely that meant that she had forgiven Maggie. "And," Sandy continued, "I swear that this shall be our secret." With that she stood up and hugged and hugged Maggie. "Thank you for telling me, my dear. You know that you need not have." With that the conversation was closed, except, before Maggie left, she asked Sandy to find out how and to whom one can make a donation to the Methodists. Whoever would receive the billion was going to get the surprise of their lives.

Two weeks later, Maggie was back in the arms of Gee. This time in her beloved Africa. No high-rise buildings, just her own patch of bush in Sabi Sands. The night sounds of Africa were, once again, her aphrodisiac. With Jimmy back at school and Sam busy with baby and husband, and having won the day with her anti-poaching campaign, Maggie felt free to join Gee for an extended stay. Maggie was a peace with the world. She now longed for a period of calm, and where better to find it than in the bush? Gee had done wonders with Sam's Camp. Business had been booming and he had really kept it in tip top condition. It was now regarded as one of the premier safari camps in the whole of

Africa and was busy all of the time. As a result, Gee's time was in constant demand, so Maggie had plenty of time for reflection, quiet reflection in the bush that she loved. At 40, Maggie was far from past her prime, but she did notice herself scrutinising the rich and beautiful 20- and 30-year-old wives and daughters that all seemed to make a beeline for Gee. Maggie knew that she had the body of a 25-year-old and the experience of a 50-year-old, but she could not help worry that Gee might be curious to take a closer look at some of the creatures that clearly lusted after him. She knew that she had no hold on him, nor him on her; that was their arrangement. And, after all, who knows what he got up to when she was not in residence? No, she realised that she had no rights over him, but she did have a special interest – she loved him. She had loved him from the day that they met and it was, after all, her fault that she had been married with children that had kept them apart. Now that this was less of an impediment, it seemed that maybe he had got so used to his freedom that he might be slipping away. He did not behave that way. He came to her bed every night. He told her that he loved her – and more often than not, proved it, at least, between the sheets. But Maggie knew. She knew that he had an eye for the ladies. She knew that she may have left it too long.

Maggie had made up her mind to confront Gee. She was now prepared to give up everything in England; her home, her friends, and her charities, to share the rest of her life with him. The question was, would he be prepared to devote himself to her? Before she could tackle the issue, there was bad news from Jimmy's school. Jimmy was going to be expelled for dealing drugs. He had not learned his lesson from Dorking High. This was a question of two strokes and you are out. Greg was in Los Angeles, battling increasingly menacing threats from NoGrow groups, so it was a bad time for him to deal with Jimmy. Maggie needed to step up to the plate. She decided to bring Jimmy to Sabi Sands to see if she could straighten him out, but she needed somebody to deal with him immediately in the UK. James, at Hope, once again, came to the rescue. Maggie knew that she could trust him. She asked him to arrange to fetch Jimmy and his belongings from school and to get him on to a flight to Johannesburg. He was to make it clear to Jimmy that he had no alternative. Jimmy, shocked at being outed, cooperated and soon he was being met by his mother at Oliver Tambo. "Maybe," thought Maggie, "I could get Jimmy interested in the wildlife business? Maybe I could get Gee to teach him? After all, you don't need a degree to take care after wild animals."

A rather sulky Jimmy stayed with Maggie and Gee for about a month. Luckily, he had been too smart to be taking the dope; he had merely seen it as a good business opportunity and he was right; he had plenty of customers. Obviously, his presence in the Royal Suite at Sam's Camp, rather put the dampeners on Maggie's love life, so it was not a situation that could last for long. It was clear to Gee that Jimmy had no interest in wildlife management or tourism. It was clear to Jimmy that Gee did not have an exclusive interest in his mother, but she did not seem to get it. Slowly it dawned on Maggie that what Jimmy wanted to do was to make money, like his dad. "In that case," she announced one day, "I am going to talk to your Dad. I am going to suggest that he teaches you the development business, like the project in Anguilla. I am going to suggest that he gives you an opportunity there to show us what you can do."

"Mum, I think I might like that," said Jimmy, much to the relief of Maggie. So, after a few phone calls with Greg, it was agreed. Jimmy would become an apprentice to his Dad. He would be required to learn how to be a quantity surveyor, a structural engineer, a designer, and a builder – all on the job. For the first time, Jimmy seemed excited. "Thank God, no more school," he thought. But before he left, he thanked his Mother profusely for rescuing him. "Thank you, Mum. For all your love and help. You always come to my rescue. I am so proud to have you as my Mum. But now I have some advice for you. I know it is none of my business, but I know that Gee has an eye for the girls. I know he thinks the world of you, but be careful. It may not be an exclusive arrangement. I am telling you because I love you, Mum." Maggie knew he was right. She was amazed at his audacity and., even more so, his maturity. She loved him for it.

When Jimmy had left to meet his dad in Anguilla, Maggie confronted Gee. Not with her planned proposal but with her sad acknowledgement that there was obviously no future in their relationship. She blamed him for nothing. She hoped that they could stay friends. She hoped that he would stay as manager of Sam's Camp, which she absolutely trusted him to do. But she acknowledged that he was a free spirit and should be allowed to fly. It was a very miserable Maggie who flew back to England.

Maggie was really downcast. Her son and daughter had gone, she had parted from her lover and she was alone. "Why," one voice within her asked, "does so much go wrong? Am I being punished for my crimes? Does it all go back to my dishonesty with the lottery ticket, because, let's face it, it was dishonest? I should have reported the truth. I was never entitled to this wealth. I deserve to be miserable. How different life might have been if I had been honest. Surely this is God's way of punishing me." Yet another voice kept saying, "You have done so much with what you were given. You have been so kind and worked for good. Stop being so down on yourself." For several days Maggie felt terribly depressed. The pessimistic voice was louder than the optimistic one. Then, all of a sudden, the depression seemed to lift. "What is done is done. Get a life. Make the most of things. Think of yourself as lucky; lucky that you can help others." Optimism seemed, for once, to be winning. Maggie determined that being sorry for herself would not help anyone. No, she should enjoy herself; she should learn to love herself. In that way she might find ways to help others.

Maggie decided to do something for herself. She decided to buy an aeroplane. She had been spending a fortune on NetJets and airline tickets. She was wealthy enough, so why shouldn't she splurge on herself? She had been chartering the Bombardier Global Express and she liked it very much. However, she thought that she should shop around the competition. Also, she did not see the point in commissioning a new jet, when there were plenty used ones on the market, so she visited an aviation broker for advice. After several trips to look over the used private jets, she kept gravitating back to the Global Express and so, after a while, instructed the broker to look out for one that was not too flashy but in good condition. Several weeks after the search began, the perfect plane, came up for sale; a three-year-old Global Express that was not plastered with gold fittings. The captain, David Turnkey, that took her on a test flight was also absolutely charming. His employer, the owner of the jet, would no longer need his services, so he 'came', so to speak, along with the plane – or at least might be available to do so. David, a handsome man in his mid-30s, might be a real bonus, thought Maggie, as she considered the purchase.

A few weeks after the test flight, and all of the mechanical checks that were needed, the gleaming Global Express was Maggie's, as, indeed, was David Turnkey. It was agreed that the plane would be stationed at Farnborough, about 30 miles from London and roughly the same from Dorking.

Chapter Thirty-Two

Farnborough Airport was the smallest international airfield in the London area. Unlike, Heathrow, Gatwick, City, Stansted and Luton airports, Farnborough only catered for private aircraft. It was a small airfield, whose claim to fame, was an annual air show, which had attained an international reputation. New aeroplane product was showcased at the air show and many multi-pound deals were concluded there every year. Outside of air show time, however, the airfield was very quiet. The departure and arrival areas were tiny rooms and there was no formal space for customs and immigration. During the day one officer was on duty to stamp in passenger's passports, but, in the evening, there was an honour system where one had to phone the local police station and wait for a local 'copper' to cycle round to act as temporary immigration officer. Most pilots would radio ahead of time to give the police their ETA's so that there were no unnecessary delays upon arrival. All of these cosy arrangements, of course, were in place before the era of drug running but when Maggie kept her plane there, the village-like atmosphere still prevailed.

David Turnkey, now Maggie's personal captain, was a familiar entity at Farnborough. Not only did he fly for Maggie, but she would allow him to moonlight for other owners or charter operators. To recoup some of her costs, she also allowed her Global Express to be charted by others, on the proviso that David captained the flights. One evening, Maggie had been returning on the plane from a trip to Geneva, where she had been addressing a World Wildlife conference, when David radioed ahead to alert the police that they would be arriving. As they touched down, David noticed the security van parked near the airport buildings as usual, but did not think anything of it. He taxied the plane into position about 50 yards from the arrivals room, lowered the automatic steps, and climbed out of his pilot's seat to accompany Maggie across the tarmac to the buildings to await the arrival of the policeman. As the two of them walked, the security van suddenly screeched across the short stretch of tarmac and four burly men leaped out and grabbed them. David, naturally put up a struggle, but one of the men quickly subdued him with a smash on his head with a truncheon. Maggie decided not to resist. Both Maggie and David were bundled into the van, which sped off at great speed towards the perimeter gates, which they had opened earlier. David's co-pilot, who had not noticed the struggle, due to the fact that he had gone to the bathroom on the plane, just caught a glimpse of the van disappearing as he returned to the cockpit to finish the flight paperwork. He did not realise that his captain and Maggie had never reached the terminal buildings. Only ten minutes later, after he had strolled from the plane to the arrivals building, did he discover that the policeman was now waiting for Maggie and David to show up. The truth suddenly hit both the co-pilot and the policeman. Maggie and David had been abducted. The policeman put out an alert for a dark blue van. The real airport security man was found bound and gagged in one of the hangers. Maggie and David were gone. The police in three counties were alerted, but the dark blue van was nowhere to be found.

A massive search began. The press was alerted and the public asked to assist with any scraps of information that might help. Maggie's disappearance was obviously big news; hers was a familiar face to readers and television audiences. The police tracked down her ex, Greg, who agreed to alert Sam and Jimmy as well as Maggie's brother in France. There was huge public interest and for two days Maggie's face never left the front pages of newspapers everywhere and the story maintained primetime on the world's television news networks. But, there was no trace of Maggie and David. Also, the police were quite puzzled. Normally, they explained to the press and to Greg, kidnappers look for a ransom to be paid by someone who has not been kidnapped, often by a loved one or relative. In this case the person who had been kidnapped was most likely the person who would have to pay the ransom. They were not sure how this would play out.

In the blue van Maggie and David had been handcuffed, gagged and blindfolded. Just before the blindfold went on David had managed to glance at his watch. It was exactly 10 pm. He was hoping that he could get a feel for the speed of the van and judge how far they had travelled if he could check the time whenever and wherever they arrived. He also tried to remember the sequence of turns, either left or right, but this became impossible to judge and to remember. Through the muffled sound of the masks he was able to ascertain that Maggie was alright. As he thought it through David realised that Maggie was obviously the target of the kidnapping, so to harm Maggie would be counterproductive from the point of view of the abductors. Maggie was a precious cargo; worth her weight in gold. He, however, was disposable.

At first, Maggie was frightened. She had never been so frightened. She wanted to live to see her children again. She wanted to live to see Gee. Why had she been so foolish as to let Gee go? Thoughts of her life raced through her head. Gradually she became calmer. Without her alive, the kidnappers, whoever they were, would be on a fruitless mission. "Presumably" she reasoned, "they are after my money. Well they can't get any if I am not alive." The thought gave her comfort and her fear subsided. "I must keep in control of the situation," she thought, "without me, they will get nothing. But, if they get nothing, I may be dead." As the van continued its journey she started to worry about David. This was not his battle. She hoped that he would not be the collateral damage.

After what seemed to be at least a two-hour ride, the van slowed considerably. Both Maggie and David were alert enough to notice. The van then seemed to make a series of left, then right turns, and the sound under the wheels was different. "Probably, an untarred road," thought Maggie. After a few minutes of this, the van stopped and the two bound passengers were bundled out and guided through what seemed like a door into a space where the sound seemed more muted. Then, they were pushed through a narrow space (they could both feel the walls on either side) and down some steep stairs that sounded wooden. When their masks were removed, they found themselves in a basement. Not a dank grimy basement, like you see on the movies, but a fairly modern one, which looked like a conversion of a basement in a normal family home; something a father might have done to get extra space.

There was even a crude bar and a darts board. "Ideal place to spend a while," thought Maggie.

Both prisoners were plonked down on kitchen type chairs to which they were tied. It all seemed a bit amateurish to David, but he kept his counsel. Three of the crooks clunked back up the stairs, all still wearing balaclavas, and one remained in the cellar on guard. He was also masked. Maggie asked to go to the bathroom. She was actually getting quite desperate. En route from Geneva, after giving a successful presentation, she had relaxed on the plane and downed half a bottle of vin rouge. Now, several hours later, she really needed to go. The guard refused to let her. Maggie was determined. "Do you want me to pee in my pants? Because that's what will happen," she yelled at the guard. "You're not going anywhere" growled the man. "Don't be so ridiculous," David chimed in, "If you want something from the lady, you had better be nice to her," he said in a very authoritarian manner. You could tell that he intended to be in command. The guard responded. "The woman wants to pee," he yelled up the narrow stairs, "one of you'd better come to take her, or Captain Smartarse down here is going to cause trouble." "Put her blindfold on and bring her up," yelled a voice from upstairs, "Leave him down there. He can't go nowhere!"

The guard replaced Maggie's mask and pushed her over to the stairs, where he guided her to the rail. He made sure that he brushed her bosom as he did so, and, since there was only room for one at a time on the steps, he made sure that he had a good look up her skirt as she mounted before him. David noticed. It made him angry. As soon as Maggie and her captor had disappeared from view, David attempted to stand up, still trapped to the chair. He was testing how tightly he was trapped. He managed to wriggle his way to the bar counter. He wondered if there were any potentially helpful tools there, but there was nothing he could see and, even if there had been, his arms were lashed to the chair, so it would have been impossible to pick anything up. "No," he thought, "we will have to defeat these punks with our brains, not our brawn." He wriggled back to the place where he had been left. It was not long before Maggie was being manhandled again down the stairs. This time the guard was quite brazen about feeling Maggie's breasts as he tied her back onto the chair. "You do that to me again, and I swear you will get nothing from me, whatever it is that you want." Maggie's voice was firm.

It was futile for David and Maggie to discuss the situation except in the broadest possible terms or the most veiled ones, because the guard was there all of the time. They just both assumed that sooner or later the thugs would tell them what they wanted, so they agreed that the best thing to do was to was to be patient. Luckily, they had not removed David's watch, so he was still able to track the time as the night ticked on. He could not understand why they just didn't get on with spelling out their demands. "What could they possibly gain by delaying things? Only to create fear," he assumed.

At three o'clock in the morning, the three burly men from upstairs clambered down the wooden stairs. Maggie had been dozing in her seat and woke up with a start. "Here we go," she thought, "now we should find out what this is all about." One of the men appeared to be in charge. He was wearing a black balaclava, with a hole for his eyes and one for his mouth. He pulled up a chair in front of Maggie. "This is a simple business transaction, Maggie ("Well, he obviously knows who I am," thought Maggie), we will let you and your fancy pilot go, for £10 million." Maggie tried to laugh. "I don't have £10 million," she replied firmly. "Then get it from your husband," the masked man shot back. "I don't have a husband." "You're a fucking liar," barked the crook. "If you don't agree to cough up the ten, then it will give us all great pleasure to take it in turns to screw you whilst you figure out how to get it. I am sure that captain here will enjoy watching that." "You lay one hand on her and it will be the last time you ever get to use it," said

David in the firmest captain voice he could muster. One of the thugs smashed him in the ribs with a blow so hard that it winded him. "Stop, stop," yelled Maggie, "you won't get anything from me if you harm either of us. I am telling you that I do not have £10 million and have no way of getting that sort of money. I will not even negotiate with you until you have untied the captain and me from these chairs. We need to stretch and we need to sleep. If you let me have my phone from my bag, I can call my banker, but he will not be there until tomorrow morning. Beating the captain or screwing me will not get you what you want." Maggie amazed herself how calmly and firmly she had spoken. She amazed David too, still smarting from the blow. The leader was silent for a moment. He knew that a dead or injured Maggie was no use to him. An injured captain, however, might be the lever he needed. What Maggie needed was time to think. The only person who had the capability of moving her funds was Shea from Stokes and Stokes. She knew that his number was in her contacts on her cell. She prayed that he would not own up to the fact that she had millions and millions more than the ten asked for.

The gang leader stepped back. He had decided to give the negotiation a little time. He would give the prisoners the freedom of movement in the locked basement; they could not escape. He would wait until banking hours the next day to see what could be achieved. If they had not made progress the next morning, he would start harming the captain. He had not really wanted the extra baggage of the pilot but now he could see what a useful tool he might be. Of course, there was no future in harming or sexually assaulting Maggie, much as he would have enjoyed the latter, but he could use David as a lever. He was pretty sure that Maggie would not want him hurt.

As luck would have it, Shea, the investment manager, had

caught the late-night news. He watched with horror as the newsreader related the story about Maggie, 'his' Maggie. He immediately grasped the fact that there could be some sort of ransom demand. As far as he was aware, he was the only person with the 'keys' to Maggie's fortune. He had routinely been investing and reinvesting her money and portfolio over a few years. Nothing moved in her bank accounts unless he signed off on it. He knew, as soon as he heard the news, that this story could lead to him. He called the police immediately, and, late as it was in the evening, within 30 minutes two detectives were ringing on his doorbell. He explained Maggie's financial set-up and his ability to move funds. All three men concurred that, sooner or later, there would be a demand for a slug of Maggie's fortune. They agreed that Maggie may be forced into a negotiation. They tried to figure out how she would react to the demands that would surely come. "My guess is that she will tell them that she doesn't have much money available," said Shea. "She's too smart to let on how much she really has. We should isolate and ringfence a certain amount, so that we can 'advise' her, if she or they contact us, what she can offer for her freedom." The detectives agreed. "The crooks will obviously have read that she is wealthy, but they cannot be sure just how wealthy. Lots of people are reported as having great wealth, but it is often greatly exaggerated, particularly wealth that is easily tapped," explained one of the policemen. "If I had to guess, Maggie, is smart enough to tell them that she can only lay her hands on a million. If they call, I am going to tell them that it would be impossible to raise any more in 'readies', okay?" That was agreed and Shea set about reorganising Maggie's cash into bundles under different titles, bar one, in Maggie's name, with just over a million pounds.

Next morning, at around 10 am, Shea received a call. It

was from Maggie, and, unbeknown to the hustlers, it was immediately being recorded by the cops. Shea had been told to keep the caller on the line as long as he could, so that it could be traced. The crooks did not think that the cops would have already got to the banker, so they were not worried about a trace for their first call. They knew that there was a possibility that the banker would alert the police later, although they would, of course, warn him off this action. The first voice on the line was that of Maggie. "Presumably you know I have been abducted. I am being asked to be brief. My captors will release me and the captain if we pay them £10 million. I have told them that I don't have 10 million. Please tell them what we have…" She was interrupted by the gang leader, who snatched the phone from Maggie. "Now listen to me. I know she is a rich broad. I want 10 million wired to an account I am going to give you. If you don't do this now or you, nor nobody else, will ever see her pretty face again. You got me?" "But I can't do that. She doesn't have 10 million in the bank. She is telling you the truth. I can send you a bank statement. The absolute maximum I could get to you would be a million. There is no more." "Well, fuck you, then. I don't suppose you will be seeing your pretty client no more. I will give you two hours to find some more dough or me and Maggie are going to start to have some fun." With that his big thumb pressed the red button and he was gone.

The detectives were ecstatic. The call had been just long enough for them to pick up a location of Maggie's phone. These crooks were evidently not the sharpest. But, had Shea not been so alert and contacted the police, this first call might not have been so useful. As it was, Maggie and David's position was pinpointed to a country house in Dorset. By the time the second call took place, the house was, unbeknown to the crooks and to their captives, surrounded by an army of police. Inside, the lead abductor called the number of the banker again. This time he knew that the call might be traced so he used a landline that would be more difficult to locate. He also determined that the call would be a quick one. Shea has been told by the detectives to try to keep the conversation going as long as he could to give the cops outside a chance to get close to the building. "It doesn't matter what you agree to," they said, "because we are going to get them before you need to send anything. So, take your time in being negotiated up." Shea agreed.

"Well, my friend, how much Tom did you pull together?" "Just a bit over a million is the best I can do. I told you already." "If you don't get real, you will never see her again," the crook threatened. "No, please, hold on a moment. There might be a way I could sell some equities and raise a bit more." "How much more?" "Maybe another million or two." "Make if five and you can have her back." "How do I get it to you? And how do we get Maggie back?" The crook, sensing that he could squeeze some more did not answer. "I think you can do better than the five. You find six. I will call you back in one hour with the arrangements." He slammed down the phone. It was the last thing he did of his free will that day, or, on fact, for many years to come. As the phone hit the cradle the doors of the cottage were rammed open at the back and the front and an army of police in riot gear with guns at the ready burst through. There was no fight. No shoot out at the corral. Four, rather amateurish, kidnappers were led away to a new life. Maggie and David were free. Maggie gave David a thankful hug. As she held on to him, she could not stop weeping. "Thank God," she whimpered through the tears, "thank God that is all over. I am so sorry, David, to have put you through this. I am so sorry." "Never mind, my dear," said David, "It's all over now. Maybe, at long last, someone will beef up the security at Farnborough. No more policemen on a bike."

The news of Maggie's release was, of course, all over the press. Once again Maggie was thrust into the limelight. Once again, she had started to think that the lottery win only brought bad luck and unhappiness. Once again, that seemed to be proved wrong. Maggie emerged from the incident a more marketable person than ever before and her bank account was intact. Except, of course, for the generous £1 million that she donated to a police charity. "After all," she told the reporters who picked this up, "I thought I had lost it anyway."

Chapter Thirty-Three

Thirteen years on and the Layburn/Coltrane family looked different. Maggie, now 55, had remarried, this time to Simon Helicon, a prominent London city banker and financier. She now lived in Eaton Square and in a rambling pile near Stow-on-the-Wold, in the Cotswolds. The family home in Dorking had long gone, as had the little red Mini. Maggie was a nationally known beauty; much loved by the nation. Her regular television programme, naturally about the plight of animals, was watched by millions throughout the world. Her Layburn Academies had set the gold standard for education in rural communities. She had worked hard to retain her good looks. She was still one of the richest women in the UK but real happiness had eluded her.

Greg was no longer alive. His life had been unbearable for several years before he died in a terrible helicopter crash between Saint-Martin and Anguilla. There had been much speculation about the cause of the crash, which, in the end was put down to mechanical failure. However, in the years leading up to the accident, Greg had been hounded by lawyers representing thousands of clients who claimed to have developed cancer after using NoGrow. More and more evidence had pointed towards the validity of their claims. For Greg, his premature death may have been a salvation.

He had left his considerable fortune to Sam, Jimmy and, surprisingly, Maggie, in equal proportions. Clearly, he had been in love with Maggie until his dying day. Clearly, the bounty he had received from the lottery had not made him happy either.

His son Jimmy, however, forced into a quick learning situation, was now a very wealthy and successful entrepreneur under his own right, at the exceptionally young age of 30. Phase one of the Sandy Point development had been completed and was hugely successful. So much so, that on the day that it opened to the public, it was immediately apparent that it was undersized, so Greg and Jimmy had launched into phase two. Now, without his Dad, Jimmy was overseeing the development of an even larger development, phase three, to include thousands of high-rise apartments, an even larger casino, multiple hotels and a new international airport. Jimmy was yet to marry, despite the string of actresses and models that had tried to land him. Maggie was not sure, but she suspected that her son was actually gay.

Sam now had three children; James and Margaret had been added to the brew. The family had been long gone from the 'house that Ellen built' to their own comfortable and less flashy family home near the Valley. John was no longer the Prime Minister, having served the maximum time allowed under the law. However, always the public servant, he had stayed in politics on an ever upward trajectory. At the age of 47 he had been appointed General Secretary of the United Nations, so Sam and the family had been uprooted to New York. Sandy, now in her mid-70s, had stayed in Anguilla, still living in the preserved village area of Sandy Point, but now surrounded with fancy apartments. For all she could now see from her porch, she might as well have been in Manhattan. Much as she appreciated the economic advantages that the development had brought to her homeland, she hated it. Her village, which Greg had promised would be preserved, was now totally surrounded with concrete and glass blocks. It was only a matter of time before the villagers caved in and sold out their precious land. Also, the commercialisation of the island had been the death knell of Sandy's precious church. Attendances at services were drastically down; effectively the influence of the church had vanished and with it, it seemed to Sandy, good manners and morals.

Pimlico Penelope still lived in Pimlico and had remained friendly with Maggie and her family. She was determined to live long enough to show her goddaughter the pubs of Pimlico. The need for Shawu to continue operating as a charity no longer existed, once the sale of tusks had been made illegal, so Penelope had closed down her fundraising efforts. Mossie Mostert, the owner of Shawu farm had passed away, and, having no direct family, had bequeathed the farm to Penelope. This had been a lovely gesture but not a particularly welcome one to Penelope, who, at her advanced years, was in no position to look after it. After consultation with Maggie, she had asked Gee to manage it for her, and it was not long before Gee put in a low offer to buy it. Penelope had accepted, with some relief.

Gee, having bought the farm moved in there with his new wife, Zandra. She was ten years younger than Gee and expected to have children. She had been brought up in Johannesburg but, like most white South African youngsters had spent a stint of her life in London, specifically in Earls Court. She was a city girl who had been courted by Gee, initially for her good looks, but over time, because of her very pleasant easy-going nature. Unfortunately, no babies were conceived and Zandra became restless and bored at Shawu. Gee invested in a small apartment in Johannesburg so that Zandra could get away from the bush from time to time, but this, of course, heralded a slow drift apart. When Maggie married Simon, Gee and Zandra were still married, but were, sadly, almost living separate lives. Gee had been convinced that had Zandra produced offspring that she would have settled down in the country. Both he and she had been tested for fertility. He had persuaded Zandra to undergo IVF treatment, but it had been unsuccessful.

Ellen was now married to a Russian, who appeared to be very wealthy, with a house in Notting Hill and a country mansion near Bagshot. Ellen, was still as vivacious as ever, but had not aged as well as Maggie. Her fabulous boobs were a little lower, although still frequently on display in the picture magazines, and she showed serious signs of Botox face. Nevertheless, she was still a great party girl and her break in friendship with Maggie seemed, at least on the surface, to have mended, particularly during the period, après Gee, when Maggie became a bit of a party girl herself, before she met Simon.

Willow had not lost her baby doll looks, but she had lost her husband, Ted. Rumour had it that he had had a heart attack in a strip club in London, although Maggie never knew if it was true or not. Maggie did know, from Willow, that from time to time, he would invite her to join him at some club or other, so, as far as Maggie was concerned, there could be some truth to the rumour. Willow soon found a toy boy, Alex, to live with her in Dorking. Maggie was sad that Ted had gone; he had always been a good turn on for her, even in her fantasies. However, as she was to find out, Alex was a pretty good replacement. In fact, when Maggie had finally broken off with Gee, she needed to find an outlet for her sexual desires, which, in her 40s, seemed to be stronger than ever. Maybe she was fearful of growing old, but particularly after Gee had called her to announce that he intended to marry a local South African girl, Maggie looked for sexual gratification wherever she could. She was rich, still beautiful, and, sadly alone. Whilst Ted had been alive, she had carried on an affair with him in front of, and behind, Willow's back. This did not feel like a betrayal to Willow because the thought of Ted enjoying himself was a huge turn on for Willow, as she had often confessed to Maggie. Alex, the new man in Willow's life, did not do the same for Maggie as Ted, but he was a young good-looking stud, so in the context of an alcohol fuelled party, he made a handy replacement, which Willow took great pleasure in sharing with her friend from time to time. Willow also introduced her old friend Trixie into the fold. Trixie could certainly be entertaining, and often arrived with the most interesting and sexy partners. Separately, Maggie had a good time with Ellen, whose husband was able to produce a long line of rich, good-looking, Russian hunks, normally surrounded by bevies of long-legged blondes. Although this scene was only on odd occasions, Maggie looked forward to it and had no inhibitions about joining in. For a period of time, in terms of a serious relationship, Maggie was drifting and this loose sexual behaviour filled the vacuum until she pulled herself together. It had been, of course, all about the loss of Gee, whom she never stopped loving, but could not have.

Maggie's wildlife television programmes had made her even more well-known than before. At the time of receiving her honour from the Queen, Maggie, being such an attractive woman, received a huge amount of press coverage. Her anti-poaching work had brought her fame, but the press publicity she received was definitely helped by her good looks. Now, through her television shows, which were broadcast and rebroadcast all over the world, she was known internationally, not necessarily because of the shows interesting wildlife content, but because of how Maggie presented the programmes. During some early filming in the bush Maggie had, on a few occasions, not worn a bra under her safari cloths, due to the lack of laundry facilities. The producer had shown her the clips, which had considerable allure since her nipples and her shapely breasts were evident under her blouse as she peered through binoculars or camera lenses. He persuaded her that the filming of her braless in the bush would not only be very natural, but also extremely appealing to the audience. Maggie had been reluctant at first and then thought, "Why the hell not? If you've got it, use it!" The producer was absolutely spot on. Viewer ratings were huge, especially of, course, with men. There had been some worry with the production company that such brazenness would severely harm female viewing numbers but, in fact, there appeared to be no negative reaction at all. In short, the show was a tremendous success and Maggie made several series over a few years, travelling across the world.

Travel, as such, was not a hardship for Maggie, since she had bought the Global Express. During her years of sexual looseness the plane had seen plenty of pleasure, but during the filming of the television shows it turned out to be extremely convenient, and Maggie had been able to offset some of the costs of running it by taking with her the production team and loads of equipment. Not to say that the film crew did not have fun. Both they and the Global Express crew had never had it so good as working and playing with Maggie.

As her 50s beckoned, Maggie wanted out. Out of the television filming with its constant travel and out of the spotlight. She felt that she was constantly on show and in demand. During the Trunk era and the international anti-poaching campaigning she had been asked to give plenty of after-dinner speeches or lectures at schools and universities. The demand for her to continue with this did not stop after the laws were changed, and even grew as a result of the television exposure. She could easily command a fee of $100,000 per speech from commercial enterprises and she was in much demand. She was also very good at it and had learned how to relax in front of an audience. It was at one of these evening events that she met her husband, Simon Helicon. Simon was an extremely successful hedge fund manager, running a fund that he had established himself some ten years before he met Maggie. Simon was mesmerised by Maggie as she spoke at a dinner where he was a guest. Simon was a man who was used to getting what he wanted and, as he watched and listened to Maggie at the podium, he decided that he wanted her. It did not matter to Simon that he was already married, actually for the second time. This, however, had not stopped him having numerous affairs, so what would be different if he succeeded in bedding Maggie? To him, this would be just another trophy. His wife, Jennie, was aware that he was a philanderer, but then so was she. In Simon's view, pursuing Maggie could not possible present any problems.

Simon was a handsome 48 years old. Jennie was a few years younger. The love had gone from their marriage a few years before Maggie's speech. In fact, whilst Simon had been captured by Maggie's spell, Jeannie was busy elsewhere with another younger banker, who worked for Simon at the hedge fund. To Maggie, from the rostrum, it seemed that the room was full of extremely well-groomed wealthy men, of all ages. She knew that she could have had any of them, such was her magnetism. Although middle aged, her beauty had matured with her; she still radiated sensuousness. Her nice personality shone through as she spoke, but so did her sex appeal. She scanned the room as she spoke. She often did this on these occasions. It had become a game with her, spotting the man she could seduce. On this occasion, her initial focus was on a young blond man, probably at least five years her junior. He was certainly very handsome and he half smiled as she caught his eye. She made no such connection with Simon at all. In the meet and greet session after the speech, Maggie made a beeline for the blond, with whom she engaged in a slightly flirtatious conversation. They were, however, rather irritatingly interrupted by Simon, who insisted on handing Maggie his card. "Please give me a call," he had said, "I have an interesting proposal for you." He looked her straight in the eyes. His look was almost challenging and rather authoritarian. "There's a man who gets what he wants," Maggie had thought at the time, but immediately turned her attention back to the blond.

It turned out that, although a handsome specimen, the blond was neither interesting nor challenging, so nothing had transpired from the encounter. Simon's card remained in Maggie's bag for a few days before she decided to call. "You took your time," Simon said, almost as if to admonish her. He was used to people doing what he asked them to do with alacrity. "Never mind, you have called now. We must meet; I have something to discuss with you." Maggie was a little taken aback by his abruptness. "You can discuss it with me on the phone," she replied. "No, I can't. It's personal," came back the response like a gun. "Are you in England?" "Yes," replied Maggie without stopping to think. "Good. We will meet tomorrow at 7 pm in the bar at the Dorchester Hotel," he stated, as if it were a done deal. "I am not sure that we will," said Maggie, "I am not sure I like being told what I am going to do." "Yes, you will. All women like it. I'll see you tomorrow." With that, he finished the call and Maggie was left looking at her phone wondering what had just happened. Since she had won the lottery, nobody had spoken to her like that. It was not something she was prepared to tolerate. "What right did any man have to talk to a woman like that?"

But, meet him she did. It occurred to her as she ruminated on the conversation, that for many years, or at least since the early days with Greg, men had allowed her to call the shots. She had a legion of men who offered advice, particularly in legal and financial matters. Even at the charities older and wiser people deferred to or sought her opinion. She had just become used to telling people what to do. She thought it was 'leading', but maybe she had just got used to ordering people about, even if it was in the nicest possible way. To have met a man who seemed to be telling her what she should do was a little intriguing. Not that she intended to put up with it, but she had to admit, it was a bit different.

"Two glasses of Klug," Simon instructed the waiter, as Maggie sat down. "I see," thought Maggie, "I am going to be told what I drink as well, am I?" Maggie had chosen exactly the right outfit for the Dorchester. A shortish tangerine coloured skirt with matching high heels, a button up the front blouse and little tangerine jacket. She had left the top two buttons of the blouse tantalisingly undone, revealing the upper part of her superb breasts. "I wonder if he is a breast man, or a leg man," she had thought. "I think I will treat him to a bit of both." The waiter appeared with the flutes of champagne. They clinked glasses. Maggie waited. "You look very nice," said Simon. "Actually, you look exceptionally nice; which is one of the reasons I wanted to see you. I intend that I become your lover. That is my proposal." Maggie was completely taken aback. Obviously, she had never before had such a direct proposition. She thought it was some strange kind of joke. She didn't know anything about the man. She wanted to get up from the chair and leave, but the statement was so bold and so surprising that she hesitated. James went on. "You probably think that this is rather forward of me, but I am a man who knows what he wants and takes immediate action. That is how I have become successful; by taking action before others; by knowing a good thing when I see it and not letting it pass. I do not intend to let you pass." Maggie sat there flabbergasted. "Was this man for real? Was this one big joke?" Apparently not. Simon appeared to be completely serious about his so-called proposal. He did not pull any punches. He told Maggie that he was married, but that this did not matter, because he was no longer interested in his wife, nor she in him. He was looking for new love and he had decided that Maggie fitted the bill.

Maggie had hardly uttered a word since she had arrived in the bar. Now she started to get up from the chair to leave. Simon put his arm out to stop her. "Don't leave. At the very least let us finish out drinks and then I will buy you dinner. If, by the end of the evening, you are not interested in my proposition, I will not bother you again." His hand was quite strong on her arm, almost pushing her down into the chair. Nobody had ever bossed her around like this. She could not work out whether she was flattered or frightened. At least it was different. For the last few years it seemed that she had been doing the chasing. Obviously not, in this case. She decided to stay.

The dinner was interesting. Simon told her all about his background and his success. He came from a long line of fairly traditional bankers, but he had understood the modern markets better than his father and his colleagues. He had been far more adventurous and extremely successful. He was definitely a darling of the City. His only failures, he admitted, were in his personal life; one failed marriage which had produced a son and a daughter, and his current failed marriage, yet to be terminated. He was not looking for a new partner to provide him with further children. He was looking for someone who could challenge his intellect and, at the same time, match his sexual adventurism. Maggie had never before, on a first date, listened to someone so frank and yet so in charge. He did not ask much about Maggie, but he certainly knew all about her. His research had been incredible. The only piece missing in the puzzle was the lottery win. He did not ask.

Maggie had never had a dinner like this in her life. Simon chose the menu and the wine, with barely a query as to whether Maggie liked his choices. Luckily, she did. For Maggie, it was almost a welcome change to have someone else in charge. Gradually she relaxed, sat back, and enjoyed being pampered. She drew the line, however, when he informed her that he had booked a suite in the hotel. "Well," she quipped, "I hope you won't be too lonely, because I am now going home." Simon had the good sense to accept that he could not have everything his way – at least, for the moment. "Let me escort you home," he insisted. "No need. I have a chauffeur outside. Thank you." "I will see you tomorrow evening then," announced James. "I might be busy," said Maggie. "Well, cancel that. I will call you to say where and when." With that he escorted her to the waiting Rolls Royce, kissed her full on the lips, and handed her over to the driver. "Phew," sighed Maggie, "I've never met a man like that."

But meet him again she did. On the second date she slept with him, not at his house in Eaton Square, but in the suite at the Dorchester. They were extremely compatible. Three months later Simon was divorced. Jeannie moved out and Maggie moved in; or to put it more accurately, was told to move in. Since selling the home in Dorking, Maggie had not bothered to find another house. She actually had no one to share it with. Jimmy had taken over the Greg's villa in Anguilla and owned a flat in Belgravia and one on the Upper East Side of Manhattan. Sam and the family, of course, were also living in New York, so there seemed little point in Maggie having a big home in England. Instead, she had paid off the staff in Dorking and moved into an apartment at Number One, Knightsbridge, where all of the apartments were provided with service from the adjacent Mandarin Hotel. She had a beautiful view over Hyde Park and the whole set-up was ideal for a single woman, especially one who often entertained. Simon had wanted Maggie to give up her flat and her aeroplane when she moved in with him, but, much as she seemed to like being bossed around by him, on these two matters she refused. He had told her that if she didn't do as he said that he would smack her bottom. She thought that he was joking, but she was wrong.

Simon's house in Eaton Square was magnificent. Its large rooms with their high ceiling were furnished elegantly and scattered with original artwork of all sorts. Maggie reckoned that there were probably over £100 million worth of art in the place. She liked the way that it was displayed, somehow giving it room to breathe. Simon was very dictatorial, but, at the same time, he was very kind and generous. Not that Maggie needed the generosity. If anything, she was richer than Simon, but it was still nice to be pampered. Simon loved Maggie to dress well. He loved her to look elegant, but he also loved her to look sexy. It was not always possible to marry the two looks, so frequently, he asked Maggie to dress in one way, when they went out and another way when they stayed in. Maggie liked it when they stayed in and she could tease him. After three months of living together Simon had announced that they were to get married. There was no such thing as a request, not even a proposal; it was very much an announcement. There was no consultation about how and when. Simon had decided. The marriage would take place at Marlon Brando's island off Tahiti. They would be using Maggie's Bombardier to get there. No guests would be invited. That was it. Maggie, of course, should have said "No," but Simon's authoritarian manner had become the norm. She actually found that is dictatorial manner was irresistible, even sexy.

It took almost a year for Maggie to wake up. The man was not robbing her. He was not trying to tap into her enormous wealth. He did not need to, because he liked to pay for things so that he could own them. He wanted to own Maggie. For a long time, Maggie was happy to be owned. It made a huge difference to her that somebody else was in charge of her life. That was fine, as long as the person owning her was devoted to her. She was willing to give up her independence to a man that, despite ordering her around, actually loved her. In some way, Maggie felt that this gave her control. It all went wrong though when Maggie discovered that Simon had not stopped wanting other woman. Once he had 'won' Maggie, it seemed he needed to look elsewhere for other conquests. This, Maggie was not going to put up with. She realised that she had never really loved him; she had just loved the idea of someone else taking charge. She had liked the fact that he ordered her around, particularly in the bedroom, but the idea that he should be free to do this with others at the same time, did not sit well with her at all. Because she was not actually in love with Simon his extra marital activity did not actually upset her emotionally as much as the break up with Gee. It just made her angry.

Rather than throw a tantrum and just leave, Maggie decided to give Simon a lesson in who was really in charge. When they were out at functions together she would flirt outrageously with other guests. When they attended affairs at his business, she would do the same with his employees. Needless to say, he would get angry and try to be forceful with her back at Eaton Square. Then, just to rub it in, she started inviting those that she had flirted with back to the house. She deliberately did not hide the evidence. Simon realised that he had lost her. He was not used to losing. Despite his behaviour he had come to adore Maggie. There was no doubt that she was a special woman, not to be replicated. He did not want to lose her. But the more he tried to change, from being a dictatorial and authoritarian bully, to a more considerate and loving man, the less Maggie liked him. His charm to her had been the fact that he was in charge. He was now behaving as if Maggie were in charge and Maggie did not like that. His appeal had vanished. Yet again, Maggie had not secured love. Once again, she was on her own. She moved back to Number One, Knightsbridge, filed for divorce, and wondered what she should do with her life.

A visit to New York cheered her up somewhat. To see Sam and John and the children was nice and gave her an opportunity to spend time with Jimmy, not that he had much free time. But, despite being surrounded by family there, she was really alone. Again. Gee was never far from her mind. Back in London, she searched for purpose. The Layburn Academies were still going strong under the guidance of a now middle-aged Peter Oxford. Maggie decided to pay them all a visit. Maybe by taking a look at something that she had successfully launched over twenty years ago would cheer her up. Peter was delighted that his long-term sponsor was showing a reignited interest in his life's passion and quickly arranged a tour of all of the (now) 14 schools. Maggie thought about using the Global Express, but then considered it too conspicuous. Instead she decided to buy a Land Cruiser and drive herself. Counselled by Peter that it would be foolhardy for a middle-aged lady to be driving herself from London to the bottom of Africa on her own, Maggie took heed and decided to ask one of her friends to accompany her. "Two middle aged ladies would be better than one," she decided. Peter stopped giving advice. The question was; who should she ask to go with her? She considered Penelope; she would be fun. But Penelope was getting on in years and suffered from arthritis, so this might make things difficult. She asked Willow to come but she wanted the toy boy, Alex, to come with, which Maggie thought would complicate things. Willow, however, mentioned it to Ellen and it was not long before Ellen called her old friend, offering her company. Maggie was not sure if she could live with Ellen in close proximity for two to three months, which was how long she estimated the trip could take. It seemed to her that Ellen could probably not go too many days without a hairdo or a hot shower, let alone a man. However, Ellen was persistent and promised to behave, so with some reluctance Maggie agreed to allow her to come. After all, she knew that Ellen was as fast a driver as she was a flirt. Maggie worked out a route with the help of some rally participants who were friends of David Turnkey on the Bombardier. They warned her that much of the route in Africa would be on dirt roads, so they had better carry a few spare wheels and be sure that they knew how to change them. Maggie thought that the sight of Ellen looking helpless with a flat would be enough to get any gentleman to stop and do the job, so she was not too fussed about this potential problem. She then googled the potential overnight stops to figure out where they could stay. Then, finally, when she thought she knew exactly what she was going to do, she responded to Ellen with the proposition.

Ellen was excited by the prospect. She had not realised that it would take so long, understood now that since the journey would be about 15,000 kilometres, they would need to cover over 160 kilometres a day to get there, or, if they travelled only one day in three, they would need to cover nearly 500 kilometres on the travel days. The Russian was a bit dubious about the thought of the two ladies taking on such a challenge. On the other hand, he would be quite happy to have a three-month break from Ellen. He suggested that they invite Maggie to dinner to discuss the whole matter before Ellen agreed to go.

Maggie had been very depressed after the split with Simon. She knew that she was one of the luckiest girls alive, but, somehow, she felt alone and abandoned. Plenty of money but nobody to spend it with. She was obsessed with the thought that she was being punished because of stealing the lottery ticket, even though she had done more than she needed to do to make amends. She could not see the good that she had done, even though others could and had rewarded her for it. The adventure that she was planning now was just what was needed to take her mind off things. This would be a challenge and Maggie never shirked a challenge. At the same time, she planned to visit the Academies where maybe, just maybe, she could inspire some African youngsters to reach for the sky. This was all good, but would it be good with Ellen? She wondered just how reliable Ellen would turn out to be. She decided to refrain from making a final decision until after the dinner with Vlad, the Russian, and Ellen.

Ellen and Vlad were staying at their home in Bagshot. They had plenty of space there, so this would be an ideal place to park the Landcruiser whilst they kitted it out for the long journey. Maggie, over dinner, laid out her plan, showing the other two the route and where she planned to stay. She would be able to visit eight of the Academies en route, most of them during the second half of the trip, since they were mostly in Sub Saharan Africa. The route would take them through France, Italy and Greece, then by ferry to Alexandria in Egypt. From there they would travel through Egypt, Saudi Arabia, Sudan, Ethiopia, Kenya, Tanzania, Zambia, Botswana, Malawi and finally South Africa. As Maggie laid out her plans, Ellen became very excited. She was definitely up for it. Vlad had plenty of practical suggestions of which Maggie took note. Maggie explained that she would finance the whole trip, since it was her idea, but Vlad would hear none of it. "We split down the middle. Whatever the cost, we pay half." Naturally, it was agreed that they would fly back and Maggie offered the use of her Global Express. She also told the others that, should anything go wrong and the trip had to be aborted for whatever reason, her plane would be available to rescue them. Vlad and Ellen were acting as if there were no decision to be made. Maggie decided not to wait, but just to accept that Ellen, her old nemesis, would now be her closest companion for a few months.

The next week, Maggie, Vlad and Ellen, went to buy the vehicle. Naturally it needed some special equipment and the Russian turned out to be extremely helpful in briefing the Toyota dealer. Basically, they were buying a vehicle that was rally equipped, with extra fuel tanks, wheels, tools, spares and so on. Ellen was a little aghast about the resultant lack of space for her clothes. Maggie told her that there were plenty of nice stores in Johannesburg. They would have to wait a few weeks for delivery of the vehicle but there was plenty of other preparatory work to be done with visas, insurance, vehicle carnets and so on. Then, just as they were almost ready, Maggie had some bad news. Sandy, had passed away in Anguilla from a heart attack. There was no question in Maggie's mind; her priority must be to attend the funeral. The pan African trip would just have to be postponed. "Thank God," thought Maggie, "that this didn't happen when we were in the middle of the Sahara. Sandy always was so considerate."

Chapter Thirty-Four

Maggie had received the news of Sandy's death from her daughter, Sam, in New York. She immediately offered to fly to Anguilla. In fact, she offered to fly to New York in her plane, pick up Sam and her family, and then proceed to the island. She could do so immediately, so, in effect, John and Sam could be in Anguilla the very next day, which would not be any later than if they flew commercial. This was agreed and arrangements made for Maggie to pick up the family at the General Aviation terminal at Kennedy, without even having to go through US immigration. Jimmy, it just so happened, was already in Anguilla, working on the project.

The Global Express was one of the first jets to land on the new runway in Anguilla. The terminal buildings were not yet complete, but the government, mindful of John's diplomatic status, gave special dispensation. This allowed the party to bypass the normal arrival procedure via Saint-Martin and sea taxi. The jet was met by all eight Members of Parliament, including the current Prime Minister, such was the esteem that the Coltrane family were held in. John, Sam and the three youngsters headed for the Coltrane's home in the Valley and Maggie went with Jimmy, who had also been at the airport, to Greg's villa, now, of course, owned and occupied by his son.

The next day John busied himself with funeral arrangements. Jimmy took Maggie to show her the progress of his
mini Monte Carlo. Although she had been opposed to the
development per se, Maggie was intensely proud of the
achievement of her son, in getting the job done. She had
to admit that the whole marina, village, apartment homes,
shops and public spaces were really beginning to look as
if they had been there forever. The new casino was just
mind-blowing and ready to open as soon as the new airport
was up and running. Maggie asked Jimmy to take her to
Sandy's little cottage. On entering, the loss of Sandy, finally
hit her. The tears streamed down her face. Jimmy held her
tightly. "She was such a lovely lady," sobbed Maggie, "and
such a wonderful friend. We were so lucky to have known
her." The little house no longer had a sea view. The salt pans
were gone, but a few other original village houses remained.
Most of them had been turned into tourist attractions,
such as shops and restaurants. Sandy's was one of the few
remaining properties that were still lived in. Maggie wondered if Sandy had left a will and, if so, would it specify
her wishes in regard to the cottage? She hoped that Sandy
had been clear about this. Maggie lingered for quite a while
in the little house. Jimmy, who normally would be itching
to get back to work, was the model of patience. He knew
that there had been a special bond between his mother and
Sandy so he wanted to give her time to mourn. He too liked
Sandy, and decided, whilst he waited for his Mum, that he
would dedicate one of the garden squares in the project to
her and would commission a statue in commemoration.
After all, she was the Sandy of Sandy Point.

The funeral took place a few days later in the Sandy Point
Methodist Chapel, which, of course, was far too small to
accommodate all who wished to attend. John, knowing
that many of the islanders would want to be there, had

arranged for rows of chairs to be placed in the grounds of the church and had arranged for a large screen to be erected on the church wall, so that those outside could follow the proceedings. The service was a true celebration of Sandy's life but, even so, many tears were shed. Jimmy had made available the largest meeting room at the Marina Hotel and all mourners were invited to a magnificent buffet, such that the islanders had never witnessed before. Even John, the seasoned politician, felt that he had never shaken so many hands in one day.

The day after the funeral the whole family had a huge surprise. John had invited his family, Maggie and Jimmy to the reading of the will in a lawyer's offices in the Valley. Nobody, least of all John, expected Sandy to have much to pass on, save for the cottage and a few pieces of jewellery. The attorney duly went through a list of small items that had been specified, naming specifically Sam, her children and Maggie. Maggie was so pleased to have been remembered. Then came the bombshell that shocked the room, especially John. It appeared that Sandy had bequeathed the sum of $1 billion, 300 million to John and his family, $1 billion to John and Sandy and $100 million each to the kids. John immediately stood up and announced that this must be a mistake. "No," replied the attorney, "your mother had a bank account with the Florida Trust in Miami, with a balance of plus minus 1 billion, 300 million. There can be no doubt. When she instructed my firm, several years ago, the amount was 1 billion. It has now grown with interest because she has not drawn one dollar from it in fifteen years. I can assure you that this is correct." John was astounded. So were the rest of the audience, bar one.

Maggie knew immediately where the money had come from. Nevertheless, she did not need to feign surprise, because she was, genuinely completely surprised too. The only difference was that Maggie knew the source of the money. She did not know, of course, that Sandy had never given it to the Church, but, in a roundabout way, ensured that it had come back to Maggie's family. Maggie wanted to laugh. This was the funniest thing that had ever happened to her. It was also an amazing thing. All the years of worry Maggie had suffered in connection with the lottery ticket, suddenly evaporated. It was as if a huge burden had been lifted from her shoulders. Sandy, God bless her, had found a way to relieve Maggie. Sandy knew that by Maggie offering a penance to the Church, as she had done, would alleviate her pain, but she could never know if she had truly been forgiven for claiming the ticket that was not hers. This was Sandy's way of letting Maggie know that she had been forgiven. Maggie was so thankful and so happy. From now on her life would be better. No more nightmares, no more guilt. "Thank you, Sandy. Thank you, so much," she whispered. The rest of the room were still incredulous about their good luck, but also absolutely incredulous about how Sandy had managed to accumulate so much wealth. "She must have won the lottery," Maggie suggested.

Epilogue

Maggie and Ellen did make the epic journey from London to South Africa by car, but that is an adventure for another book. It didn't go exactly as originally planned because they decided to take along a television crew for fun, but also for their security. Even so, it was an epic journey and one which they, nor the camera team, would ever forget. When they finally reached Johannesburg, Ellen had a ball in the Sandton shops and Maggie reunited with Gee in the Intercontinental corner suite. Ellen flew back to her waiting Russian and Maggie stayed with Gee, this time, forever.

Who is to say whether Maggie made the right choice in claiming the lottery ticket? For years, despite her massive wealth, she was tormented with guilt and suffered horrendous nightmares. There is no doubt that she did her best to use the winnings unselfishly, but, deep in her heart, she believed that she had done wrong. Only at the reading of Sandy's will did she feel that her God had forgiven her, and she lived out her old age in peace with her beloved Gee at Shawu Farm, where she participated in the saviour of many suffering animals.

What would you do if you were to pick up a lost lotter ticket? Would you keep it to see if it is a winner? And, if it is, would you claim the winnings? Just as Maggie said, it is not an important question, because it is not going to happen. Or is it?

Lightning Source UK Ltd.
Milton Keynes UK
UKHW010439271122
412865UK00004B/68